MW01250943

Dear Je[illegible]
They s[illegible]
start somewhere—
Thank you for being
a special part
of mine ♡
Blessings & Love,
Diana

The Forever Heart

DIANA BOLIANAZ

The Forever Heart
Copyright © 2022 by Diana Bolianaz

All rights reserved. No part of this publication may be reproduced, distributed, or transmitted in any form or by any means, including photocopying, recording, or other electronic or mechanical methods, without the prior written permission of the author, except in the case of brief quotations embodied in critical reviews and certain other non-commercial uses permitted by copyright law.

Tellwell Talent
www.tellwell.ca

ISBN
978-0-2288-8307-4 (Hardcover)
978-0-2288-8306-7 (Paperback)
978-0-2288-8308-1 (eBook)

Dedication:

I dedicate this book to my brave, dear friend Rita, who allowed me to tell her story. Her capacity for love, compassion and forgiveness as well as her strength and determination inspire me greatly. Throughout the process of writing this book, she was my constant cheerleader and encourager.

Acknowledgments:

I want to thank my niece Haley who happily took on the role of my trusted personal assistant. Without her skills in technology I would not have been able to navigate the necessary steps in the publishing process.

Finally, to my family and friends who walked with me and prayed for me throughout this journey.

Table of Contents

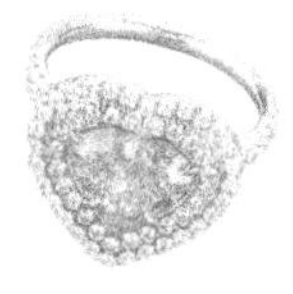

Chapter One

The Beginning

1974

LIZA WAS NINETEEN YEARS OLD when she met him. Every morning she would go to the same coffee shop. As she stood in line waiting to order the usual venti decaf soy milk latte, extra hot, extra foam, she sensed someone staring at her. She glanced over her shoulder and saw *him*. His eyes twinkled as he smiled and winked at her. She felt her face flush and quickly turned her head.

He wore black pants, a black cardigan, and black boots. He looked like a famous basketball player, almost like Michael Jordan, but not quite as tall. He got up to leave and walked right past her. He came so close to her that she felt the heat from his body and inhaled the sweet fragrance that lingered in the air. Still breathing in his scent, Liza stood with her eyes closed. She snapped back to reality when the girl behind her in line tapped her on the shoulder and motioned for her to step forward. The clerk took Liza's order. She left, sipping her coffee. She only had a block to walk before she turned the corner and arrived at work.

For the rest of the day, Liza daydreamed about Mr. Tall, Dark, and Handsome! She secretly hoped she might see him again the next morning.

Liza went straight home after work. Her mom greeted her at the door as usual.

"How was your day, dear?"

"Fine, Mom."

"You look a little flushed. Are you feeling okay?"

"I'm fine, Mom. Call me when dinner's ready, please. I'm going to my room."

When Liza's brother, Junior, came home, her mom called her to say dinner was ready. Her father was out of town working, so only three places were set. When Klaus was away, the conversation around the dinner table was easy and light-hearted. At dinner, Liza seemed a bit distracted, lost in her own thoughts.

"How was your day, Junior?"

"Pretty good, Mom. We had a test in math today. I think I did pretty well. Liza, did you have Mr. Lanky when you were in grade twelve? Liza? Liza!"

"What?"

"Where were you just now?"

"What do you mean, where was I? I'm right here!"

"I asked you a question."

"What was the question?"

"Did you have Mr. Lanky for math?"

"No, I didn't. Why?"

"I have him for math this year. He's a pretty good teacher, but not everyone likes him."

"Why not?" Helga asked.

"Because he's kinda tough, and he gives a lot of homework."

"Well, hard work never hurt anyone."

"Oh Mom, now you sound like Dad."

"Just keep up with your homework and I'm sure you'll do just fine, dear. If you need any help with your homework, I'm sure your sister will help you. Won't you, Liza? Liza? Liza!"

"What?"

"What are you thinking about, dear?"

"Nothing, why?"

"You must be thinking about something. You haven't been paying attention to anything we've been saying."

"It's just stuff at work, Mom."

"Everything is all right, isn't it, dear?"

"Everything is just fine. I think I'll go to my room now if you don't mind."

"That's fine, dear. It's Junior's turn to help with the dishes anyway."

"I helped last night."

"No, you didn't, that was two nights ago, brother dear."

Liza went to bed early that night, hoping to have a good night's sleep. Per chance to dream about *him*. Unfortunately, she hardly slept at all. Her alarm rang at seven, about an hour after she fell asleep. She got up immediately, showered, and put on her favourite "little black dress." She hurried past her mother in the kitchen, as she could hardly wait to go to the coffee shop.

"You sure dressed up this morning, dear. What's the occasion?"

"No occasion, Mom. I have to run. See you later."

Liza hadn't worn that dress to work before. In fact, it was only the second time she had ever worn it. The first time was to her friend's bar mitzvah.

Liza got to the coffee shop about the same time as she always did. She took a quick look around but didn't see him. She stood in line with her back toward the door. She waited her turn, and as she did, she felt someone come and stand behind her.

The same sweet fragrance she remembered from the day before enveloped the air around her. She was too nervous to turn around. *It has to be him*, she thought. He leaned in, and his cheek brushed against her long, dark, silky hair. For the first time, she heard his beautiful velvety voice.

"Good morning, Princess, how are you this fine morning?"

He was right, it sure is a fine morning, she thought. *Did he just call me Princess?* She turned her head and felt the same flush come over her as she had experienced yesterday. This time though, she didn't turn away.

"Fine, thank you," she managed to say.

"That little black dress you're wearing looks amazing!"

Perfect, she thought, *it worked!* "Thank you."

"I have a confession to make," he said.

"What do you mean?"

"I've been watching you."

"You've been watching me?" *Uh oh, he's a stalker,* was the first thing that crossed her mind. "You're not a stalker, are you?" Immediately she though better of asking that question. If he was a stalker, he wouldn't admit to it.

He just smiled and said, "Well, it's more like admiring you." He held out his hand to her and said, "My name is Melvin, Melvin Jr."

"My name is Liza," she replied as she slipped her hand into his. She looked down at the floor, blushing once again.

He lifted her chin gently with his strong fingers. Her eyes were half-closed as she stood, lost in the moment.

Melvin whispered, "It's your turn."

"It's my turn," Liza whispered back, with her eyes completely closed.

"It's your turn, Miss. May I take your order?" the clerk said loudly.

"Oh, it's my turn!"

"That's what I said, Princess." He ordered for her. "She'll have a venti decaf soy milk latte, extra hot, extra foam."

Melvin paid and handed the coffee to Liza. "A treat for you, Princess."

"You *have* been watching me! Yummy," she said as she sipped her coffee.

"I agree," he said as he looked into her beautiful brown eyes.

"Pardon me?"

"I'd like to walk you to work, if you don't mind."

"I don't mind. I work just around the corner."

Their conversation began, as many do, with comments about the weather. It hadn't progressed too much when Liza stopped in front of a two-storey, stone building.

"Here we are," she announced.

"It kinda looks like an apartment building."

"You're right, Melvin. There are apartments on the main floor, and the office is on the second floor. Room 222."

"Really? Interesting."

Melvin held the door open for Liza as she walked past him to enter. She turned slightly as he touched her arm.

"By the way, Princess, do you have any plans Saturday night?"

"Saturday night?" *He's asking me out on a date!* She knew the answer immediately, but didn't want to appear overly anxious. "Not really, why?"

"I know the best place for great food and groovy music."

"Did you say, groovy music?"

"Yup. Blame it on Melvin Sr., my pops. That's his favourite word."

"Let me get this straight. I just met you, and you're already asking me out on a date."

"Yes, I believe I am."

"I don't even know you."

"Yes, but you like me."

She didn't answer. She felt her cheeks flush.

"I feel like *I* know *you*, Princess."

"Well then, you seem to have the advantage."

"Please say yes, I promise you won't regret it."

"Yes."

"Good answer! I'll pick you up at your place. Where do you live?"

He definitely couldn't pick her up at home. Her father would never approve. There is no way a white girl from a strict Mennonite background would ever be allowed to date someone who is Black. Her mom may agree eventually, but Liza would have to ease her into it. Klaus, being the strict father he was, thought Liza should start dating when she was about thirty or so, and then marry a nice Mennonite boy.

"Liza?"

"Yes, uh, I was thinking. Could you pick me up at the office? I have to go in and do some work," she lied.

"On Saturday?"

"Yes. It doesn't happen too often. Sometimes I go in and catch up on some filing."

"Okay. I'll pick you up at eight, and don't be late," he said with a grin. He waved as he turned to leave. "See you then, Princess!"

"See you then, Melvin."

Liza walked upstairs to the office, sat down in her chair, and stared out the window. She couldn't concentrate enough to start typing. Normally, she could type 150 words a minute. When she finally began, she averaged ten. When the phone rang, she didn't hear it. Her boss thought she was away from her desk, so he answered it. He hated answering the phone because it interrupted his train of thought. He was a writer and was writing books, mainly manuals for business systems. After answering phone call number three, he went out to the front office to see where Liza was. He startled her when she turned from the window and saw him standing right in front of her desk. He usually stayed in his office unless it was lunch time. That's when he took a break from writing.

"Marcus? Is it lunch time already?" she said as she straightened out her reading glasses that sat perched on the end of her nose.

"Where *were* you?"

"Where was I?" she repeated.

"That's what I just said! Better still, where have you been?"

"I've been right here, why?"

"If you were right here, why didn't you answer the phone?"

"Well, if it rang, I would have answered it."

"If it rang? I've taken three calls in the last half hour. You look a little flushed ... are you okay?"

"Why does everyone keep asking me that?" she said under her breath.

"What?" Marcus said, straining to hear what Liza said.

"I'm fine, really."

"All right then. Please answer the phone, and if anyone calls for me, just take a message."

"Yes, Marcus."

He turned on his heel and walked quickly down the hallway to his office. Marcus was about six feet tall, with a slim build. He had brown, wavy hair, green eyes, and was about fifty-four years old, which he would neither confirm nor deny. He was a snappy dresser, up on all the latest fashions. Ethel, his wife of thirty years, made sure of that.

Marcus and Ethel had only one child, Bishop. Who names his kid *Bishop*? He was, as they say, "To the Manor Born," (which means he was spoiled rotten). Marcus was a very generous, doting father and made sure that Bishop had everything he wanted. It's amazing Marcus didn't walk around holding a silver platter in front of Bishop.

Bishop and Liza didn't see eye to eye on anything. (Not just because she was a lot shorter than he was, either!) Bishop thought he could boss Liza around whenever he wanted to. Liza basically ignored him. She only did what Marcus instructed her to do. That didn't sit too well with Bishop. Bishop was about five-feet-ten and skinny. He had mousey brown hair, squinty eyes, and wore thick glasses. Liza considered him pond scum. He obviously did not inherit his father's good looks.

Liza didn't miss any more calls that day. She counted down the hours until she could go home. Four-thirty couldn't come soon enough.

When she got home, she dropped her purse and keys on the table beside the back door.

"Hello? Anybody home?" she called out.

No one answered. She went to her room and stared at the clothes in her closet. What was she going to wear Saturday night? She decided she had to go shopping and buy something new to wear.

Liza heard her mom in the kitchen. "Liza, why did you leave your purse and keys on the table? I've told you a thousand times, take them to your room!"

"Hi, Mom. Sorry, I forgot."

"You always forget."

Liza's mom was a fanatic about cleaning. Obsessive, you might say. Everything had to be "just so." Liza thought her mom went overboard most of the time. Her mom was fifty now and seemed to be getting pickier the older she got. Helga had short, curly, greyish-white hair. She was about five-feet-two inches tall and squarely built. She came from a German Mennonite background, just like Klaus. She was an excellent cook and loved to bake. Liza loved her mother's cooking. Helga always stocked the freezer full of food and lots of baking. Her favourite trick around Christmas time was to put all the baking in special containers in the big freezer in the basement and label it "liver" so no one would find and eat the delicious treats she hid so cleverly. Or at least she thought she did. Everyone knew her little tricks, and soon the "liver" started to disappear. Liza blamed the disappearance on her brother, and her brother blamed it on her. They were careful not to leave any trails of crumbs anywhere. When

Helga would find the empty containers, she would just sigh and bake some more.

Liza went into the kitchen, picked up her purse and keys, and said, "Mom, can I use the car for a couple of hours? I want to go and meet Sarah at the mall."

Sarah was Liza's best friend and had been since kindergarten.

"What about dinner? It's almost ready."

"I'll grab something at the mall."

"Fine, dear, just be home by nine."

"Thanks, Mom! See you later."

Of course, she wasn't meeting Sarah. She couldn't tell her mom that she had to go shopping for an outfit to wear for her hot date on Saturday night.

Liza never had trouble finding clothes *or* spending money, and this day was no exception. In only a few hours, Liza managed to buy a sweater set, a pair of capri pants (even though it was the end of spring and not super warm out yet), and strappy sandals to die for—not Manolo Blahniks, but they were hot, and more in line with Liza's budget.

Helga was already looking out the window to see if Liza was nearing home when she pulled up in the driveway. Helga looked at her watch. It was 8:55. She waited for Liza as she came through the back door.

"Liza, I was beginning to worry."

"I'm okay, Mom. Just shopping. And you know what girls are like when they get shopping!"

"Yes, dear, I know. What did you buy?"

"Oh, just a couple of things. Liza folded everything so that it all fit into one bag, except for the shoes. "Got some pretty good deals too."

Helga didn't agree with Liza's spending habits. Helga was very "frugal," which Liza openly called "cheap." Liza devised a crafty trick to avoid her mother's "spending too much money" lecture. She would take a red pen with her, and before she brought her purchases home, she'd put a red line through the ticketed price and mark it down 50 percent. This way, Helga didn't get angry with Liza for spending too much money, and Liza bought whatever she wanted. Liza called this "hassle-free shopping."

"Mom, may I use the car Saturday afternoon? I have some errands to run."

"You barely made it home on time tonight and you're asking for the car again?"

"You always told me to make sure that I ask ahead of time. This is Tuesday, and that's ahead of time, right?"

"You have a point there. You may use the car, but you'll have to drop me off at the church. I have to help at the bazaar."

"Okay, but could you get a ride home from church? I don't know what time I'll be done."

"Yes, dear, I will."

"What time will you be home from the church bazaar, Mom?"

"Oh, probably not until six or so."

"I'm going out with Sarah Saturday evening. She's going to pick me up from the office. I have a bit of filing to do."

Her mom really liked Sarah and never hassled her about anything she and Sarah did together.

"Yes dear, that's fine."

"Ok. I'm going to bed now. Good night, Mom. See you in the morning."

She kissed her mom on the cheek and went down the hall to her bedroom.

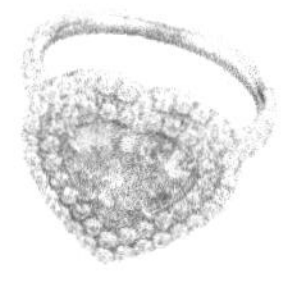

Chapter Two

Speedy Freddie and Old Lady Meedemeyer

SATURDAY FINALLY ARRIVED, and Liza dropped her mom off at the church bazaar. Liza made an appointment for a manicure, pedicure, a wash and blow dry at a salon close to the mall. If she was going to be called "Princess," she wanted to look like a princess.

"How do you want me to do your hair today, Liza?" her stylist asked.

"Nothing fancy. Something that looks natural, almost like I did it myself. (She didn't want to look like she was trying too hard.) Liza probably could have done it herself, but her hairstylist could make it stay nicely for the whole evening. She always felt so much more confident having her hair done.

After her appointment at the salon, Liza stopped in at the mall to buy a new lipstick and bumped right into Sarah.

"Liza, wow, do you look great! You really did a nice job on your hair today."

"Sarah, hi, thanks!"

"What are you doing here, Liza? Do you want to have lunch?"

"I don't really have time today. How about if I call you tomorrow?"

"Sure, no problem. Gee, you look so happy."

"Thanks, I am." Liza could feel her cheeks start to get a bit flushed.

"You look a little flushed. Are you okay?"

"I'm *fine*," Liza said adamantly. She wanted to spill the beans to Sarah, but she didn't want to jinx things for her date. She wasn't really superstitious. She just thought she should keep things to herself until they actually came true.

"I'll call you, Sarah. I really have to run now."

"Well, okay. Uh, talk to you later, Liza."

"Don't call me, I'll call you," Liza added.

"Oh, okay," Sarah said hesitantly. Sara walked away with a slight frown on her face, but she shrugged it off.

As soon as Liza got home, she went straight to her room and laid out her new clothes on her bed. She picked up her sweater, held it in front of her, and stared in the mirror. She chose a few different pairs of earrings and held them up while holding the sweater to see if they would match. She couldn't decide. She put the sweater down, applied fresh lipstick, and then held one pair after another up to her ears to see which would look best. She chose her favourite small, silver, dangly pair. Not too small, just right. (Goldilocks would have been proud.) Liza also chose a pretty little chain link bracelet that matched the earrings quite well. Helga always said, "Less is more." Liza always said, "If less is more, how much better can more be?" Helga did have good taste, so she went with less.

Liza sat down in her favourite chair beside her bed. It was a comfy, oversized chair that had belonged to her grandmother. She closed her eyes for a little wink before having her bubble bath. Her little wink turned into a full-blown hour-long sleep. Liza woke with a start and looked at the clock on the table beside her bed.

She ran to the bathroom. No time for a bubble bath now. A quick bath was all she had time for. She put on her favourite lotion, dressed, and went downstairs to leave a note for her mom.

> *Dear Mom,*
>
> *I'll see you later. Sarah and I are going to dinner and a late movie.*
>
> *Love you,*
> *Liza*

Liza had just finished writing the note and placing it on the kitchen table when her mom came in the back door. She went out the front door. *Excellent*, she thought. *A clean getaway.*

Liza decided to take the bus to the office. She normally walked to work, but she was wearing her new shoes. They were "good-looking" shoes, not "good-walking" shoes.

When she got off the bus and approached the office, Liza could see a light on. Who could be there now? She unlocked the door and called out, "Hello?"

No answer.

"Hello?"

"Liza?"

"Marcus? What are you doing here?"

"What am I doing here? This is my office. What are *you* doing here?"

"I came in to do some work."

"Wearing that outfit?"

"Well, I'm going out to dinner and a late movie with Sarah, and she's picking me up here in a little while."

Marcus liked Sarah. They had met on a few occasions, and he always enjoyed talking to her.

"What time is she picking you up?"

"Why do you ask?"

"If she arrives before I leave, I'd like to say hello."

"I'm not exactly sure when she'll be here." *He will be here in forty-seven minutes, but who's counting?* "How much longer are you planning to work, Marcus?"

"Actually, I'm almost done. Why?"

"Oh, no reason. I was just wondering."

Liza sat down at her desk and opened a couple of folders. She pretended to look through them. Marcus went back into his office. Liza stared out the window, watching for Melvin.

At about 7:50, a black BMW pulled up in front. Liza didn't want Marcus to see her date, so she ran outside and didn't even say goodbye.

A woman got out of the driver's side, and upon seeing Liza, she said, "Could you please direct me to Union Street?"

Liza was a bit unnerved when she realized that it wasn't Melvin. She was trying to process the whole thing and didn't hear a word the woman said.

"I'm sorry, what did you say?" Liza asked.

"You look a little flushed, dear. Are you okay?"

"Yes, I am," Liza said sternly. She gave the woman instructions to Union Street. The lady got back into the BMW and drove away.

Liza looked up and down the street. No other cars in sight. She was getting a bit anxious and wanted to bite her nails, but she'd just had a manicure, after all, and decided not to. She was looking in her purse for a mint and didn't see Melvin pull up. He got out of his car and started walking toward her.

"Hello there, beautiful Princess." He leaned in and kissed her on the cheek. "Mmm, you smell good! Is that Chanel Number 5?"

"How did you know?"

"My sister wears the same fragrance. Why were you waiting out here? I would have come in to get you. Room 222, right?"

"Yes, that's right," Liza confirmed.

"See, I remembered."

"Oh, I just needed some fresh air."

They walked over to the car. Melvin opened the door for Liza, took her hand, and helped her in. He ran around to the driver's side, got in, and said, "Okay, Speedy Freddie's, here we come!"

Liza was trying not to stare at him. He was so handsome. She kept looking straight ahead and would just glance over at him from time to time. He smelled good too.

"What is the name of the fragrance you're wearing, Melvin?"

"Do you like it?" he said with a little smirk.

"Yes, I do."

Every time Liza took a breath, she felt like she was floating on air.

"It's called Black Knight."

"Black Knight?"

"Yes, as in knight in shining armour, not the opposite of day."

"It's yummy," she muttered.

"Pardon me?"

"It's lovely."

"Thank you."

Melvin wore a navy t-shirt and jeans. *Man, what a body! Wide shoulders, muscular arms— my favourite combination. Nice, luscious full lips. I don't trust guys with skinny lips. How do you kiss a guy with skinny lips? You can feel his teeth right through his lips. Full lips, soft lips, lips you could get lost in. Oh, ya!*

Melvin had been talking to Liza for about ten minutes, and she hadn't heard a word he'd said. She was nodding and smiling, daydreaming about his sexy body up against hers, kissing those delicious lips, when she heard him say, "Well?"

"Well what?" she answered.

"Well, what do you think?"

"I uh, well, I uh, I agree with you."

"You do?" he said in disbelief. "You are the first woman that ever agreed with me on that subject."

Liza had no idea what he was talking about.

A half hour later, they were still driving. They drove through parts of town Liza had never seen before, and then they took an exit onto the highway. She started to get a bit nervous. Thoughts of being kidnapped crossed her mind. No one knew where she was, or for that matter, who she was with. The note she'd left for her mother told a completely different story. She didn't even tell Sarah about the date. Now she wasn't listening to what Melvin was saying because fear had set in. They took another exit into a place she didn't recognize. They rounded the next corner, and Liza saw a large blinking sign that said "Speedy Freddie's" straight ahead.

She breathed a sigh of relief. Melvin parked the car, got out, and walked around to the passenger side to open Liza's door.

"Here we are; you're going to love it! Are you okay? You look a little pale."

"That's a switch," she muttered.

"Pardon?"

"Nothing. I'm starved!"

They walked in and took a look around. To their left was a little kiosk for gifts. Straight ahead was a circular bar. To the right was a long counter where people lined up for food. Beyond that was a dance floor where a band was playing fifties music. In front of the band were tables and chairs. Behind those tables and chairs were bar stools up against a long counter that spanned the length of the wall.

"Let's get some food," Melvin said, rubbing his hands together.

The menu was simple and the food was cheap. A large chalkboard hanging behind the counter listed all the menu items: hamburgers, cheeseburgers, hotdogs, shrimp, pork, chicken and beef kabobs, and french fries. The prices were the same as they were back in the fifties. Liza couldn't believe her eyes.

While they were trying to decide what to order, a young boy walked by with a huge bucket of shrimp. He handed it to the girl behind the counter and she dumped it into the shrimp bin.

"We sure go through a lot of these!" she said.

"What would you like to eat, Princess?"

"I don't know, Melvin. Everything looks so good."

"That settles it. We'll have one of everything and a dozen shrimp. You do like shrimp, don't you?"

"Love them," Liza said eagerly.

"Let's go grab a table and order some beer. They'll call us when our order is ready."

They took their number and went to find a place to sit. The waitress came by the table promptly to take their drink order.

"Beer okay, Princess?"

"Fine with me." Liza had never had beer before, but now was as good a time as any to start.

"How do you like it here so far?"

"It's ... what's that term? Oh, yes, groovy!"

Melvin laughed.

The waitress put a beer in front of each of them. "That'll be three dollars," she said.

"For both?" Liza said in disbelief.

"Yes, Princess, for both! I told you this was a great place!"

"Yes, you did, Melvin."

"Here's to our first date and to my beautiful Princess!"

"Thank you," Liza said as she blushed. "Mmm, this is good ... refreshing."

"Do you have a favourite?"

"No, not really." She didn't want to admit that she was a bit of a novice when it came to drinking. She really didn't drink much at all. Wine with dinner on special occasions. Her father frowned on drinking, of course. He frowned upon almost everything. Her mother was a bit more lenient.

Liza finished half of her beer and was starting to feel a bit tipsy when they heard their number being called out at the food counter. Melvin jumped up to get the food while Liza waited at the table.

"Will you be able to carry everything by yourself?"

"Oh sure, no problem. If the waitress comes by, order another couple of beers for us."

"Okay, Melvin."

Carrying the food wasn't difficult because they placed it in such a way that the tray was loaded evenly. Melvin placed the tray on the table and began to unload it.

"Wow, do you think we'll be able to eat all of this, Melvin?"

"I don't know about you, Princess, but I'll have no trouble. I really didn't eat much today. To tell you the truth, I was a bit nervous," he confessed.

"*You* were nervous?"

"Yes, does that surprise you?"

"A little."

"When you have a date with a Princess, that's a tall order to fill."

"Oh Melvin, you say the nicest things. I have to admit, I was a bit nervous also."

"Well, we're not nervous now, are we? Let's eat."

As they ate, stories and beer flowed. They shared details about their lives. Melvin shared first. He was twenty-three years old and had a degree in journalism. He worked for the local newspaper and did freelance writing. He lived alone in an old stone apartment building across from the coffee shop, where he did a lot of his writing and "Liza watching."

Melvin's only sister, Alicia, three years older than he, was married and had a three-year-old little boy named Max. Melvin's mother had left his father when he was ten, and there was no room for him or his sister in her life. She was a singer and had travelled all the time before the children had come along. The road was her home and her first love. After being at home with them for thirteen years, she joined a band and left. His father swore that he'd never marry again, but changed his mind when he met Lola. (She was a showgirl.) Once a week Melvin Sr. would get dressed in his "Sunday-go-to-church" suit, slap on some cologne, and go to a little cabaret on the outskirts of town. That's where he first laid eyes on her. (Alicia was fifteen by then, and Melvin was twelve.) Lola was the headliner. Melvin Sr. would slip the hostess twenty dollars so she would seat him at his favourite table right in front.

About a year after they met, Melvin Sr. and Lola were married. Lola is still the headliner at the club on Saturday nights and Melvin Sr. still sits at the table in front. He just doesn't have to tip the hostess twenty dollars anymore. He has his reserved table and parking—a perk that comes along with being married to the headliner.

Melvin turned to Liza and said, "Okay, Princess, your turn."

"My life isn't as exciting as yours, Melvin. I hope you won't be bored."

"With you, Princess? Never!"

"Okay, here goes." Liza graduated from high school when she was seventeen, as she had skipped grade three. She went to a local business college for a one-year business/accounting diploma course. She applied for a job with Marcus a week after she graduated and had been working for him for a year now. Her job requires some accounting and general office duties, banking included. Because she's an excellent typist, she will be typing all of Marcus' manuscripts. She'll get an annual bonus when the proceeds from Marcus' book sales come in.

Liza lives at home with her mother, Helga, her father, Klaus, and her brother, Junior, who is a year younger. Her father is the owner of a company that builds custom homes. The home they live in was one of the first, her mother's "dream home." When her father is away, it really is a *dream home*. Peaceful, happy, fun, and calm. She describes him as a mean tyrant with lots of rules, his main rule being, "Do as I say, not as I do." He has an expensive gun collection, which he keeps in a glass showcase under lock and key in his study. The only person besides her father allowed in his study is her mother. He allows her to go in and clean and dust once a week.

Liza stopped talking and stared off into space.

"Are you okay?"

Liza looked at Melvin and said, "I'm really glad you had the courage to talk to me, Melvin."

"Well, it did take me a couple of weeks." The band started to play a slow song. Melvin stood up and offered his hand. "May I have this dance, Princess?"

"I'd love to."

He pulled her chair out, took her by the hand, and led her onto the dance floor. Melvin pulled Liza in close to him, pressed his chin against her temple, and breathed in the scent of her soft, wavy, long, brown hair. He ran his hand from the top of her head, through her hair, to the small of her back. Liza's legs wobbled for a minute. Melvin felt her wobble and caught her.

"Are you okay, Princess?"

"I'm fine, Melvin, thank you."

"You look a little flushed."

"I think I'll have to start wearing less blush and more powder."

"Pardon me?"

"I think the band should play a little louder."

They danced to a few more songs until the band stopped to take a break. Liza's feet were tired and sore. Her new shoes were a bit stiff. As she walked off the dance floor, she was limping a bit.

"New shoes?"

"No, not really. I've had them for a while." *Three days,* she thought. "I just haven't worn them much." *At all ...*

"They sure look good on those cute little feet of yours."

Little, she thought. *They're size nine!* "Thank you, Melvin, you're so kind."

He led her off the dance floor and back to their table.

"That was fun, Melvin—you're a good dancer!"

"So are you, Princess. We'll have to do this more often."

"Fine with me."

"I know this great little place with a groovy band, not far from my place. How about if we check it out this Thursday?"

"Thursday?"

"Yes. Thursday is *the* night to be there."

"Okay, Thursday it is! What time?"

"Things don't get started until at least ten."

"Ten o'clock?"

"Is there a problem?"

"No, no problem at all."

"Okay, Princess, I'll pick you up at nine-thirty. How about if we meet for a drink before we go to the club?"

"Sure, if you want to."

"What time should I pick you up then?"

"How about if we meet at the coffee shop and go from there?"

"That's easy for me, but are you sure I can't pick you up?"

"Sometimes on Thursdays I have dinner with my friend Sarah," she lied. "I'll get her to drop me off at the coffee shop."

"I've got a better idea. Why don't you come over to my place instead?"

"Your place?"

"Sure, why not? It's across the street, remember? I promise I'll be on my best behaviour. I'll treat you like the Princess you are."

"Okay, Melvin, if you insist."

"I do."

They stayed to hear the band play one more set and then decided to leave. By this time, it was about twelve-thirty.

"I know a great little after-hours coffee joint," Melvin said as he opened the door to leave.

"It sounds good, but I really should be getting home."

"Just one quick nightcap," he pleaded.

Liza really couldn't resist. She wanted this night to go on forever but knew it couldn't. Even though she was nineteen, she still had a curfew—strictly enforced when her dad was home, but he wasn't scheduled to be home until late the next day.

"Could I take a rain cheque?"

"Sure, Princess," he said with obvious disappointment. "What street do you live on?"

"Mulberry Street."

"Oh, I know where that is."

They drove along, not really saying too much. Just happy to be together. Melvin reached across and held Liza's hand. She held on and didn't want to ever let go.

"Turn right here," Liza said when they got to Mulberry Street.

She pointed to a house about halfway down the block, which happened to belong to Old Lady Meedemeyer. Liza couldn't risk having Melvin drop her off in front of her own house. If her father *was* home, he'd probably shine his big floodlight into the car and come out wielding one of his shotguns.

"Thank you for a lovely evening. I can't say when I've had a better time." *Basically never*, she thought.

"I feel the same way, Princess." He leaned over, lifted her hand, and kissed it. Then he kissed her on the cheek.

"Good night, fair maiden. Until we meet again."

He was just going to get out to go and open her door when Liza said, "No need to get out."

"As you wish, Princess," he said and handed her a piece of paper. "Here's my number. Call me any time."

"Thank you, Melvin."

Liza got out of the car and walked down the driveway to the back door. She waved to him, and just then the motion sensor light went on. Melvin thought she went in and turned the light on and he drove away. She tiptoed back down the driveway and looked up and down the street. Just then Old Lady Meedemeyer opened the back door.

"Is that you, Liza? Is everything all right?"

"Yes, Mrs. Meedemeyer. Nothing to worry about here." She waved and Mrs. Meedemeyer went back into the house.

When Liza got to her house three doors down, she tried to open the back door as quietly as she could, all the while praying her father wasn't home. She took off her shoes and tiptoed into the kitchen. *So far so good,* she thought. She just had to make it down the hallway. Luckily her bedroom was the first door on the right.

Just then, the light went on in the kitchen. She almost had a heart attack. She turned around to see who it was.

"Where have you been? Why are you sneaking in here at this late hour, young lady?"

"Junior! You scared me half to death! What are you doing up anyway? And why are you sitting in the dark?"

I couldn't sleep and thought I'd get myself a snack. I heard the door open and thought I'd have a little fun."

"At my expense?"

"Liza, is that you?"

"Yes, Mom."

"Oh, good—you're home. What time is it?"

"It's eleven-thirty."

"Okay, dear."

Junior tried to say something, but Liza put her hand over his mouth to stop him. She gave him five dollars and told him to keep quiet.

"Good night, Junior," she whispered and went to her room and closed the door.

She threw her clothes over the chair and fell, exhausted, into her bed. The curtains were open and the moonlight shone across her bed. She opened the window a bit for some fresh air. The cool, fresh evening breeze put her right to sleep.

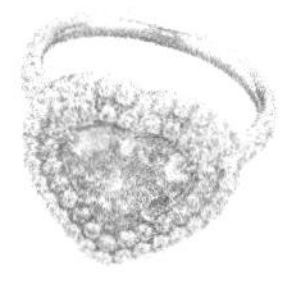

Chapter Three

Father Knows Less

LIZA AWOKE TO THE SOUND of her father's voice coming from the kitchen. She turned over to look at the clock on the nightstand beside her bed. It was only seven-thirty. She got up to go to the washroom and caught sight of herself in the mirror. She realized she hadn't taken her make-up off before she went to bed. She always made a point of washing her face no matter what time she came in. Not this time, though. Her mascara had smudged, and she looked like a raccoon. She washed her face, brushed her teeth, and put on a fake smile, pretending to be happy to see her father.

"Good morning, sleepyhead," her father said in his thick German accent.

"Sleepyhead? It's only seven-thirty! When did you get in?"

"This morning around five," he answered.

"How long will you be home? When do you leave again, and how long will you be gone?" Liza thought she would cover all the bases and get the lowdown forthwith.

"I'll be home for a couple of days. Then gone for three weeks."

"Only a couple of days? We hardly ever see you," she said, feigning sincerity.

"What would you like for breakfast, Liza?" her mom asked.

"I think I'll just make myself some toast, Mom. I'm not very hungry."

"Will you be coming to church with us?"

"I have a bit of a headache, Mom. I'm going to eat, take an aspirin, and lie down for a while."

"Gee, Liza, not enough sleep last night?" Junior said as he sat down at the table.

Liza gave him a look that would turn water into ice.

"What did you say, Junior?"

"Oh nothing, Dad."

Liza took the toast to her room, closed the door, and turned on her radio. She didn't want to hear the way her father spoke to her mother. The truth was, Liza wanted to spend as little time as possible around her father. His cold-hearted sarcasm always cut to the bone. He was always complaining about her mother's cooking, ordering her around, and generally showing her a lack of respect.

Why did Mother marry him in the first place? How could she stand being married to him for twenty-five years? She couldn't figure it out.

Liza lay on her bed, daydreaming about Melvin. She was thankful her father was leaving in a couple of days, as he wouldn't be around on Thursday when she had her next big date. If he was home, there's no way she'd be able to get away with anything. It would be hard enough to work around her mother, but not impossible.

Liza spent most of Sunday in her room cleaning out her closet and her drawers, which she absolutely hated doing, but it kept her busy and away from her father. He didn't bother her when she was busy doing something. He always told her she had to have a strong work ethic. She had that, but according to him, not much else.

"Liza, what are you doing in there?" her father said as he knocked on her bedroom door.

"I'm organizing my closet and drawers," she said as she opened the door.

"Oh, I thought you were being lazy and sleeping."

"Sleeping isn't being lazy; it's being tired."

"Why should you be tired? You don't do anything."

"What do you mean, I ..." she almost started arguing with him but thought better of it. "I wasn't sleeping. Now if you don't mind, I'd like to finish what I started."

"That will be a first," he added sarcastically.

Before her father could say anything more, Liza closed the door. She screamed into her pillow and felt like throwing something. Instead, she sat down on the edge of her bed and closed her eyes. She chanted to herself, *Breathe in breathe out, breathe in breathe out.* She saw Marcus doing that when he was having a particularly difficult day. It actually worked. Before long, she felt calm again. She finished organizing and decided to call Sarah.

"Hi, Sarah! Do you have any plans for tonight?"

"Why, what's up?"

"My father is home and I don't want to be here. I can't bear to watch him talk with his mouth full or listen to him slurp his coffee and burp out loud."

"Say no more. What do you feel like doing?"

"How about dinner and a movie?"

"Sounds good to me. What time?"

"As soon as possible."

"It's three o'clock now. How about I pick you up at four?"

"Perfect, thanks for coming to my rescue."

"Don't mention it!"

***

Liza changed, put on fresh make-up, and styled her hair. It looked just as nice as it did the day before.

She heard the doorbell ring and her mom answer it.

"Sarah, hi! What are you doing here?"

"I'm here to pick Liza up."

"Really? She didn't mention anything."

Liza came around the corner and said, "Don't you remember, Mom? Sarah and I are going out tonight."

"I thought you two went out last night."

Liza hurried out the door. "Gotta go, Mom! See you later!"

"What did your mom mean when she said we went out last night?"

"I'll explain later. Where do you want to go and eat?"

"How about burgers at Duda's?"

"You always want to go there."

"I've never heard you complain."

"Sure, let's go."

On the way to the restaurant, the girls decided to see the new chick flick at the local theatre.

They sat in a booth at the restaurant. It was early, so the usual dinner crowd wasn't there yet. When it was busy, the noise level was so high you had to shout to be heard.

Liza and Sarah ordered and while they waited, Sarah told Liza all the latest details about the "Sarah and Farley" romance. Sarah was a few months older than Liza and six months older than Farley. He often referred to Sarah as "the older woman." Sarah and Farley were talking about getting married. Sarah was graduating from college with a Childcare Certification Diploma. She was looking forward to working with kindergarten children ideally. Farley worked full-time for his uncle, who owned a successful construction company. One day Farley would take over and run the company.

While Sarah spoke, Liza's mind wandered to thoughts of Melvin. Sarah went on and on. Liza drifted in and out, partly listening, but mostly daydreaming.

"What do you think, Liza? Liza? *Liza!*"

"What?"

"I said, what do you think?"

"Think about what?"

"*Liza,* did you hear *anything* I said? Where were you?"

"I was right here."

"Coulda fooled me! You look a little flushed. Are you okay?"

"Yes, *I am okay!*"

"You don't have to snap at me!"

"I'm sorry, Sarah. I didn't mean to."

"What's really going on with you?"

Liza leaned forward across the table, the way people do when they have something important to say. Sarah leaned forward also.

"There's something I have to tell you, Sarah."

"What? What is it? You're okay, aren't you?"

"I'm fine."

"Then what is it?"

"I met someone."

"*You met someone?*" Sarah said as she stood up.

"Ssh, sit down."

"Who? When? Where?"

"Slow down. I met him a week ago."

"You met him a week ago and you're just telling me this now? I can't believe you kept this a secret from me this long!"

"I met him at the coffee shop around the corner from the office. He lives across the street and said he had been watching me for a couple of weeks."

"Watching you? That's kinda creepy."

"Sarah, do you want to hear the story or not?"

"Yes, I do."

"Now where was I? Oh yes. He was sitting at the coffee shop on Monday morning. He stared at me as I walked in. I caught him staring and then he winked at me."

"He winked at you?"

"Yes, he winked at me. I went back the next morning hoping to see him again, but I didn't see him at first. Then he came and stood behind me in line. He leaned forward and complimented me on my dress."

"Your dress? Since when do you wear a dress to work?"

"*A-n-y-w-a-y,* he complimented me on my dress and asked if he could walk me to work. Oh, and he ordered my coffee and paid too."

"Then what?"

"Then he walked me to work and asked me out on a date."

Sarah stood up again. "He asked you out?"

"Ssh, will you sit down! He asked me out and we had our first date last night."

"Wait a minute!" Sarah said slowly. "When I bumped into you at the mall, your hair looked so nice—you were getting all gussied up for your date? You said, 'Don't call me, I'll call you!'"

"Are you done? I'll explain everything if you'll just let me!"

"I can't believe you kept this a secret! I thought I was your best friend!"

"You *are* my best friend! I was going to tell you eventually."

"*Eventually*?"

"Okay, fine! His name is Melvin. He's twenty-three, and he's gorgeous!"

"Do tell!"

"He looks like Michael Jordan."

"You mean he's Black?"

"Yes, and he wears this awesome cologne called Black Knight. Suits him perfectly. He's six-foot-two and an excellent dresser!"

"Your father isn't going to like this one little bit! You know he'll never agree. Your mom won't be too happy either!"

"I know, that's where you come in."

"Where I come in?"

"Yes, I really need your help."

"You know I'll help you in any way I can, Liza. That's what best friends are for!"

"I knew I could count on you."

"If you knew you could count on me, you would have told me sooner!"

"Sarah—"

"Sorry, I just couldn't resist."

"We have another date this Thursday. I'm meeting him at his place, and then we're going to a club."

"You're meeting him at *his* place and then you're going to a club?"

"Why do you keep repeating everything I say?"

"Sorry. Continue."

"I told him he couldn't pick me up at home, because I was going to be out to dinner with you, and you would drop me off."

"Where did he pick you up yesterday?"

"I told him I had some filing to do, and he could pick me up at the office."

"Filing? On Saturday?"

"Work with me, will you?"

"Where did he take you?"

"We went to a place called Fast Freddie's."

"Fast Freddie's? I've never heard of it. Where is it?"

"I have no idea. He drove to places and took exits I've never seen before. It's a really groovy place with great fifties music and cheap food at prices from the fifties. Beer was only a dollar and fifty cents."

"Beer? You drank beer?"

"Yes, it was *so* good! You'll have to try it some time."

"Did he drive you home?"

"Sort of ..."

"Sort of?"

"When he turned down my street, I pointed to Old Lady Meedemeyer's house."

"Why?"

"Why? Because there's no way he could pull into the circular driveway of my house and drop me off at the front door. What if my father had come home early?"

"Okay, you pointed to Old Lady Meedemeyer's house. Then what?"

"He dropped me off in front. I walked down the driveway to the back door and waved goodbye. When I waved, the sensor light came on. I guess he thought I'd opened the door and put the light on, so he drove away."

"Honestly, Liza, the things you come up with! What have you got cooked up for Thursday night?"

"I'm going to tell my mom you and I are going to volunteer at a fundraiser."

"A fundraiser?" Sarah said as she rolled her eyes. "What time are you supposed to be at Melvin's?"

"I'm supposed to be at his place at eight-thirty, and we're going to the club for ten."

"Ten? You're usually in bed by ten!"

"I'll make an exception! Pick me up at six. I'll say we have the dinner and fundraiser at six-thirty and also that we have to clean up, so we'll probably be late."

"Where is this fundraiser supposed to be?"

"How about the Lakeside Community Centre? They always have stuff going on Thursday night. If anyone drives by, there will be lots of cars in the parking lot."

"Okay, it's a plan. Hey, look at the time, Liza. The show starts in thirty minutes."

"Do you still want to go?"

"I do. Do you?"

"Sure, let's go."

***

After the movie, Sarah dropped Liza off and went home. When Liza came in through the back door, she saw her mom sitting at the kitchen table, having a cup of tea.

"Hi, dear. How was your evening?"

"Good, Mom. What are you doing sitting here all by yourself?"

"Your father left sooner than expected."

"Really? Why?"

"He got a call from Sylvia earlier this afternoon. In fact, he was on the phone with her when Sarah came to pick you up. He came in the kitchen just as you went out the front door. He called to you, but I guess you didn't hear him. In any case, Sylvia was working at one of the show homes and said your father had to go over there and do some type of inspection for a prospective buyer."

"Sylvia is the agent he hired to co-ordinate the sales, right?"

"Yes, that's correct. On his way out, he said he'd be leaving after that to go to Merisfield."

"Merisfield?"

"Yes, that's where he'll be for the next three weeks. He also said he was going to be picking George up on the way."

"George? Who's George?"

"He's the head foreman for the project in Merisfield."

"He always travels alone."

"Who am I to say?"

"Where's Junior?"

"He went to bed already."

"I have a busy day tomorrow, so I'm going to bed also. By the way, Mom, Thursday night Sarah and I are going to volunteer at a fundraiser at Lakeside Community Centre."

"A fundraiser for what?"

"I don't know, to raise funds."

"What time does it start?"

"We have to be there by six-thirty."

"What time will you be home?"

"I'm not sure. We'll have to help clean up and stuff when it's over."

"I hope it's not too late; you have to work the next day."

"I know, Mom."

"Why couldn't the fundraiser be on a Friday night instead?"

"I don't know. I'm going to bed now. Good night. See you in the morning. Love you."

"Love you too, dear."

Liza was looking forward to dreaming about Melvin, and she was happy that she wouldn't have to see her father in the morning.

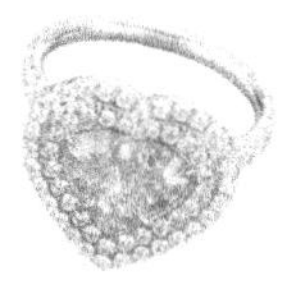

Chapter Four

Roberto

LIZA ARRIVED AT WORK Monday morning an hour earlier than she normally would. As she unlocked the door, she saw an envelope lying on the floor.

"To My Princess," she read. She sat down at her desk and opened it.

Mirror, mirror, on the wall,
Who is the fairest Princess of them all?
Princess Liza!
Love, Melvin

Just then, Marcus walked in. "Good morning, Liza. What are you smiling about?"

"Oh, nothing," she said as she slipped the letter into her purse.

"What were you just reading?"

"Just a note from a friend."

"A *boy*-friend?"

The phone rang and she answered *it* and not Marcus. *Saved by the bell.* "Good morning, Mr. Buckleworth. Yes, he is, one moment, I'll put you through."

Marcus motioned for Liza to put it through to his office.

Liza worked quickly all day without stopping to take a lunch or coffee break. She was just about ready to leave for the day when Marcus came around the corner.

"Heading out, Liza?"

"Yes."

"Me too."

"Marcus, I have a favour to ask."

"Sure, what is it?"

"If I come in early every morning and get all caught up on my work, can I leave early on Thursday?"

"Shouldn't be a problem. Do you have a hot date?"

"Yes."

"Aha, I knew it!"

"With Sarah."

"With Sarah?"

"Yes. Sarah and I are volunteering at a fundraiser, and I'd like to have enough time to get ready."

"A fundraiser? For what?"

"Why does everyone keep asking me that? I'm not sure. I just volunteered to help."

"Okay, Liza. By the way, where is it?"

"It's at the Lakeside Community Centre."

"Really? Maybe I'll stop by on my way home. I always like to donate to a good cause."

"Uh, well, uh, it's for women only."

"For women only?"

"Yes, I just remembered. It's to raise funds for the new women's shelter."

"A new women's shelter? I haven't heard anything about that. I'll have to look into it."

"*No!*" Liza said sharply.

"No?"

"I mean, no, you don't have to look into it, Marcus, I'll get some information for you."

"All right, Liza."

"So I can leave early?"

"Sure, no problem."

"Thank you, Marcus."

***

By the time Thursday rolled around, Liza was all caught up on her work. At three-thirty she tidied up her desk and announced to Marcus that she would be leaving.

Liza's Mom had been at a church bake sale, and Liza didn't expect her home until about five-thirty. She was looking forward to having a nap before getting ready for her date with Melvin. Liza was singing as she opened the back door and walked into the kitchen. She always sang when she was happy. She put her purse on the counter and took a soda from the fridge. She popped it open and it sprayed a bit.

"Liza? Is that you?"

"Mom?"

"Yes."

"What are you doing home so early, Mom?"

Helga set a batch of clothes on the counter and said, "I didn't sleep too well last night and had a headache when I woke up this morning. I came home early to take an aspirin and have a little rest before going to work at the bake sale tonight. What are you doing home so early, Liza?"

"I have the fundraiser tonight, remember?"

"Yes, that's right."

"I went to work early every day this week to catch up on all of my work. Since I'm actually ahead on some things, Marcus said I could leave early today."

"That's good, dear."

"I'm going to have a short nap now, Mom."

"What time are you leaving, dear?"

"Sarah is picking me up at six o'clock."

"Would you and Sarah mind dropping me off at the church? I'm not sure I feel up to driving."

"We could drop you off, but we can't pick you up afterwards. I don't know what time we'll be leaving the fundraiser."

"That won't be a problem, dear. I'm sure one of the ladies can drop me off later."

"Sounds good, Mom. I'm going to have my nap."

***

Sarah rang the doorbell promptly at six o'clock.

"Mom, Sarah is here," Liza announced. "Hi, Sarah, come on in."

"I'll just get my purse and be right there," Helga called out.

Sarah whispered, "Your mom is coming with us?"

"No, we just have to drop her off at the church. She's working the bake sale tonight."

"Ready, girls, let's go!" Helga said as she hung her purse on her shoulder.

They got into the car and Liza turned on the radio. If the radio was on, maybe her mom wouldn't ask any questions about the fundraiser.

"Sarah, would you mind turning the music down, please? I still have a bit of a headache."

Liza turned it down and then said to Sarah, "How is your grandmother?"

"My grandmother?" Sarah said as she frowned at Liza.

"Yes, your grandmother!" Liza said as she winked at Sarah.

"Oh, my grandmother. Good. Yup, better than ever!"

"What was wrong with your grandmother?" Helga asked.

"Uh, she uh, stubbed her big toe. Yes, that's it."

"She stubbed her big toe?" Helga sounded concerned.

"Yes, and her nail was all black too."

"Oh, the poor thing. Give her my best, will you, Sarah dear."

"Yes, I will definitely. She's much better now."

"Here we are!" Liza announced.

"That was quick. Just drop me off right there at the front door, please."

Sarah parked the car and waited for Helga to get out of the car.

"Good luck at the fundraiser, girls! Liza, don't be too late. Thank you for the ride, Sarah!"

"Bye, Mom!"

"That was close! She stubbed her big toe, Sarah?"

"Liza, you put me on the spot. I didn't understand what you were talking about."

"I didn't want my mom to ask a question about the fundraiser, so I thought I'd steer the conversation a bit."

"There is no fundraiser," Sarah said jokingly.

"I know that!"

"Where should we go for dinner, Liza?"

"Let's go somewhere we're not likely to run into anyone we know. How about that new Italian restaurant on First Avenue?"

"Fine with me," Sarah said.

They drove for about twenty minutes and then Liza spotted it. "There it is, Sarah, Café Guido."

"Looks like a nice place, Liza."

They parked the car, and as they walked up the steps to the front door, a young Italian boy about sixteen years old held the door open for them. As he did, they were greeted inside by a very handsome waiter.

"Buona Sera." *Good evening.* "Per due?" *For two?*

Liza and Sarah looked at each other. They didn't understand what the waiter said.

"Welcome, lovely ladies. Come-a right-a this way. My name is Roberto, and I will-a be-a your-a waiter tonight-a."

Roberto was about six feet tall. He had dark brown eyes and thick, black, curly hair. He looked very athletic, a soccer player perhaps.

As they followed Roberto to the table, they couldn't help but stare at him.

Liza whispered to Sarah, "Wow!"

Sarah nodded in agreement.

Roberto stopped at a cozy little table off to the side, toward the back of the restaurant.

"It's-a okay for-a you?"

"Oh yes, this is just fine!" Sarah said as she stared at Roberto.

"Allow-a me-a Senorina," he said as he pulled out a chair for Sarah.

Liza began to pull out her own chair, and then Roberto turned to her and said, "Wait-a for-a me-a." He pulled out the chair for Liza and she sat down.

"May I-a tell-a you-a the specials for-a tonight?"

"Yes, please!" they answered in unison as they leaned forward and stared up at Roberto.

"We have-a pasta primavera, pasta fagiole, and chicken cacciatore."

"Okay," Liza said.

"Okay what?" Roberto asked, slightly confused.

"Okay, that's what I'll have," Liza confirmed.

"All-a three-a?"

"No, the last one." Liza didn't have a clue what it was. Just listening to him speak made her weak in the knees. Good thing she was sitting down.

"And-a for-a you-a, Bella?"

"My name is Sarah, but you can call me Bella if you want to!"

"Bella means beautiful in Italian."

"By all means, call me Bella!"

Liza rolled her eyes.

"What-a would-a you-a like-a, Bella?"

"Could you please repeat the specials?"

"Certo!" *Sure.* Roberto proceeded to repeat them.

"Which one do *you* think I should have?" Sarah said as she batted her eyes at him and pursed her lips.

"My-a favourite is-a the pasta primavera."

"Then that's what I'll have. Thank you, Roberto."

"I will-a be-a right-a back with-a some-a water for-a you."

"What do you think Farley would say, Bella?"

"Oh, be quiet, Liza! You were staring at him too!"

"Not like *that*, I wasn't!"

***

They ate their dinner, and afterwards Liza went to the washroom to powder her nose and freshen up her lipstick. While she was gone, Roberto came back to the table and talked to Sarah.

"How was-a your-a dinner tonight-a, Bella?"

"It was delicious, thank you, Roberto."

"I hope-a to-a see-a you again, Bella. Please-a come-a back-a soon!" he said as he took Sarah's hand and kissed it while he stared right into her eyes. His lips lingered on her hand.

Liza returned to see what was happening. "I don't mean to interrupt, but we really must be going now, Sarah," Liza said as she stood by the table. Liza handed Roberto the money to pay for their dinner.

"Keep the change," Sarah offered.

"Grazie, Bella." *Thank you, beautiful.* "I hope-a to-a see-a you-a both again-a soon!" Roberto walked them to the door, and they waited as he opened it for them. Liza went first.

"Ciao, Roberto," Sarah said as she walked past him.

"Ciao, Bella!"

Liza waited at the bottom of the steps for Sarah. "Ciao, Roberto?" Liza said. "All of a sudden you know how to speak Italian?"

"I've always loved the language. I'm thinking of taking a course," Sarah said decidedly.

"Earth to Bella! Earth to Bella! What about *Farley*? You remember ... the love of your life? Or have you forgotten about him?"

"No, Liza, I haven't forgotten about Farley."

"Ciao, Roberto." Liza imitated Sarah again as she took Sarah's hand and pretended to kiss it.

"Oh Liza, stop that!"

They both laughed as they got into the car.

"Where should I drop you off, Liza?"

Liza looked at her watch and said, "We're going to be a bit early, so just drop me off at the coffee shop and I'll go powder my nose."

"Didn't you just do that?"

"Doesn't hurt to look my best!"

Sarah stopped in front of the coffee shop. Liza got out as Sarah said, "Have fun, and don't do anything I wouldn't do!"

"What does that mean, Sarah?"

"Never mind. I want to hear all about it tomorrow, and I do mean *all*!"

"I'll call you after work."

Sarah waved and drove away.

Chapter Five

Apartment 307

LIZA WENT INTO THE COFFEE SHOP and headed straight to the washroom. She took her time, fluffed her hair, touched up her lipstick, and decided she had enough powder on her nose. *Better get going now,* she thought.

She knew the girl working at the counter and just waved as she headed for the front door. As she reached for the door, she heard a familiar voice.

"Where are you going, beautiful Princess?"

Liza turned around and saw Melvin sitting at his usual table.

"Melvin, what are you doing here?"

"I was just going to ask you the same thing."

"I was a bit too early to come over, so I thought I'd make a quick stop and go to the ladies' room and freshen up."

"You look pretty fresh to me. I saw you and Sarah drive up. I thought you'd come straight over, then I saw you walk in here instead. For future reference, you can never be too early. Come on, let's go." He took Liza's hand, opened the door for her, and they walked across the street.

"By the way, you look very pretty tonight, Princess."

"You look pretty *pretty* yourself, Melvin."

"I've been called a lot of things before, but *pretty* wasn't one of them."

Melvin lived on the third floor. No elevator. They walked up the stairs to apartment 307.

"Here we are," Melvin said as he stopped to unlock the door. "After you, Princess."

The apartment was large and very tastefully decorated. In the living room was a large, black leather couch and matching loveseat. A glass-top coffee table sat in front of the couch, and two matching end tables were on either side of the loveseat. A large floor lamp curved over the right side of the couch to light the corner of the living room. A large area rug in grey and black covered most of the living-room floor. There were three white pillar candles placed on a silver tray in the middle of the coffee table. Another tray held chocolate-covered strawberries. On the wall in front of the couch was a large bookshelf filled with books, pictures in frames, and ornaments that looked like they came from Africa.

"Come in, Princess, make yourself at home."

Liza stood in front of the bookshelf, looking at the pictures.

"Feel free to take a little tour while I pour you a drink. Champagne?"

"Champagne is perfect."

Liza walked over to a little nook where Melvin's desk sat in front of a large window that overlooked the street, with a clear view of the coffee shop. The large desk faced the window, just as Liza had imagined.

The kitchen was sparkling clean with only a few glass containers on the counter that held tea, coffee, and sugar.

"How do you like it so far?"

"It's lovely, Melvin. Who does your decorating?"

"I do!"

"Really?"

"You sound very surprised, Princess."

"No, not really ... well, okay, maybe a little!"

Melvin smiled as he took a glass of Champagne and handed it to Liza. "Have you ever had Champagne before?"

"I had Champagne on my mother's birthday last year."

Melvin leaned in close to Liza as he stood next to her in the kitchen.

"A toast. May this be the beginning of many magic moments with my Princess."

"Mmm, this is good," Liza said as she took a sip.

"There's more where that came from, my sweet. Let's go into the living room."

Liza walked over to the bookshelf and looked at the pictures again. Melvin walked up and stood behind her.

"Who is this?" Liza asked at she pointed to the picture of a little boy wearing a football uniform.

"Yours truly," Melvin answered.

"You played football?"

"Yes, until my last year in university, when I got sidelined."

"Sidelined? What does that mean?"

"I got injured and couldn't play anymore. I had to watch from the sidelines."

"I'm so sorry."

"Thanks. Now I concentrate on writing."

"Who is this pretty lady?"

"That's my mom. She calls every once in a while, from wherever she might be, but she never seems to have time to get together."

"I'm sorry," Liza said again.

"It's okay, thanks. Lola is a really good mom to me, so it makes up for a lot." Melvin pointed to another picture and said, "This is my sister, Alicia, her husband, Ritchie, and my nephew, Max."

"What a nice family! Your sister looks like your mom."

"Yes, she does, doesn't she?"

"Max is adorable. I think he looks like you."

"You think?"

"Definitely," Liza said as she looked at the picture more closely.

"Are you saying I'm adorable too?"

"Definitely."

"You look a little flushed, Princess. Are you okay?"

"I'm fine, Melvin."

"More Champagne?"

"Yes, please."

"Let's sit down and relax, Princess."

Liza sat down on the couch and put her drink on the coffee table. Melvin put some music on and then sat down beside her. He turned his body toward her and rested his arm on the top of the couch behind her.

"Princess?"

"Yes?"

"You sure are pretty."

"Thank you, Melvin, you are so kind."

"Kind? It has nothing to do with being kind; it's simply the truth."

He leaned over, lifted her chin up gently, and kissed her. Liza was a bit surprised, and she pulled back.

"Oh, I'm sorry. I didn't mean to offend you."

"You didn't offend me, Melvin. I just wasn't prepared for that."

"Well, get prepared, because I'm going to kiss you again."

Melvin put his glass on the coffee table. He put his arms around Liza and pulled her closer to him and kissed her. After the kiss, Liza sat in the same position with her eyes closed and her lips still puckered.

"Princess?"

"Mmm, that's the best kiss I've ever had," she said with her eyes still closed.

Melvin laughed. Liza opened her eyes. They talked and drank lots of Champagne.

"How do you like the music, Princess?" He got up and turned it up a bit. "Would you like to dance?" he said as he offered his hand.

"Yes, I believe I would." Liza stood and took Melvin's hand.

"What time are we going to the club, Melvin?"

"The best time to be there is about ten, or ... if you're comfy, we could just stay here. I've got lots of music and more Champagne."

"I'm not sure if I need too much more Champagne. I do have to work tomorrow."

"Don't worry about that now. Now is the time to relax and enjoy yourself, Princess."

"You do have good music," Liza said as she swayed back and forth with the music as Melvin held her close to him. Liza continued, "I *am* relaxed, and I *am* enjoying myself."

"In that case, what have you decided? Stay in or go out?" Melvin asked.

"Stay in," Liza confirmed.

"Stay in it is! Have a seat, Princess, and I'll go and get the other bottle of Champagne." He turned the first one upside down in the bucket of ice.

Liza sat down and picked up one of the chocolate-covered strawberries. She was just about to take a bite.

"Hold on, Princess," Melvin said as he walked over to her. He set the Champagne on the table and took the strawberry from her. "Allow me," he said, placing the strawberry against her lips. "Open up."

Liza opened her mouth, and Melvin fed the strawberry to her.

"Yummy," she said. "Now it's my turn to feed you, Melvin." Liza took a strawberry and fed it to Melvin.

"You're right, that is yummy," he said as he chewed and swallowed. "You know what that tastes like?"

"No, Melvin, what does it taste like?"

"It tastes like more!" He leaned over and said, "Now give me a sweet strawberry kiss."

Liza leaned in and Melvin kissed her.

"There's something to be said for those strawberries, Liza, but you taste even better!"

Liza felt slightly embarrassed, but she smiled and took a sip of Champagne.

"Maybe we should dance a little, Melvin."

"My pleasure, fair maiden; after all, the dance floor is empty."

Liza wobbled a little as she stood up.

"Steady there, Princess."

"Melvin?"

"Yes?"

"I think I need to sit down."

"Is the Champagne making you feel a little tipsy?"

"A bit," she confessed.

He kissed her neck and then led her to the couch. "You know you're irresistible, Princess."

"You say all the right things, Melvin. I feel the same."

"You think you're irresistible too?" he joked.

"No, silly. I think you're irresistible."

"Why, thank you, my dear." He leaned in and kissed her in a way she had never been kissed before. He pushed her backwards gently as he kissed her again.

She pushed him back up.

He pushed her backwards again.

She pushed him back up.

He pushed her backwards again; this time she gave in.

"I just want to feel your body against mine and hold you for a while, Princess."

"Just for a little while then, Melvin. I need to be getting home soon though."

They lay in silence, listening to the music for what seemed like quite a long time. Liza opened her eyes suddenly and said, "Melvin, what time is it?"

He checked his watch and said, "It's eleven-thirty. What time do you want me to drive you home?"

Never, she thought.

Melvin smiled.

Did I say that out loud? she wondered. "Pretty soon, I have to w—"

He didn't let her finish; he kissed her instead. Liza moaned. Melvin kissed her again, this time with more passion than the last. Liza let out a big sigh.

When she caught her breath, she said, "That was amazing!"

"Amazing?" Melvin repeated.

"Amazing!" Liza confirmed. "I really should be going, although I don't want to."

"I understand, Princess. We'll have more nights like this, I promise."

"If you promise."

"I do," he said. "It's midnight, Princess. Your fairy godmother isn't going to suddenly appear, is she?"

"Don't be silly, Melvin. Your car won't turn into a pumpkin, will it?"

"I have referred to it as a lemon a few times, but never a pumpkin! One last toast," Melvin said as he raised his glass. "To my Princess, this magical night, and many more to come!"

"I'll drink to that," Liza said as she raised her glass to his.

"On that note, I better drive you home."

***

Melvin held Liza's hand all the way to the car.

As he opened the door for her, he said, "Your chariot awaits m'lady."

"Thank you, Melvin."

Melvin didn't need any directions this time. He pulled up in front of Old Lady Meedemeyer's house and announced, "Here we are."

"You have a very good memory, Melvin."

"When it comes to you, Princess, I remember everything!" He leaned in and kissed her. "Until next time. Can I call you tomorrow night?"

"Call me tomorrow during the day at work, Melvin. My brother has a habit of picking up the extension at home and listening in on people's conversations."

"We wouldn't want that now, would we? You have my number. Call me whenever you want to. There's no chance anyone will be listening in."

Liza got out of the car and, just as before, walked down the driveway toward the side door. She waved, but the sensor light didn't come on right away. Melvin waited.

"Uh, oh," Liza said under her breath. "Please turn on."

Just then the light turned on, and Melvin drove away. Liza waited a few minutes before walking down the driveway and over to her own house.

Liza talked to herself as she walked. *This sucks. Why do I have to lie to Melvin? Why do I have to hide him from my family? Why can't I just be honest about him? My father would have my head if he ever found out, that's why. I think Mom would be a bit more understanding, but she has a hard time keeping secrets from my father. He can read her like a book and would drag it out of her somehow. I just can't take that chance. In the meantime, this will just have to be my little secret ... and Sarah's.*

Liza was still muttering to herself as she walked into the kitchen. She stopped and listened to make sure that no one was up. She quietly closed the door, took off her shoes, and tiptoed into her room. She heard her mom get up and quickly closed the bedroom door. Liza got into her bed, still wearing all of her clothes, and turned on her side facing away from the door as she pulled the covers over her. Her mom opened Liza's bedroom door, saw her in bed, and closed the door again. *That was close!* She got up, got undressed, and slipped back into bed.

Chapter Six

"Oh, What a Tangled Web We Weave"

LIZA'S ALARM WENT OFF at 7:00 a.m. She hit the snooze button, which gave her an extra ten minutes.

Helga knocked on her door. "Come on, sleepyhead, time to get up or you'll be late for work."

"I'm up, I'm up," Liza said as she slid one foot onto the floor. She slipped into the shower and turned on the water. The shower felt good, but she still had a hard time opening her eyes. Afterwards, she got dressed and went into the kitchen.

"Good morning, dear. I didn't hear you come in last night. What time did you get home?"

"I'm not exactly sure, Mom."

"I got up around one o'clock to get a glass of water and checked your room. You were already fast asleep."

In bed, yes, but definitely not asleep.

"I think it was about eleven-thirty or so, Mom."

"How was the fundraiser?"

"Great! We had a lot of fun."

"What was it f—"

Liza cut her off. "I gotta go, Mom. I'll pick up a muffin on the way to work. See you later."

"Wait a minute! Do you want a ride to work? I have to go right past there on my way to the dentist."

"No thanks," Liza said as she went out through the front door. She caught the bus and got off in front of the coffee shop. She went in and ordered her coffee and a muffin to go. She left the coffee shop, and as she turned the corner, Melvin was waiting for her.

"Melvin! What a surprise! What are you doing here?"

"Waiting for you, Princess!"

Liza did a quick check to make sure her hair was in place as she looked in the barber shop window. For a minute, she didn't remember what she was wearing. *Oh good, it's my pink and white two-piece skirt outfit.* Pink was her favourite colour, and she always got compliments when she wore it.

"You look beautiful this morning. May I walk with you to work?"

"I would love for you to walk me to work."

"I was going to call you today and ask if you'd like to go out with me tomorrow afternoon, but I decided to come and ask you in person."

"Tomorrow afternoon?"

"I thought it might be fun to go to an afternoon matinee."

"That does sound like fun, Melvin. I've never been to an afternoon matinee."

"Really?"

"Really!" Liza confirmed.

"I'll pick you up at one o'clock. The movie starts at two."

"You've already chosen the movie? Pretty sure of yourself, Melvin!"

"I'm sure I want to see you as much as I can."

"Here we are again, Melvin," Liza said as she stopped before walking up the stairs to work.

"I wish I could spend more time with you today, Princess."

"I'll spend more time with you tomorrow, Melvin."

"Yes, you will!" he confirmed.

Melvin leaned in and kissed Liza on the neck and whispered, "Until tomorrow."

All of a sudden, they heard the sound of tires screeching, as if someone was trying to stop suddenly. It was Helga! She screeched to a halt at the stop sign a half block past where Liza and Melvin were standing. They looked over to see what was happening.

"Oh no, it's my mother!"

"Your mother? What's she doing around here?"

"I don't know." Then Liza remembered her mom said she had a dentist appointment.

"I forgot my mom said she was going to the dentist this morning. It's just two blocks from here."

"Do you think she saw us?"

"It's possible. I'm sure I'll find out when I get home after work today."

"Will it be a problem?"

"Don't worry, I can handle my mother. It's just a good thing it's not my father!"

"Pardon me?"

"I said, it won't be too much of a bother."

"Call me later, Princess, and let me know how it goes."

"I will, Melvin."

"I'm sorry about shocking your mother."

"I'm not."

"You're not?"

"Why would I be? My mom has always said my happiness is important to her. You make me very happy, Melvin."

"You make me very happy too, Princess."

"I'm glad. I really have to go in to work now, Melvin. I'll call you later."

"I'll be expecting your call, Princess!"

Liza walked into the office singing. Marcus commented on her good mood and listened to her humming as she worked. He didn't comment any further; he was just happy she was happy. The day seemed to go very quickly, and before she knew it, Liza was on her way home.

Liza wasn't sure what to expect when she got home. As she walked through the back door, she saw her mom sitting at the kitchen table.

"I've been waiting for you to get home, Missy."

Uh oh, I'm in trouble; she's calling me Missy! Liza thought.

"Who were you talking to in front of your office building this morning, Missy?" Helga asked.

"How was your dentist appointment, Mom?"

"Don't change the subject! Who *was* that? I saw a young man there with you."

Liza had to think for a moment about whether she should tell her mom the truth now or ease her into it later. She didn't want her mom to know the truth and blurt it out to her father. She decided to wait.

"Oh *him*! Just someone asking for directions."

"It sure didn't look like that to me!"

"That's all it was Mom, really."

"Do you know him?"

"No, Mom, I don't know him. I may have seen him at the coffee shop a time or two."

"Really?" Helga said, somewhat suspiciously.

"What's the harm in talking to someone, Mom?"

"There's no harm in *talking* to someone, as long as that's all it was."

"That's all it was," Liza assured her mom, then added, "How was your dentist appointment?"

"It was fine, dear. I just have to go back next week for a filling."

"Oh really, what day?"

"Friday at nine.

Note to self... don't stand in front of the office with Melvin that day!

"What's for dinner, Mom?"

"Chicken, potatoes, and your favourite salad with romaine lettuce, blue cheese, almonds, and that creamy dressing you love so much."

"Sounds delicious! What time will Junior be home?"

"He won't be home this weekend. He went to the lake with John and his family."

"It's just you and me, then! We haven't had dinner alone in a long time. Can we use the good china and have some wine?"

"I suppose so."

"I'll set the dining room table."

"You really want to get fancy, don't you, Liza?"

"It's a special occasion when it's just the two of us, Mom."

"Okay, go ahead and set the dining room table."

"How about candles?"

"If you're going to do it up fancy, you might as well pull out all the stops!"

***

Liza and Helga had a wonderful dinner together. Helga even had a second glass of wine. Usually she didn't drink much at all. After dinner, Liza took out a photo album with her baby pictures and they reminisced and laughed.

Helga stopped looking at the pictures, and in a sombre tone she said, "Your father wasn't home much when you kids were young. He was always working."

"What brought that on, Mom?"

"I don't know. Looking at these pictures reminded me of all the hopes and dreams I used to have. I always hoped that once you kids got older and we had more money, your father wouldn't have to work so hard or be away as much. Now he seems to be away just as often, if not more."

"Do you miss him? It seems when he's home, you two don't get along."

"I do miss him and I know we argue, but after twenty-five years of marriage, I still love him. I guess I'm used to him too."

"When is he going to come home again?"

"Actually, your father called earlier today and said there was a change of plans. He'll be home next weekend and he wants all of us to go to the lake."

"Next weekend? I thought he was going to be away much longer! Isn't it a bit early in the season?"

"It's the last weekend in April; that's when we always open the cottage. Oh, and one more thing, Sylvia and her husband will be joining us."

"Sylvia? Why? I'd rather invite Sarah."

"You can invite Sarah. There will be plenty of room. They won't be bringing their three kids."

"I still don't understand why *she* has to be there."

"Now dear, you know your father and Sylvia work together."

"Just because they work together doesn't mean he has to invite her to the cottage too."

"You know your father—once he's made up his mind about something, there's no changing it."

"I know. Anyway, let's change the subject. I'm going to go to an afternoon matinee with Sarah tomorrow and then out for a bite to eat."

"You've been doing that a lot lately."

"I guess I have." *I should make up a new story,* Liza thought.

"Okay, dear. I've made plans to go out with Aunt Sadie tomorrow. We're going to a flea market downtown, and then Aunt Sadie and I are having dinner together."

"Where's the flea market, Mom?" The last thing Liza wanted to do was bump into her mom and Aunt Sadie when she was out with Melvin.

"I'm not exactly sure, dear. Aunt Sadie just discovered it. She's picking me up at noon tomorrow."

"Really? Can I use the car?"

"Sure, dear. That would be fine. What movie are you and Sarah going to?"

"I'm not sure. There are a few we haven't seen yet. They all start around the same time."

"I see."

"I feel really tired, Mom. Can we do the dishes in the morning?"

"I'll wash the china and put the rest into the dishwasher. I'm not tired."

"Thanks, Mom, you're the best! Have a good sleep. Love you."

"Love you too, dear."

Liza went to her room and called Melvin. She was whispering so her mom wouldn't hear her.

"Hello, Princess," he answered.

"Hello, Melvin," Liza whispered.

"Princess? Is that you? Why are you whispering? Is everything okay? I was getting worried."

"Everything is okay. I was having dinner with my mom, and this is the first chance I've had to call you."

"Are we still on for tomorrow?"

"Yes. I'll have my mom's car, so I'll come and pick you up."

"Great!"

Just then, Helga knocked on Liza's door. "Liza, who are you talking to?"

"Melvin, I have to go. See you tomorrow. Bye."

"B—" He didn't have a chance to say goodbye.

"Liza, what are you doing? Who are you talking to? Is that Sarah?"

Liza opened her bedroom door. "Yes, Mom, that was Sarah."

"I wanted to ask her how her grandmother was doing."

"Her grandmother?"

"Yes, remember? Her grandmother hurt her toe."

"Her toe?"

"Liza, your memory isn't what it used to be. Remember when you and Sarah gave me a ride to the bake sale? Sarah said her grandmother had hurt her toe."

"Oh, *that* toe! She's fine!"

"Tell Sarah to give her my regards."

"Sure, Mom. Good night."

"Good night, dear; see you in the morning."

I'm going to have to try harder to remember which stories I tell my mom from now on. I wish I could tell my mom the truth. When you tell the truth, you don't have to have a good memory.

Chapter Seven

"Missy" and Melvin

LIZA WAS UP, dressed, and ready to leave by noon. She wanted to go to the office and give Sarah a call to tell her about her movie date with Melvin and fill her in on the details about their date the other night.

"I'm leaving now, Mom," Liza called out.

"It's only noon. I thought the movie didn't start until two."

"I thought I'd stop in at the office and catch up on a few things."

"Since when do you go to the office on a Saturday?"

"When I have a few things to do."

"All right, dear. Say hi to Sarah for me."

"I will, Mom. Say hi to Aunt Sadie for me."

"I will."

Liza drove to the office and parked in Marcus' spot. She went inside and dialled Sarah's number. Busy. She turned the radio on, sorted through some papers on her desk, and tried Sarah's number again. Still busy. She kept trying about every ten minutes until she had to leave to go and pick up Melvin. She called him to say she was on her way. He agreed to meet her downstairs.

"Hi, Princess," Melvin said as he got into the car. "Are you sure you want to drive? We could leave your car here and take mine if you'd rather."

"No, I don't mind driving; it's not too often I get the car."

"Okay, you're the boss."

They parked in the lot across from the movie theatre and walked across the street.

"We have a number of movies to choose from. What tickles your fancy?" Melvin asked.

"Why don't we see that new suspense movie?" Liza suggested.

"Sounds good to me," Melvin agreed.

They bought popcorn and drinks and went to take their seats.

Melvin held Liza's hand during the movie. Holding hands with Melvin felt so right, she never wanted to let go. She kept looking over at him, making sure she wasn't dreaming.

Liza missed most of the movie, concentrating more on how wonderful it felt to hold hands with Melvin, how handsome he was, and how lucky she felt.

When the movie ended, they sat and watched the credits while others left the theatre.

"How did you enjoy the movie, Princess?"

"I thought it was great, Melvin."

"What was your favourite part?"

"Umm, I couldn't really say for sure."

"Me either. I thought it was really well done, but I couldn't narrow it down to just one part. I have a surprise for you, Princess."

"You do? What is it?"

"I'm going to cook dinner for you!"

"You're going to cook dinner for me?"

"Yes. You don't have to go straight home or anything, do you?"

"No, I told my mom I was going to be out for the evening."

"Perfect. Let's go back to my place so we can get started."

"What are we having?"

"It's a surprise. You're not allergic to anything, are you?"

"No."

"Excellent. There's a parking lot behind the apartment. Pull in there and park in one of the visitor's spots."

***

When they got into the apartment building, Melvin took Liza in his arms and kissed her passionately.

"I've been wanting to kiss you all afternoon," he confessed.

"You have?" Liza said innocently.

"I have to confess, I missed parts of the movie, fantasizing about kissing you."

"I have to confess the same."

"Great minds think alike, Princess. Next time we go to a movie, we'll make sure to watch it."

"We can try," Liza replied.

Melvin unlocked the door and ushered Liza into the living room. "Why don't you choose some music to play while I get some wine for us. Red or white?"

"Red for me."

"Me too. Good choice."

Liza chose to play an R&B mix from the fifties.

"That's about my favourite selection," Melvin called out from the kitchen.

He walked into the living room and handed Liza a glass of red wine.

"Here's your wine, Princess. May I propose a toast? Here's to days *and* nights of wine and roses." From behind his back, Melvin produced a single red rose.

"Oh Melvin, it's so beautiful."

"Not as beautiful as you, my Princess."

He kissed her on the cheek and took her by the hand.

"Come and keep me company in the kitchen."

"I'd love to."

Liza watched as Melvin chopped, cut, seasoned, sautéed, and prepared the dinner. He put it in the oven, set the timer, and poured more wine.

"It won't be long now and dinner will be ready," he announced. "I hope you're hungry."

"I'm starved!"

"That's good. Me too! Wait until you see what I have for dessert, Princess!"

"Dessert too?"

"Of course! What's a dinner without dessert?"

"I didn't realize you were a chef, Melvin."

"I wouldn't say I'm a chef, but I manage. I do love to cook!"

"We'll get along just fine, because I love to eat."

"I knew we were perfect for each other."

They sat in the living room drinking wine and listening to the music. About an hour later, the oven timer sounded.

"Come with me, Princess." Melvin took Liza's hand, led her into the dining room, and pulled out her chair.

"Thank you, kind sir."

Melvin brought the dinner and salad and placed it on the table. "We have for your dining pleasure, chicken in mushroom and wine sauce, rice pilaf, mixed vegetables, and finally, a tossed salad."

"It looks wonderful, Melvin."

"Let's hope it tastes wonderful!"

"Mmm, this is really good, Melvin."

"I'm glad you like it."

"In fact, I think I'll eat here again! The only other person who has ever cooked for me before is my mother."

"Get used to it, my Princess; it's going to be a regular occurrence."

"How did I get so lucky, Melvin?"

"I am the lucky one!"

There was no shortage of conversation at the dinner table. Afterwards, Melvin cleared the dinner plates and brought out the dessert.

"Strawberry sundaes to cleanse the palate."

"I *love* ice cream," Liza said as she took the first spoonful of her dessert.

"This is not just *any* ice cream, Princess. I made it myself."

"You're kidding!"

"I wouldn't kid you."

"This is amazing, Melvin!"

"Thank you. I'm glad you like it."

They hadn't quite finished dessert when Melvin stood up and said, "Come with me, Princess, and bring your wine."

"Where are you taking me, Melvin?"

"You'll see."

Melvin led Liza out of the apartment, through the doorway at the end of the hall, and up a flight of stairs that led to the roof.

"Close your eyes, Princess."

Liza closed her eyes. Melvin opened the door to the roof, took her hand, and walked forward about six steps.

"Open your eyes now."

"Oh Melvin, it's beautiful. What a lovely rooftop garden."

There were small trees, flowers too many to count, a waterfall pouring fresh water into a fish pond, and twinkle lights in the trees and all around the garden.

"I love twinkle lights."

"It's my neighbour's garden. She's away and asked me to water the plants for her."

"I've never seen such beautiful flowers."

"Let's go and sit down."

There were two reclining lawn chairs in the middle of the garden. Melvin lit the candles on the table between the chairs.

"A night fit for a Princess," he said.

"You're my knight, Melvin."

"Thank you, Princess."

They were having so much fun, they lost track of time.

"What time do you have to be home, Princess?"

"What time is it now?"

"It's midnight."

"I'm going to have to cut our night short. My mom is picky about what time I come home when I have her car. I'm sorry, Melvin."

"I'm sorry too, Princess. I wish this night could go on forever."

"If only ..."

"Come on, I'll walk you to the car."

"I'll call you tomorrow, Melvin," Liza said as she unlocked the car door.

"I'm going to my pop's place tomorrow. Alicia and Max are coming for a visit. Hey, do you want to come with me and meet them?"

"I don't think I can. Can we make it another time?"

"Sure, Princess, anything you say. Call me tomorrow night. I should be home by nine or so."

This time Liza leaned in and kissed Melvin first.

"Oh, I like that," he said.

"I'll miss you, Melvin."

"I'll miss you more, Princess."

"Talk to you tomorrow night."

"I can't wait."

***

Liza drove home seemingly on auto pilot. She didn't know how she got home. She just did. In her mind, she replayed the events of the day and evening, rewinding and replaying her favourite parts.

As she drove up to the house, she noticed the kitchen light was on. *That's not a good sign.* Liza pulled into the garage and waited until the overhead door closed before going into the house. *I wonder if Mom forgot to shut the light off before she went to bed.*

Helga was sitting at the kitchen table, wearing her pyjamas and housecoat. She had curlers in her hair.

"Well, Missy! Where have you been until this late hour?"

"Out with Sarah. We went to a movie and then for dinner."

Helga walked over to the answering machine and pressed "play."

Liza heard Sarah's voice: "Hi, Liza, it's me. It's two o'clock Saturday afternoon. I haven't spoken to you in a couple of days. Call me and let's make a date to get together soon. Miss you."

Liza's mouth got very dry. Her face turned ghostly white as her heart sunk.

"Do you want to try that again, Missy? I want the truth this time."

Liza didn't know what to say. This was not how she wanted the perfect day to end. All of a sudden, it wasn't so perfect anymore.

"I'm waiting," Helga said as she crossed her arms.

"I met someone," Liza whispered as she stared at the floor.

"You what?"

"I met someone."

"You met someone? Look at me when I am speaking to you."

Liza looked up at her mother.

"How long has this been going on? Wait a minute! Is he the young man I saw you with in front of the office? The one you said was just asking for directions?"

"Yes."

"How dare you lie to me, young lady! Just when were you going to tell me about him?"

"I don't know. I didn't *want* to keep it a secret from you, Mom. I wanted to tell you, but I don't want Father to find out.

You know you can't keep secrets from him. He'd probably shoot me if he found out."

"Oh Liza, don't exaggerate. I won't tell your father, I promise."

"You have to cross your heart and promise that, no matter what, you will never tell him."

"I promise. Now tell me about this young man."

"His name is Melvin. He's twenty-three years old and he's a journalist."

"A journalist?"

"Yes, he writes for the local paper, and he also does some freelance writing."

"Tell me about his family."

"His dad and his stepmom don't live too far from here. They have a house just outside the city. His sister and her husband and their little boy, Max, live about two hours from here."

"Where does he live?"

"Melvin lives in an apartment."

"Liza, tell me you haven't been alone with him!"

"Mother, I *am* nineteen years old!"

"I don't care. You are forbidden to go to his apartment."

"Whatever."

"Don't *whatever* me, young lady! Did you hear me?"

"Yes, I heard you."

"How long have you been seeing him?"

"Not long."

"What does that mean?"

"It means not long."

"What else have you been keeping from me?"

"Nothing, Mom."

"I hope he treats you well."

"He treats me like a princess."

"A princess?"

"Yes, a *princess*."

"Your father used to treat me that way."

"What changed?"

"I don't know. He's gone most of the time, and I think we drifted apart. When he's home, it's almost as if he's a stranger. He acts like a tough disciplinarian. He doesn't show love much anymore."

"He doesn't show any love at all. When was the last time he told you he loves you?"

Helga thought for a minute and said, "I can't remember. We weren't talking about your father and me. We were talking about you."

"I think we're done talking about me, Mom."

"When are you going to be seeing him again?"

"I don't know. He invited me to his father's place for dinner and to meet his family."

"Meet his family? Is it serious already?"

"I told him I wouldn't be able to go with him this time. All I know is that I feel wonderful when I'm with him, and I miss him when we're not together." Liza paused, took a deep breath, and said, "He's the nicest guy I've ever known."

"The nicest guy you've ever known? You're only nineteen. You haven't dated anyone before."

"There was Billy Blackford in grade seven!"

"Oh Liza, really!"

"Like I *said*, he's the nicest guy I've ever known."

"Just promise me you'll take it slow."

"I promise, Mom. And *you* have to promise to keep this a secret."

"I promise, dear."

"I'm tired, Mom. I'm going to bed."

"Okay, good night, dear."

Liza went to her room. She heard her mom go to her bedroom and close the door. Then she called Sarah.

"Hello," Sarah said in a sleepy voice.

"I was trying to call you this afternoon, but the line was busy."

"Liza?"

"Who else would it be?"

"You sound upset!"

"I needed you to cover for me while Melvin and I went to a movie. I called you from the office, but I couldn't get through. Who was on the phone?"

"Slow down, you're talking too fast. My mom was on the phone with my aunt. When my aunt gets talking, she never stops."

"No kidding!"

"What happened?"

"My mom went out with Aunt Sadie for the day and let me use the car. When I couldn't get through to you, I left to go pick Melvin up. We went to the movie and then afterwards he made a special dinner for me at his place. We went up to the roof where there was a beautiful garden and we drank wine together. When I got home, my mom was sitting in the kitchen waiting for me."

"Oh no!"

"Oh yes!"

"And I called and left a message..."

"I didn't know that." Liza said.

"Oh no!"

"Oh yes! My mom asked me where I was, and I told her I was with you. Then she played the message you left."

"What happened then?"

"I told her about Melvin."

"You did?"

"What else was I going to do?"

"What did she say?"

"She asked a lot of questions and told me to take it slow. I am forbidden to go to his apartment."

"Too late for that!"

"I left that part out. I forgot to tell you that my mom sort of saw us on Friday morning."

"What do you mean she sort of saw you?"

"Melvin was waiting for me outside the coffee shop after I got my coffee. He walked me to work and kissed me. Just then my mom drove by on her way to the dentist. She was staring at us and almost drove through a stop sign. She screeched to a halt and that's when we noticed her. She questioned me when I got home after work."

"What did you say?"

"I tried to smooth things over and told her it was just someone asking for directions. She didn't quite buy it."

"Not if she saw him kiss you."

"I don't know how much she really did see."

"Your mom isn't going to tell your father, is she?"

"She promised to keep it a secret."

"That may be difficult considering what your father is like when he wants information."

"I know, but she did promise."

"When is your father coming home?"

"He's coming home next weekend, and we're supposed to go to the lake. Do you want to go with us?"

"I'll check with my parents and Farley. Who will be going?"

"My family, Sylvia, and her husband."

"Sylvia? Who's Sylvia?"

"She's a real estate agent who works for my dad at the show homes."

"I have a better idea, Liza. Why don't you ask your mom if you could stay at my house for the weekend instead?"

"Sarah, you're a genius! Then I could spend more time with Melvin. I'll ask my mom tomorrow."

"I'll check with my mom too. I'm sure it will be fine."

"I think I'll go to church with my mom and Junior in the morning. I'll call you when I get home."

"Okay, Liza, good night."

"Night, Sarah."

Chapter Eight

Antonia

"LIZA," Helga called as she opened her bedroom door. "Are you going to church this morning?"

"Yes, Mom."

"Hurry up then; we have to leave in half an hour. Junior, are you ready?"

"I'm ready," he replied.

***

Liza didn't really like the pastor of the church. He was an old fuddy-duddy. He stood about five-feet-five-inches tall and had a big stomach that made him look like he was nine months pregnant. Liza didn't know how he stood upright and didn't fall over. He had grey, wavy hair with a bald spot on the top of his head. His wife, on the other hand, was a "big" woman. Her name was Bertha. She stood almost six feet tall and had blonde hair almost as thin as her husband's. She probably outweighed him by about fifty pounds.

When Pastor Klassen spoke, people fell asleep. His sermons were filled with lots of statistics. B-O-R-R-ing!

Liza sat in the pew next to her mom on one side and Junior on the other. She pretended to listen as she daydreamed about Melvin, her favourite pastime. She replayed things in her mind. Things they did together, things Melvin said, the way he kissed her. Before she knew it, the service was over.

Pastor Klassen stood at the door to shake hands with the members as they left the church.

"Good morning, Helga. Good morning, Junior. Good morning, Liza. I'm glad you joined us this morning; it's been a couple of weeks."

"Excellent sermon, Pastor," Liza said.

"Which part did you find most meaningful?" he said as he kept shaking her hand.

Liza wished she hadn't said anything, considering she didn't hear a word he said.

"Really, Pastor, the whole sermon was meaningful to me today."

"We need more members like you, Liza," he said as he finally stopped shaking her hand.

"Have a nice day, Pastor."

Helga and Junior were waiting for Liza outside.

"Where do you kids want to go for lunch today?"

"We're going out for lunch, Mom?" Junior sounded very surprised.

"What's the occasion?" Liza asked.

"Do I need an occasion to take my own children out for lunch?"

"No, you sure don't," Junior said.

"When Father is home, we never go out," Liza added.

"That's because he's too cheap," Junior said.

"Junior, cut it out."

"Sorry, Mom."

"What your father doesn't know won't hurt me."

Liza and Junior looked at each other, trying to compute what Helga had just said.

"If we're going out for lunch," Junior said, "I vote we go to that new Italian restaurant. Café something."

"Liza, how does that sound to you?" Helga asked.

"I'm not sure I want to go there." She didn't want to be recognized and was afraid she would be if Roberto was there.

"You love Italian food, dear."

Liza agreed to go but prayed Roberto wouldn't be working.

***

As they walked up the steps, someone opened the door, just as before. This time it was an older Italian man.

"Welcome," he said as they entered.

A hostess came to greet them and escort them to a table. Liza looked around as they were being seated. She didn't see Roberto anywhere. She quietly asked the hostess if he was working. She told Liza that he didn't work on Sundays.

"Your server will be right with you," the hostess said and turned to leave.

A couple of minutes later, a beautiful young girl walked over to their table and handed each of them a menu.

"Good afternoon. My name is Antonia. I will be your server today."

Junior couldn't stop staring at her. "*Antonia*," he whispered to himself as he took a deep breath.

Antonia was about five-feet-two-inches tall with blonde hair and blue eyes. She looked about eighteen or so.

"Would you like to hear what the lunch specials are for today?"

Junior couldn't manage to say anything. He just nodded.

Antonia described three different specials and then turned to Helga and said, "What would you like to order?"

Helga chose the spaghetti with meatballs and garlic toast.

"Who would like to order next?"

Junior put up his hand, still unable to utter any words.

"You're not in school now, Junior; put your hand down and tell Antonia what you want."

"Shut up, Liza," he muttered.

"Junior, behave yourself," Helga added.

"I'll have the spaghetti also," he managed to say.

"And for you, Miss?"

"I'll have the pasta primavera."

"That's my favourite," Antonia said as she collected the menus.

"Anything to drink?" she asked.

Once again, Junior could only nod.

"He'll have a Coke," Helga said. "I'll have a coffee with cream and sugar. Liza, what would you like?"

"I'll have a Coke also, please."

"I'll be right back with your drinks."

Junior stared as she walked away.

"Junior, snap out of it!" Liza said.

"Shut up, Liza."

"We don't say *shut up* in this family," Helga scolded.

"Dad says it all the time," Junior muttered under his breath.

"You are staring at the waitress and acting like a school boy," Helga said.

"I *am* a school boy," Junior said.

Antonia brought the drinks, and not long afterwards, she brought their lunch order. Everywhere Antonia went, Junior's eyes followed. He didn't say a word throughout lunch. He quietly ate as he sat and watched her.

Just before they finished eating, Antonia came back and said, "Will there be anything else for you today? I'll be finishing my shift now."

"No, thank you, we won't be needing anything else," Helga answered.

"You may stay as long as you like, but if you wouldn't mind, I'll just leave your bill here. I've enjoyed serving you today and hope to see you again soon."

As Antonia walked away, Junior said, "Did you hear that? She said she hopes to see me again soon!"

"She meant all of us, little brother."

Helga took the bill and studied it for a minute. "It's very reasonable," she commented.

"That means we can come here again ... right, Mom?"

"Down, boy," Liza said as she patted Junior on the back.

"Stop bothering your brother, Liza."

"Ya, stop bothering your brother!" Junior repeated.

"That is enough, you two. It's not very often we go out to lunch together, so behave yourselves," Helga said as she stood up to leave.

Junior saw Antonia going out the front door and he hurried to follow her. He was just about to say something to her when he saw her walk over to a tall, handsome, muscle-bound guy standing by a silver convertible parked across the street. Junior watched as Antonia jumped into the other guy's arms.

Liza came out of the restaurant just in time to witness the embrace and watch them start kissing.

"Still wanna come here again, little brother?" Liza said as she put her arm around Junior's shoulder.

"Shut up, Liza."

"Junior, I told you to stop saying that."

"But, Mom!"

As Junior crossed the street and walked past them, he said quietly, "Get a room!"

Helga saw them kissing and said, "Things have certainly changed since I was that age."

"That's for sure, Mom," Liza agreed.

They got into the car. Junior sat silently, turned his head, and stared out the window. He didn't say a single word all the way home. Liza didn't say anything to him. She thought he'd had enough torture for one day.

Chapter Nine

Helga the Brave

HELGA UNLOCKED THE BACK DOOR, and Liza followed her in.

Junior called out, "I'm going to John's for a while, Mom."

"Okay, Junior, don't be late. Liza, would you like a cup of tea?"

"Sure, Mom, that would be nice. By the way, I asked Sarah if she'd like to join us at the cottage this weekend."

"Is she going to come along?"

"Actually, Mom, she had another idea."

"Oh, what was that?" Helga asked as she placed Liza's tea in front of her.

"Sarah invited me to spend the weekend at her place instead."

"Your father wants us to go out to the cottage to spend some quality time together."

"If he wanted to spend *quality* time together, why did he invite *what's her name* and her family for the weekend?"

"Her name is Sylvia."

"That's what I said, *what's her name!*"

"Liza, behave yourself!"

"Fine."

"I don't know why he invited Sylvia and Fred for the weekend. Their three children won't be coming with them. They're going to camp, I think."

"Thank goodness!" Liza exclaimed.

"I know it's not the way you'd like it to be, but it's your father's decision."

"Why does it have to be *his* decision? It's *your* cottage too! You could tell him we want to go to the cottage to spend quality time together, and he can invite Sylvia and Fred some other time."

"Your father doesn't always listen to what I say."

"No kidding."

"Liza, mind your manners."

"I'd really like to spend the weekend at Sarah's, Mom."

"Your father will be calling later. I'll mention it to him then. Now drink your tea; it's getting cold. Wait a minute—you're not planning to spend time with Melvin, are you?"

"I probably will see him sometime on the weekend. Remember, you can't say *anything* to anyone. I mean not one thing!"

"Yes, Liza, I know."

"I'm going to call Sarah now."

"Hold off for a bit, dear; your father should be calling shortly."

"I'll go to my room and read while I finish my tea."

A few minutes later, the phone rang. Liza called out, "I'll get it, Mom! Hello," she answered in her pleasant telephone voice.

"Liza?"

"Yes, who is this?" Liza said, knowing full well who it was.

"What do you mean, who is this? It's your father, that's who! Were you expecting someone else to be calling?"

"No, why would you ask me that?"

"You don't normally answer the phone that way."

"What way?"

"Never mind. Put your mother on the phone."

"I'll see if she's available," Liza continued in her pleasant voice.

"If she's avail—"

Liza didn't wait for him to finish. She called out, "Mom, the phone is for you. It's him!"

Helga picked up the extension in the kitchen. Liza stayed on the line and listened in.

"Hello," Helga said.

"Hello, Helga. What's going on with Liza?"

"What do you mean, Klaus?"

"I don't like her attitude."

"I think her attitude is perfectly fine, Klaus."

"We'll talk about it later. I'll be home Thursday evening. We'll leave Friday when Junior gets home from school and Liza gets home from work."

"Junior and his friend John will be coming with us. Liza will be spending the weekend at Sarah's."

"What do you mean Liza will be spending the weekend at Sarah's?"

"The girls made plans and I gave Liza permission to stay at Sarah's for the weekend. Besides, you were supposed to be away for another week."

"Why would you give Liza permission without consulting me?"

"I make decisions all the time when you're away, Klaus, based on what I think is best."

Liza cheered silently, *Yay, Mom!*

"How are we supposed to have quality family time together, Helga?"

"I was wondering the same thing," Helga answered.

"What do you mean by that?"

"If you wanted to spend quality time together, then why did you invite Sylvia and Fred?"

"It's my cottage, and I can invite whomever I want, Helga!"

"It's *your* cottage? I thought it was *our* cottage!"

"Your thinking isn't always correct."

"I beg your pardon! If that's the way you feel, Klaus, you can go and have your quality family time with Sylvia and Fred."

"Stop giving me aggravation, Helga."

"Stop being a tyrant, Klaus."

"What's gotten into you, Helga?"

"Nothing, Klaus."

"Something has. I have to go now, Helga. I'll see you Thursday."

"Not if I see you first," Helga muttered.

"What? What did you say?"

"I said, I'm getting thirsty. See you Thursday, Klaus. Goodbye."

Before Klaus could reply, Helga hung up.

Liza waited for a minute after Helga hung up before she hung up the extension in her room. She headed into the kitchen and put her tea cup into the dishwasher. Helga was wiping down the counters, even though they didn't need wiping. She always did that when she was upset or preoccupied.

"Mom, how did your conversation go?"

"It went fine."

"Fine?"

"Fine."

"Did you ask if I could stay at Sarah's for the weekend?"

"Sort of ... I didn't *ask* him. I *told* him."

"You did? Yay, Mom! I'm proud of you."

"I can make decisions around here. I don't have to ask his permission. I'm not a child, and I have decided it's high time I made some changes around here."

Liza put her arms around Helga and gave her a kiss on the cheek.

"You are absolutely right, Mom!"

"Thank you, dear."

"You should finish your tea, Mom. I'm going to call Sarah now."

"Okay dear."

***

"Hi, Sarah. I wanted to tell you the good news. I can stay at your place on the weekend."

"That's perfect. My mom said she would be happy to have you come and stay with us."

"Okay, great. Talk to you tomorrow."

***

Melvin said he would be home from visiting his parents by nine o'clock. Liza sat and watched the second hand on her watch tick along until it was exactly nine. She dialled his number and sat back on her bed and waited for him to answer.

"Hello, Princess."

"How did you know it was me?"

"Lucky guess!"

"I have some good news, Melvin."

"Give it to me straight up."

"Next weekend my family is going to our cottage."

"That's not good news."

"*They're* going. I'm going to stay at Sarah's for the weekend. That means you and I can spend a lot more time together."

"That *is* good news, Princess. You didn't want to go to the cottage with them?"

"No, Melvin. I'd much rather spend time with you. Besides, they'll have more than enough guests. Junior has invited his friend John, and my father has invited another couple."

"If you're sure."

"I am more than sure, Melvin!"

"We'll have to make every moment count, won't we, Princess?"

"We certainly will! How was your visit with your family?"

"It was lots of fun! I told them all about you, and they can hardly wait to meet you."

"You told them all about me?"

"Yes, I did."

"What did you say?"

"I told them you are perfect for me in every way, I miss you when we're apart, and I want to spend as much time with you as I can. I may have told them a few more things."

"What things?"

"Now *that* would be telling!"

Liza laughed. "I can hardly wait to meet them too!"

"This week I'm going to have to work a bit of overtime. I've got a piece I'm working on and the deadline is Friday."

"That's no problem, Melvin. We can chat on the phone and make plans for next weekend."

"I don't know how I'll make it through the week without seeing you, Princess."

"I feel the same way, Melvin, but knowing we have next weekend to look forward to will make it easier."

"You're right."

"Call me tomorrow at work, Melvin. Marcus always goes out for lunch at noon. We can chat freely then."

"You can count on it! Good night, Princess."

"Good night, Melvin."

***

Marcus walked past Liza's desk on his way out to lunch when the telephone rang. "If it's for me, Liza, take a message and I'll call back after lunch."

"I will, Marcus."

"Hello," Liza answered.

"Hello, Princess," Melvin said.

"You sound happy, Melvin."

"I'm always happy when I hear your sweet voice. I'm also happy because I've thought of a couple of things we can do this weekend that I think you'll enjoy."

"Don't keep me in suspense."

"How about if we start by going out for a nice dinner Friday night?"

"That sounds lovely, Melvin. What restaurant did you have in mind?"

"It's a surprise, Princess."

"I do like surprises. What else have you got planned for us?"

"I thought we could drive out to my parents' place and spend the day with them on Saturday. How does that sound?"

"I would love to meet your parents."

"It's settled, then. How about dinner for six-thirty on Friday?"

"It's a date, Melvin. I'll get Sarah to drop me off at your place. She'll probably be going to Farley's and it's on the way."

"See you at six-thirty, Princess."

"See you then, Melvin."

***

Liza was busy at work and the week went by very quickly.

She packed a bag for the weekend Thursday morning and planned to go over to Sarah's right after work to avoid having to see her father. When she got downstairs, her mother was already sitting at the kitchen table.

"Mom, you're up early!"

"I didn't sleep very well. I see you have your weekend bag packed and ready to go. Not planning to come home tonight?"

"I thought I'd go straight over to Sarah's after work, if that's okay with you."

"I understand, dear, and I don't blame you. Sometimes your father isn't very nice to be around."

"Mom, I've never heard you say anything like that before."

"Don't worry, dear. I'm sure everything will be fine. You just have a nice weekend at Sarah's."

"I will, Mom, and thanks. I love you."

"I love you too, dear."

Liza gave her mom a hug and left for work.

***

Helga was making dinner, and Junior was sitting at the kitchen table doing his homework after school when Klaus came in.

"Hi, I'm home," he called out.

"Hi, Dad," Junior answered.

"Hello, Klaus," Helga said as she continued chopping vegetables.

"Where's Liza? Shouldn't she be home from work by now?"

"I told you she's spending the weekend at Sarah's."

"It's only Thursday," he said.

"Sarah and Liza have a function they're attending this evening and it was easier for them to get ready and leave from Sarah's."

"A function? What kind of function?"

"Something related to Sarah's class at school," Helga said matter-of-factly as she knowingly lied.

"That's not a lot of information, Helga."

"It will have to do, Klaus, because it's all I have. I guess you can ask her next time you see her."

"When will that be?"

"I'm not sure. It depends on when you'll be spending more time at home with us."

"What is that supposed to mean, Helga?"

"Nothing, Klaus. It just means that you'll see her when you're at home for a longer period of time."

"I'm away working to earn money to pay the bills and put food on the table. I'm trying to provide for our family, Helga."

"The house is paid in full, the business is successful, and we have money in the bank. Now that things are better, Klaus, I thought you'd be able to spend more time at home with us and not have to be away as much."

"I still have to run the business, and that means I have to be away to do that. I have meetings all the time and I don't have much time to spend at home."

"I guess that's your choice, Klaus."

Klaus banged his fist on the table, which always shook everyone up. "I am doing my best, and if you don't like it, that's too bad!"

"Dad! Don't yell at Mom!"

"It's okay, Junior," Helga said.

"I'm going out," Klaus said as he turned to go.

"Dad, you just got here."

"I'll see you later, Junior."

Helga sat down at the table and started to cry. Junior put his arm around her and said, "Are you okay, Mom?"

"I'm okay, Junior."

"I'm sorry Dad yelled at you."

"I guess I shouldn't have said anything."

"You have to speak up for yourself and us, Mom."

"Your father will cool down and be better when he gets home later."

"It's not your fault, Mom. You can't help that Dad has a temper."

"Your father always enjoys going to the cottage. Let's look forward to a nice weekend away, Junior."

"Sure, Mom. You're right. When Dad's at the cottage, he's in a much better mood."

"I guess when he's away from the stress at work, he has a chance to calm down and relax," Helga said.

"Then he should act that way when he's at home too. When he comes home, he's away from the stress at work here."

"I don't know, dear. It may have something to do with the calming effect of nature. He loves to take the boat out on the lake."

"We'll make the best of it, Mom. John and I will be there to help you."

"You are a good son," Helga said as she patted Junior on the back.

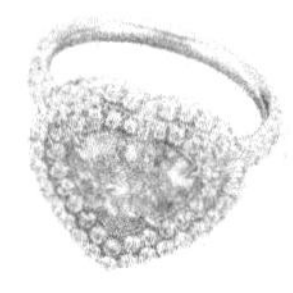

Chapter Ten

Opposites Attract

THE TRIP TO THE COTTAGE took about three hours and was bearable at best. The two boys sat in the back seat and chatted quietly. Helga and Klaus sat in silence in the front seat. Klaus turned on the radio and tuned it to his favourite station to listen to the farm reports.

After they had driven for about two hours, Helga said, "Klaus, please stop at the next gas station. I'd like to use the washroom."

"Why didn't you use the washroom before we left home?"

Helga was just about to answer when Junior piped in, "I'd like to use the washroom too, Dad."

"Me too," John added.

Klaus mumbled something and pulled into the next gas station. Helga got out first, and John and Junior followed.

"I didn't really have to go to the washroom," Junior said once they were inside.

"Me either," John replied.

"I just didn't want my dad to be angry with my mom."

"I picked up on that. You wanna get a drink or something?"

"Sure, John, that's a great idea."

They picked up a couple of sodas and headed back to the car. Helga was just a couple of steps behind them.

"Great timing, Mom."

"I'll say!"

As they got into the car, Klaus said, "Are *youse* ready now?"

"Youse?" John whispered to Junior.

"Dad, you do know that *youse* is not a real word, don't you? Our English teacher would have a fit if she heard anyone say that."

"Well, she's not here, is she?" Klaus snapped back.

Helga sat quietly and didn't say a word. She smirked as she stared straight ahead.

***

When they arrived at the cottage, Junior and John helped carry in groceries and suitcases. Klaus went to the boathouse.

Helga looked out the kitchen window and saw him pull the boat out and drive across the lake toward the General Store. The General Store was a kind of one-stop shopping place: groceries, books, magazines, bait, tackle and lures for fishing, an ice cream parlour, and general odds and ends.

"Where's Dad going, Mom?"

"He's probably going to get fuel for the boat."

"Why didn't he ask John and me if we wanted to go too?"

"I don't know, dear. Don't worry, you can take the boat out when he gets back."

***

Junior heard a car drive up and called out, "Mom, Sylvia and Fred are here."

"Hellooo," Sylvia called out as she came in through the back door. "Hi, Helga, how are you?" she asked.

"Better if you weren't here," Helga whispered. Junior and John heard what she said and snickered.

"Pardon me?" Sylvia said.

"I said, it's nice to see you, dear."

Sylvia was a tall blonde. A real beauty. Like one of the beauties you'd see in a glamorous movie. Her hair was styled impeccably, makeup done to perfection, nails and toes always polished. She had a knack for dressing with a certain flair. Like the right little sweater to throw over her shoulders. Accessories to complement her outfit: earrings, bracelet, matching necklace. The perfect little handbag and high heels.

Sylvia and Fred were opposites. It has been said, "opposites attract." Fred was six-feet-two-inches tall with brown hair and blue eyes. He was the "outdoorsy" type and could be described as ruggedly handsome.

"Here, Helga, these are for you," Sylvia said as she handed Helga a small bouquet of flowers. "They're from my garden. I hope you like them."

"Thank you, Sylvia, how thoughtful."

The back door swung open as Fred came in carrying their bags.

"Sylvia, where do you want these things?" Fred asked as he set the bags down.

"You and Fred can take the bedroom down the hall, the last door on your left. Junior, could you and John please give Fred a hand?" Helga added.

"Sure, Mom, no problem."

Sylvia walked over to the living room window. "What a beautiful view of the lake," she said. "This is such a beautiful cottage, Helga."

"*We* think so too!" Helga replied, with a little added emphasis on the *we*.

"Where's Klaus?" Fred asked as he came into the kitchen.

"He went across to the store to get fuel for the boat," Junior replied as he followed behind Fred.

"I think I'll go outside and enjoy the view and get some fresh air," Sylvia said and then added, "Does anyone want to join me?"

"Thank you, Sylvia, but I'm going to get dinner started," Helga said.

"How about you, Fred?"

"No thanks, Sylvia. I noticed some wood out back that needs chopping. I'm going to go out and do that now."

"That's nice of you, Fred, but you don't have to. I'm sure Klaus can do that tomorrow sometime."

"It's no trouble at all, Helga. I like to keep busy and earn my keep. You boys wanna come and keep me company?"

"Sure, Fred, lead the way," Junior said.

***

Just as Sylvia put her sunglasses on and arranged her lawn chair on the deck out front, Klaus pulled up alongside the dock.

"Yoo-hoo!" Sylvia called out as she waved to him and watched as he tied the boat up.

"Hi, Sylvia, how are you?" he said as he approached the deck. "Where's Fred?"

"I'm fine, Klaus. Fred is out back, chopping wood. He likes to keep busy."

Junior and John heard the motor from the boat and came running from around the back.

"Hey, Dad, can John and I take the boat out for a ride?"

"I would prefer if you didn't."

"But, Dad—"

"Why don't you let the boys have some fun, Klaus," Sylvia interceded on their behalf.

"All right. You have one hour. Don't go near Sherbit Cove. The water is shallow and the rocks are jagged and sharp.

"I know, I know. You tell me that every time. Come on, John, let's go."

"Be careful, and don't go too fast."

His instructions fell on deaf ears because Junior and John had already walked away. They walked down to the dock, untied the boat, and got in. Junior puttered away slowly until they were around the bend, and then they sped away.

Klaus turned to Sylvia and said, “Can I get you something to drink?”

“That would be nice, Klaus. I’ll have what you’re having.”

“Beer it is then,” he said as he offered his hand to her. “Let’s go in and see what kind we have. Watch out! Don’t get those high heels stuck in the cracks of the deck. You know, you really should wear more sensible shoes.”

“I will next time.”

Helga stood at the living room window and waved to Klaus, beckoning him to come in. Klaus waved back. He and Sylvia came in through the front door. At the same time, Fred came in through the back door.

“Hi, Fred, I heard you’ve been chopping some wood out back,” Klaus said.

“That’s right. Got it all done too! That oughta keep you stocked up for a while now.”

“Thank you, Fred, I really appreciate the help. I was just going to have a beer. Can I interest you in one?”

“Sure, Klaus. All that choppin’ made me pretty thirsty.”

Klaus went over to the fridge in the porch where they kept all the drinks and took out three cans of beer. He handed one to Sylvia, one to Fred, and kept one for himself.

“What about me?” Helga said.

“You don’t drink beer, Helga,” Klaus answered.

“I think now is a good time to start, Klaus.”

“I’ll get another one. Here, you can have mine, Helga,” Fred offered. He walked over to Helga, looked over her shoulder, and said, “Something sure smells good. Whatcha cookin’?”

“You’ll see, Fred. Dinner will be ready shortly. Would you please pass me a glass from that cupboard to your right?”

He passed her the glass and went to the drink fridge and chose a beer for himself.

"Can I help you with anything, Helga?" Fred asked.

"You can set the dinner table if you like."

"Sure thing."

"The dishes and placemats are in that cupboard beside the pantry. Set the table for six, please."

In the meantime, Klaus and Sylvia sat and watched as they drank their beer.

"Where are the boys?" Helga asked.

"They went for a boat ride," Klaus answered. "They should be back shortly."

Klaus walked over to the wine rack, chose a bottle of red wine, and set it on the dinner table.

"Here come the boys now," Fred called out as he saw them heading toward the dock. About ten minutes later, the boys walked in.

"How was the boat ride, guys?" Fred asked.

"It was great, Fred. Thanks for asking!" Junior said. "Hey, Mom, what smells so good?"

"You'll see. Go and wash your hands, you two."

"I'm starved," Junior said.

"Me too!" John added.

When everyone was seated, Klaus said grace and then started passing the food around.

"Everything looks so delicious, Helga," Sylvia commented.

"Who would like a glass of wine?" Klaus asked.

Sylvia answered first. "I would!"

Klaus stood up, went over to her, and poured the wine as she handed him her glass.

"I'd like a glass of wine too, Klaus," Helga said.

"You just had a beer, Helga," Klaus said as he frowned at her.

"So did everyone else," Helga answered.

"Mom, you had a beer?"

"Yes, Junior, I did."

Fred spoke up. “We all had a beer, and now we can all have a nice glass of wine with our dinner. I heard wine is good for the digestion!”

“In that case, John and I will have some too,” Junior said as he held up his glass.

“You most certainly will not,” Helga scolded.

“But Mom—”

“Don’t ‘but Mom’ me, Junior. Go and get a couple of sodas. There’s a good selection in the drink fridge.”

“Okay, Mom.”

“Where is Liza this weekend, Helga?” Sylvia asked.

“She’s staying with a friend,” Helga replied.

“Ya, I wonder *which* friend,” Junior muttered to himself.

“What did you say, Junior?” Klaus demanded.

“I said she’s staying with her best friend.”

“That’s too bad. I was looking forward to seeing her,” Sylvia added.

Now it was Helga’s turn to mutter. “She didn’t want to see *you*.”

“What did you say, Helga?”

“Nothing, Klaus. Pass the potatoes, please.”

After dinner, Helga started clearing the dishes.

“Would you like some help?” Sylvia offered.

“No, thank you, Sylvia. The boys can help. Go ahead and relax a little with your husband. You two haven’t spent much time together today, with Fred chopping wood all afternoon.”

“It was my pleasure, Helga,” Fred said.

Klaus turned to Sylvia and Fred and said, “How about if I take you out for a boat ride? It won’t be dark for another couple of hours.”

“That would be lovely, Klaus,” Sylvia said as she stood and walked over to him.

“How about you, Helga?” Fred asked.

“I’m going to clean up here. You and Sylvia go ahead. It’s a nice night for a boat ride.”

"All right then," Fred said.

"If you're sure," Sylvia added.

"Oh, I'm sure," Helga answered.

"Let's go then," Klaus called from the front door.

After they left, Junior said, "Didn't you want to go with them, Mom?"

"No, dear. I'd rather clean up and spend some quiet time here with you and John."

"I understand, Mom," he said as he put an arm around her.

***

The weekend weather turned out to be beautiful. Helga spent most of her time cooking for everyone. Fred helped with chores and dishes, while Sylvia sunned herself on the deck. Junior and John kept themselves busy having as much fun as possible. As Helga earlier predicted, Klaus was in a very good mood.

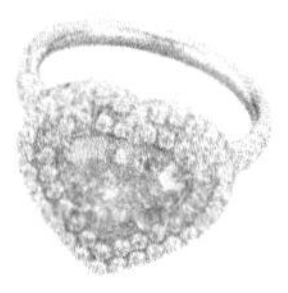

Chapter Eleven

A Good Cause

MEANWHILE, BACK IN THE CITY ...

Sarah dropped Liza off at Melvin's Friday evening at six-thirty. He was waiting outside and waved when he saw them pull up.

"That's Melvin? He's gorgeous!" Sarah said as she parked in front.

"Yes, he is, isn't he!"

Melvin opened Liza's door and offered his hand to help her out.

"I can't remember the last time Farley opened the car door for me."

"Jealous?"

"A little."

Liza got out of the car. Melvin hugged her tightly and gave her a big kiss.

"I really missed you, Princess."

"I missed you too, Melvin."

Sarah got out of the car and walked around to where Liza and Melvin were standing. She extended her hand to Melvin.

"Hi, I'm Sarah."

"Nice to meet you, Sarah," Melvin said as he extended his hand as well.

"I've heard a lot about you, Melvin."

"All good, I hope," he said as he smiled at Liza.

"All good," Sarah confirmed.

"We'll have to go now. We have dinner reservations at seven. I'll drop Liza off later, Sarah, so you don't have to worry about picking her up."

"Sounds good. Nice meeting you, Melvin."

"Likewise, Sarah."

"See you later, Liza."

"I won't be late, Sarah. Probably around eleven."

"That's perfect. See you then."

"Your friend Sarah seems very nice," Melvin said as they walked to his car.

"She is, Melvin."

"I thought we'd try a new restaurant I just discovered, Princess. I hope you like Italian!"

"I love Italian," Liza said hesitantly.

"You don't sound too convincing."

"I really do like Italian, Melvin."

Liza had a funny feeling that they were heading for Café Guido. They drove for about twenty minutes when Melvin announced, "Here we are."

Liza was right.

"You've been here before?"

"Yes, I have."

"I wanted to share it with you for the first time."

"Being here with you, Melvin, will make it feel as if it is the first time."

"Thank you, Princess, that's very kind of you to say."

Liza walked up the steps ahead of Melvin. A young girl she hadn't seen before opened the door and greeted them. Once inside, the hostess checked the reservation and then led them to a private area where there was a reserved table for two. In the centre of the table stood a beautiful, ornate silver vase that held a dozen red roses. Melvin pulled out Liza's chair for her as he always did.

"Those roses are beautiful, Melvin. I don't see roses on any other table, though."

"The roses are for you, Princess."

"How did ... when did—?"

"I was here this afternoon and had the owner reserve this table for us and place the roses here especially for you."

"What's the occasion, Melvin?"

"*You* are the occasion. I missed you and wanted to show you just how much."

"Thank you, Melvin. You really are my knight in shining armour."

Just then, Roberto appeared carrying a large ice bucket and in it, a bottle of Champagne. He set it in a floor stand next to Melvin. Then he noticed Liza.

"Senorina. How-a nice-a to see-a you again! How is-a your-a friend?"

"What friend?" Melvin asked, slightly puzzled.

"A beautiful-a young-a lady," Roberto answered.

"He means Sarah."

"Yes, Sarah. Bellissima" *Beautifullest.*

"She's fine, Roberto."

"Please-a say-a hi for-a me!"

"Yes, I will."

"Your-a server will-a be-a right-a back with-a your-a menus."

"Sarah seems to have made quite an impression on Roberto," Melvin observed.

"It was mutual. He made quite an impression on her too. After our dinner here, Sarah was ready to sign up to take Italian lessons."

"He must be quite a charmer."

"He certainly is."

Antonia walked over to their table and handed Melvin a menu. She recognized Liza.

"Hello, Miss. Nice to see you again."

"Nice to see you too, Antonia."

"How is your family?"

"Your family? You were here with your family too?"

"Just my mom and Junior. My mom surprised us after church the day you went to visit your family. It really wasn't a big deal. Please don't be upset, Melvin. It's so much nicer being here with you."

"Shall I pour the Champagne for you?" Antonia asked.

Melvin's mood lightened and he nodded in agreement.

"The specials for today are attached to the front cover of the menu. I'll give you a few minutes to decide and come back shortly to take your dinner orders."

"I'd like to make a toast," Liza said. "May each day we are together be as special as today."

"I'll drink to that, and to our future."

Our future ... wow, he's thinking about our future.

A few minutes later, Antonia came back. "Are you ready to order now?" she asked as she took out her order pad and pen.

"Princess, what would you like?"

"I'll have what you're having, Melvin."

"I'll have the pasta primavera," he said as he handed the menu to Antonia.

Liza smiled at Antonia, happy for Melvin's choice, since it was secretly what she wanted too. Antonia topped up their Champagne and took their menus.

"Can I get you anything else?" she asked.

"That's all for now, thank you," Melvin replied.

***

"I have something to tell you, Princess."

"What is it, Melvin?"

"I got a promotion at work!"

"Oh Melvin, that is wonderful news. Congratulations! Here's to your new promotion!"

They raised their glasses and sipped their Champagne.

"There's a small hitch," he said hesitantly.

Liza set her Champagne glass down and stared at Melvin. "What do you mean, a hitch? What kind of hitch?"

"I'll be the head of the editorial department now."

"That doesn't sound like a hitch, Melvin."

"I'll be the head of the editorial department at our sister office in Waterford."

"Waterford? That's nine hours away from here."

"Ten, actually."

"When do you start?"

"In a couple of weeks."

Liza's heart sank.

"It's a smaller newspaper but a good career move for me, and more money too."

"I'm happy for you, Melvin."

"Why so glum, chum?"

"I didn't realize when you said you got a promotion that it would mean you were going to leave me. That's not good news at all. You've gone to a lot of trouble this evening, roses, Champagne, dinner ... just to say goodbye."

"Goodbye? I'm not saying goodbye. I want you to come with me."

Liza sat in stunned silence.

Antonia came in carrying their dinner. "Can I offer you more Champagne?"

"Yes, please," Liza said immediately.

"Another bottle, please," Melvin confirmed. "Princess?"

"How am I going to go with you, Melvin? I have a job here. What am I going to tell my parents? I *knew* this was too good to be true." Liza started to cry.

"Don't cry, Princess." He reached over and wiped the tears rolling down her cheeks. "I've got it all worked out."

"How can you have it all worked out?"

"My Aunt Joanna owns a daycare in Waterford."

"So?"

"So you like kids, don't you?"

"Yes, Melvin. What does that have to do with anything?"

"It has everything to do with everything. My aunt owns the daycare, and they always hire people for the summer. A lot of the staff take holidays then, as the enrolment is much lower."

"My parents wouldn't let me go with you. What about my job?"

"You have holidays, don't you?"

"Yes, but only a couple of weeks."

"Then ask for an extended leave. Tell your parents and your boss that you heard of a great opportunity to work in a Christian daycare."

"Melvin, did you say that it's a Christian daycare?"

"Yes, why?"

"My parents usually approve of anything *Christian*. Where would I stay?"

"Aunt Joanna lives next door to the daycare. She provides rooms for the girls who come and work for the summer. That's where you'd be staying."

"I think my parents would be okay with that. I'd just have to convince Marcus."

"I've already spoken to Aunt Joanna, and she can hardly wait to meet you!"

"You've already what?"

"I've already spoken to my aunt. She'll take good care of you. Actually, there's a job for Sarah too if she's interested."

"That's right up Sarah's alley. She's almost completed her childcare certification."

"Well, all right then!"

"Where will you be staying, Melvin?"

"The newspaper has rented a house for me there. We can spend tons of time together, all of our evenings and weekends. Of course, Aunt Joanna will still have a curfew for you girls, but she's reasonable."

Antonia brought the Champagne and put it in the ice bucket without interrupting their conversation. Melvin poured Liza another glass.

"Do you trust me, Princess?"

"I trust you, Melvin."

"There's one more thing I wanted to tell you, Princess ... I love you."

Liza stared at him for the longest time and then she said, "I love you too, Melvin."

"Now *that's* something to celebrate! Here's to love, Princess."

"Here's to love, Melvin."

"We should probably eat our dinner, Princess; it's getting cold."

They ate in silence for a while. Liza's mind was racing a million miles an hour. *How am I going to pull this off?* she thought. She couldn't bear to be away from Melvin and desperately wanted to go with him.

Melvin broke the silence and said, "Still want to go with me to visit my parents tomorrow?"

"Yes, of course, Melvin."

"I wanted you to be with me when I tell them about my promotion."

"I'm looking forward to it. Do you mind if we make it an early evening tonight, Melvin?"

"I don't mind at all. May I ask why?"

"When Sarah comes home from Farley's, I'd like to be there so I can tell her about Waterford."

"Sure, Princess, whatever you want."

They finished their dinner but not all of the Champagne. Melvin paid the bill and they thanked Antonia for wonderful service. On the way out, they noticed Roberto sitting at a table holding hands with a pretty girl. He kissed her hand and they heard him say, "I hope-a to-a see-a you-a again, Bella!"

Liza said, "I'm not going to mention this to Sarah."

"Good idea, Princess."

It was about nine o'clock when Melvin dropped Liza off. The plan was that he would pick her up the next morning at ten-thirty to go to his parents' place.

Liza went into Sarah's room, lay down on the bed, and stared up at the ceiling. *Mom might give me permission, but there's no way Father will. What will Marcus say?* She didn't want to lose her job. Her mind was on overload, and at some point, she fell asleep.

Sarah came in about an hour later, turned on the light, and was startled to see Liza asleep on the bed, still dressed in her clothes.

When the light went on, Liza was startled too and sat straight up.

"What's wrong? What's happening?" Liza said, still bleary-eyed and not quite coherent.

"Liza, it's me, Sarah. I didn't mean to startle you. I didn't expect you to be home yet. What are you doing home already? Is anything wrong?"

"Yes and no."

"That's confusing. What do you mean?"

"Melvin got a promotion. He's going to be the head of the editorial department."

"That's fantastic!"

"In Waterford."

"Waterford? That's nine hours away."

"Ten, actually."

"I think that's actually really good news," Sarah said, smiling.

"Why do *you* think that's really good news?"

"You know Farley works construction, don't you?"

"Of *course* I know that, Sarah."

"Let me finish," Sarah said somewhat impatiently.

"What you don't know is that Farley will be working in Waterford this summer. His uncle's company got a big contract out there, *and* he wants me to go with him!"

"Melvin wants me to go with him!"

Liza told Sarah about the daycare and housing arrangements.

"Sounds amazing! If we pull this off, we're going to have the most amazing summer ever!"

"My mom might go for it, Sarah, but I'm not sure about my father."

"Piece of cake!" Sarah said.

"Better be chocolate!" Liza joked.

Sarah seemed to have formulated a plan already. "This is what we'll do. I'll tell my parents that you know of a Christian daycare that's hiring for the summer and you really want to go. We'll jazz it up and say they really need people to work this summer because so many of their staff are going on holidays."

"We don't really have to jazz it up. That's actually true."

"Then you can tell your parents that I heard of this great opportunity to work at a Christian daycare, etc., etc.! We'll go from there."

"Sarah, you seem to know what you're doing."

"Do you trust me, Liza?"

"That's what Melvin said."

"Great minds think alike."

"What am I going to tell Marcus?"

"Tell him the same thing. I'm sure he'll recognize that it's a good cause and will give you some extra time off."

"We're not as busy in the summer, and Marcus *does* support a good cause."

"It's settled then."

"I'll talk to Marcus on Monday."

"What are you and Melvin doing tomorrow?"

"We're going to his parents' place so he can tell them about his promotion and so I can meet them."

"Ooh, meeting the parents!"

"Yes, and I better get my beauty sleep. Melvin is picking me up at ten-thirty."

"Okay, Liza. Do you want me to set my alarm?"

"Sure, Sarah, but I'll probably wake up early anyway."

Chapter Twelve

Made in the Shade

LIZA WAS EAGERLY AWAITING Melvin's arrival as she stood outside watching for him. He surprised her when he approached from the opposite direction.

"Hey there, pretty girl, need a ride?" he called out.

"Melvin, I thought you'd be coming the other way," Liza said as she got into the car."

"I took a wrong turn at Albuquerque."

"Albuquerque?"

"Never mind, old joke."

"I have some interesting news, Melvin."

"What is it, Princess?"

"Remember when I told you Farley works for his uncle's construction company?"

"I remember."

"The company got a big road construction contract in ... wait for it ... Waterford! He invited Sarah to go with him this summer!"

"Amazing how things work out, isn't it? If you and Sarah are able to work at the daycare, you might just get there before Farley does."

"What do you mean, Melvin?"

"When I spoke to Aunt Joanna, she said the term will be from May to September. Maybe longer depending on the fall enrolment."

"Just think, Melvin, we could spend four glorious months together."

"It would be a dream come true, Princess."

***

Melvin turned into a driveway off the highway just past the city limits. The house was hidden by trees that lined the winding road. As they got closer, they could see Melvin Sr. and Lola sitting on the front porch. Melvin parked in front of the detached double garage on the left side of the house.

"Hey, you two!" Melvin Sr. called out as they got closer.

"Hi, Pops! Hi, Lola! This is Liza!"

"It's very nice to meet you, Liza," Melvin Sr. said. "You're even prettier than Melvin described."

Liza blushed and said, "Thank you."

Lola walked over to Liza, put her arm around her shoulder, and said, "Welcome, Liza. We are so happy to finally meet you." Lola opened the front door and led Liza into the house.

"Let's all have something to drink, shall we? What would you like, Liza?" Melvin Sr. asked.

"What are you having, Melvin?"

"I think I'll have one of Pop's famous cocktails."

"Okay, me too," Liza said.

"Me three," Lola added.

Melvin Sr. said, "A round of cocktails coming right up."

"Your house is lovely, Lola. It looks like a picture in a magazine."

"Thank you, Liza."

"I can tell where Melvin gets his decorating talent from."

Lola smiled and said, "Our home is your home. You are welcome to come and visit anytime."

Melvin Sr. came into the living room with a tray of fancy cocktails in tall glasses, each with a little umbrella for decoration. He leaned over and presented the tray to Liza. "Please help yourself, young lady."

"Thank you. They look so pretty."

"Take a sip and tell me how you like it."

"Mmmm, this is delicious. What's in it?"

Melvin answered, "Pops has never told anyone what's in his special cocktails, and we gave up trying to figure it out."

"I know what it tastes like," Liza said as she took another sip. "To quote your son, it tastes like more!"

"My son stole that line from me."

"Shh, Pops, don't give away my secrets! Something sure smells good!"

"Lunch will be ready in about an hour," Melvin Sr. said.

"Your dad has been cooking since early this morning," Lola said.

"Now who's giving away secrets?" Melvin Sr. joked.

"Melvin gets his decorating skills from you, Lola, and he gets his cooking skills from his dad. What a winning combination."

"You're very kind, Liza," Melvin Sr. said. "I hope you two brought your appetites."

"I did, Pops. I only had a piece of toast for breakfast."

"That's all I had too," Liza confessed.

"Good, because there's plenty of food for everyone, and there will be some leftovers for you to take home, son. I know how much you love leftovers!"

"I'll be happy to help you eat those leftovers, Melvin," Liza offered.

"I'll be happy to share them with you," Melvin said as he winked at Liza.

"When are you going to tell them your good news, Melvin?" Liza whispered.

"What good news, son?"

"How did your dad hear that?"

"He has super-sonic hearing, just like Aunt Joanna," Melvin whispered back.

"Mine is actually better than Joanna's."

"I got a promotion, Pops!"

"Congratulations! Come over here and give your old Pops a big hug!"

"Don't forget me," Lola said.

"Fill us in on the details, son."

"I'll be heading up the editorial department."

"We're so proud of you."

"Thanks, Pops. There is one little hitch."

"Oh, what's that?" Lola asked.

"The position is in our other office in Waterford."

"Waterford?" Melvin Sr. repeated.

"It's a good career move for me, Pops, and it comes with a nice raise too!"

"I suppose our loss is Joanna's gain."

"It's not a loss, Pops. You and Lola can come and visit any time you want. I'll be in Waterford for a year to gain the experience I need, then I can come back and run the editorial department here."

"I like the sounds of that," Lola said.

"Me too," Liza agreed.

"Me three," Melvin Sr. added. "Your Aunt Joanna will look after you while you're there."

"I spoke to Aunt Joanna and—"

"You told my sister about your promotion before you told us?"

"Let me finish, Pops. I called Aunt Joanna, but I didn't tell her about my promotion. I called her to see if there may be any openings at the daycare for summer term. She said there were and asked if I knew anyone who would be interested. I told her I had someone in mind. I want Liza to go with me, Pops, and I wanted to get the information from Aunt Joanna so Liza and I could make plans for the summer. Liza is going to ask her parents' permission tomorrow when they get back from their cottage."

"I see," said Melvin Sr. "It seems everything is falling into place for you, son. A promotion, a new beginning in a new town, and a beautiful, charming, and intelligent young lady by your side. I think you've got it made in the shade!"

Liza blushed. Melvin graciously thanked his dad and put his arm around Liza and said, "I really am lucky."

"I think I just heard the timer on the oven. Make your way to the dining room and get comfy. We've got a lot of lunch to munch!"

"Come and sit beside me," Lola said as she ushered Liza into the dining room.

By the time all the food was on the table, there must have been twelve platters heaping full. Liza sat in silence as each one was carefully placed in the centre of the table.

"Now you see why we have such a large dining room table," Lola whispered to Liza.

"Who would like to say grace?" Melvin Sr. asked as he set the final platter on the table.

"Melvi, you go ahead," Lola said.

"Heavenly Father, we are grateful for this special family time today. Bless us and the food we are about to receive. Thank you for your provision. In Jesus' name we pray, amen."

"Don't be shy now. Dig in! I made sure there is a lot to choose from. I didn't know what kind of food you like, Liza."

"I like everything!"

"Make sure you take some of everything then," Melvin Sr. said as he passed the first platter to Liza.

As they ate lunch, Liza told Melvin Sr. and Lola about Sarah and Farley. She explained Farley would be working in Waterford on the construction project for the summer, and if she and Sarah get permission, they would both go and work at the daycare.

Melvin Sr. and Lola agreed it would be a wonderful opportunity and very beneficial for Joanna to have people she can trust to fill the positions.

"Hey, Pops, what's for dessert?" Melvin said as he finished the last bite of his lunch.

"Dessert? I am so full, I don't think I could eat another bite," Liza said, patting her stomach.

"Would you like coffee, Liza?" Lola offered.

"Coffee would be perfect, Lola, thank you."

"I'll have coffee too, Lola, *with* my dessert!" Melvin said.

"Me too, honey," Melvin Sr. said.

Lola went into the kitchen and reappeared a few minutes later with the dessert.

"Banana cream pie!" Liza exclaimed. "That's my all-time favourite dessert!"

Melvin winked at Lola. He'd requested it especially for Liza to surprise her.

"It's one of Lola's specialties," Melvin Sr. bragged.

"I'm still too full to have any right now."

"I will pack some up for you, Liza, and include it with the leftovers."

"Thank you, Lola."

"Lola is the pastry chef in our house, and I'm in charge of the meat and potatoes."

"Oh Melvi, I wouldn't call myself a pastry chef."

"I would, honey. When it comes to baking, I don't know anyone who can compete with you!"

"I still can't make a peach cobbler as well as Joanna."

"Joanna has my mother's secret recipe. I looked for it after Momma passed away, but I couldn't find it. I have a feeling Joanna tucked it away somewhere."

"Joanna also has your grandmother's recipe for her famous sticky ribs!"

"Yes, she does," Melvin Sr. confirmed.

"We'll have to see about getting those recipes from her. Maybe when you two are in Waterford, you can butter her up, and maybe she'll give them to you."

"We'll see what we can do, Pops."

"More coffee, anyone?" Lola offered.

"I think we should be going shortly," Melvin said. "Liza is staying at Sarah's while her parents are at the cottage. Before I drop her off, I'd like to take the leftovers home."

Melvin Sr. winked at Lola and said, "In other words, you want to have some time alone with your sweetie."

"Oh Pops."

"Don't *Oh Pops* me, young man. I was young once too!"

Melvin just shook his head.

***

They packed up the food and took it out to Melvin's car.

"You and Melvin come by again soon," Lola said as she walked alongside Liza.

"We will, Lola," Melvin promised.

"We've really enjoyed having you here, Liza," Melvin Sr. said as he hugged her. "Until next time."

"Until next time," Liza repeated.

"Drive safe now, son."

"We will. Thank you, guys, for everything; it sure was fun!"

Melvin Sr. and Lola stood waving until the car disappeared at the end of the driveway.

As they drove away, Melvin said, "You're awfully quiet, Princess. A penny for your thoughts."

"I wish I had a happy family like yours."

"You do. My family is your family."

"You make it sound so simple, Melvin."

"It is simple. Pops and Lola love you already and they just met you. Stick with me; you'll see everything will work out just fine."

"Your dad and Lola are wonderful. Lola is sweet and kind. Your dad is pretty funny."

"Don't forget handsome!"

"Yes, he is handsome," Liza agreed. "I don't mean to change the subject, Melvin, but when we get back to your place, can I have my dessert?"

"You mean some of my delicious kisses or the banana cream pie?"

"I will have ... *both*! Kisses first, then pie."

"Good choice!"

***

Once inside the apartment, Melvin didn't waste any time collecting kisses from Liza. He'd barely set the bags down when he took her in his arms and started kissing her.

In between kisses, Liza managed to say, "Don't you think we should put the food away?"

"Nope," was all Melvin said and he kept kissing her.

"Your kisses really are delicious, Melvin. You know what they taste like?"

"Let me show you ... more." And he kissed her again.

"Melvin?"

"Yes, Princess?"

"Can we have some pie now? I seem to have worked up an appetite."

Melvin started to unpack the food and called out, "I found it! Lola packed enough for both of us, so I'll have a second helping and join you."

"I could eat banana cream pie every day and never get tired of it," Liza admitted.

"I know what you mean. What would you like to do tomorrow, Princess?"

"After breakfast, Sarah and I are going to tell her mom about Waterford and the daycare."

"What about her dad?"

"Sarah's mom is really good at convincing her dad about things. If she thinks something is a good idea, then he thinks it's a good idea too."

"That sounds like a good plan. How about the afternoon?"

"The afternoon will be perfect. Let's plan for one o'clock, Melvin. I'll call you after we talk to Sarah's mom."

"Okay, Princess."

"Sarah and I made a plan to meet back at her place in about half an hour. Farley will be dropping Sarah off. If we leave now, we should arrive at the same time."

As they turned the corner toward Sarah's house, Liza said, "There they are now, right in front of us!" Melvin parked behind Farley.

"I'll call you tomorrow. Good night, Melvin, I had a wonderful time today."

"Good night, Princess," Melvin said and kissed her.

Liza waved as Melvin drove away. Sarah waved as Farley drove away.

They went into the house, took off their shoes, and tiptoed to Sarah's room. Sarah closed her bedroom door quietly behind them.

"How did things go with Melvin's parents?"

"Amazing. They are both so nice. Lola is beautiful. She's petite and has the biggest brown eyes. When she smiles, she lights up the room. You know she's a singer, right?"

"I think you mentioned that," Sarah recalled. "What about Melvin's dad?"

"He's handsome and a bit taller than Melvin. He's an excellent cook and makes the best cocktails! He's in great shape, just like Melvin. He wears his hair short like Melvin does, but his hair is salt and pepper—you know, grey mixed with black. He's got a good sense of humour and likes to joke around. Melvin's dad and Lola are really good together. You can feel they love each other very much. They are so easy to be around."

Sarah just listened and smiled as Liza rambled on.

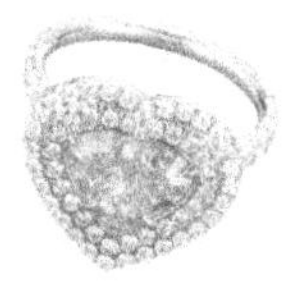

Chapter Thirteen

Convinced, Part One

"YOU AWAKE?" Liza said as she gave Sarah a little nudge.

"No."

"I smell bacon."

"Good for you," Sarah said without moving an inch.

"I *love* bacon."

"My mom always make bacon and pancakes every Sunday morning," Sarah said with her eyes still closed.

"You're so lucky. Now I want to be lucky too. Get up, I'm hungry."

Sarah stumbled to the table for breakfast, still half asleep. Liza followed behind her, fully awake, perky, and cheerful.

"Good morning, girls. Sleep well?"

"Yes, Mom, until the aroma and crackling bacon woke Liza up and then she woke me up. Where's Dad?"

"He went out to get the newspaper and said he was going to drop by the golf course and have breakfast with the boys at the clubhouse."

"Perfect," Sarah said.

"What's perfect?"

"Liza and I have something to ask you, Mom."

"I'm listening," Sarah's mom said as she flipped pancakes on the griddle.

"Liza found out about a Christian daycare in need of childcare workers for the summer term."

"I know we have a private Christian school here in town, but I didn't know we have a Christian daycare, too."

"That's just it, Mom; it's not here in town. It's in Waterford."

"Waterford? That's nine hours away!"

"Ten," Liza and Sarah both said.

"You mentioned the *summer term*. What does that mean?"

"The summer term starts in May and goes until August," Liza said.

"When in May? It's already the end of April."

"The sooner the better," Sarah said.

"Where would you girls stay?"

"My friend's aunt owns the daycare and is the director. She lives next door and will provide rooms for us ... girls only."

"Girls only?"

"That's right, Mom, girls only."

"What do your parents say about all of this, Liza?

"You know my parents, they're all in when it comes to furthering the Christian cause."

"What about your job?"

"I'm sure Marcus would be agreeable. We're not nearly as busy in the summer months, and I do have some vacation time coming."

"Assuming I can convince your dad, Sarah, and I'm sure I can, I have a few conditions."

"What's that, Mom?"

"Your dad and I will drive you and Liza to Waterford. We'll want to meet the director and see where you'll be staying. I'll also be calling your mom, Liza."

"My mom? My mom is at the cottage. She won't be back until later this evening."

"I didn't mean today. I'll give her a call tomorrow sometime. That's not a problem, is it?"

"No, no problem at all! Sarah, we're going to have to work fast!" Liza said through clenched teeth.

"Did you say something, Liza?"

"I said, great breakfast!"

"Who wants more bacon?"

Sarah and Liza hugged each other as Sarah's mom turned back to the stove to get the frying pan.

"Can I use your car today, Mom?"

"Sure, dear, I won't be needing it."

Once they were back in Sarah's room, Liza said, "That went really well, don't you think?"

"I knew my mom would be pretty easy to convince, but I had no idea it would be *that* easy."

"Now all we have to do is convince my parents. My mom should be a pushover, but my father is another story."

"We'll convince them together. I'm sure it will work out. If we're all going to be working in Waterford, I think Farley and Melvin should meet, don't you, Liza?"

"Let's not put the cart before the horse. I don't have permission yet."

"I still think they should meet. Farley and I don't have any plans for this afternoon."

"Melvin and I don't have any plans either."

"We should do something together then," Sarah said excitedly.

"I'll call Melvin and tell him your mom gave you permission to go to Waterford and see if he wants to go on a group date."

"While you're doing that, I'll have a quick shower and get ready, then I'll give Farley a call. You should probably pack too. We'll put your bag in the trunk; that way we can go straight to your house later."

***

"Hi handsome," Liza said when Melvin answered.

"Hi yourself, Princess."

"I have good news, Melvin. We talked to Sarah's mom this morning and she's on board."

"That's great news!"

"Sarah's mom and dad will drive us to Waterford. Her mom wants to meet your Aunt Joanna and see where we'll be staying."

"I'm sure Aunt Joanna would love to meet Sarah's parents."

"Sarah suggested we all get together this afternoon, so you and Farley can meet."

"I'm in. What did you have in mind?"

"Sarah will have her mom's car, so we'll pick Farley up first and then we'll come and pick you up. We can decide then what we want to do."

"It's a date, Princess."

"We'll pick you up in an hour, Melvin."

***

Sarah slid over to make room for Farley to get in on the driver's side. He kissed Sarah and then turned to say hello to Liza.

"I hear we're on our way to pick up the *Mysterious Melvin* Sarah has told me so much about."

"I think you guys will hit it off," Liza said.

"I'm sure we will. He sounds like a *groovy* guy," Farley said as he winked at Liza.

Liza gave Farley directions to Melvin's place. When they arrived, Liza got out of the car to go and get him. Melvin was already walking toward her. "Hello, Princess," Melvin said as he hugged Liza and kissed her. "I saw you guys drive up and thought I'd save you a few steps."

After introductions were made, the group decided to go bowling.

After three games, Sarah and Liza were leading. Strike, spare, strike, spare. Melvin and Farley were stunned. Neither of them could get a strike *or* a spare.

"Whose idea was it to go bowling anyway?" Farley said as he took off his bowling shoes.

"There's always next time," Sarah said.

"I don't know about the rest of you, but I've worked up an appetite. Anyone want to go for a burger?" Melvin asked.

"I could eat!" Farley replied. "Winners have to buy!"

On the way to the restaurant, they passed Liza's mom and her father driving in the opposite direction. Liza caught sight of them.

"Melvin, what's that on my shoe?" she said as she pushed him over.

"What's what?" he said as he sat up again.

"Sorry, I thought I saw something weird on my shoe. I guess I was wrong."

"I guess you were."

When they got to the restaurant, Liza pulled Sarah aside. "Do you think my parents saw us, Sarah?"

"I doubt it. They looked pretty stoic from what I could tell. They didn't look over at all. If they did, they would have only seen Farley and me in the front seat. It's not that easy to see anyone in the back seat when you're driving by so quickly."

"I sure hope you're right."

"We better go and sit down. Farley likes to ask a lot of questions if he thinks I'm away too long."

"I'm really looking forward to going to Waterford," Farley said as Sarah and Liza sat down.

"I still have to talk to my parents this evening," Liza said.

"When will they be home from the cottage?" Melvin asked.

"I have a feeling they may already be home," Liza answered.

"After we eat, we'll drop you guys off. Liza and I will head over to her place and talk to her parents about Waterford."

"Wish us luck," Liza said.

"Luck!" Farley replied.

"I don't think I'll be able to fall asleep tonight until I find out what your parents decide. I definitely won't be able to wait until you get to work tomorrow morning to call me," Melvin said.

"Maybe you won't have to. I have an idea. When Sarah gets home later, she can call Farley and tell him the verdict and he can call you, Melvin."

"Works for me! Pass that napkin, Farley. I'll write my number on it for you," Melvin said.

Chapter Fourteen

Convinced, Part Two

"HELLO, ANYBODY HOME?"

"Yes, we're home, Liza," Helga answered.

Sarah and Liza peeked around the corner into the kitchen.

"Hi, Sarah, I didn't expect to see you this evening."

Liza whispered, "Where's Father?"

"He's in his study making a phone call."

"Good," Liza said as she breathed a sigh of relief.

"Sarah and I have something we want to tell you about, Mom."

"Sounds serious, dear. What is it?"

"Liza and I have an opportunity to go and work at a Christian daycare," Sarah began.

"Christian daycare? What are you talking about?" Klaus said as he walked into the kitchen.

Liza poked Sarah.

"Like I was saying, Liza and I have a chance to work at a Christian daycare. A lot of staff start taking holidays in May. They're looking to hire for the summer term."

"Where is this Christian daycare?" Klaus asked.

"It's in Waterford," Sarah answered.

"That's ten hours away," Klaus said.

Sarah and Liza were just about to correct him and say "ten," but they didn't have to.

"I think that sounds like a great opportunity, girls."

"What are you talking about, Klaus?" Helga said. "You don't know anything about it!"

"I know that it's a Christian daycare, and that's good enough for me."

Liza stared at her father in utter shock and disbelief. Sarah poked Liza. Liza poked Sarah right back.

"I need a lot more information, Klaus," Helga said adamantly.

Sarah filled in the details. "My friend's aunt owns the daycare and is the director. She lives next door and provides rooms for those she hires ... girls only. Liza and I will have our own rooms. My parents have offered to drive us to Waterford. They think it's a good idea and agree it's for a good cause."

"I agree with your parents, Sarah. Anything to further the Christian cause! When do you girls have to be there?"

"The sooner the better," Sarah answered.

"Wait a minute," Helga said. "What did Marcus say, Liza?"

"I'll find out tomorrow when I go to work."

"Don't things slow down at the office right about now?" Klaus asked.

"Yes, Father."

"Shouldn't be a problem then!"

"When will you come back, Liza?"

"The term is from May until the end of August, Mom."

"You'll be away that long?" Helga lamented.

"Don't worry, Helga, the girls will be just fine," Klaus said.

Liza couldn't believe what just transpired.

"By the way, Mom, Sarah's mom is going to call you tomorrow. I'm sure she'll put your mind at ease."

"I should be going now, Liza," Sarah said.

"I'll walk you out, Sarah."

"Goodbye, Sarah," Klaus said.

"Goodbye," Sarah replied.

Helga turned around and started wiping down the counters.

***

"Can you believe your father, Liza?"

"No, can you? Why do I feel like I just hit a jackpot, Sarah?"

"We kind of did. Freedom from rules, except the ones Joanna has. No parents to tell us what to do—independence!"

"The biggest jackpot ever! I get to spend all my spare time with Melvin."

"I get to spend all my spare time with Farley!"

"You and I get to work together. The four of us can also hang out whenever we want to! What are you doing, Sarah?"

"I'm pinching myself to see if this is real."

"Oh, it's real all right," Liza said, and then she pinched Sarah.

"Ouch! Liza, what did you do that for?"

"I thought I would pinch you too, to be sure it's real."

"Oh Liza, stop it!" Sarah said and laughed.

"Don't forget to call Farley when you get home so that he can tell Melvin the awesome news!"

"I will, Liza."

"We make a good team, Sarah."

"We sure do! As we always say, that's what friends are for!"

"I'll call you tomorrow when I get a chance and let you know what Marcus says. Drive safely, Sarah."

"Thanks, Liza. Talk to you tomorrow."

Liza walked into the kitchen, took the cloth Helga was wiping the counters with, and sat her down at the table. Liza sat down across from her.

"If it will make you feel better, Mom, you can come along when Sarah's mom and dad drive us to Waterford. Sarah's dad has a van, so there will be plenty of room."

"Do you think they will mind?"

"No, Mom. I don't think they will mind at all."

"That would be very nice, dear. I will really miss you, Liza. It won't be the same here without you."

"The time will go quickly, Mom. Besides, Junior will be here to keep you company."

"That's true," Helga said.

"We just have to wait and see what Marcus will say tomorrow," Liza said.

"What do you think he will say?"

"I think he will be okay with it."

Chapter Fifteen

Full Speed Ahead

LIZA WAS PACING BACK AND FORTH in front of her desk, rehearsing what she would say to Marcus, just as he walked in.

"I have something to tell you," they said simultaneously.

"I'll go first," Liza offered. "Sarah and I have an opportunity to go and work in Waterford at a Christian daycare."

"Waterford is a very nice town. Ethel and I stayed there for a weekend a couple of summers ago. The diner is amazing!"

"Marcus, I just told you I'd like to go away and work in Waterford—"

"When do you start?"

"As soon as possible."

Marcus hesitated and then said, "That's perfect, Liza."

"It is?"

"Yes. Ethel and I are going to go on an African safari. We leave next week. That's what I was going to tell you when I came in."

"Wow, an African safari!"

"It just sort of came up. I finished writing the manuscript for my next book, so Ethel and I thought it would be a perfect time for a holiday."

"What are you going to do about the office?"

"I was going to have you keep up with the basics, taking in the mail and the usual duties, but Bishop can manage around here. Things are starting to slow down now, so there won't be much for him to do. Ethel and I will be back at the end of August."

"That's when Sarah and I will be back too."

"Well then, things will work out just fine. You have my permission to take the position and I support you in your decision."

"Thank you so much, Marcus!"

"I'm surprised your father agreed to let you go."

"He was all for it! My mom was the one who needed convincing."

"That's a switch."

"It sure is. It seems everything is falling into place, Marcus."

"You know, Liza, that does happen from time to time."

"Marcus, would you mind if I call my mom? I told her I'd call her after I spoke to you."

"Sure. Say hi to her for me. I've got a number of things to wrap up before Ethel and I leave next week. I better get started."

Liza called her mom. It took a number of rings before she answered. "Hello," Helga said, slightly out of breath.

"Hi, Mom. Are you all right?"

"Yes, dear, I'm fine. Your father was just leaving, so I walked out to the car to say goodbye. I heard the phone ringing as I was walking back to the house."

"I called to tell you that Marcus gave me permission to go to Waterford."

"How will he manage without you?"

"Turns out he's leaving too."

"What do you mean, dear?"

"He and Ethel are going on a vacation. They leave next week and will return at the end of August. Bishop will take over in the meantime."

"I see," Helga said.

"I know you don't really want me to go, Mom. I'll call you and you can call me too. You'll see, it will be all right."

"I suppose. I know it's important to you, dear."

"I have to call Sarah now, Mom. I want to tell her we're cleared to go. Her mom will be calling you sometime today."

"I'll be home. Tell Sarah I'll look forward to hearing from her mom."

"I will. See you after work."

"Bye, dear."

Marcus walked over to Liza and handed her a stack of files. "How's your mom today?"

"Not bad. She's having a hard time adjusting to the idea that I'll be going to Waterford."

"She'll be okay; she's very resilient. I have to go out and take care of some banking and pick up some things for Ethel. I may or may not be back today."

"No problem, Marcus. I'll hold down the fort."

"I know you will."

"Marcus, would you mind if I take a longer lunch tomorrow? I want to have lunch with Aunt Sadie, and traffic going downtown is unpredictable."

"Why don't you take the afternoon off. You've earned it, always working at your desk through your lunch hour. Besides, Bishop will be coming in, so I can brief him on what he'll have to do around here."

"Thank you, Marcus."

"I'll see you in the morning, Liza."

"See you then."

Liza quickly did the filing and called Sarah.

"Hey there, gal pal," Liza said as Sarah answered the phone.

"Hi, Liza. My mom was just about to call your mom."

"Glad I caught you first then. Marcus gave me the green light to take the job in Waterford."

"Waterford, here we come!" Sarah said happily.

"One more thing. I invited my mom to come along for the ride."

"That's a good idea."

"You think so?"

"Yes, I do. My parents and your mom will have a chance to meet Joanna. They'll see where we'll be staying, maybe even take a little tour of the daycare. Then your mom will have a good idea of what it's all about. That will put her mind at ease. On the way back home, my mom will convince your mom that it will be a good experience."

"If anyone can convince her, it's your mom!"

"You got that right! I gotta go; my mom is calling me. She wants to use the phone so she can call your mom now. Call me later."

The next call Liza made was to Melvin.

"Guess what, Melvin!" Liza said, barely giving him enough time to say hello. "Marcus has given me his blessing to go to Waterford! In fact, he and his wife, Ethel, have been there and think it's a great place! He said the food at the diner is awesome!"

"I've heard that too, Princess. I had a feeling Marcus would be on board. I have a meeting with my boss tomorrow at lunch, to go over the details for my new position and finalize the start date."

"That answers my question."

"What question?"

"I'm going downtown to have lunch with my Aunt Sadie at her hotel and was going to invite you to join us."

"Your aunt owns a hotel?"

"My aunt and my father own it. Aunt Sadie holds the majority shares. My father is the silent partner, which is ironic, because he's never silent."

"I wish I could, Princess. If you call me after lunch tomorrow, I'll have the information we need to go forward with our plans."

"I'll call you from the hotel after lunch."

"I love you, Princess."

"I love you too, Melvin."

Chapter Sixteen

Helga Stays, Liza Goes

JUNIOR WAS OUTSIDE cutting grass when Liza got home from work. He shut down the lawnmower when he noticed her walking toward him. "Hey, Liza! How was work today?"

"It was good. How was school?"

"Good too!"

"You missed all the excitement around here last night," Liza said.

"Dad let me stay over at John's."

"How did you manage that? Today was a school day."

"I didn't have to *manage* anything. Dad was in a really good mood and was totally okay with it."

"When Sarah and I proposed the plan to go to Waterford, he thought it was a great idea, so he definitely was in a good mood."

"When I get home after school, I overheard Mom on the phone with Sarah's mom discussing the trip."

"Mom doesn't like the idea that I'm going to be away so long."

"Don't worry about Mom. You and Sarah go and have fun! I'll spend more time at home. Instead of going to John's, he can come here. Mom really likes John. We'll keep her busy cooking for us. She won't even miss you."

"Now you're going a little too far, little brother!" Liza said as she punched Junior in the arm.

Helga came outside to see how Junior was doing with the grass and saw Liza punch him.

"Liza, don't hit your brother!"

"It was all in fun, Mom. We're not fighting."

Junior started rubbing his arm and said, "Ouch, that hurt!"

Liza punched his other arm, a little harder this time.

"That's enough, you two! Liza, I had a nice conversation with Sarah's mom earlier today."

"I was going to ask you about that, but Junior distracted me."

"Don't blame me for your bad memory."

Liza was just about to punch Junior again when he jumped behind Helga and used her for a shield.

"Coward," Liza said jokingly.

"Bully," Junior called out, still hiding behind Helga.

Helga stepped away from Junior and pointed out the lawnmower. "Get a move on, Junior."

Junior waved her off and started up the mower.

Helga and Liza went inside. "Do you and Sarah know when you'll be leaving?"

"I'll know tomorrow afternoon."

"I've given a lot of thought to going along for the ride to Waterford and have decided not to go after all."

"Really, Mom? Why not?"

"For a number of reasons. Your father is away for two weeks. If I did go, I'd want Junior to come along too. I won't leave him at home on his own. Having four people in the van is quite comfortable. Adding two more would be a bit too crowded, although Sarah's mom assured me that there is more than enough room for all of us. If you and Sarah happen to leave on a weekday, your father won't allow Junior to miss school. Sarah's mom promised to take pictures of the daycare and the place where you girls will be staying.

We'll get together when they get back and she'll tell me all about it."

"Are you sure, Mom?"

"Yes, dear, I'm sure."

"Would you help me get my suitcases from the basement storage room?"

"I brought them up earlier and put them in your room, dear. I'll help you do some packing while Junior finishes cutting the grass."

"That would be great, Mom."

"By the way, Liza, Aunt Sadie called this afternoon and said you'll be joining her for lunch at the hotel tomorrow."

"Yes, that's right. It's been a long time since I've seen Aunt Sadie, and even longer since I've been at the hotel. I want to see her before we leave for Waterford."

"Aunt Sadie and I had a bite to eat at the hotel after our afternoon at the flea market. You're going to love what they've done! I won't give you any details. You'll see for yourself tomorrow."

"I'm looking forward to it."

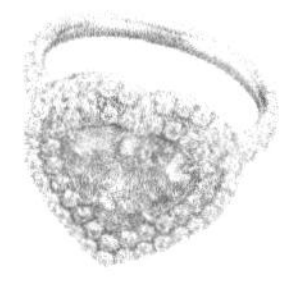

Chapter Seventeen

The Hotel

"THERE'S MY FAVOURITE NIECE!" Aunt Sadie said as she hugged Liza. "How are you, my dear?"

"I'm doing really well, Aunt Sadie. How are you?"

"I'm fine, dear. Busier than ever, now that renovations are complete. When was the last time you were here?"

"The renovations were just at the beginning stage."

"I think you'll really like all the changes we've made, and there are a lot of them," Aunt Sadie said. "I've reserved our favourite table."

"Aunt Sadie, this is incredible! The dining room looks like a grand ballroom!"

"Like it?"

"Like it? I *love* it!"

Liza walked through the dining room and couldn't believe the transformation: chandeliers sparkling in the sunlight; round tables with high-backed black leather chairs, seating six; square tables seating four; and cozy tables for two. Champagne-coloured table linens with ornate silverware framing each place setting. Crystal water glasses gleamed and seemed to absorb the hue from the colourful bouquet of fresh flowers, the centrepiece of each table.

"The dining room is beautiful, Aunt Sadie!"

"Wait until you see the new wing!"

"There's a new wing?"

"Yes. Now there are three deluxe honeymoon suites in addition to the other rooms. We can take a tour after lunch if you have time."

"I have all afternoon."

"Wonderful, dear!"

Aunt Sadie motioned for her personal attendant, Helana, to come to the table.

"Hello, Miss," Helana said as she greeted Liza.

"Hello, Helana. So nice to see you again."

"Helana, I would like tea, please."

"And for you, Miss?"

"Tea would be lovely, and may I have honey also?"

"Would you like to see our new menu, Liza?"

"I'll take a look at it, but I already know what I'd like."

"We'll have two roast beef specials, Helana, please. Just leave one menu."

"Yes, Ma'am."

"Here you are, Liza," Aunt Sadie said as she gave the menu to her. "We've added a number of new treats to the dessert section. I had to hire another pastry chef to keep up with the demand. Gloria has simply revolutionized the way our desserts are prepared. For example, she changed your favourite banana cream pie—for the better, I might add."

"Aunt Sadie, how could banana cream pie get any better?"

"Gloria lines the pastry shell with fresh slices of banana before she pours her homemade banana pudding on top. When the pudding has cooled, she tops it with a generous dollop of fresh whipping cream. Just before serving, she garnishes it with freshly sliced pieces of banana. I took the liberty of ordering a couple of slices for our dessert today. I hope you don't mind."

"On the contrary, I'm glad you did. It sounds so good, I'd like to have dessert first!"

"Your tea, Ma'am," Helana said as the served Aunt Sadie. "Your tea and your honey, Miss."

"Thank you, Helana," Liza said.

"There's something different about you, Liza. I can't quite put my finger on it, but you are glowing," Aunt Sadie said.

"I *am* very happy, Aunt Sadie. I have a boyfriend; he's a journalist and is going to work in Waterford, and I'm going too, and I'm going to work at his aunt's daycare, and Sarah and Farley are going too, and everything is just perfect, and he's perfect too and I'm in love," Liza said in one breath.

"Slow down; breathe and start over. You say you have a boyfriend?"

"His name is Melvin. He's amazing, Aunt Sadie."

"Do your parents know?"

"Yes and no."

"Let me guess. Your mom knows, but your father doesn't."

"Mom knows a bit —"

"I hope she can keep a secret."

"She's been doing a good job so far, *and* she's been standing up for herself lately."

"It's about time! I'm proud of your mom. I know my brother, and I know he's not easy to get along with."

"Easy?"

"You know what I mean."

Helana arrived with their lunch order. "Will there be anything else?" Helana asked.

"Please bring a bottle of sparkling water."

"Yes, Ma'am."

"Now, Liza dear, tell me more about this young man of yours."

As they ate, Liza told Aunt Sadie about Melvin. When it came to the part about Helga almost running the stop sign, Aunt Sadie couldn't contain her laughter.

"Poor Helga! That must have been quite a shock. To see her little girl kissing someone she knew nothing about."

"Technically he was kissing me. I managed to convince her he was just asking for directions. Unfortunately, a couple of days later, I told Mom I was out with Sarah. I couldn't reach Sarah ahead of time to tell her to cover for me."

"Uh, oh."

"Uh, oh is right! Sarah called and left a message. Mom listened to it, and when I got home, she was waiting up for me."

"At that point, did your mom change your name from Liza to Missy?"

"You know it!"

"What happened then?"

"I had to come clean ... sort of. I told her about Melvin, but I left out a few details. When Mom almost ran the stop sign, she was too far away to get a good look at him, so I didn't tell her that he's Black."

"I think that's wise. What your mother doesn't know, your father can't pry out of her. If you're happy, I am happy for you."

"Thank you, Aunt Sadie. That means a lot to me. Sarah and I didn't tell our parents about the *real* reason we want to work in Waterford. As far as they know, we're going to work at a Christian daycare. What they don't know is that Melvin is being transferred there for work, and his Aunt Joanna owns the daycare. Farley will be working on a big construction project there for the summer."

"If you're going to all this trouble to follow your young man, it must be quite serious."

"I love him, Aunt Sadie."

"I'm very happy for you, dear."

"Excuse me, Ma'am," Helana interrupted. "Sylvia Moore is here and she's asking to see you."

"Sylvia Moore? What is *she* doing here?" Liza demanded.

"Tell her I'll be there in a minute, Helana."

Aunt Sadie turned to Liza and said, "Sylvia is booking rooms for an upcoming event. I believe it's a family reunion. I'll be right back, Liza."

Helana returned to clear away the lunch plates. "Your aunt instructed me to tell you she has enlisted Lazlo, our new Events Coordinator, to take the meeting with Mrs. Moore. She said I should serve the dessert, as she will be along momentarily."

"I would love to have dessert now, Helana. Thank you."

Within a couple of minutes, Aunt Sadie returned. "Sorry about that, dear. I explained to Sylvia I won't be handling the event bookings anymore. Lazlo is very capable and is handling things beautifully. I went over to introduce him. I hired fifteen new staff so I can have free time to do things like have lunch with my favourite niece and take an afternoon off to go shopping with your mom, my favourite sister-in-law."

"Aunt Sadie?"

"Yes, dear?"

"I don't like Sylvia."

"That's all right, dear. We don't have to like everyone. Here's our dessert. Doesn't it look delicious?"

Liza took a bite and said, "It *is* delicious. I didn't think anyone could improve upon good ol' banana cream pie. I was wrong. Gloria is a genius. I bet this is going to be your best seller!"

"It's right up there with the double chocolate fudge lava cake," Aunt Sadie bragged.

"I think I'm gaining weight just thinking about it.

After dessert, they toured the new wing. Each of the new rooms was even more beautiful than the last. The tour ended with the honeymoon suites.

"I saved the best for last," Aunt Sadie announced. "This one is my personal favourite."

Liza followed Aunt Sadie into the luxurious honeymoon suite. As she did, her thoughts turned to Melvin. She pictured him carrying her over the threshold on their wedding night. Melvin wore a black tuxedo and a white silk shirt and tie. Liza wore a white satin wedding gown, a floor-length lace veil held in place with a beautiful multi-layered crystal tiara, a bouquet of white roses cascading down the length of her gown. The vision she imagined played out in slow motion, just as she had seen in the movies so many times.

The king-sized bed lay covered in red rose petals. Champagne was chilling in a silver ice bucket, her favourite chocolate-dipped strawberries on the night stand next to the bed. On each pillow was a single wrapped chocolate.

Melvin carried her over to the bed and ... the romantic music Liza imagined playing was interrupted by someone calling her name.

"Liza?"

"Yes, Aunt Sadie?"

"You look a little flushed, dear."

"I'm fine."

"Were you just daydreaming about your own wedding night, dear?"

"Me? Nah!"

"How do you like the honeymoon suite?"

"I didn't realize a honeymoon suite could be this beautiful!"

"That's the end of our tour. I should be getting back to the dining room. I have to go over tonight's dinner special with the chef."

"I told Melvin I'd call him after our lunch. He had a meeting with his boss to discuss final details about Waterford. He should be finished his meeting by now."

"Go ahead and use the phone on the nightstand. You'll have all the privacy you want here. I'll head downstairs. Close the door when you leave; it will lock automatically.

Have Helana inform me when you return to the dining room. I'll say goodbye then and walk you out."

"I won't be long, Aunt Sadie."

"Take as long as you like, dear. Tell your young man I look forward to meeting him."

"I will."

Chapter Eighteen

Departures

LIZA PROPPED HERSELF UP on the bed and dialled Melvin's number, excited to tell him about her lunch with Aunt Sadie, the hotel renovations, and the beautiful honeymoon suite she was calling from. Instead, Melvin began by telling Liza his news first.

"Melvin, guess where—"

"Princess, I'm so glad you called," he said with an urgent tone in his voice. "The meeting with my boss ended not long after it began."

"Why?"

"There was only one thing on the agenda."

"What was that?"

"My boss handed me a plane ticket and said I'm booked on the nine o'clock flight to Waterford Thursday morning. I've been packing all afternoon. The moving company will be here tomorrow morning to pick up the furniture and anything I didn't finish packing today. Do you think you could come over and help me?"

"I'm on my way!"

"Oh, one more thing. I called Aunt Joanna, and she wanted to know if Sarah's parents could drive you out to Waterford on Saturday."

"I'll call Sarah and then I'll leave the hotel to come to your place. It will take me about half and hour to get there."

"No problem, Princess. See you soon."

***

"Hello," Sarah said, sniffling.

"Sarah, are you crying?"

"Farley is leaving tomorrow for Waterford. They extended the contract to include more road construction, which means they need more time in order to complete it." Sarah blew her nose and it was so loud, Liza had to move the phone away from her ear.

"Dry your eyes, my friend! I just spoke to Melvin. He's flying to Waterford Thursday morning. His aunt wants us there on Saturday."

"MOM!" Sarah yelled.

Sarah's mom came running, thinking something was wrong. "What is it, Sarah?"

"Liza is on the phone. She just found out a few minutes ago that the director of the daycare would like us to arrive in Waterford on Saturday."

"What about your graduation dinner?"

"We'll have it when I get back."

"I'll go tell your dad."

"I better start packing, Liza."

"Don't panic. You have time. I had lunch with Aunt Sadie at the hotel and I'm just leaving to go to Melvin's and help him with his packing. The movers are scheduled to do a pickup tomorrow morning. I'm going to tell my mom that I'm going to your place to help you."

"Good plan ... hold on, Liza, my mom wants to tell me something. Okay, Mom, I'll tell her. My mom said my dad is good to go for Saturday. He said we'll have to get an early start on the day, so we'll pick you up at six."

"I'll be ready."

"I'm going to start packing now, Liza. I'll talk to you tomorrow."

"I'll call you when I get a chance, Sarah."

Liza couldn't help smiling as she called home, thinking that in a few days, she and Sarah would be on their way to Waterford. "Hi, Junior. Is Mom there?"

"She just left to go to the store. John's coming for dinner, and she didn't have enough ingredients for her spaghetti sauce."

"Make sure you save some for me."

"I can't promise anything. You've seen the way John eats."

"I found out today that Sarah and I have to be in Waterford on Saturday. I'm almost packed because I started a while ago. Sarah is just starting, so I'm going over to help her. Can you explain that to Mom for me and tell her I won't be late?"

"Sure, no problem."

"Thanks, Junior, see ya later."

Liza left the honeymoon suite and headed back to the dining room. She spotted Helana at the reservation desk.

"Helana, hi! Could you please tell Aunt Sadie I'll be leaving now?"

"Yes, Miss. Your aunt is in the kitchen, I'll let her know."

***

"On your way, dear?"

"Yes, Aunt Sadie. I'm going over to Melvin's to help him pack. Although I just told Junior that I was going to Sarah's. At the meeting today, Melvin's boss informed him that he has to report to work in Waterford on Thursday. He flies out Thursday morning."

"That's short notice!"

"It's a week earlier than he expected. His aunt requested Sarah and I arrive in Waterford on Saturday."

"That's short notice too!"

"We knew the term would be from May to August; we just didn't know the exact date we would be starting. That is, until today."

"I'm so glad we were able to spend some time together today," Aunt Sadie said.

"Me too! Aunt Sadie?"

"Yes, dear?"

"I'm really going to miss you."

"I will miss you too. You know where to find me, so don't hesitate to pick up the phone and call. Your mom is in good hands here, so nothing to worry about."

"That means a lot to me, Aunt Sadie."

"Have a wonderful time in Waterford."

"I love you, Aunt Sadie," Liza said as she hugged her.

"I love you too, Liza dear."

Liza waved goodbye as Aunt Sadie stood outside and watched as she drove away.

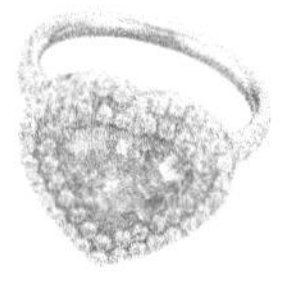

Chapter Nineteen

The Heart

"YOU'VE CERTAINLY GOTTEN A LOT OF PACKING done in such a short time, Melvin," Liza said as she walked the path Melvin cleared through the maze of boxes.

"I did some organizing the last couple of days to prepare, after my boss hinted at a quick departure."

"Where should I start, Melvin?"

"You should start right here," he said as he pointed to his lips. "I didn't get my hello kiss yet."

Liza kissed him, stepped back, smiled, and said, "I get to kiss you every day when we are in Waterford."

"I can't wait, Princess! My new position is going to be fun and exciting, but being with you is what I'm looking forward to most." Melvin kissed Liza again and then said, "Morning comes early, so we better get the rest of the packing done."

"Just point me in the right direction!"

"I could use your help in the kitchen. I'll hand things to you from the cupboards. You can place them on the counter. Then together we can wrap and pack them."

Liza laughed. "That's funny, Melvin! Wrap them and pack them!"

"I'm so glad you're here, Princess. Things always go faster when there are two people working together."

"We make a good team, Melvin!"

"We sure do! How was lunch with your aunt this afternoon?"

"It was great! You should see the hotel. They've completed a huge renovation. Now everything is new and improved ... right down to the banana cream pie!"

"How can banana cream pie be new and improved?"

"I said the same thing! Aunt Sadie's new pastry chef somehow managed to do it!"

"Don't tell Lola; she prides herself in having the best banana cream pie!"

"I might tell her Gloria's secret, and Lola can decide if she wants to make any changes to her recipe. After dessert, Aunt Sadie took me on a tour of the new wing."

"I'm sorry I had to miss it. I would have liked to meet your aunt."

"Aunt Sadie said she's looking forward to meeting you sometime."

"It won't be for a while now."

"That's okay, she understands completely. I told her you're leaving Thursday morning and you still had some packing to do."

"I'm glad you could spend some time with your aunt today, especially since you leave on Saturday."

"It was perfect timing!"

"Speaking of spending some time together, I've made plans to go to my pop's place tomorrow after the movers leave. Since they'll be taking all the furniture, Pops suggested I stay overnight. He and Lola will take me to the airport on Thursday morning."

"Your pops is right. I'm sure they'd be happy to have you all to themselves."

"Thank you for understanding, Princess."

"Give them my love. Hopefully they'll come and visit us in Waterford."

“As a matter of fact, they’re already planning their trip. Pops hasn’t seen Aunt Joanna in a couple of years.”

“That’s a long time!”

“Yes, it is. They get together as often as they can. They’ve always been close.”

“Just like you and Alicia.”

“That’s right. You and Junior seem pretty close too.”

“Junior and I look out for each other, and Mom. Since my father is away most of the time, Junior and I have a much closer bond with my mom.”

“Makes sense,” Melvin said as he closed up the last box of kitchen stuff, taped it shut, and labelled it “kitchen stuff.”

Within a couple of hours, they had everything done.

“That’s just about does it, Princess. I have a few things left from my office to pack, but I’ll do that later. How about if we take a little drive and get some fresh air?”

“What did you have in mind?”

“There’s a little spot called Camper’s Beach about half an hour from here. I though we’d go there.”

“I’ve never been there before.”

“We used to go there when we were kids. I think you’ll like it.”

“I’m sure I will, Melvin. If you like it, I’ll like it.”

“Leave your car here, we’ll take mine.”

***

The beach was deserted, except for a man walking a dog. Melvin opened the trunk and took out a blanket and a little basket.

“When did you have time to pack for our little excursion?”

“I picked up a few things after my meeting. Just before you got to my place, I ran out and put the basket in the cooler I have in my trunk.”

“You’re so thoughtful, Melvin.”

"You make it easy, Princess. One for you and one for me," Melvin said as he handed Liza a miniature bottle of wine. "Since you have to drive home later, and I still have a little packing to do, we'll toast with these."

"I've never seen wine in miniature bottles. They're so cute!"

Melvin laughed. A black Labrador retriever came bounding up and went straight to Liza. He knocked her over and started licking her face.

"Hey! Get your own girl; this one's mine!"

"Charlie, come here! Sorry, folks, I didn't know anyone was here. Charlie loves to run along the shore and chase birds. If I'd seen you, I would have put his leash on," Charlie's owner said.

"No harm, no foul," Melvin replied.

"He's a beautiful dog," Liza said.

Charlie licked Liza's cheek as she petted him.

"Okay, Charlie, let's go and let these people have their picnic in peace."

"Bye, Charlie," Liza called out.

He turned to look at Liza and then ran after his owner on the shoreline.

Melvin reached into the basket and took out a container. "The lid on this container sticks a bit. I'll hold the bottom, Princess, and you take the lid off."

"What did we say before, Melvin? Team work, right?"

The lid came off very easily. In the container were cheese and crackers, grapes, and a small blue velvet box tied with a blue velvet ribbon.

Liza noticed the blue velvet box immediately. She did a double take. She looked at the box, then at Melvin, then again at the box, and at Melvin. Melvin took the box and held it in front of her.

"This is a symbol of my love for you, Princess. It's a promise of forever." He untied the ribbon, opened the box, and revealed a heart-shaped, diamond-studded ring.

"Melvin, it's beautiful!"

Melvin took Liza's left hand and placed the ring on her finger. "This is a promise ring, Princess. I promise to love you all the days of my life. Eventually, I'll replace it with a BIG diamond ring, but for now, this ring will hold the place for an engagement ring. Why are you crying, Princess?"

"These are happy tears, Melvin. I accept your promise, and I promise to love you all the days of *my* life."

"There are times we may have to be apart, but all you need to do is look at this ring to be reminded of my heart and all the love it holds for you, and you alone."

Liza wrapped her arms around Melvin's neck, hugged him, and kissed him. Just then Charlie came running back and jumped in between them.

"Charlie! Charlie! Come back here!"

Liza and Melvin were laughing so hard, Charlie's owner started laughing too. Charlie knocked over Liza's little wine bottle. Before he could start lapping it up, Melvin grabbed him by his collar.

"Oh no you don't! That's not good for you," Melvin said.

"Come on, Charlie, leave the nice people and their wine alone. I have some water for you back at the truck."

"We were going to toast with our wine. I still have a couple of sips left," Liza said. "Charlie didn't spill it all."

"Here's to you, and here's to me, and now here's to *us*. One plus one in our case does not equal two. It equals one. From this day forward, we are one."

"Thank you for your beautiful words, Melvin. I'll never forget this night."

"Look at the sunset, Princess. What a perfect backdrop for our romantic evening."

"You've made me the happiest girl in the world! I know our future will be bright and sparkle just like my ring."

Melvin leaned over and kissed Liza and said, "I hate to leave, but we should be heading back now."

Liza stared at her ring all the way back to Melvin's place.

***

"I guess this is goodbye until Saturday, Princess," Melvin said as he walked Liza back to her car.

"I'll miss you until then, Melvin."

"I'll miss you more! I need a bunch of your kisses to tide me over, Princess."

They stood beside the car, kissing and holding on to each other for dear life, neither one wanting to let go.

Melvin kissed Liza on her neck and on her forehead and on her cheek and said, "Until Saturday, my Princess!"

"Until Saturday, Melvin!"

On the way home, Liza stopped off at Sarah's. She wanted to ask Sarah to hold on to her ring for her until they arrived in Waterford. She wanted to keep it a secret from her family.

"Hi, Liza. What brings you here?" Sarah's dad said as he answered the door.

"I just wanted to see how Sarah is doing with her packing."

"I think she's packing the kitchen sink right about now. She's been in her room for hours. Sarah! Liza's here to see you!" her dad called out. "You know where her room is, so go ahead."

Sarah and Liza rounded the corner at the same time and bumped into each other.

"Liza, what are you doing here? I thought you were helping Melvin."

"Shh," Liza said as she pushed Sarah into her room and shut the door. "Melvin had done almost all of the packing before I got there. We just had to pack things from the kitchen and then took a little drive to Camper's Beach."

"I *love* Camper's Beach! We used to go there when we were kids."

Liza threw up her hands and said, "Seems like everyone except my family has been there!"

As Liza threw her hands in the air, Sarah caught a glimpse of something that sparkled. She followed Liza's hands as she waved them around. Sarah grabbed hold of Liza's left hand, held it, and stared at the ring *and* Liza.

"What are you wearing on your finger?!"

"It's a promise ring. I came here to show it to you and ask if you would hold it for me until we get to Waterford."

"A promise ring? It looks like an engagement ring with all those diamonds!"

"Melvin gave it to me when we went to the beach, as a promise of his unending love for me. He said that even when we are apart, I will have his heart."

"Sarah started crying. I'm SO happy for you. How romantic! I'll have to talk with Farley and tell him it's about time he got *me* a ring. After all, we've been together for three years!"

"You and Farley are talking about *marriage*. Marriage is a lot more serious than a promise."

Sarah didn't say anything; she just stared at Liza's ring.

"You know I'm right, Sarah."

"I hate it when you're right!"

"Yes, but you love me anyway."

"Fine, I love you anyway."

Liza took off the ring, put it in the box, and handed it to Sarah.

"I'll put it in my purse right now. It will be safe there."

Liza noticed that Sarah's suitcases were all packed. "Ready to go?"

"Yup. I just zipped the last zipper when I heard my dad calling to say you were here."

"What did Farley say when you told him you'd be in Waterford Saturday evening?"

"He was speechless at first and then he couldn't stop saying how happy he was."

"I can't stop smiling! I have to contain myself so that my mom doesn't think I'm up to something," Liza said.

"It's okay to be happy. I'm glad you stopped by, Liza."

"If my mom asks me any more questions when I get home, I can honestly say I was at your place tonight! See you Saturday, my friend!"

"See you then ... bright and early!"

Helga was on the phone when Liza got home. She waved hello.

Helga whispered, "It's Aunt Sadie."

Liza whispered back, "Hi, Aunt Sadie. I'm going to bed now, Mom."

Helga nodded.

***

Liza's morning alarm went off and then the phone started ringing. She lay in bed waiting for someone to answer it. When it became clear no one was making an attempt, Liza answered.

"Hello," she said in a gravelly voice.

"Good morning, Liza. I hope I didn't wake you."

"Hi, Marcus. No, you didn't wake me. I had to get up to answer the phone anyway."

"Even half asleep, you're still sharp witted."

"What's up, Marcus?"

"I called for a couple of reasons, the first one being to ask when you're leaving for Waterford."

"We're leaving early Saturday morning. I found out yesterday."

"Good for you, Liza! The second reason is to tell you I won't be in the office for the next few days, so you needn't come in either."

"Are you sure, Marcus?"

"Quite sure. I met with Bishop yesterday afternoon, as you know, and we got things squared away at the office. I thought you could use the time to pack and get ready for your trip."

"You thought right, Marcus."

"I hope you and Sarah have a wonderful time in Waterford. Please say hi to Flo at the diner for Ethel and me."

"You got it! Have fun on the safari!"

"Thank you, Liza. I'll get in touch with you mid-August."

Liza hung up and went into the kitchen. She found a note on the table from her mom explaining that she'd left to drive Junior to school for an early basketball practice. Afterwards, she was going to have breakfast at the hotel with Aunt Sadie.

Liza spent the next few days doing some shopping and finalizing her packing. Friday evening, Helga prepared a special farewell dinner for Liza with all of her favourite foods.

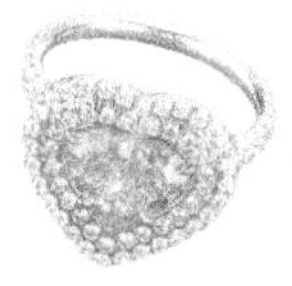

Chapter Twenty

"Lucky"

SARAH'S DAD PULLED INTO THE CIRCULAR DRIVEWAY at precisely six o'clock. Helga was watching for their arrival and called out to Junior to get Liza's luggage and take it to the van. She opened the door for Junior just as Sarah's dad rang the bell.

"Let me help you with those, son," he said.

"Gee, thanks. Looks like a nice day for a road trip!"

"Supposed to be good weather all the way through," Sarah's dad said as he reorganized Sarah's bags to make room for Liza's.

Sarah, her mom, Liza, and Helga gathered and watched as the bags were loaded.

"Wait until you hear your dad's plan for our trip today, Sarah."

"The plan is to drive for about three hours, stop for breakfast, and stretch our legs. The next leg of the trip, we'll drive four hours and then stop at Billy Joe Bob's Burger Bonanza. It's a great roadside diner. I've been there before. They have twenty different burgers on the menu! My favourite is Billy Joe Bob's signature burger. Billy Joe Bob cooks them up himself with some kinda special sauce. I heard he keeps the recipe in a safe in the back office. He shot a bear that tried to eat him for dinner one night and had the thing stuffed. That darned ol' bear stands guard over that safe. Billy Joe Bob went and named him "Lucky." Ever since he put that ol' bear back there, business has been booming! Not only is Lucky stuffed, but so is the safe ... full of cash!" Sarah's dad closed the back door of the van and said, "We'll have three hours left after that, which will get us to Waterford just in time for dinner."

"The plan you made seems to revolve around eating," Sarah's mom said.

"Driving makes me hungry, what can I say?"

"I think a destination eating plan is a great idea!" Junior said. "If I was going with you, I'd be all in!"

Helga stood in front of Liza, reached over to fix the collar on her white blouse, and said, "Now you go ahead and have a nice time in Waterford. Enjoy the children and the people you'll be working with. I'll miss you, dear, and I love you." Helga hugged Liza tightly.

"I love you too, Mom."

Junior stepped up next and wrapped his arms around Liza.

"Take good care of our mom, little brother," Liza whispered.

"You know I will!" Junior whispered back.

"We'll make sure he does," Sarah's mom promised.

"Time to go," Sarah's dad said. "All in that's getting in!"

"One more hug for the road!" Liza said. "Goodbye, Mom; goodbye, Junior."

"Drive safely," Helga said.

"When it comes to driving, I'm the best!" Sarah's dad bragged.

Liza looked back to see Junior put his arm around Helga as they walked toward the house. She felt sad to be leaving but happy to be off to a new adventure.

***

"How about if we make some breakfast, Mom? And by *we*, I mean *you*."

"I thought you were going to go back to bed, since you had to get up so early."

"First things first. You know I'm a growing boy!"

"That I know for sure, Junior. You're taller than any of the men in my family, and your father's too."

"Since I play basketball, my height is definitely an advantage. If you want to see me slam dunk the ball and hang on a hoop from time to time, you better keep feeding me, Mom!"

"I have *always* fed you, Junior. I'm not about to stop now!"

"May I also add, now that Liza is away, that I don't mind if you dote on me a little more."

Helga rolled her eyes and laughed.

"Just so you know, John is going to be spending a lot of time over here. You'll probably have to cook twice as much food as you usually do, because he has a pretty big appetite."

"Yes, Junior, I've seen John eat when he stays with us at the cottage. I am more than happy to cook for you both and have John visit, as long as I get some help with the dishes."

"Actually, Mom, John is really good at doing dishes ... well, loading the dishwasher anyway. He uses a stopwatch to time himself. A full load takes him four minutes, *including* the pots and pans!"

"I'd like to see that!" Helga said.

"I'll get him to show you. Now how about that breakfast?"

"All right, Junior."

"I'll make coffee, Mom. It will keep me awake so that I don't fall asleep before the grub is ready."

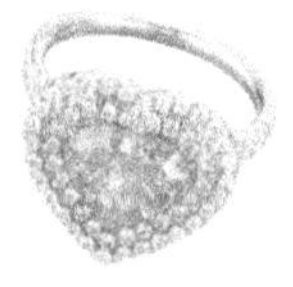

Chapter Twenty-One

J. J. House

SARAH'S DAD WAS RIGHT. The burgers at Billy Joe Bob's were dee-licious. In his honour, Billy Joe added burger number twenty-one to the menu—a triple decker burger Billy Joe named "The Hungry Man's Burger." It consisted of three hamburger patties, bacon, tomato, cheese, pickles, caramelized onions, and of course, Billy Joe's special homemade sauce.

While Sarah's dad finished his burger, Billy Joe took the girls on a tour of the restaurant and showed them the pictures on the wall of fame. Many famous and not so famous people passed through the restaurant doors, and Billy Joe had a story to go along with each one. For the grand finale, Billy Joe introduced the girls to Lucky.

"I've had nothin' but good luck ever since I stopped Lucky here from eatin' me," Billy Joe said as he patted the bear on the back. Sarah could have sworn that Lucky winked at her, and she ran back to where her father was sitting. Billy Joe checked Lucky's left eye and saw that the eyelid had closed halfway. "They didn't sew that sucker properly, and every once in a while it droops. He lifted the lid and tucked it under. By now, Sarah's mom and Liza had seen and heard quite enough and announced they would be heading back to their table.

"That was the best burger I've had in a long time," Sarah's dad said.

Billy Joe took care of their tab and said, "Stop by on your way back home."

"Thank you, Billy Joe. I'm stuffed ... but not like Lucky! I don't think I'll be eating another burger for a while."

"You know where I'll be if you change your mind!"

"Thanks, Billy Joe, we'll be seein' ya!" Sarah's dad said.

Sarah fell asleep not long after they got back on the road. Liza was too excited to sleep. When they got closer to Waterford, Liza helped navigate, using the directions Melvin had given her.

You are Now Entering Waterford
Population 15,000

"Perfect," Liza said. "That's our first landmark. We're looking for Jones Road next. Drive past the diner, the drugstore, the bakery, the florist, the veterinary clinic, and the church by the cemetery. When you see the sign "J. J. Daycare," take the next right, which will be Jones Road.

"Sarah, wake up," Liza said as she shook her shoulder gently. "We're almost there."

Sarah sat up, rubbing her eyes, and looked around. "That was fast!" she said.

"Nothin' fast about it," Sarah's dad said. "You've been asleep for a couple of hours."

Sarah's mom pointed to a sign and said, "There it is—J. J. Daycare."

"I see it!" Sarah's dad said.

"There's Jones Road," Sarah called out.

As soon as they turned the corner onto Jones Road, they could see two large buildings side by side. A six-foot-tall, strikingly beautiful Black woman stood in front of the house directing them to park in the VIP spot. She wore a colourful floral silk top, white silk pants, large gold hoop earrings, and an ornate cross that hung from a gold chain around her neck.

"Hello, I'm Joanna Jones," she said as she extended her hand to Sarah's mom.

"It's very nice to meet you. I'm Charlene," Sarah's mom replied.

"You must be Liza, and you must be Sarah," Joanna said.

"How did you know?"

"It's quite obvious, Liza. Sarah closely resembles her mom," Joanna explained.

"I'm Sarah's dad; great to meet you."

"Nice to meet you, Sarah's dad."

"It's Jeffrey."

"It's nice to meet you, Jeffrey. Leave the suitcases and I'll have Eli bring them in. Let's go in and have a bite to eat and some refreshments. Sam has set the dining table for us."

Liza walked alongside Joanna as she led the way to the house and ascended the large stone staircase.

"I had no idea that Jones Road was named after you, Joanna."

"Well, Liza, when you've been around as long as I have, they start naming things after you. J. J. House and J. J. Daycare were named after my late husband, Joshua."

They stood in a large foyer and stared in amazement at the beautiful surroundings. To their left was a library with a huge wood-burning fireplace. Oversized, overstuffed easy chairs, a large couch, and a chaise lounge were placed in cozy areas in front of the fireplace.

"I promised my mom that I would call when we got here, Joanna. Do you mind if I call now?"

"Not at all. There's a phone in the corner next to the chair by the window."

"Thank you, Joanna."

Sarah took her shoes off, went into the library, and plopped herself down on the chaise lounge. "I've always wanted one of these," she said.

"Sarah, come here!" her mom said.

"Relax and enjoy," Joanna said. "That's what it's there for!"

"Okay, that's done," Liza said as she hung up the phone.

Joanna led them to a large dining room adjacent to the library. The long oak table was set for five, although there were twelve chairs, five on each side and one at either end. Light blue padded chairs were simple, elegant, and comfortable. Navy blue and gold brocade curtains hung across each of the six large rectangular floor-to-ceiling windows, which overlooked the lush and beautifully landscaped yard and flower garden to the rear of the house.

"Please sit down," Joanna said. "I'll have Sam bring the refreshments." Joanna disappeared into the kitchen for a few minutes and returned with Sam.

"This is Sam," Joanna announced. "He's our amazing cook!"

"Pleasure to meet you nice folks," Sam said.

Joanna sat at the head of the table. Sam pushed a cart loaded with drinks and five dinner plates. He served Joanna first by removing the large silver dome covering the plate, revealing a beautiful meal.

"I hope you all enjoy what I've cooked up for you. These are some of Miss Joanna's favourites."

As Sam served the others, Joanna said, "Sam has been here as long as I have. What's it been now, Sam?"

"Goin' on twenty years, Miss Joanna."

"That sounds about right. I have twenty years of Sam's excellent cooking stuck on these ol' hips of mine to prove it! Dig in, everybody. I don't want to be the only one gaining weight around here," Joanna joked.

After they had eaten, Joanna said, "I'll show you to your rooms now if you've had enough to eat and drink."

"I've had more than enough," Sarah's dad said. "I didn't think I could eat anything else for a while after that burger I had at Billy Joe's."

"Billy Joe is quite the character," Joanna said.

"You know Billy Joe?"

"He's a legend in these parts, Sarah. I always stop for one of his famous burgers when I take a trip to visit my brother and his wife, Lola, back home. Billy Joe didn't scare you with Lucky's winking eye, did he?"

Sarah's mouth dropped open.

"Don't worry, Sarah, you're not the only one. The first time I met him, he played that silly trick on me. He pats lucky on the back, which causes one eyelid to fall, making it appear that he's winking at you. Your rooms are this way," Joanna said as she led them down a long hallway around the corner from the library. There were two doors on each side. Joanna stopped and gave Liza a key and one to Sarah. "Here are your bedrooms. You girls are going to find it quiet around here. I hired two other girls, but they won't be staying here. They decided to rent a little apartment in town. Go ahead, check out your rooms."

Sarah opened the door to her room, and her mom and dad followed her in.

Liza opened the door across the hall from Sarah's. She stopped int her doorway and said, "This is beautiful. It's twice the size of my room at home."

"Go on in," Joanna said.

Liza walked in and flung herself across the queen-size bed. She sunk into the big feather quilt that covered it. Beside the bed was a round night table with a fresh bouquet of flowers in a tall-standing vase.

"The flowers are so pretty, Joanna."

"I find fresh flowers always bring cheer to a room."

"I totally agree," Liza said.

"Your washroom is here, fresh towels in the linen closet. Soap, shampoo, conditioner, hair blower, tissues, and other miscellaneous things are in the vanity drawers, if you forgot to bring your own. If you find you're getting low in supplies, just fill out the order form in the top drawer of the desk. Put it in my mailbox in the hallway next to the kitchen. Three days' notice will suffice. If you have special preferences, the grocery, drugstore, or gift shop will have everything you need."

Liza walked over to the desk, opened the drawer, and found the order forms Joanna mentioned. She stood gazing out the window in silence.

"A penny for your thoughts," Joanna said.

"Earlier today I was in *my* bedroom. Now I am in *this* bedroom."

"Are you feeling a little homesick?"

"Not really. I'm happy to be here. It's just that it's all new to me, because I've never been away from home before."

"We'll take good care of you, Liza, don't worry. Let's go and check on Sarah, shall we?"

"Sure."

"How do you like your accommodations, Sarah?" Joanna asked.

"I may never want to leave!"

"Wait, what?" Sarah's mom said.

"Just kidding, Mom."

"You're welcome to stay here as long as you like. That applies to both you and Liza." Joanna turned to Sarah's parents and said, "Would you like to have coffee or tea while the girls settle in a bit?"

"About an hour outside of Waterford, we noticed a cute little bed and breakfast and thought we'd get a room for tonight. Jeffrey doesn't like driving when it gets dark, so we were going to head out."

"I understand, I don't like driving at night either. The bed and breakfast that you mentioned ... would that be The Rosebud?"

"Yes, that's the one," Sarah's dad said.

"My friend owns The Rosebud. I'll call her and let her know you'll be coming and to hold a room for you. You'll really like it there. As a matter of fact, Sam's brother is the cook. The breakfast he whips up is equal to none ... except for Sam's! I'll go make the call."

"That's very kind of you, Joanna."

"It's my pleasure, Charlene."

Sarah hugged her mom and dad, and Liza hugged them too. Her mom turned away as she started crying. Sarah knew her mom well enough to know why she turned away.

"Don't cry, Mom."

"You know your mom is an old softy."

"I know, Dad. I've seen her cry at sappy movies."

Sarah's dad looked at his watch and said, "Time to shove off."

Joanna reappeared and said, "It's all set. Your room is booked and my friend Rosalinda is expecting you."

"Thank you, Joanna. We're so glad we made the trip with the girls," Sarah's mom said as she wiped the tears from her cheeks.

"I'm glad you did too. Here's my card. I check my messages regularly, so feel free to call anytime."

Sarah walked out to the van with her parents. Liza and Joanna sat in the library waiting for Sarah.

"I hope you don't mind, Liza, but I took the liberty of calling Melvin after I spoke to Rosalinda. I explained that Sarah's parents were leaving shortly and if he and Farley would like to come over, it would be all right with me."

"Melvin and Farley are on their way ... now?"

"I told Melvin to give Sarah's parents about fifteen minutes' head start."

"I gotta go comb my teeth and ... I mean brush my teeth and comb my hair."

"Go ahead," Joanna said, smiling.

"Where's Liza?" Sarah said when she came in and saw Joanna sitting alone.

"She went to freshen up. Melvin and Farley are on their way over."

"Over here?"

"Yes, over here."

Sarah ran out of the library and down the hall to her room. She fumbled with her key and let out an exasperated groan. Liza left the door to her room and said, "Hurry up, Sarah, they'll be here any minute."

"I'm going as fast as I can!"

Joanna went to the kitchen, poured herself a cup of coffee, returned to the library, and sat down on the easy chair by the fireplace. Melvin didn't ring the doorbell when he and Farley arrived. They tiptoed inside and joined Joanna.

Liza hurried out of her room, stopping in Sarah's room momentarily. "I'm ready," she said. "I'll meet you in the library."

"Wait for me, Liza. I'm almost ready."

"Okay, hurry up."

"Here's your ring, Liza," Sarah said as she took it from her purse.

Sarah was applying lipstick as they walked down the hallway.

"Is it on straight?" Sarah said as she smacked her lips together and puckered them to show Liza.

"Looks good to me," Liza said.

"Looks good to me too!" Farley said as Sarah entered the library.

"How did ... when did—"

Farley didn't let Sarah finish. "These are for you," he said as he handed Sarah a bouquet of flowers.

"These are for you, Princess," Melvin said.

"While all of you get reacquainted, I'll go put those in some water for you. They'll be in your rooms for you."

"We're going to go out for a while, Aunt Joanna."

"I thought you might," she replied. "Word to the wise," she continued, "it's Saturday night, so your curfew is twelve o'clock, same as it is on Friday night. Sunday night curfew is eleven o'clock. Now go and have some fun!"

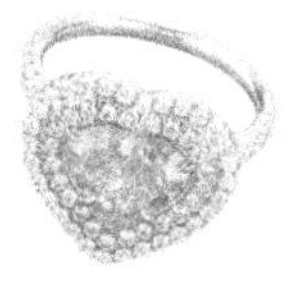

Chapter Twenty-Two

Together Again

"SARAH, WE'LL MEET YOU and Farley back here just before midnight," Liza said as they got into separate vehicles.

Farley was driving a company truck. Melvin had a company car for the year that he would be in Waterford.

Melvin held Liza's hand tightly as he drove. "Wait till you see our house."

"Our house, Melvin?"

"Yes, Princess. We'll be spending most of our time there, so I consider it *our* house."

"I like the sound of that!" Liza said.

They drove for about twenty minutes and then Melvin parked in front of a quaint little cottage-style house. "Here we are," he announced.

"Which one is it?" Liza asked.

"The white house with the light blue trim."

Just before they went in, Melvin picked her up and carried her over *the threshold*.

"Melvin, what—?"

He put her down, closed the door, and held her in his arms, kissing her as though it had been an eternity since he last saw her. They stood kissing so long, Liza's feet were getting sore. She pulled away slightly.

"What is it, Princess?"

"Do you think we could sit down, Melvin?"

"Yes, of course. Come with me."

The house was dark inside, as the sun had already set. Melvin took Liza by the hand as they walked through the screened-in porch that faced the back yard. He sat down and guided her to sit beside him on a swing built for two.

"You can't *see* it because it's dark outside, but if you listen closely, you will *hear* it."

"Hear what?"

"There's a brook that runs behind the house. Close your eyes and listen. I'll be right back."

Liza sat with her eyes closed. Melvin lit some candles, turned lights and music on, and returned with two glasses of wine.

"I can hear it," Liza said as she opened her eyes. "Is that what you call a *babbling brook*?"

"Yes and no."

"What do you mean?"

"I work with a girl named Brooke. She talks non-stop! That's what I call a *Babbling Brooke*!"

Liza started to giggle.

"A glass of wine for you, my Princess. To *us*," Melvin said as he leaned his glass against hers.

"To us," Liza repeated.

Melvin looked at Liza lovingly as he gazed into her eyes, brushed her hair back from her shoulders, and said, "You are so beautiful. I missed you something awful."

"I missed you too, Melvin. I can't believe we're here together."

"Believe it, because it's real," he said as he took her hand and looked at the ring he had given her, the heart illuminated in the candlelight. "It's as real as this heart, solid and true."

"I've never known love like this before," Liza confessed.

"That's because up until recently, you didn't know me."

"This feels like heaven on earth, Melvin."

"Heaven sure feels good, Princess."

"I feel better than I have in a very long time."

"I think it's because you're free to relax and enjoy yourself."

"I think it's because I'm enjoying you, Melvin."

He kissed her and said, "Listen, the band is playing our song. May I have this dance?"

Liza sipped her wine and walked toward Melvin as he stood with open arms.

"It feels so good to hold you, Princess."

"It feels so good to be held. Melvin?"

"Yes?"

"Could we dance every night?"

"If you promise you'll be my partner."

"I promise."

"Then we will dance," he said as he kissed her forehead and lingered. He pressed his cheek against hers, closed his eyes, and whispered, "My days and nights have been filled with thoughts of you, Princess. Not a minute goes by that I don't think of you."

Liza drifted into a dream-like state, lulled by the gentle swaying of their bodies and a cool, sweet, clover-scented breeze. The candlelight flickered and danced along with them.

After they had danced a few more songs, Melvin said, "What would you like to do tomorrow?"

"As long as I'm with you, anything we do is fine with me."

"Would you like to go to the Sunday brunch at the diner?"

"Sure."

"Farley and I have already been there for brunch. You'll love it!"

"Sounds like a good plan."

"Afterwards I'll show you where I work; we can do a little touring around town and then come back here."

"That would be very nice, Melvin. I think we have to be heading back to Joanna's now, if we want to get back in time."

"I want you to stay."

"I have to go."

"I know."

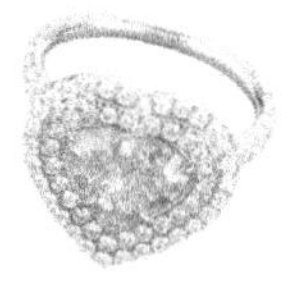

Chapter Twenty-Three

Mr. Mittens

LIZA WAS WALKING UP the front steps when Farley dropped Sarah off.

"Hey, wait up!" Sarah called out. "Farley and I want to know if you and Melvin want to join us for Sunday brunch at the diner?"

"Melvin and I planned to do the same and were going to invite you and Farley. We have to get there by eleven to beat the church crowd, so Melvin is picking me up at ten-thirty."

"Farley should be here at ten-thirty also."

Liza opened the door quietly as Sarah followed. A grey cat with white front paws greeted them. "Meow."

"Who do we have here?" Liza whispered.

A voice coming from the library answered, "That's Mr. Mittens."

Liza and Sarah peeked around the corner and saw Joanna sipping tea. She put her bookmark, a grey ribbon with a silver cross attached to it, into her Bible and closed it and placed it on the table next to her.

"Did you girls have a nice evening?" Joanna said knowingly.

Sarah was wearing lipstick when she left, and Liza was wearing lip gloss. There was no trace of lipstick or lip gloss on either of them.

"Yes, thank you. Melvin and I had a lovely evening."

"Farley and I did too."

"I didn't know you had a cat, Joanna," Liza said.

"Technically, he's not mine. He just showed up one day and never left. He's shy around people and usually hides until the coast is clear to come out."

"Meow," Mr. Mittens confirmed.

"You didn't have to wait up for us," Liza said.

"This is my quiet time. Mr. Mittens keeps me company while I have my evening tea."

"Hello, Mr. Mittens," Liza said as she walked over to the window ledge to pet him.

Mr. Mittens put his paw out and touched her hand.

Joanna looked surprised and said, "He's never done *that* before! He obviously likes you, Liza."

"I think that's what they call *animal magnetism*," Sarah joked.

"Really, Sarah!" Liza said as she sat down in the easy chair beside the window.

"Would you girls like to join me in a cup of tea?"

"I don't think Liza would fit!"

"You have quite a sense of humour, Sarah," Joanna said.

Liza rolled her eyes and said, "I would love to join you."

"Me too."

"There's plenty of tea in the pot on the kitchen table. Cups are in the cupboard beside the pantry. Sugar is on the counter by the coffee pot. Cream is in the fridge." They returned with their tea, sat by the fireplace, and watched the wood crackle and burn.

"What are your plans for tomorrow, girls?"

"We're going to go to the diner for Sunday brunch at eleven," Liza answered.

"Best to beat the church crowd! The food is fresh, tasty, and there's lots of it," Joanna said.

"Actually, my boss and his wife stayed in Waterford when they travelled a couple of years ago, and they ate at the diner. He said it was excellent."

"He's correct," Joanna replied.

"After brunch, Melvin and I are going to do some sight-seeing around town, and then he'll show me where he works."

"Maybe he'll show you where our churches are too," Joanna added.

"Is that a hint?" Liza asked.

Joanna didn't answer. Instead, she walked over to Mr. Mittens and picked him up. "Time for bed, Mr. Mittens."

"Meow."

"Mr. Mittens says, *good night*."

"Thank you, Joanna. Good night," Liza said.

"Sweet dreams," Sarah added.

***

"How was your evening with Melvin?"

"It was perfect. We sat in the back porch, listened to the trickle of the brook behind the house, drank wine, and danced. I didn't want to leave. How was your evening?"

"Farley and I drank wine and talked about getting married."

"You did?"

"We're planning a June wedding next year."

"Oh Sarah, I'm so happy for you."

"The construction industry is booming, so we'll be able to look at buying a house too."

"We'll have to go to the pharmacy and buy some of those bridal magazines. They say you have to order a wedding dress a year in advance," Liza said.

"Really?"

"Yes, really!"

"I'm not going to tell Farley about dress shopping just yet."

"He probably won't be too interested. It's not a guy-thing."

"You're probably right."

"I'm always right, remember?"

This time it was Sarah's turn to roll her eyes.

"I'm exhausted, Liza. How about you?"

"I was exhausted when we arrived today. I revived a bit when Melvin and I were dancing. The breeze in the porch was so refreshing."

"Let's call it a night."

"It's a night!" Liza replied.

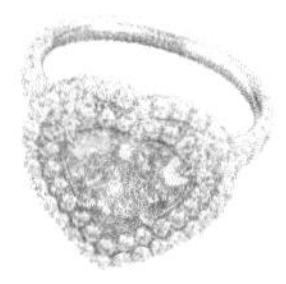

Chapter Twenty-Four

The Engagement

"COME ON, PRINCESS, let's hurry in and get a table. Farley and Sarah just parked right behind us."

"Hi, Flo," Melvin said as he and Liza rushed in. "We'll need a table for four, please."

"Follow me," Flo said. She let them to a booth beside the jukebox. She picked up the reserved sign on the table and put it in her pocket.

"I thought it was first come, first serve. I didn't think we were allowed to make reservations," Melvin said.

"*Yer* not," Flo said. "Joanna Jones is. She called and told me to keep this one fer you, honey. Seein' as yer her favourite nephew and all."

"That's so nice of your aunt," Liza said.

"She does have her connections, that's for sure."

Farley and Sarah sat down across from Melvin and Liza.

"Looks like yer gang's all here now," Flo said. "Who are these young ladies ya'll brought with ya?"

"This is Liza and Sarah," Melvin explained.

"Mighty nice to meetcha. Here's yer menus. Can I git y'all some coffee?"

"Coffee would be great, thank you, Flo," Melvin answered.

Liza and Sarah looked over their menus, while Melvin and Farley put their own off to the side.

"What are you guys going to have?" Liza said as she peered over the top of her menu.

"The Sunday Special is really the only choice," Melvin said.

"That's right," Farley agreed.

"If we all order the special, we'll get it quickly. Melvin and I have been here a few times, and Flo always gives us extra-big helpings. They always have more than enough ready."

Flo came back carrying a pot of coffee in her right hand while balancing a tray with four cups, cream, and sugar in her left. She put the cups down, poured the coffee, and said, "Waddle ya have?"

"We'll have four specials, please," Melvin said.

"How didja want yer bacon?"

"Crispy!" they all answered.

"Well then, I guess it's anonymous."

"You mean unanimous," Sarah corrected.

"Isn't that what I just said?"

Farley spoke up, "Yes, Flo. That's what you said." He squeezed Sarah's hand under the table.

Sarah looked at him and frowned.

Flo walked away with the menus and placed them on a shelf beside the cash register.

"Sarah, just go along with Flo. Don't correct her. We're on her good side. If you get on her bad side, she'll make you wait, and you get less food."

"Okay, Farley."

"I don't really know what I'm getting for the Sunday Special. I was too busy looking at the dessert menu to see if they had banana cream pie, before Flo took the menus away. Melvin, did you notice? They *do* have banana cream pie!"

"Yes, I noticed."

"Can we order some for dessert?"

"I don't think you're going to need dessert when you see how much food you'll be getting."

"By the way, what are we getting?"

Melvin began:

Baked three cheese macaroni
Home fried potatoes
Bacon
Honey ham
Deep fried battered pickles
Garlic toast
Coffee or tea

"Deep fried pickles?"

"Yes, Princess. Wait until you taste them! Trust me, you're going to love them!"

"I'll take your word for it, Melvin."

They barely had time to put cream and sugar in their coffees when Flo returned.

"Okie dokie, here's yer Sunday Specials," Flo said as she rolled up with a cart loaded with food and parked it alongside their table. "I asked Frankie to give ya a buncha extra bacon, since y'all are so polite."

"That's so nice of you, Flo," Sarah said.

"Don't mention it," she replied, and rolled the cart away.

"Try one of the deep fried pickles, girls," Farley said.

"Here goes," Sarah said and took a bite.

"Mmmm," was all Liza managed to say.

"See, I told you," Melvin said.

They sat in silence as they ate. Fifteen minutes later, Flo came around with a fresh pot of coffee.

"Y'all wanna warm up?"

They each nodded and held up their cups. Flo filled their cups and turned to walk away. She winked at Frankie as she walked toward the kitchen. Their signal, confirming happy customers.

"Sarah told me some happy news last night," Liza said.

"What news is that?" Melvin asked.

"Go ahead, Sarah," Farley said.

"We're planning to get married next June," Sarah said excitedly.

"That's wonderful news!" Melvin said, equally excited. "Congratulations, you two!"

"We're not really telling anyone until we're officially engaged," Farley said.

"That's totally understandable. We won't mention it to anyone," Melvin said.

"There's nobody to really mention it to," Liza added, "since we're basically out here on our own."

"Are you going to have a big wedding?" Melvin asked.

"We want to be reasonable about the number of people we invite. We haven't added it all up yet, but we have the same number on each side to invite, so it will be fair."

"With the money I make from the project we're working on, plus the work we have lined up, we'll be able to put a nice down payment on a house."

"That's the way to do it!" Melvin said.

"By the way, you are the first couple on our guest list ... after our parents, of course," Sarah said.

"Go ahead, ask her," Farley said as he poked Sarah.

"Ask me what?" Liza said.

"Liza, would you be my maid of honour?"

"Umm, let me think about that for a minute. Of COURSE I will be your maid of honour! It is my honour to be your maid of honour. Is that too many honours?"

"Never too many!" Sarah said.

"This calls for a celebration," Melvin said. "Why don't you and Sarah follow us back to our place. I've got some champagne in the fridge, chilling."

"*Our* place?" Sarah said.

"What's mine is hers," Melvin explained.

"I don't care *whose* place it is," Farley said. "Let's go drink Champagne and celebrate!"

"Would you guys mind if Sarah and I go to the pharmacy for a few minutes? We have to pick something up," Liza said.

"No problem. Meet you at the car," Melvin said. "We'll just settle up with Flo."

Flo was standing behind the counter as Sarah and Liza were leaving.

Liza said, "That's the first time we've ever had deep fried pickles. They sure are good, and we'll be back for more! Thank you, Flo."

"Yer welcome. Have yerselves a good day now."

Melvin and Farley stayed to finish their coffee.

"Anything else I can git ya?" Flo said as she took her note pad from her pocket, her pencil from behind her ear, licked the tip, and put pencil to paper to tally up their bill. She put the receipt face down, took the plates and Sarah and Liza's empty cups, and put them on her tray.

"Them girls ya got fer yerselves are sure perty!"

"We're very lucky, Flo," Melvin said.

"Don't ya forgit it, neither. Nice girls are perty hard to find. Treat 'em right or yer gonna have to answer to me, ya hear?"

"Yes, Flo," Farley said.

"We'll see you tomorrow for lunch," Melvin said.

"See ya then, boys!"

Melvin took out his wallet and then turned the receipt over. It read, *Paid in full, compliments of Joanna Jones.*

"Here, let me see how much I owe for Sarah and me," Farley said.

"My Aunt Joanna paid it for us," Melvin said.

"Give me that," Farley said as he took the receipt from Melvin. "Your aunt is very generous," Farley said.

"Yes, she is," Melvin agreed. "Aunt Joanna is one of a kind. Somehow she always knows exactly the right thing to say and do. She also *sees* everything, *hears* everything, and *knows* everything. It's hard to put anything past her. Aunt Joanna just has that extra sense, or you might call it intuition."

"You're really lucky to have such a wonderful aunt. Do you think she would consider being my aunt too?"

"I'm sure she'd be happy to be your aunt too! Aunt Joanna loves children of all ages!"

"Very funny, Melvin."

Liza and Sarah were leaning up against Melvin's car, looking at one of the bridal magazines, when Melvin called out, "What are you looking at?"

"Just a fashion magazine. Always nice to keep up with the latest styles!" Liza said as she put the magazine back into the bag.

"Everybody ready?" Melvin said. "Let's go!"

***

"This is a really nice little place you have here," Sara said. "Maybe we can look at buying a house like this, Farley."

"We can look at any house you like."

"Come with me, Sarah. I'll show you the brook that runs behind the house," Liza said.

"Go ahead, girls; we'll bring the Champagne outside," Melvin said.

"I love this little brook, Liza. I could watch it trickle over the rocks all day long and not get tired of it."

"It's nice, isn't it?"

"Here's the Champagne," Melvin said as he set a tray of Champagne flutes on the patio table. He handed one to Liza and took one for himself.

Farley pulled out a lawn chair for Sarah to sit on. "Allow me," he said. He handed a glass to Sarah.

"Aren't you having any?"

"I will in a minute; there's just something I need to do first."

Farley knelt down on one knee in front of Sarah as he took a ring box from his shirt pocket.

"I've loved you from the minute I laid eyes on you, and every day I love you even more. I promise to love you for the rest of my life." He opened the box that held an exquisite solitaire diamond. "Sarah Ann Morgan, will you marry me?"

"Farley, I've loved you from the minute I met, and YES, I *will* marry you."

Farley placed the ring on Sarah's finger. They both stood as Melvin and Liza started clapping and cheering. Farley and Sarah kissed and kept kissing.

"Okay, you two! You have a lifetime of kissing ahead of you," Liza said. "Let me see that rock you've got on your finger!"

Sarah and Farley didn't budge. Sarah just held her hand out for Liza to see.

"Looks like we'll just have to drink this Champagne ourselves, Princess."

Farley stopped kissing Sarah and said, "Oh no you don't. We'll have some too!"

"Here's a glass of Champagne for you, Farley," Liza said.

"A toast to the happy couple, from us, *the other happy couple*," Melvin said.

"Here, here," Farley said. "I'll drink to that!"

"So will I," Sarah said. "When did you put this surprise together, Farley?"

"I had a few days to plan before you and Liza arrived," Farley explained. "Melvin and I had dinner at Joanna's Thursday night. I told her I wanted to propose and asked if she could suggest where to go to buy the ring."

"Aunt Joanna is good friends with Simon. He owns the jewellery store around the corner from the florist. Joanna called him Friday morning and arranged for an after-hours appointment for seven o'clock."

"I held on to the ring here for Farley and slipped it to him when you girls went outside."

"I have to hand it to you both, it was a very good plan," Sarah said as she admired her ring. "I'll have to thank Joanna for her part in all of this."

"I love you so much," Sarah said and kissed her ring.

"Hey, what about me?"

"I love you too, Farley."

"I suppose you two will have some calls to make to tell your parents," Liza said.

"Sarah's mom and dad already know," Farley admitted.

"My mom and dad already know?"

"I called your dad Friday just before I met with Simon and asked for his permission to have your hand in marriage."

"You did?"

"Aww, that' so sweet," Liza said.

"What did my dad say?"

"He gave his blessing and so did your mom."

Sarah started to cry.

"He also said that he recognizes that I'm a hard-working young man, and he knows I will be able to provide for you ... and a family one day."

"My dad said all that?"

"He sure did!"

Melvin handed Sarah a box of tissues.

"Dry your eyes; we're celebrating, remember?" Liza said. "You are so lucky, Sarah. Your mom and dad are the best!"

"It's more than luck, Liza. I feel so *blessed* to have an awesome family, but more than that, I'm blessed to have you for my best friend, and Melvin as a new friend."

"We're really happy you and Melvin are here to celebrate with us," Farley said.

"We wouldn't have it any other way, buddy. How about a bit more Champagne?"

"Coming right up."

"I'd like to call my mom and dad, Farley. After we finish our champagne, do you mind if we go back to the apartment?"

"I don't mind at all. I'm sure your parents are eager to hear from you. I didn't tell my parents yet, so I'll have to call them also."

"I'd also like to get back to Joanna's earlier than curfew tonight. Tomorrow is the first day at work, and I want to be rested."

"That's a good idea, Sarah. What time do you have in mind?" Liza said.

"Curfew is eleven tonight, so I was thinking ten o'clock would work. I'm hoping to see Joanna and thank her for making the arrangements with Simon."

"I'll plan to be back for ten o'clock as well," Liza said.

"Okay, Sarah. I'm ready to go," Farley said as he finished the Champagne. "Thanks for all your help, Melvin. I couldn't have pulled it off without you!"

"My pleasure."

Melvin and Liza stood in the doorway as Farley and Sarah walked out to their car.

"Don't lose track of time, you two lovebirds," Melvin said.

"We'll try! The good news is, we have a lot *more* time to lose track of this summer!" Farley said.

***

Melvin and Liza sat on the swing in the back porch. Liza sipped her Champagne and sat in silence.

"Something on your mind, Princess?"

"I have an idea of what the future looks like for Sarah and Farley. What does our future look like?"

Melvin looked into Liza's eyes and said, "It's you and me against the world."

"Is it really?"

"Where is this coming from?"

"I'm here just for the summer and then I have to go back to a life I really can't stand most of the time."

"You just got here! We have the whole summer to spend together. Let's just take it one day at a time. We'll make some plans before the summer is over and maybe you won't have to go home."

"You mean it?"

"Yes, I do. I wouldn't say it if I didn't mean it. I want to spend my whole life with you, not just one summer. I thought you knew that."

"Now I know it."

"Good. Can we please relax and enjoy each day as it comes?"

"I'll try."

"That's my girl!"

On the way back to Joanna's, Melvin gave Liza a tour of his office. On his desk were three framed pictures: one of his pops and Lola; one of Alicia, her husband, and Max; and one of Liza.

"Where did you get *this* picture, or should I say when did you take this picture of me?"

"I snapped it when we were at my pop's place. You were in the kitchen with Lola."

"I didn't know you had a camera with you."

"I didn't. It's Pop's camera. I know where he keeps it. Besides, a good newspaper man doesn't reveal his sources. I've said too much already."

Liza sat down in Melvin's chair at his desk. "This is a pretty nice office, *Mr. Newspaper Man.*"

"Thank you. It's a nice place to work too. I think I'm really going to like it here."

"Time will tell," Liza said.

"Speaking of time, we should head back to Aunt Joanna's."

"You're right, Melvin."

"You have a big day ahead of you with all those little kids."

"I'll be ready."

"Aunt Joanna is really happy you and Sarah have come to work for her. She really likes you both. AND she's happy for me too. Happy I found you."

"I'm happy you found me too! All kidding aside, I really like your aunt too. She's kinda mysterious, but in a cool way."

"She's lived a very interesting life, which you'll find out as you spend more time with her."

"I look forward to it."

***

Melvin shut the headlights off as they approached Joanna's so they wouldn't shine in the front window. He parked and kissed Liza goodnight, and as he walked over to open the door for her, he noticed the curtains flutter a bit.

"I guess Aunt Joanna is reading in the library," Melvin said.

"It could be Mr. Mittens. He loves to sit on the ledge there."

"You're probably right, Princess."

"I'll see when I go in."

"Have a good day tomorrow, and play nice with the kids!"

"I will. Have a good day too, Melvin."

"I'll pick you up tomorrow around five. You can tell me all about your first day then. One more thing ... I love you."

"I love you too, Melvin."

***

Mr. Mittens jumped down from the window ledge and brushed up against Liza's leg as she took off her shoes.

"Well, hello, Mr. Mittens. I missed you too," Liza said as she picked him up.

"Liza? I'm in here," Sarah called from the kitchen. She had the refrigerator door open and was looking inside. "I'm looking for a snack," Sarah said. "Would you like something?"

"Sure."

Liza and Sarah were sitting at the kitchen table when Joanna came in calling for Mr. Mittens. When she saw the girls sitting at the table, she said, "I hear congratulations are in order. Let me see your pretty engagement ring."

Sarah held out her hand. Joanna took her hand and turned it from side to side.

"It is absolutely stunning. I hope you and Farley will be very happy."

"Thank you, Joanna. Thank you also for introducing Farley and Simon. Making the appointment was very kind of you."

"Anything I can do to help. I also noticed the lovely heart-shaped diamond ring you are sporting, Liza."

Melvin surprised me with it the day before he left for Waterford."

"My nephew is a true romantic," she said as she poured herself a cup of coffee. "Would either of you care for coffee?"

"I would," Liza said.

"How about you, Sarah?"

"None for me, or I won't sleep tonight."

Joanna sat down next to Liza. Mr. Mittens jumped up on her lap. "I'll meet you girls in the foyer at eight-thirty tomorrow morning. We'll go across to the school together. You should probably wear comfy clothes. Pants would be good. Sam will have your breakfast ready at seven-thirty."

"Will you be joining us?" Liza asked.

"I don't usually eat breakfast. I have a bite in my office or with the children at snack time around ten. I'm off to bed now, girls," Joanna said. She poured a bit more coffee in her cup, emptied the rest from the pot into the sink, and rinsed the pot. "Sleep well, you two. See you in the morning. Let's go, Mr. Mittens."

"Meow."

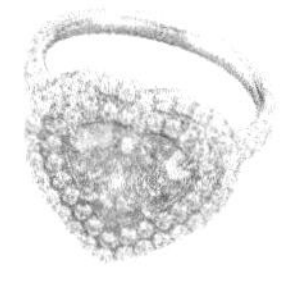

Chapter Twenty-Five

J. J. Daycare

JOANNA WALKED A COUPLE OF STEPS ahead of Liza and Sarah, opened the first door, and then swiped her ID card to open the second. There was a security guard sitting behind a large desk with a panel of monitors in front of him.

"Good morning, Isaiah. How are you today?"

"Just fine, Miss Joanna. How are you?"

"I am well, thank you."

"So these are the new recruits," Isaiah said. Liza detected an accent, Jamaican maybe.

"This is Liza and this is Sarah."

"Isaiah stood, came around the desk, and shook Liza's hand and then Sarah's. He looked shorter when he was sitting behind the desk, but when he stood, he towered over them at about six-feet-four-inches tall. He had a deep baritone, silky smooth voice. Isaiah wore a uniform typical of security personnel, military style, with his last name on the right side of his shirt, *FRANKLIN*. In large bold letters across the back of his shirt was *SECURITY*.

"Have a good day. I know you'll be happy here," he said.

Joanna took Liza and Sarah to her office. She unlocked a cabinet behind her desk and put her purse in it and locked it again.

"You'll each have a locker in your classrooms where you can store your purses."

Joanna pressed an intercom button and said, "Luther, please come to my office so that you can take Liza and Sarah for their photographs.

"Luther will take your pictures. He'll give you temporary ID tags for now. Your permanent photo ID tags will be ready at the end of the day."

Within a few minutes, Luther appeared. He wore a navy, long-sleeved shirt with *J.J. Daycare* embroidered in white lettering on the right side of it. Underneath the navy shirt, just a bit of it showing at the neck, he wore a white t-shirt. Liza's maternal grandfather always wore an undershirt underneath whatever shirt he happened to be wearing. It brought back a lot of childhood memories. Now if he only wore Aqua Velva aftershave, Liza would have been transported in time. Luther was about the same height as Joanna, which would make him six feet tall. His hair was cut short, brush-cut style.

"Okay, girls, follow me," he said. "Which one of you is Liza?"

Liza put up her hand and said, "That's me."

"Then by process of elimination and the fact that I have an uncanny knack for the obvious, you must be Sarah."

"You would be right," Sarah said.

"Are you girls just here for the summer?"

Sarah answered, "Yes."

Liza said, "Maybe."

Sarah turned quickly and looked at Liza. "What do you mean, *maybe*?"

"We'll talk about it later," Liza said as she turned to Luther and smiled.

"We're here. Who wants to go first?"

"I will," Liza volunteered.

"Sit down on that stool. I'll just take a minute to get the camera ready." Luther stood behind the tripod and adjusted the camera lens. "On the count of three, say *potatoes*!"

Liza could barely get the word out without laughing.

"It's your turn, Sarah," Luther said. "Same procedure. Ready, one, two, thr—"

Before Luther gave the final count of three, Sarah called out, "Potatoes!"

That made Luther laugh. "Let's try that again, Sarah. This time on *my* count." Sarah got it right on the second try. "That wraps it up for now. Here are your temporary tags, which simply say, *STAFF*. You can clip them onto your shirt pocket, or you can wear them around your neck. Here are two clips and two braided cords, one for each of you. Joanna is waiting for us, so I'll take you back to her office."

"Special delivery," he said as he knocked and then opened the door to Joanna's office.

"Thank you, Luther."

"I'll bring the tags to you by three o'clock or so."

"That will be just fine. Okay, girls, now the fun begins! Let's go take a look around. I'll show you where your classrooms are and introduce you to the teachers you'll be working with."

Liza and Sarah put on their ID tags and followed Joanna as she gave them directions and explained the school layout.

"The rooms in the school are built around the library, which is the hub of the school. The classrooms are down this hallway. There are five rooms with an average of fifteen to twenty children in each. The gymnasium is down that hallway, as are the change rooms and washrooms. Here is the staff room. Feel free to help yourself to coffee or tea any time you like. Sam provides morning snack for the children at ten, lunch is at twelve, afternoon snack is at two. Dismissal is at four-thirty. Lunch is provided for the staff, just put your order in the day before. The menu is on the bulletin board in the staffroom. On Fridays, a lunch truck arrives at noon. It allows Sam to take the afternoon for grocery shopping and menu prep for the coming week. The food truck offers a wide variety of meal items, like sandwiches, wraps, soup, french fries, salads, burgers, hot and cold beverages, etc. During your lunch hour, you can choose to eat in the staffroom, outside at the picnic tables, or you can go back to the house if you like. There are volunteers to do lunch supervision in the classrooms. Staff meetings are the first Wednesday of each month. The students are dismissed at three-thirty on those days. The staff meeting usually wraps up by four o'clock. Any questions so far?"

"I can't think of any," Liza said.

"Me neither," Sarah added.

"Let's go into your classrooms, this way."

"Just lead the way," Liza said.

"We can take a shortcut through the library. Here is your classroom, Liza."

Alice had her back turned and didn't see Joanna at the door. One of the children walked over to Alice and pulled on her jacket and said, "Miss Alice, Miss Joanna and some other people are at the door."

Alice Franklin was the assistant director of the daycare, as well as a teacher and Joanna's trusted friend and confidant. Alice was five feet tall and weighed about 110 pounds. She was small in stature but had a big presence and kept everyone in line ... including the adults. Alice had big brown eyes, more than the windows to her soul—they spoke volumes. One look and you knew exactly what she was thinking and where you stood with her.

Isaiah and Alice were a package deal. When Joanna hired Alice, she explained to Joanna the myriad of reasons why it was necessary for her to hire her husband, Isaiah, also. So she did.

"Sit down on the carpet please, boys and girls," Alice directed.

"Alice, this is Liza. She'll be working with you this summer."

"We're happy to have you, Liza. Come and meet the children."

"This is Sarah. She'll be working with Lilah. I'll check in with you later, Alice."

"See you later, Sarah," Alice said as she closed the door to the classroom. "Come over to the carpet with me, Liza. Boys and girls, this is Miss Liza. She will be working in our classroom with me this summer. Can you say *good morning* to Miss Liza?"

"Good morning, Miss Liza," they all said in perfect cadence.

Joanna took Sarah to the classroom next door and knocked. A tall four-year-old boy named Wendell opened the door. "Good morning, Wendell," Joanna said. "I'd like to see Miss Lilah please."

Wendell said, "I'll get her," and closed the door.

Joanna could hear Wendell call out to Lilah. "Miss Lilah, you better hurry. Somebody is at the door, and they look like they got something to tell you."

"I'm sorry Wendell closed the door, Joanna," Lilah said as she opened the door again.

"No problem at all," Joanna said. "Lilah, I'd like to introduce Sarah."

"Welcome, Sarah. We were just lining up to go to the library." Lilah held up her hand, and the children stood still and listened.

"Boys and girls, this is Miss Sarah. Let's all welcome her." Lilah held up three fingers for the countdown. "Three, two, one," she said. "All together now, 'Welcome, Miss Sarah.' Very good, boys and girls. Now let's show Miss Sarah how quietly we can walk to the library."

Lilah turned to Sarah and said, "Would you mind following at the end of the line? Please shut the lights off and close the door behind you."

"Yes, of course," Sarah replied.

Each of the students carried one book with them. As they entered the library, they put their books on a cart next to the checkout desk, then they went to sit on the carpet. The librarian was sitting in a rocking chair in front of the students as they sat down.

"Is there anyone who forgot to bring their book back?" she said.

No one put up their hand.

"That's very good, boys and girls."

The librarian asked Sarah if she would like to read the story to the children.

"I'd *love* to read to the children."

Lilah handed the storybook to Sarah and said, "This is my favourite storybook."

"*Heidi*. That's my favourite too!" Sarah sat down in the rocking chair and held up the book for the children to see. "Can anyone guess what the story is about?"

Each of the children were wearing name tags, so Sarah could call them by name.

"Penelope, what do you think it's about?"

"I think it's about a little girl."

"Very good answer. Anyone else? What do you think it's about, José?"

"I think it's about nature."

"Another very good answer. Now let's read it and find out. Once upon a time ..."

Joanna and Lilah stood off to the side and observed as Sarah read to the children.

"I think she'll do just fine," Joanna said.

"I agree," Lilah said. "She's fitting in nicely."

"Lilah, don't forget the meet and greet at lunch in the staffroom."

"I've got it marked on my calendar."

At the end of the day, Liza and Sarah met Joanna in her office. She gave them their picture ID tags.

"You are both very photogenic," Joanna said.

"They turned out pretty well, considering Luther told us to say *potatoes* to make us smile," Sarah said.

"It usually makes people *laugh*, then he has to do retakes. Luther gets a kick out of it. What do you say we closeup shop for today, girls?"

"I'm ready," Liza said.

"Ready," Sarah said.

Joanna put her arms around the girls as they walked down the path to the house.

"How would you like to invite your sweethearts for dinner tonight? It's *Meatloaf Monday.* I happen to know it's Melvin's favourite."

"Farley *loves* meatloaf," Sarah said. "I've tried to make it for him, but it always turns out like mush loaf instead."

Joanna stopped in her tracks and bent over in laughter. When she recovered, she said, "I'll have Sam set a couple of extra places at the dining room table."

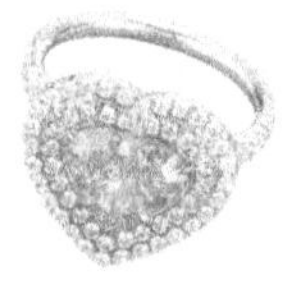

Chapter Twenty-Six

Who Doesn't Like Meatloaf?

"HELLO, MELVIN SPEAKING."

"Hi, Melvin."

"Princess, hi! Is everything all right?"

"Everything is fine. Joanna wanted me to invite you to dinner this evening, it's *Meatloaf Monday.*"

"I *love* meatloaf."

"That's what your aunt said."

"She knows me too well!"

"Dinner's at five-thirty."

"I'll be there. Afterwards, we'll still have some time to spend together. I want to hear all about your first day."

"We'll probably talk about it over dinner. Joanna said she wants to hear all about it too."

"Spoiler alert—Aunt Joanna has eyes and ears everywhere. By now, she's gotten a full report from everyone at the daycare. She's just looking for *your* report."

"I only have good things to report," Liza said.

"I wouldn't expect anything less from my Princess. I'm going to have to let you go now. I have another call coming in. See you at five-thirty."

"Can't wait!" Liza said.

***

"Something sure smells good," Farley said as he and Sarah walked into the dining room.

"It not only smells good; it tastes good too! Sam makes the best meatloaf!" Joanna said.

"You didn't start without me, didja?" Melvin asked as he came in through the front door.

Liza went to greet him. "I didn't hear the doorbell ring," she said.

"That's because I didn't ring the doorbell. I just followed my nose and it led me right here," Melvin said and then gave Liza a kiss hello. "Hi, Farley. Hi, Sarah," he said.

"Hi back at ya," Farley answered.

"Liza tells me that you love meatloaf too, Melvin," Sarah said.

"Yes, I do," Melvin replied.

"I'm just glad it's not *mush loaf*!" Farley said.

Joanna let out a little giggle. "Let's say grace now so that we can start eating. God bless this bunch as we munch and munch."

Liza opened one eye to see if Joanna had finished praying.

Joanna said *amen* and then continued, "Help yourselves! There's plenty to eat, so take as much as you like. Just make sure you leave some gravy for me!"

"How was your day, Sarah?" Farley asked.

"The day was filled with so many activities, I don't know where to begin."

"I always say, begin at the beginning," Joanna offered.

"All right. The teacher I work with is Delilah, although everyone calls her Lilah."

"It's not as much of a mouthful for the children," Joanna said.

"Lilah is super-organized and runs a tight ship. I thought I knew a lot, considering I completed my course in childcare, but I learned a lot more today. Lilah taught me little tricks about how to get *and* keep the children's attention. I learned that *snack time* and *lunch time* is their favourite part of the day."

"That's because some of the children come from single parent, low-income families. We provide nutritious snacks and lunches, so they don't go hungry. They can learn better and enjoy being here. We also provide clothing for those in need. Tuition is based on income. If they can't afford much, they don't pay much," Joanna explained.

"I didn't know that, Aunt Joanna."

"We hold fundraisers a couple of times a year and have generous contributors."

"I think it's more like you are very persuasive," Melvin said.

"Shh, child, now don't you go giving away your auntie's secrets!"

"People should know the great things you do here for the children," Sarah said.

"Bragging is not the Christian way," Joanna said. "As long as the children have a safe, happy, and positive learning environment and they're fed and clothed, that's all that matters."

"You are very modest, Joanna," Liza said.

"Aunt Joanna got the *modesty trait* my pops didn't get," Melvin joked.

"Don't let my brother hear you say that."

"I wouldn't dream of it, Aunt Joanna."

"I know that, dear. Now, Liza, tell us how your first day went."

"Okay, sure. I work with Alice, who is assistant director of the school and a super-cool teacher! She's really great with the children and keeps them on their toes. She may be five feet tall and only weighs a little more than a hundred pounds, but you'd swear she's six feet tall! I have my own group of eight children out of the sixteen. They have a strict routine and lots of opportunities for learning, interaction, and play. Alice makes sure of that. It felt like the day just got started and the next thing I knew it was home time."

"You're not kidding! I don't know where the day went!" Sarah said.

Sam came to clear the dishes and said, "Is anyone still hungry for some dessert?"

Liza put up her hand. Sarah, Farley, Melvin, and Joanna followed suit.

"How 'bout some coffee to wash it down with?"

They all raised their hands again.

"From what you've said so far, it seems like you're both off to a good start," Melvin said.

"You couldn't tell it was only their first day," Joanna said.

"I love it already," Sarah said.

"Not as much as you love me, though," Farley said.

"Umm ..."

Farley frowned.

"Not as much as I love you, Farley," Sarah said and kissed him on the cheek.

Farley smiled.

Liza heard a faint meow. She looked under the table to find Mr. Mittens lying at her feet, his tail swirling up against her leg.

"What is it, Liza?" Sarah asked.

"It's Mr. Mittens," Liza said as she picked him up and put him on her lap.

"Mr. Mittens can't have none of this here dessert," Sam said as he put a large piece of banana cream pie in front of Liza.

"Banana cream pie!" Liza exclaimed.

"I thought you might enjoy having your favourite dessert tonight," Joanna said.

"How did you know?"

"I have my sources," she said as she stirred her coffee.

Melvin looked at Liza and winked.

"This pie is amazing," Liza said as she took a big bite.

"It sure is," Farley said. "I think this is my new favourite."

"I forgot to tell you, Sarah, Lilah told me that you did a great job at story time today," Joanna said.

"Thank you, Joanna. I had fun."

"Your class has story time and book exchange tomorrow, Liza. If you want, you can read to the children."

"Sure, that would be great!"

"It's Harvey's birthday tomorrow. Alice made a special storybook for him, using his name for the main character."

"Harvey is going to *love* it! He seemed to take a liking to me very quickly," Liza said.

"Who wouldn't?" Melvin said.

"Harvey has had a difficult time lately. His mom and dad are separated and he lives with his dad and his grandmother. His mom is pursuing her singing career and left to go on the road with a band she joined," Joanna explained.

"I know what that's like," Melvin said in a serious tone.

"His grandmother is very kind and loving. Harvey is her only grandchild, so he gets extra-special care. His dad works full-time in construction. In fact, I think he's working on the same construction project you are, Farley," Joanna said.

"Maybe I know him," Farley said. "What's his name?"

"Hector Ruiz," Joanna answered.

"I know Hector! Great guy, hard worker too," Farley said.

"He's very dedicated to Harvey," Joanna added.

"Sam has prepared a special treat for snack time tomorrow. Birthday cupcakes with sprinkles."

"Can I come?" Melvin asked.

"If there are any cupcakes left, we'll be sure to save some for you."

"Melvin, phone call for you," Sam announced.

"Who is it?" Melvin asked.

"It's your pops."

"I hope he's okay."

"Go ahead and take the call in the library," Joanna said.

Mr. Mittens jumped off Liza's lap and followed Melvin to the library.

"Pops? Are you okay?"

"Hi, Junior. I'm fine. I called you a number of times at home and thought I'd try you at Joanna's. I'm calling to say we're planning to drive out this weekend for a visit."

"I would love to see you guys, and there's plenty of room! When will you arrive?"

"We'll be there Friday about four and head back Monday morning."

"That's perfect! Bring your golf clubs. I'll book a round for us on Saturday morning."

"Already in the trunk, son."

Melvin laughed. "Okay, Pops, have a safe drive and we'll see you on Friday."

Melvin came back to the dining room with a big smile on his face.

"Looks like you got some good news."

"Yes, Aunt Joanna. Pops and Lola are coming for a visit this weekend."

"That's fantastic," Liza said.

"Yes, it's good news. I haven't seen my big brother in almost two years. I'll have to make my mother's famous peach cobbler, assuming I'll be invited for dinner."

"That goes without saying, but I'll say it anyway—you're invited for dinner. Farley, you and Sarah are also invited. Let's make it Friday at five."

"How long will your parents be staying?" Sarah asked.

"Just for the weekend; they'll be leaving Monday morning. Pops doesn't like to drive at night."

"If you don't mind, I'm going to look for my peach cobbler recipe and see if I have all the ingredients," Joanna said. "Enjoy the rest of your evening. Oh, by the way, Sam packed up some leftovers for you two boys to take home."

"Aunt Joanna, you're the best! Thank you!"

"Don't thank me, thank Sam!"

"We sure will!" Farley said.

***

"I can't believe how tired I am," Liza said.

"If it wasn't for the coffee, I might not have made it through dinner," Sarah said as she yawned.

Farley watched Sarah yawn, and he yawned too.

"Princess, how about if we make it an early night. I'll see you tomorrow. I could use some time to get the guest room ready for Pops and Lola."

"Okay, Melvin. I'll walk you out."

Sam came into the dining room with two brown paper bags, one for Melvin and one for Farley. "Don't forget these," he said.

"Thanks, Sam. You're a life-saver," Melvin said.

"I shore know what it's like to live alone and cook for yourself, or get some take-out. When I met my wife, she changed all that and all *this*," he said as he pointed to his slightly rounded belly. "Have yourself a good night, now. See you girls in the mornin'!"

***

Melvin held Liza in his arms as they stood outside. "I'm really proud of you, Princess. You really put your heart and soul into those kids today."

"Thank you, Melvin."

"I can tell Aunt Joanna is pleased."

"How can you tell?"

"Oh, just by the way she looked so relaxed at dinner."

"That's good to know."

"There is one other thing I noticed."

"What's that?"

"She might be a tad jealous."

"Of what?"

"You're getting a lot of attention from Mr. Mittens ... that's usually her domain."

"In case you didn't notice, Mr. Mittens left *me* to follow *you* into the library when you went to talk to your Pops. What do you have to say about that?"

"I say, that cat has good taste!" Melvin smiled and kissed Liza. "I'll be counting the hours until I see you tomorrow. Five-thirty okay?"

"Yes, that's good," Liza said.

"I'll have to do a little grocery shopping for the weekend. Wanna go with me?"

"Sounds like fun."

He pulled her closer and whispered, "I could be holding you tonight."

"I know."

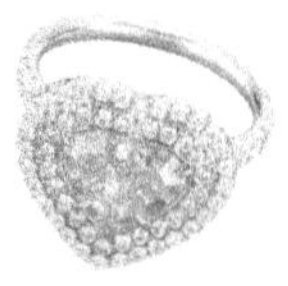

Chapter Twenty-Seven

Sam

"YOU AND I HAVEN'T SPENT MUCH TIME TOGETHER," Sarah said as she and Liza approached their rooms.

"No, we haven't. Wanna come in and hang out for a while?"

"Sure. We'll have to plan to spend more time together when we get back home."

"I don't want to go back, Sarah."

"I know, but I'm going to need help from my maid of honour to plan wedding stuff with me."

"Of course I'll help you."

"Do you think your parents would let you stay on here for a little longer?"

"I highly doubt it. Besides, Marcus wants me to be back at work mid-August."

"The manuscript, right?"

"Yup."

Liza's phone rang and she answered it, thinking it was Melvin.

"Hi M—"

"Liza?"

"Mom?"

"Yes, dear. How are you?"

Sarah whispered, "I'll come back later. I'm going to call my mom."

Liza nodded.

"Is someone there with you?"

"It's just Sarah. She's going to call her mom. As a matter of fact, I was just going to call you."

"I waited until your father left before calling."

"It's nine o'clock. Doesn't he usually leave first thing in the morning?"

"There's nothing *usual* about what your father does anymore."

"What do you mean, Mom?"

"He was only home for a few days and he's gone again. He's away for two weeks now. He's been spending a lot of time in his study, on the phone."

"He's always done that. He's usually talking to clients, drumming up more business."

"He sure knows how to talk, that's for sure."

"Is he spending time with Junior?"

"If Junior is home, they watch sports together."

"That's good."

"When we're having dinner, I try to start a conversation. He says he just wants some peace and quiet."

"Lucky you."

"Pardon me?"

"I said, it must be hard on you."

"I'm not sure what to do anymore."

"Ignore him. Talk to Junior instead. Don't try so hard, Mom." Liza heard her mom complain about her father in the same way so many times. She hoped this time her mother might actually take her advice.

"Enough about that. I didn't call to talk about your father. I called to see how you are and to tell you that Junior and I miss you very much."

"I miss you guys too!"

"How do you like working at the daycare?"

"I *love* it! Everyone is so nice, and the children are so cute!"

"That's nice, dear. When do you think you'll be coming home?"

Liza could tell by Helga's comment that she really wasn't listening to what she said.

"I will be home in mid-August to prepare the manuscript for Marcus to submit to his publisher."

"That means you'll be home before Junior leaves for college."

"What do you mean, *before Junior leaves for college*? I thought he was going to a local college."

"He hasn't decided yet, but he applied here at home and out West. I want him to stay and attend college here."

"Don't worry about Junior. I'm sure he'll make the right decision when the time comes."

"As long as he decides to stay here. I have to go, Liza. Junior just came home from basketball practice. I better go and make him something to eat."

"Say hi to Junior for me. I'll call you next week."

"Call me anytime you want, dear. I'm usually home."

Helga hung up before Liza could say goodbye. She sat down at the desk and stared out the window. She thought about her mom, Junior, her room back home, Melvin, and her dreams about what may be. The knock at the door broke her train of thought.

"Coming, Sarah," she called out.

She opened the door to find Joanna standing in front of her.

"I hope I'm not interrupting anything."

"No, please come in. I just spoke to my mom. My brother came home from basketball practice so my mom cut our conversation short."

"I won't stay but a minute. Since Melvin's parents are arriving Friday, I thought you might like to pack a bag and enjoy the weekend with them."

"You mean it?"

"Yes. You'll be properly chaperoned. Lola and my brother actually suggested it."

"They did?"

"Don't look so surprised. They love you and want to spend time with both you and Melvin."

Liza threw her arms around Joanna and hugged her.

"What did I miss?" Sarah said as she walked in.

"Joanna suggested I spend the weekend with Melvin and his parents!"

"That's a great idea!" Sarah said.

"Mel and Lola should arrive sometime Friday afternoon."

"Mel?"

"Yes, Sarah. That's Melvin's dad's name. Melvin Senior, actually."

"I didn't know that, Liza. You always refer to him as Melvin's dad, or Melvin's Pops."

"One more thing," Joanna added. "If you think I have an uncanny ability to know what's going on at any given time—and I *do*—Melvin's dad is sharper than I am."

"Thank you, Joanna. I'll keep that in mind. I'm looking forward to seeing them."

"They feel the same way. I also know they have high hopes for the two of you."

"How do you know that?"

"I have my sources."

"I get it," Liza said.

After Joanna left, Sarah said, "*What* do you get?"

"What?"

"You said, 'I get it.'"

Melvin probably told her and she's not saying *who* told her. So I'm not asking."

"Ohhh ... I get it."

"Do you?"

"Not really."

"How is everything going with your family, Sarah?"

"Good. My mother is making the wedding guest list for our side of the family already. I didn't know we had so many relatives! She's having fun with it. My dad is just happy he doesn't have to help."

"That's nice."

"You sound sad, Liza."

"When I compare your parents or Melvin's parents with mine, I feel even worse."

"Your mom is pretty nice."

"She has her moments."

"Nobody's perfect, Liza."

"I'm not asking for perfect. I'll settle for normal."

Sarah put her arm around Liza and said, "Don't think about any of that now. Just look forward to the weekend and all the fun you'll have!"

"You're right. I do worry about my mom, though."

"She'll be okay. After almost twenty-five years, she's pretty used to your dad."

"My father is away for two weeks, so my mom gets a break."

"Your mom will have Junior and John to keep her company. They'll keep her busy cooking, I'm sure of that. Now stop worrying and start planning what you're going to pack for the weekend."

***

Liza barely slept at all. She got up before her alarm went off. She put on her favourite dress and went to the kitchen to have coffee. Sam was frying bacon and greeted her as she sat down at the table.

"Good mornin', Miss Liza. You shore look pretty today, and you're up mighty early, too!"

"Good morning, Sam. Actually, I didn't sleep much ... well, at all."

"Would you like coffee?"

"Yes, please, Sam."

"Now, what's troublin' you, Miss Liza?" Sam said as he poured the coffee.

"I don't want to ruin your day and bore you with dramatic details."

"I don't bore easy, Miss Liza."

"It's about home, Sam. My father is extremely difficult to get along with, and he's pretty mean too."

"I know somethin' about that too, Miss Liza."

"You do?"

"My daddy was a military man. Oooh child, was he strict! Didn't say much, but when he looked at you, his face said everythin' he was thinkin'."

"My father is like that too."

"I don't remember him ever huggin' me or my little sister neither. And Mama? Well, forget that! He just bossed her around and made her cook three meals a day, with no thanks for nothin'! Stubborn as all heck. I suppose he learned that from his daddy. Two peas in a pod, you might say."

"You are describing my father. How did your mom handle him?"

"Mama? Why, she just worked around him. Didn't say much. He couldn't get angry with her if she never said nothin'. She just put the food in front of him and went about her business. I will say one thing for my daddy, he did pay the bills and paid for the food Mama made. He had a soft spot for my little sister, and he was real nice to her. She used to watch football with him Sunday after church. Daddy loved that. I stayed in the kitchen with Mama."

"So that's where you learned to cook."

"That's right. I remember Mama's secret recipes too. Me and Mama stayed out the way of Daddy and we did just fine."

"My mom called me yesterday, and I basically told her to do what your mama did—ignore him and talk to my brother instead. My father watches sports with my brother. Junior plays basketball, which my father likes. He doesn't like me too much. Luckily, my father travels a lot, so my mom gets a break from him."

"If I know anythin' at all, Miss Liza, it's this—how he treats you ain't your fault. Whatever happened to him is makin' him angry inside, and then he acts nasty on the outside."

Liza got teary-eyed and sniffled.

Sam handed her his handkerchief and said, "Now don't worry yourself for nothin'. You gonna be all right, Miss Liza. How 'bout some strawberry waffles and crispy bacon?"

"That sounds so good, Sam."

"Mama always said, Ain't nothin' like a home-cooked meal to heal what's ailin' ya!"

Liza smiled. "Your mama sounds like a really smart lady, Sam."

"She shore 'nuf was!"

"She passed away?"

"Daddy went to be with the Lord first, then Mama a few years later."

"I'm sorry, Sam."

"I didn't cook for a long time after Mama passed. Then I met my wife. She's a pretty good cook, but I'm better! My wife is grateful I know how to cook, cuz she shore 'nuf likes to eat!"

Liza and Sam were laughing when Sarah came into the kitchen, followed by Joanna.

"What were you two talking about?" Sarah asked.

"Oh, this and that," Sam answered.

"Gee, Liza, how long have you been talking to Sam?"

"I guess about an hour or so."

"I'm makin' Miss Liza strawberry waffles and crispy bacon. Can I make some for you too, Miss Sarah?"

"Yes, please!"

"Don't forget the whipping cream, Sam," Joanna said.

"I never forget that!"

"I'll take some to go. What's the special occasion, Sam? You haven't made waffles in over a year now."

"No special occasion, Miss Joanna."

Sam placed Liza's plate in front of her and patted her on the shoulder. Then he served Sarah.

"Thank you, Sam," Sarah said.

"Like Mama always said, 'When you feed your belly, you feed your brain.'"

"I learned that in my childcare course, but they didn't say it as well as your mama. She must have been a very smart lady."

"She was," Sam and Liza said.

Chapter Twenty-Eight

Spy Stuff

LIZA SPENT THE WHOLE DAY just going through the motions in activity with the children while thinking about Melvin.

They didn't go to the library for story time. Instead, they stayed in the classroom so they could have the cupcakes Sam made for Harvey, right after the story.

As Liza read Harvey's special birthday book, she read the *words*, but her thoughts were a million miles away. The children listened intently as she read, and when she read the final two words, *The End*, the children clapped. That's when Liza clued in again. Harvey was beaming with a smile from ear to ear. Alice had never seen him so happy, *except* when she brought out the tray of birthday cupcakes. Harvey's eyes got really big and he started clapping again.

"Harvey," Alice began, "since you are the birthday boy, you may have the first choice."

He chose a cupcake with blue icing and white sprinkles.

"Thank you, Miss Alice," he said politely.

"You're welcome, Harvey."

Harvey turned to Liza and said, "I love sprinkles, and blue is my favourite colour!"

"Blue is my favourite colour too!" Liza replied.

Harvey smiled and began eating his cupcake happily.

As Alice handed out the cupcakes, Liza followed, handing out plates and napkins. Alice and Liza sat off to the side at the art table and enjoyed a cupcake with the children.

"You seem a bit preoccupied today, Liza. What's on your mind?"

"Oh, nothing really. I'm a bit tired. I didn't sleep well."

"I completely understand. Before Isaiah and I were married, I used to daydream about him *all* the time."

Liza looked at Alice as if she had two heads.

"How did I know you were daydreaming about Melvin?"

Liza nodded.

The blank look in your eyes and the lack of expression on your face. I recognize that look, because I used to have the same one and sometimes still do! Isaiah and I have been married a long time now, and I still think of him throughout the day, even though he works right here in the building *and* we have lunch together every day!"

"You're so lucky, Alice."

"I wouldn't call it *lucky*. I would say *blessed*. Isaiah and I have found true love, and true love is a wonderful blessing."

"I agree."

"Hold on to each other and enjoy the ride! There are some ups and downs of course, but as they say, *love conquers all*!"

"Thank you, Alice, that is very good advice."

"Happy to help," Alice said as she glanced up at the clock. "It's time for recess and I have duty. Let's get the children ready to go outside. We could all use some fresh air."

***

When five-thirty rolled around and Melvin came to pick Liza up, she was already waiting outside. He barely stopped the car when she opened the door and got in.

"You look—"

Before he could finish, Liza leaned over and kissed him.

"Hello to you too, Princess."

"Let's get out of here, Melvin."

"Your wish is my command, your highness. I was about to say, you look beautiful."

"Thank you, Melvin."

"Is that a new dress you're wearing?"

"Sort of. I bought it a while ago, but I've never worn it before. Are we still going grocery shopping?"

"No, we don't have to. I left work early today, went shopping, and picked up the things I needed."

"Great, now we can just relax and spend a nice evening, just the two of us."

Liza didn't wait for Melvin to come around and open the car door for her. She got out and walked quickly to the front door. He hurried to keep up with her to unlock the door. Once inside, Liza walked over to the fridge, took a bottle of wine from the shelf, opened it, and drank some.

"Would you like a glass for your wine, or would you prefer to just continue drinking from the bottle?"

Liza put the bottle down on the counter, took out a coffee mug, and poured until the mug was full.

"Tough day?" Melvin said as he stood watching her.

"It's starting to get better," Liza said.

"Shall we sit down, Princess?" Melvin took the mug from her as he took her by the hand and sat down beside her on the couch. Liza put her head on Melvin's shoulder and sighed deeply.

"I'm glad we have a few evenings to spend together before your pops and Lola get here on Friday."

"About that ..."

Liza sat up and stared at Melvin.

"Remember that piece I worked on before I got the transfer to Waterford?"

"Yes, I remember. I didn't see you for a few days."

"Turns out I have to take a break from the editorial department and put my journalism skills to work again. My boss wants me to delve deeper and do more research for the same project."

"What's it about?"

"I'm not at liberty to say."

"Sounds like spy stuff."

"It kinda is. That's all I can tell you."

"No problem. I'd rather talk about *us*, anyway."

"After tonight, I won't be able to see you for the next couple of evenings until Friday. I have to concentrate on my research, which I have to confess is extremely difficult, because my mind wanders to thoughts of you."

"I have the same problem, Melvin—that is, if you can call it a problem. It's more like my *happy place*. We'll have plenty of time together all weekend."

"Uh, except for a few hours on Saturday morning. Pops loves to golf, so I made a reservation for nine o'clock."

"Golf sounds like fun. I'll have to give it a try sometime."

"I'll be happy to teach you."

"It's a deal."

"In the meantime, Lola said she's looking forward to having some *girl time* with you while Pops and I are golfing."

"Lola is really easy to be with; your Pops is too."

"What am I, *chopped liver*?"

"Don't be silly, Melvin. This weekend is going to be a family weekend I always dreamed of having but never did."

"It definitely will be a family affair. I may have to share you with everyone this weekend, but I don't have to share you tonight. Pass the wine."

Chapter Twenty-Nine

Weekend in Waterford

WHILE MELVIN CONTINUED RESEARCHING the spy stuff, Liza spent time with Mr. Mittens each evening after work. She carried him in her arms as she walked in the flower garden. She went to bed early and got up early. She was the first one in the kitchen for breakfast.

"Good morning, Sam," Liza called out.

"Good mornin' to you, Miss Liza," Sam said as he turned and looked over his shoulder. He did a double-take and turned around to face her. "Miss Liza, you shore look beautiful this mornin'! Is that makeup you're wearin'? Must be a special occasion ... your birthday?"

Liza giggled. "It *is* a special occasion, but it's not my birthday."

"Do tell, Miss Liza!"

"Melvin's pops and Lola are arriving today and are staying at Melvin's until Monday. I get to spend the weekend with them."

"Does Miss Joanna know?"

"Believe it or not, Lola suggested it and Joanna gave her permission."

"I never figured Miss Joanna would allow such a thing."

"We'll be properly chaperoned by Melvin's parents."

"I see."

"You know Joanna has extra-sensory perception."

"I shore do, Miss Liza."

"Melvin's pops has extra-extra-sensory perception."

"Ooh child, now I know why Miss Joanna is sayin' you can stay there. Ain't nothin' gonna tempt you two kids while his pops is stayin' there. Watch out for flour on the carpet at bedtime!"

"Why would there be flour on the carpet, Sam?"

"Flour on the carpet will catch any footprints if anybody wants to be a sneakin' to a different bedroom in the middle of the night."

"I never heard of anything like that before!"

"Back in my day, some folks got caught that way!"

"What happened?"

"Let's just say, they didn't do it again anytime too soon!"

"That's not something I would be doing, but thank you for warning me."

"Do you want strawberry or blueberry sauce for these here pancakes, Miss Liza?"

"Blueberry, please, Sam."

"Good morning," Joanna said as she poured herself a cup of coffee. "Liza and I will be going to dinner at Melvin's this evening, Sam. My brother and his wife are in town for the weekend. We'll be leaving right after work today."

"Miss Liza was just fillin' me in about that."

Sarah came into the kitchen, sat down, and joined the conversation. "Farley and I are invited for dinner also."

"That's real nice. Gotta spend time together when you can," Sam said. "Here's your pancakes, Miss Sarah."

"Thank you, Sam. How did you know I love blueberry sauce on my pancakes?"

"I must confess," Liza began, "it was I who informed our Royal Chef."

"It's too early in the morning for your theatrics and English accent," Sarah said as she promptly dropped blueberry sauce down the front of her blouse.

"Ye shall not criticize one's companion, fair maiden, for it results in sloppiness and the need for a costume change."

Sarah ignored Liza. "I'll be right back," she said.

"Eat up, Liza. I know you're excited to see Melvin and his parents, but we still have to go to work today."

Liza quickly finished her breakfast. Joanna took coffee to go.

"I'll see you at recess break, Sam."

"I'll have your sandwich ready for ten o'clock, Miss Joanna."

"Thank you, Sam."

Liza and Joanna walked over to the daycare together.

"Good morning, ladies," Isaiah said. "Where's Sarah?"

Liza answered, "We had pancakes with blueberry sauce and instead of *eating* hers, Sarah wore them."

Isaiah laughed and said, "Alice has to change her clothes lots of times because she does the same thing. Seems to always happen when she's wearing white."

"At least I'm not the only one," Sarah said, slightly out of breath as she ran in behind Liza.

"Have a good day, girls. Liza, I'll pull the car around front at four-thirty. See you then," Joanna said and then disappeared into her office.

***

At four o'clock, Joanna was going out the front door as Liza was coming in from the daycare.

"Oh my goodness, Joanna, am I late?"

"No, dear, I left school early to pack up the peach cobbler and a few extra little things to take along with us. I'm going to load up the car and I'll meet you outside shortly.

"I'll go and get my bag."

***

"I'm so excited to see Mel and Lola," Joanna said as they drove away.

"Me too," Liza replied.

Joanna turned on the radio and started singing with Aretha Franklin. *R.E.S.P.E.C.T.*

"You have an amazing voice, Joanna. Have you ever thought of pursuing a career in music?"

"I was in a band for many years. In fact, for a very brief time, Lola and I were in the same band."

"I didn't know that!"

"Lola was the headliner at a club when Mel met her. He told me how marvellous she was and made arrangements for us to meet. She auditioned for the band and got hired. We played a few clubs in town. When it came to doing a gig out of town, Lola said she really loved staying at home but would give it a try. She only came out on the road with us once."

"Only once?"

"After the accident, I stopped touring. Lola quit the band and stuck to performing at the club. I'll tell you more about it some other time. Now I sing in the shower, in the car, and at church for special occasions."

"Seems like a waste of your talent."

"Music will always be a part of me, but now I have the children and the daycare. Joshua and I always loved children and thought we'd have a family of our own one day. Unfortunately, that didn't happen. I did, however, manage to save some money working all those years with the band. With the money from the sale of the house, I was able to buy the daycare and J.J. House. I know Joshua would approve.

"Do you miss performing?"

"Sometimes, but for the most part, I'm happy at the daycare with the children."

"Have you ever thought of getting married again?"

"The thought crossed my mind, but I haven't met anyone who holds a candle to my Joshua."

"You never know! When you least expect it, you'll meet someone."

"You never know."

***

Joanna honked the horn to announce their arrival at Melvin's. Melvin Sr., Lola, and Melvin Jr. rushed out to greet Joanna and Liza. Joanna ran toward them with outstretched arms. Melvin Sr. and Lola hugged Joanna while Melvin Jr. walked past the group and hugged Liza. When the group hug ended, Melvin Sr. walked over to Liza and Melvin Jr. and said, "Excuse me, son, but it's my turn to hug this lovely young lady. Come here, little Liza," he said.

Lola pushed her way in, "Okay, Melvi, step aside, it's my turn!"

"Hello, sweet Liza," Lola said.

"Come, girls, let's go into the house. Those big, strong, handsome men can collect our things."

"We're on it, Aunt Joanna!"

"Mmmm, mmm something sure smells good in here," Joanna said.

"Oh, you mean something besides me, Sista Girl!" Lola said.

"All right, Miss Thing, you still got it!" Joanna replied.

"Tell me something I don't know, girlfriend!"

Joanna and Lola laughed and hugged each other again.

"Who wants a glass of wine?" Melvin Jr. asked.

"Baby boy, do you really have to ask? Just pour, sweet thing!"

"I forgot who I was talking to for a minute, Aunt Joanna."

"Here's to this great family of ours," Melvin Sr. said.

"Here, here," Joanna said.

Melvin Jr. sat down beside Liza. Melvin Sr. chose the easy chair. "Ahh," he said as he took a sip of wine, "that's what I call mighty fine!"

The doorbell rang. Joanna went to the door, opened it, and ushered Sarah and Farley in.

"Come on in, you two, you're just in time for a glass of wine! Lola, Mel, this is Sarah and Farley."

"Pleased to meet you," Sarah said. "We've heard a lot about you."

"Here's a glass of wine for each of you," Melvin Jr. said.

"One more toast then," Melvin Sr. said. "To forever family, old and new."

"Good one, Pops."

"Thank you, son. Excuse me for a minute, I have to go check on dinner."

"You're all in for a treat tonight. Since we got here much earlier than we originally planned, Melvi has had time to cook dinner. He's made all of Joanna's favourite dishes."

"What's the menu?" Liza asked.

"You'll see. Dinner is almost ready," Lola said.

***

Liza sat quietly while conversation was going on all around her. She loved listening to all the stories and hearing laughter. She was soaking it all up while thinking about her own family. Melvin Jr. put his arm around her shoulder and pulled her in closer to him.

"You kids haven't said much at all," Joanna said.

"Just happy to listen, Aunt Joanna."

"Works out perfectly, son, because we like doin' all the talkin'!"

"This food is delicious," Farley commented.

"Better save room for my peach cobbler," Joanna said.

"After eating roast beef with gravy, roasted potatoes, honey glazed carrots, and Caesar salad, I don't think I have room for dessert," Sarah said.

"Wait a minute, I see a little space right here," Farley said as he poked Sarah in the stomach.

“Cut it out, Farley,” Sarah said as she brushed his hand away.

“I could use a little help with the dessert,” Melvin Jr. said to Liza.

“Sure, I’ll help you.”

Once in the kitchen, Melvin turned and hugged Liza tightly. “I’ve been waiting all day to hold you in my arms and kiss your sweet lips,” he said and kissed Liza passionately.

Joanna, Lola, and Melvin Sr. were carrying on lively conversation. Sarah and Farley joined in from time to time.

Melvin and Liza were hoping no one would notice the silence in the kitchen.

“Howz that dessert coming along, son?”

“Melvi, don’t bother them. Don’t you remember what we used to do?”

“Of course I do, sweetheart. That’s why I’m interrupting them!”

“Coming right up, Pops!”

Melvin and Liza brought out a tray of peach cobbler and started to serve it.

“You look a little flushed, Liza. Are you feeling all right?” Melvin Sr. said.

“She’s fine, Pops!”

“Excuse me, please,” Liza said. She went to the washroom and put a cold towel on her forehead and then on her neck, to cool down and calm down.

“Melvi, did you have to embarrass Liza?”

“I didn’t *have* to, but I couldn’t resist.”

“Don’t you remember how Daddy used to embarrass us?” Joanna said. “You hated it!”

“Well, my dear sister, now it’s my turn. Why do you have children if you can’t embarrass them sometimes?”

“Cool it, Melvi. Can’t you tell Liza is sensitive?”

“Her parents don’t joke about things. Her father is very serious and controlling. He’s also very critical of her.”

"Sorry, son, I'll go easy on her. You know we love Liza."

"I know, Pops, and she loves you guys too. We are the complete opposite of her family. She just needs some time to get used to us."

"I understand."

Liza returned looking refreshed and having regained her composure.

"I'm sorry if I embarrassed you in any way, little Liza. My son is used to my humour. I realize you may need more time."

"No harm done. I'm happy to get used to your sense of humour."

"That's our girl," Melvin Sr. said.

Chapter Thirty

Smoking Will Kill You

SARAH AND FARLEY LEFT SHORTLY after dessert, while Joanna stayed on a little longer.

"One visit is not enough to catch up with my favourite sister-in-law," Lola said.

"I'm your *only* sister-in-law," Joanna said matter-of-factly.

"That's beside the point. We aren't leaving until Monday morning and thought we would have a barbeque Sunday afternoon around two o'clock. We can spend more time together then, if you'd like to join us."

"I would love to join you," Joanna said.

"It's a date! I'll need help with the sauce for the ribs," Melvin Sr. said.

"Ribs? You know that's my specialty!"

"No one makes ribs like you do, Aunt Joanna."

"Except Grandma Annie," Melvin Sr. added.

"I learned from the best! On that note, it's time for me to say good night. See you all on Sunday."

"I'll walk you out," Melvin Sr. offered.

***

"Joanna is looking very well," Lola commented.

"Yes, she is," Melvin Sr. agreed.

"On the way over, Joanna was singing along with an Aretha Franklin song on the radio. She's an amazing singer," Liza said.

"Aretha is Joanna's favourite artist," Lola said.

"She told me there had been an accident and she stopped touring and performing after that."

"What did she tell you about the accident?"

"She didn't tell me anything, Lola. Just that she would explain some other time. She did mention you were on that road trip."

"Yes, I was," Lola began. "It was our last night of a ten-day gig. We were all exhausted and couldn't bear the thought of another night in a hotel. We all agreed that we would leave after the last show and do the three-hour trip home. Melvi had driven out the day before, so we could make the trip home together.

"We finished the last set and the guys started to pack up the equipment. Joshua and Joanna went to the office to get our money from Mac, the club owner. This was the first time we'd played this club. So far, Mac seemed like a stand-up kind of guy. When they went to collect our pay, Mac handed Joshua an envelope with the cash. Joshua counted it and saw that Mac had shorted us three hundred dollars. Joanna called Mac on it. He told her that was all he was going to pay. Joanna had the original signed contract, which clearly showed the amount he'd agreed to.

"Joshua was a big man—six-foot-six and he weighed 240 pounds, all muscle. Just the sort of person you'd be glad to have as your manager. Joanna made all of the deals and did all of the talking. He was there to back her up and make sure club conditions were up to par. He took care of all the little details.

"Joshua stepped between Joanna and Mac. He looked down at Mac and said in his deep, low voice, 'Pay the lady proper.' Mac pressed a button under his desk and three 'security guards,' a.k.a. 'thugs,' showed up.

"Joshua said, 'We don't want any trouble. We just want what's rightfully ours.'

"'You got what's rightfully yours. Now take it and get out,' Mac said.

"Joanna didn't want to fight. She took Joshua by the arm and said, 'It's not worth it; let's just go.'

"One of the thugs said, 'You should listen to the lady, if you know what's good for you.' Then he moved his jacket aside to show a gun in a shoulder holster.

"'I know what's good for me. Getting paid our due is what's good for me!' Joanna tightened her grip on Joshua's arm and pulled him toward the door.

"'Let's go,' she said sternly. Reluctantly, Joshua turned around and left with Joanna. They heard laughter coming from the office as they walked down the hallway.

"By this time, the equipment had been loaded and everyone was on the bus. Melvi and I were waiting in the car. Joanna and Joshua went on to the bus to pay everyone. They didn't say a word about what happened and paid everyone in full.

"When they got into the car, I asked what took them so long. Joanna said Mac was just talking too much. Joshua was too angry to keep quiet.

"'That's not what happened," he said. Joanna tried to quiet and calm him down. He wouldn't have it and told us the whole story. I told Joanna that we needed to split whatever money she had, fifty-fifty. It wasn't fair that she should be left short.

"Joanna took Joshua's hand and said, 'It's over, forget it. We're out of there safely and we'll never go back there again.' He finally started to relax a bit.

"We drove for about an hour and saw an all-night diner on the right-hand side of the highway, so we stopped for a bite to eat and some coffee. The coffee you get at road-side diner always tastes so good for some reason. It's the kind of place where you get good coffee, lots of food, and only pay a little. Not like those ultra-fancy restaurants where you get a little food and pay a lot!

"By the time we finished eating, everyone was in good spirits. Food always makes a body feel better. Melvi picked up the tab, which he and Joshua argued over who was going to pay. Melvi promised to let Joshua pay the next time.

"As we left, Joshua offered to drive the rest of the way home. Melvi didn't mind, because it meant we could snooze a little in the back seat. It was about four in the morning by then.

"About twenty miles from the city limits, Joshua pulled over to have a cigarette. We were all sleeping at that point. He walked around to the front of the car and leaned against the hood, lit his cigarette, and watched as the sun started to come up. He finished his cigarette, walked back, and was just about to reach for the door when a passing car hit him. He died instantly. The driver said he was blinded by the sun coming up and didn't see him in time to swerve around him. We woke up when we heard the screeching tires."

Tears were streaming down Liza's cheeks as she listened. Melvin put his arm around her and held her close.

Liza whispered, "That's so awful."

Melvin Sr. had his head down in his hands. He shook his head and said, "I should have been driving. This never would have happened."

"Melvi, it's no one's fault. It was a tragic accident. We don't understand why things happen, and there are no words to explain it."

"I miss him so much."

"I know; we all miss him," Lola said.

"Aunt Joanna always says we'll be reunited with him in heaven sone day."

Melvin Sr. lifted his head and said, "Knowing Joshua, he's having a really good time up there! You know him, he's *living large!*"

"He's probably having more fun in heaven than we're having here on earth," Melvin Jr. said.

"Then it's time to change all that," Lola said.

"Melvin?"

"Yes, Princess?"

"Could I have a bit more wine? I'd like to make a toast."

"Of course."

"Here's to Joshua and to living large!"

"To living large!" they all said.

Lola said quietly, "I don't know if Joanna will ever get over Joshua's death. He was the love of her life."

"People say *time* heals, but I say *love* heals," Liza said.

"Joanna may find love again," Melvin Sr. said.

"If the right person comes along," Lola said.

"They say that when you know, you know," Liza added.

"Never say never!" Melvin Jr. said.

The conversation went on until the early hours of the morning, when Lola glanced at her watch and said, "This can't be right! It's three-thirty!"

"Time flies when you're having fun, honey!"

"I guess we're having fun because that's the fastest night I've ever spent."

"Time to go to bed, Pops. I don't want you to fall asleep on the golf course."

"That's right, son, morning comes early!"

"As my grandmother used to say, we better sleep fast!" Lola said.

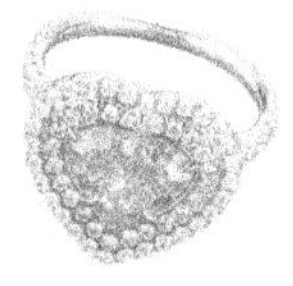

Chapter Thirty-One

A Girl's Gotta Have Some Secrets

MELVIN SR. WAS THE FIRST ONE UP. He brewed a pot of coffee, took it, and walked down the hallway, fanning the aroma as he went. He walked back to the kitchen, poured himself a cup, opened the newspaper, and sat down to read it. Liza was the next to get up.

"For some reason, I just can't wait to have coffee," she said.

"You don't say," Melvin Sr. said with a grin. "You're in luck; it's hot and ready."

"What are you two talking about?" Melvin Jr. said as he leaned over and kissed Liza.

"Nothing much, son."

"I hope there's some coffee for me!"

"Your dad and I already drained the first pot. The second one is just about ready."

Melvin Jr. was pouring his coffee when Lola came into the kitchen, yawning. She opened the cupboard, chose the biggest mug she could find, and filled it almost to the top.

"Is there any flavoured cream left?" she said as she leaned halfway into the refrigerator.

"It's over here on the table, sweetheart. Come sit beside me," he said and poured the cream into the coffee for her.

"What shall we have for breakfast?"

"We don't have time for breakfast, Pops. We'll have to get a bite at the course."

"Okay, son. What are you girls doing today?"

"We're going to relax and have some girl time. You boys better hurry along now!"

"If I didn't know better, I might think you're trying to get rid of us!"

"Who me? Melvi, I love having you around. Here's your cap," Lola said as she kissed him on the cheek and walked him to the door.

"We'll be home around four," Melvin Jr. said.

"Perfect, cocktails at four. Dinner at five," Lola said.

"What are we having for dinner, honey?"

"It's a surprise."

"See you later!" Melvin Sr. said.

"Have fun, Melvin!"

"Thank you, Princess."

Lola and Liza waved goodbye at the window.

"Liza, go put your lipstick on; we have a manicure and pedicure in half an hour."

"We do?"

"Yes. I'll call a taxi. We should just make it!"

"I've never done anything like this with my mom."

"That's too bad, sweetie. I'll be your mom today. Come on, let's go have some fun!"

***

"Where to, ladies?" the cab driver said.

Lola read the name on the meter. "*Your driver is Rocky.*"

"We're going to the Sunset Salon, Rocky."

"Sunset Salon it is," he said as he started the meter.

"The last time we visited, Joanna and I treated ourselves to a little pampering."

"My wife loves this place. Comes home in a much better mood too, if you don't mind my saying so," Rocky said, joining in their conversation.

"Happy to hear that," Lola said.

"Here we are, ladies."

"That was fast; it only took fifteen minutes," Liza said.

"I took a few short cuts to avoid some of the construction goin' on around here."

"Here you go," Lola said as she paid him. "Keep the change."

"That's real generous. Thank you!"

They were greeted by the receptionist as they entered the salon.

"Lola and Liza, I presume."

"Yes, that's correct," Lola confirmed.

"Right this way, please. Would you ladies like something to drink? Here we have our coffee bar. If you prefer tea, there's an assortment of herbal and regular tea. Cookies, fruit, cream and sugar, as well as honey. Feel free to help yourself. Chantal will be right with you."

"How fancy is this!" Liza commented.

"These cookies look yummy," Lola commented.

They had a few minutes to enjoy their coffee and then a very beautiful, very tall girl with long, black hair appeared. "Hi, I'm Chantal. I'll take you over now. Follow me, please. Are you ladies new in town?"

"I'm visiting for the weekend," Lola answered.

"I'm here for the summer," Liza said.

Chantal seated Lola next to Liza at the manicure station. They didn't discuss anything too personal ... salons are typically a place where people eavesdrop on other people's conversations. News travels fast in a small town.

Two hours later they were seated in the lounge, where they could allow for extra drying time.

"What are we fixing for dinner tonight, Lola?"

"It's all been taken care of, my dear. When Melvi and I visited Joanna a few years ago, we ate at the diner and got to know Flo. I called Flo last week and told her we'd be coming for a visit. I ordered ahead for dinner tonight, and Flo was more than happy to help. We'll pick up the food when we leave here. All we have to do is transfer it to baking dishes when we get to the house, get rid of the containers, and relax. Later on, we'll reheat, set the table, and eat! The boys will never know."

"I never would have thought of that," Liza said.

"We have to have *some* secrets," Lola said.

***

Rocky happened to get dispatched back to the salon to pick them up after their appointment. "Where to now, girls?"

"We're going to the diner to pick up our take-out order."

"Sure thing. I love the mac and cheese myself," Rocky said.

"Did you try the deep-fried pickles?" Liza said enthusiastically.

"Did I! My wife and I get a *double* order! Say *hi* to Flo for me," he said as Lola and Liza got out of the cab.

"Will do," Liza said.

Flo was filling up the sugar bowls when Lola and Liza walked in.

"Hey there, girlies! Haven't seen you in these parts for a while! How ya bin keepin'?"

"I'm very well," Lola answered. "How have you been, Flo?"

"Can't complain. Even if I did, ain't nobody gonna listen!" she said as she slapped Liza on the back and laughed.

Frankie motioned for Flo to come to the kitchen. "Looks like yer order is ready." Flo put four big bags on the cart and rolled it out. "Here ya go, girlies!" Flo glanced out the window and saw Rocky. "Looks like ya got Rocky out there waitin' on ya."

"Oh yes. We were supposed to say *hi* from him."

"Tell him, right back at ya!"

"Thank you for everything, Flo. We're going to be eating well tonight," Lola said.

"Ya shure are!"

"Melvin speaks very highly of you, Flo."

"Nice kid. Shure got a good appetite!"

"He takes after his pops," Lola said.

"See you soon, Flo," Liza said.

"See ya, girlie,"

Rocky was waiting outside by the taxi and opened the door for Lola. They put the bags of food in the back seat first, then Lola got in. Liza sat in the front seat.

Rocky helped them to the door when they got to the house. Lola tipped him twenty dollars.

"Thank you very much," he said as he put the twenty in his pocket.

"Don't mention it," Lola said, "And I *mean, don't mention it!* You know nothing about this food coming from the diner."

"Gotcha," Rocky said.

"Let's get the food out of these containers and into the baking dishes. Except for the deep fried pickles—we'll eat those right now. I also got a tray of snacks for us to have with our wine."

"You think of everything, Lola."

"I try. There's a big garbage bin at the end of the street; let's take the containers and dump them there."

***

"Now that's done, let's relax and have some wine," Lola said.

"I'm on it," Liza said. "It's a good thing we both like red, or we'd have to open two bottles."

"I actually don't see a problem with that."

"This has been such a wonderful day, Lola."

"It's important that we pamper ourselves every once in a while."

"I feel like I've missed out on so much."

"You are still very young, Liza. You have more life ahead of you than you do behind you."

"I've said it before and I'll say it again, I wish my family was more like yours."

"I didn't have a very good family life growing up, either."

"You didn't?"

"Nope. My life changed for the better when I met Melvi."

"Really?"

"My dad left my mom and me when I was four years old ... but let's begin at the beginning. I came from a musical background. Dad was the lead singer in a very popular band. Mom was one of their back-up singers. Mom said it was love at first sight. You and I both know how that feels!"

"We sure do!"

"They got married after only six months. They had so much fun and were so happy touring, travelling, and performing together. The challenge of being performers didn't bother them, because they had each other.

"After their second wedding anniversary, Mom found out that she was pregnant. Mom's pregnancy was a bit difficult. In her last trimester, the doctor recommended she not go back on the road but take it easy at home. Dad took a little time off to be with Mom closer to her due date. When I was born, he was home. Mom said it was the happiest time of their lives.

"Instead of reading to me at bedtime, Mom and Dad would take turns singing me to sleep each night. Mom sang all the time, especially when she was cooking. When Dad was home, he would help in the kitchen and sing along with her.

Of course, I would join in. I was about one or so. They would get such a kick out of it. Back then, Mom said she knew I would be a star one day.

"After my third birthday, something changed. Dad would come home from his latest gig, and although he'd spend time with us, he wasn't as attentive to Mom as he used to be. Mom noticed a difference but didn't say much at first. Dad was a very handsome man. Mom saw firsthand the way girls would swoon over him and throw themselves at him. Dad didn't take the bait. He and Mom would actually laugh about it. Most of the other band members were single and partied pretty hard. Mom knew the lifestyle very well. They would do a show, and if they didn't have to get on their tour bus and drive to the next gig the same night, they would party. Since they always played the same circuit, they'd get to know people wherever they went. There was never a shortage of people—mainly girls—ready to party with them.

"One night when Dad was home, I heard them arguing. Mom accused Dad of cheating. He would never disrespect her by lying to her. He knew she had probably figured things out and he told her the truth. Turns out, he and the girl who took Mom's place had started spending time together. One thing led to another and, as they say, the rest is history. Dad slept on the couch that night and left the next morning.

"I didn't understand it at the time, but as I got older and started to perform, I began to see things more clearly. The entertainment business is *some* hard-living. If you're not grounded, it can eat you up. Long days, even longer nights, being on the road, takes a toll. Things were great when Mom and Dad travelled on the road together, but after I was born and Mom stayed at home, Dad was lonely without her and gave in to temptation. She saw the signs but chose to ignore them because she loved him so much.

"After a while, the changes she saw in him were too much for her. She had to face reality. His life was on the road and her life was at home. Dad married the back-up singer after the divorce. Mom never did remarry. Dad didn't want to have any more children. I was his one and only.

"Mom and I had a very good life; Dad made sure of that. Probably because he felt so guilty, and I think deep down inside, he really still loved her. She passed away about five years ago now. She took up smoking after Dad left. Complications from smoking took her in the end.

"On the day of the funeral, the church was packed, with standing room only. Old people, young people, church people, neighbourhood people, entertainers, family, and Dad. I sang her favourite song, 'How Great Thou Art.' There wasn't a dry eye in the whole place, including Dad. In a way, I feel that if I hadn't been born, their love story would have continued forever."

"If you hadn't been born, you wouldn't have met Pops. You are the love of his life, and from what I can see, he is the love of your life."

"That is true, Liza. The day I met Melvi, my life began ... the life I'd always dreamed of in my secret dreams."

"I have those too."

"You and Junior were meant to be together! Uh, oh ... look at the time! We better set the table and put the food to warm. The boys should be home any time now. They better smell some food cookin' up in here, or they'll wonda what we been doin' all aftanoon. That's how Momma used to say it!"

"I wish I could have met your mom, Lola. She sounds like a very special lady."

"Thank you, Liza. I know she would have loved you, just like we do. Now come on, girl, we don't want those boys all up in our business."

***

"Smells like you girls have been cookin' up a storm," Melvin Sr. said as he walked in.

"Something like that, Melvi," Lola said as she gave him a big hug and kiss hello.

"Hi there, Princess. You sure look pretty."

"Thank you," Liza said as she hugged and squeezed Melvin tightly.

"We should leave these girls alone more often," Melvin Sr. said. "A nice welcome home and food cookin'. It just doesn't get better than this!"

"You two should go and get washed up."

"Yes, Pet," Melvin Sr. said.

***

"Wanna beer, Pops?"

"You know it!"

Melvin Jr. got two cold ones from the fridge. He left one on the counter and took one for himself, opened it, and sat down beside Liza on the couch.

"Melvin, is that the fragrance you were wearing the day I met you?"

"Sure is, Princess."

"You haven't worn it in a while."

"It's been sold out and on back order, so I couldn't get it until now."

"I hope you stocked up, since it's my favourite."

"I bought two."

"Your dad used to wear that fragrance when we first met. Black Knight, right?"

"That's what I used as my secret weapon," Melvin Sr. said as he kissed Lola on the cheek. "It worked too! She found me irresistible and said *yes* when I popped the question!"

"It had nothing to do with his good looks and charming personality," Lola joked.

"Did you two have fun golfing?" Liza asked.

"I haven't golfed or even gone to the range since last year, but I could hit 'em pretty darn good; right, son?"

"I was actually surprised at how well we both did, Pops."

"Natural talent never goes away!"

"I lost a ball on the eighth hole, but I think the guy in the blue shirt ahead of us hit my ball instead of his."

"What did you two girls do besides cook all day?"

"We relaxed and had a glass of wine, Melvi."

"Good for you! All work and no play is never good."

"You can say that again, Pops!"

"All work and—"

"Melvi, you are so funny. Come on, dinner is ready."

"It looks like Thanksgiving with all this food, honey."

"Liza and I thought you boys would appreciate a hearty dinner after golfing."

"This food is so good, I think I'll eat here again," Melvin Jr. said.

"This is your house, Melvin."

"I know, but if this is the kind of food you girls cook when you're together, I want more of it."

"We'll see what we can do tomorrow when Joanna comes over," Lola said. "She has some pretty good tricks up her sleeve."

"That's because she has a lot of our momma's recipes."

"She learned how to make your grandmother's sticky ribs. She won't share the recipe with anyone. I tried to figure out the ingredients, but there's something I'm missing," Lola said.

"I've never had sticky ribs before," Liza said.

"You've lived a very sheltered life, little Liza."

"I guess I have."

"We're about to change all that. Get ready for some lip-smackin' sauce on your face; can't get enough of grandma's sticky ribs," Melvin Sr. said.

"I'm ready!" Liza said.

Chapter Thirty-Two

What a Difference a Day Makes

MELVIN AND HIS DAD were having a conversation in the kitchen, and that's what woke Liza up.

"Yikes," she said to herself. "It's nine-thirty already."

She had taken Joanna's advice about packing clothes that were comfortable and made her feel good. She put on an outfit she hadn't worn yet. In fact, the price tag was still on it. It was a white two-piece skirt outfit with navy trim on the collar of the blouse and along the bottom of the long-flowy skirt.

Melvin whistled as she walked into the dining room. "You look beautiful, Princess."

"Thank you, Melvin."

"That is a lovely outfit you are wearing," Lola said.

"Thank you, Lola. Since it's Sunday, I thought I'd dress up."

Melvin kissed her on the cheek and pulled out a chair for her. "I'll get your coffee and breakfast. We kept it warming for you," he said.

"Looks like a beautiful day for a barbeque," Melvin Sr. said.

"I can't wait to try the ribs," Liza said.

"For now, how about trying Pops' famous apple pancakes. Here's your coffee too."

"Am I the only one eating breakfast?"

"Lola and Pops have already eaten, but I waited for you."

"Melvi, would you like to go out for a walk with me?"

"Sure, honey."

***

"I think Lola wanted to give us some time alone before Joanna comes over," Liza said.

"Kinda obvious, wasn't she?"

"They are so thoughtful."

"Here's a thought, Princess." Melvin took her fork, set it on her plate, and offered her his hand. "I think you should kiss me."

"Oh, you do, do you?"

As Liza stood up, Melvin didn't waste any time; he brushed her hair back, looked into her eyes, and kissed her as though it was their last kiss. This time, Liza's knees didn't wobble. She stood strong and kissed him back just as passionately. They were still kissing twenty minutes later when Lola and Melvin Sr. came back.

"Looks like we'll have to reheat those pancakes!" Melvin Sr. said.

Liza pulled away from Melvin. "We didn't hear you come in," she said.

"You were busy," Lola said.

They all started to laugh.

"We decided to cut our walk short and come back to start prepping the food before Joanna gets here."

"Good thinking, Pops. We'll help!"

Liza set the dining room table while Melvin Sr. helped Lola peel potatoes. Melvin Jr. chopped vegetables and started making the salad. Music was playing, Lola was singing along, and everyone was busy. No one heard the doorbell. Neither did they hear Joanna come in, until she was in the kitchen standing face-to-face with Lola.

"Is this a private party, or can anyone join in?"

"Aunt Joanna, let me help you with your bag. It's so heavy! What do you have in here, bricks?"

"Very funny, sonny boy. I brought my favourite Champagne, a couple of other good things, and the sauce for the ribs."

"You already made the sauce?" Lola said, somewhat disconcerted.

"I thought it would save a little time."

"We were hoping to make the sauce *with* you," Liza said innocently.

"In case you want to make it again sometime, I brought something for you. Now where did I put it?" Joanna said as she winked at Liza. She took two recipe cards from her purse and handed one to Liza and the other to Lola. On the top of each card she wrote, "Annie Mae's Sticky Ribs."

Melvin Sr. could not believe his eyes. "You mean to tell me after all these years of keepin' this recipe a secret, you're just going to give it to us now?"

"I thought it was time."

Melvin looked at the recipe with Lola. He skimmed over the ingredients and then he said loudly, "*Root beer*!" That's the secret ingredient? *Root beer*!"

"And look," Lola said. "Honey too!"

"I guess it ain't no secret no more," Joanna said, imitating Annie Mae. She took a large bottle of root beer and a jar of honey out of her bag. "Here you go. Thought I'd get you started for next time."

"It says here, put the dry rub on the ribs and bake at 325 degrees for two-and-a-half hours," Lola read.

"Oh yes, I almost forgot ... here's the package of dry rub I made up for you. Pretty simple. Bake 'em slow, eat 'em fast," Joanna said as she sat down. "The ribs are basically ready after you bake them. You can just put them on the barbeque for fifteen minutes to grill them. Underside first with some sauce on them. Flip them over, put a little more sauce on. There's lots of sugar in that ol' sauce because of the root beer, so you don't want to burn 'em. You can serve up some sauce on the side, too. Now how about some Champagne? All this talkin' has got me pretty thirsty. Here you go, young fellow. Pour your auntie a glass of bubbly. Who's going to join me?"

"It's still early," Melvin Sr. said.

"What's that saying people use as an excuse to have an afternoon cocktail: 'It's five o'clock somewhere!'"

"All right then," Lola said. "A round for the house!"

They spent the afternoon cooking, singing, laughing, and having fun. Melvin Sr. barbequed the ribs—with Joanna's supervision, of course. Joanna brought adult-sized bibs for everyone. She said, "You can't enjoy ribs the proper way if you're worried about gettin' sauce on your clothes."

"These are the best ribs I've ever had in my whole life," Liza said as she licked sauce off of her fingers.

"Annie Mae is listening and dancin' cuz she always loved feedin' people her ribs," Lola said.

"I've lived a lot longer than you have, little Liza, and these are the best ribs I've ever tasted, hands down!"

Melvin Jr. stood up, raised his glass of Champagne, and said, "To my dear grandma, Annie Mae—" He hadn't quite finished the toast when the phone rang.

"Who could that be? Everyone who is anyone is already here."

"You better answer it, son, and find out."

"Hello? Hi, Boss." He put his hand over the receiver and whispered, "It's my boss."

Liza whispered, "I think we figured that out!"

"What? Where? When? I can't? Are you sure? For how long? I see. Yes, I'll be in at nine. Okay, goodbye." Melvin hung up the phone and sat down.

"What was that all about, son?"

"Before I was transferred here to Waterford, I worked on a special project back home. This past week, my boss called me into his office and said they'd uncovered some new information as a result of my preliminary research. He assigned three other guys in our office to the same project. He read all of our reports and found that we have inadvertently stumbled upon something significant. He wants me to take the lead on the investigation."

"Does this have anything to do with the *spy stuff* you've been working on?" Liza said.

"I can neither confirm nor deny."

"*Spy stuff*? It sounds very intriguing, son."

"It is, Pops."

"What else did your boss say when he called?" Lola said.

"Since you're my family, I'll tell you what I can, but you are sworn to secrecy ... understand?"

"We understand," Melvin Sr. replied.

"He said our group is being reassigned to a new location, which I'm not allowed to divulge, because it's classified. For all intents and purposes, we're just newspaper geeks working for a newspaper."

"We're not allowed to know where you are going?"

"I'm afraid not, Princess. The less you know, the better."

"When is this transfer going to happen?"

"That will be discussed at the meeting tomorrow morning, but my boss said it may happen as soon as Friday."

"Friday," Liza said as she began to cry.

"Don't cry, Princess. It's not forever."

"How long *will* you be away?"

"My boss said we have to proceed carefully so that we don't risk getting found out. The time frame he mentioned was a year."

"A *year*! A *year is forever, to me*!" Liza said as a steady stream of tears fell down her cheeks and landed on her blouse.

"I'm sorry, Princess. I'm in shock too!"

"If it means your career, I guess you have no choice," Joanna said.

"When I was in my last year at the university, I always dreamed of travelling to unknown places and doing exactly this type of investigative journalism. Now that this opportunity has presented itself, I must admit, I feel torn."

Liza stopped crying and said, "Melvin, you have to go. I'm not going to hold you back from doing what you're meant to do."

"You are so understanding."

"There is no other option," she continued. "If you don't go, you may regret it for the rest of your life. I wouldn't want you to blame or resent me for what *could* have been."

"I really don't deserve you."

"We'll just have to have long telephone conversations."

"Unfortunately, you won't be able to contact me. When I can, I'll contact you. We can't risk anyone tracing your calls."

Liza sat in silence as she stared at Melvin. He reached over and held her hand.

"It's a lot to process, I know. We'll work it out, Princess, you'll see."

"What do I tell Sarah and Farley? I'm sure they'll have some questions."

"As little as possible. Just say I'm being transferred to a somewhat remote location where we'll be setting up a new office. That will explain why you won't be able to contact me and why I'll be away for that length of time."

"That sounds like a plausible explanation," Joanna said.

"I've said more than I really should have. It's imperative you all tell the same story."

"You can count on us, son."

"On that note, I think I'll take myself home," Joanna said. "I'd offer to take you along with me, Liza, but it seems you and my nephew may have to continue this conversation in private. Take your time getting back."

"Come on, Melvi, let's go walk Joanna out."

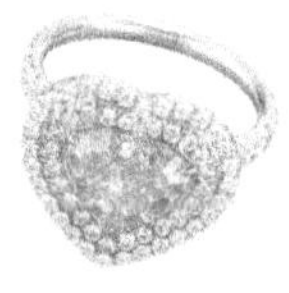

Chapter Thirty-Three

Memories Are Made of This

"I'M REALLY SORRY OUR WEEKEND had to end this way," Melvin Jr. said.

"There's no need to apologize, son. Sometimes work takes people away for a while."

"You're right, Pops. It's just bad timing, that's all."

"Maybe your project won't take a year and you can come back sooner," Liza said.

"Maybe."

"I'm glad we were able to spend this weekend together. This was *good* timing!" Lola said.

"We made a lot of good memories I'll be taking with me," Melvin Jr. said.

"I hate to say this, because I don't want to leave, but I should get back to Joanna's. That way you can spend some time alone with Lola and your pops, since they're leaving in the morning. I'll go pack my bag," Liza said.

"Would you like some company?" Lola offered.

"That would be nice," Liza said.

***

"We're going to miss you, son."

"I'll miss you too, Pops. I'll call you when I can."

"You can call us anytime, day or night."

"I will."

Liza came around the corner, carrying her bag.

"All ready to go, little Liza?"

"Yes. I just wanted to tell you how much I have enjoyed our time together. I have happy memories to take with me too."

"It's been our privilege to be with you these last few days," Melvin Sr. said.

"Thank you," Liza replied.

"I especially loved our girl time," Lola added.

"Me too!" Liza said and managed a smile. "Have a safe trip back!"

"We will, and we'll call you when we get home tomorrow, son."

"Sounds good, Pops."

"I better hug you guys and get going before I start crying again," Liza said.

"Take care of yourself, little Liza. We'll call Joanna and check up on you."

"Okay."

"See you guys shortly," Melvin Jr. said.

"Don't worry son, take your time."

As he drove, Melvin held Liza's hand tightly. Liza leaned over and put her head on his shoulder.

"I can't believe this is happening to us, Melvin."

"I can't believe it either, Princess."

"Now that you're leaving, there's no reason for me to stay here."

"Of course there is, Princess. Joanna loves you, sings your praises, and has really come to depend on you. You're great with the kids; they love you, and your best friend is here."

"Those are all good reasons, I'll admit. The main reason I came here in the first place was to be with you. I'm going to be lost without you! It might be different if Sarah was here on her own, but she has Farley."

"I'm sure they will invite you to do things with them."

"I don't want to be a third wheel."

"I'm sure they won't see it that way."

"They may not, but I do."

"Mr. Mittens would be happy to have you all to himself."

"That is not helping, Melvin."

"It's just for a little while."

"A year is a very *long while*."

"It's a little while compared to the rest of our lives together," he said.

"It still seems like an eternity to me! Things can change in a year. Look how much they've changed already."

"I know one thing that won't change, Princess."

"What's that, Melvin?"

"My love for you. Someone once said, *Absence makes the heart grow fonder.*"

"Yes, I've heard that. I don't think absence could make *my* heart grow fonder."

"Why is that, Princess?"

"Because all of me already loves all of you."

"I feel the same way, Princess. You know I'd stay if I could."

"I believe you, Melvin. I just feel helpless, that's all."

"You're not alone. We might feel helpless, but we are not *hopeless*. We have hope for a happy future ahead of us. We just have to do the best we can until then."

"You're right, Melvin."

Melvin turned the corner onto Jones Road, and Liza said, "Why does it seem like the time it takes to get back to Joanna's is a lot shorter than the time it takes to go to your house?"

"I don't know the answer to that, but I know what you mean."

"You don't have to walk me in," Liza said.

"I'll call you after the meeting tomorrow."

"Okay, Melvin."

"Sleep well, Princess," he said and kissed her.

"You too," she said.

He waited until Liza was inside and lingered for a few minutes before he drove away.

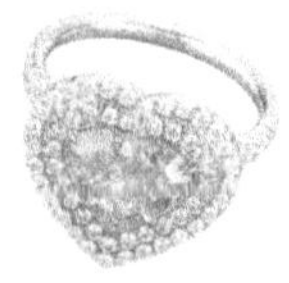

Chapter Thirty-Four

Plans Do Change

LIZA'S THOUGHTS WERE RACING as she unpacked. *A year? He's going away for a year! What am I going to do? How can this be happening!*

She heard a gentle knock at her door and went to answer it.

"Can I interest you in a cup of tea?"

"Sure, Joanna. Please come in."

"How are you doing?"

"I'm not sure."

"It's a lot to process."

"I haven't been able to process anything, really. It all seems so surreal. The plans we made are ruined."

"Plans do change."

"How am I supposed to respond to all of this?"

"Just breathe and keep putting one foot in front of the other. My vocal coach, Roy, who was my very dear, very wise friend, once said, 'Jo, just say your prayers, go on about your business, and the rest will take care of itself ... and don't take it back again!'"

Liza took a deep breath and a sip of her tea.

"I know the reason you came here was so you and Melvin could spend the summer together, unencumbered by parents. Working at the daycare was just a means to an end. Although Melvin is being called away for work, you still have a place here. Spending the summer with us will be the best thing for you. It will give you something meaningful to do and keep you busy. You've made an indelible impression on the children, and you have new friends and formed some meaningful relationships ... namely with Sam and me.

"That takes care of the days. What about the evenings?"

"If you're okay spending time with an old fuddy-duddy like me, I'm sure we'll figure something out."

"You are anything *but* a fuddy-duddy, Joanna! You've lived a very interesting life, and I for one would love to hear more about it!"

"I'll be happy to oblige. I'm sure Sarah would love to spend more time with you."

"Farley might have something to say about that. Sarah should be getting in soon. Would you stay with me while I try to explain Melvin's sudden transfer? I don't want to mess up and say the wrong thing."

"If it would make you feel better."

"It would."

Less than five minutes later, Sarah knocked on Liza's door and quietly said, "Liza, are you still up?"

When Liza opened the door, Sarah immediately sensed something was wrong. Then she saw Joanna and knew her inkling was correct.

"Who wants to tell me what's going on?" Sarah said.

"Melvin got a call from his boss earlier this evening," Liza said.

"And?"

"He and three others are being transferred to a somewhat remote location, where they will be tasked with starting up a new office," Joanna explained.

"Why does Melvin have to go?"

"His boss feels he is the right one for the job. In fact, he'll be in charge of the whole project," Liza said.

"When will he be leaving?"

"There's a meeting tomorrow morning to confirm the date, but Friday was mentioned," Liza said.

"How long will the project take?"

"They estimate a year," Joanna answered.

"A YEAR!" Sarah yelled out. "Liza, what are you going to do?"

"Joanna and I were just discussing that. I'm going to stay on for the term."

"Oh, thank goodness! I'm so sorry Melvin is being transferred, but I'm glad you're staying. I could use your help and yours too, Joanna. The wedding plans are getting more and more complicated ... there are so many little details. I need help with all of the decisions."

"I'd be happy to help," Joanna said.

"Me too," Liza added. "Suddenly I feel very tired. If you both don't mind, I'd like to go to bed now."

"Of course, dear. Sleep well."

Sarah hugged Liza and then followed Joanna out. "See you in the morning," she said as she closed the door behind her.

"Liza seems to be handling this quite well," Sarah whispered to Joanna.

"I don't think she's handling it at all. I think she's still in shock. In the days to come, she'll need a lot of moral support."

"I'll plan to spend more time with her."

"I'm sure she'll really benefit from having you to lean on."

Sarah nodded in agreement.

"See you in the morning, Sarah. Sleep well."

"You too, Joanna."

***

Sam was singing in the kitchen when Liza sat down to have her coffee.

"Good mornin', Miss Liza. I have something for you," Sam said as he handed her a long-stemmed red rose.

"What's this for, Sam?"

"Miss Joanna didn't seem herself this mornin'. When I asked her why, she told me that your Melvin has to go away for a time."

"Yes, that's right. Thank you for the lovely rose, Sam."

"I cut it from the garden out back, to remind you there's still beauty all around, and to bring you some cheer."

"Can I ask you a question, Sam?"

"Anything you want, Miss Liza."

"How long have you and your wife been married?"

"Gonna be thirty years come this September."

"What's the secret of your success?"

"We love each other, plain and simple. She was the prettiest girl I ever did see—still is! I loved her the minute I laid eyes on her. *She* took a little longer, needed a little convincin'. I just kept showin' up everywhere she was, so she'd notice me. I started writin' love poems and givin' her flowers and such. I think that's what did it. She liked that I was romancin' her. I still write love poems just like I did thirty years ago. She kept every last one of 'em, too!"

"That's so romantic!"

"Just cuz you're married don't mean you don't have to try no more."

"You are very wise, Sam."

"Thank you, Miss Liza. What can I fix you for breakfast?"

"I'm not hungry, Sam. I'm just going to take my coffee with me and go to the daycare now."

"All right, have a nice day, Miss Liza."

Liza walked past Sarah on her way out.

"Hey, where are you going?" Sarah said.

"I'm going to the daycare. I'll see you at lunch."

"Okay," Sarah said.

***

Alice was putting art paper, crayons, and paints at each of the tables in the classroom when Liza arrived. She looked up at the clock on the wall and said, "Liza, you're here awfully early! What's the matter, couldn't sleep last night?"

"There's been some new developments."

"What do you mean?"

"Melvin has been informed that he, along with three other guys, are being transferred to set up a new office. He'll be leaving this week and will be away for a year," Liza said without emotion.

Alice looked perplexed. "That's a lot to take in," she said.

"I've decided to stay and keep working here with you. Joanna thought it would be best."

"Joanna always knows what's best. She helped me through some pretty tough times. The good news is, I'm still standing!"

Isaiah walked into the classroom carrying a brown paper bag and handed it to Liza.

"Sam dropped this off and said to give it to you. He thought you might need a snack for recess. There's a sandwich in there for your lunch too."

Liza smiled, shook her head, and said, "Oh, that Sam!"

"I know, I know," Isaiah said. "Brought me some lunch too."

"I packed a lunch for you, Isaiah."

"I forgot it at home, Alice."

"I swear, if I didn't put it in your hand, you'd forget it every time."

"We're lucky Sam looks after us," Liza said.

"We sure are, Miss Liza. We sure are." Isaiah turned to Alice and said, "I'll see you at recess."

Alice waved and continued with the art supplies.

Joanna knocked on Alice's classroom door just before the lunch bell rang. Alice answered. She and Joanna stood facing each other in the doorway. At one point, Alice turned to look at Liza. When the conversation ended, Alice walked toward Liza. Liza could tell by the look of consternation on Alice's face that she had something important to say.

"Joanna wants you to meet her in her office. Take your purse with you."

Liza's face turned ghostly white. She went to the cabinet, unlocked it, and took her purse. She cut through the library and hurried to Joanna's office.

"What is it, Joanna?" Liza said hesitantly.

"Melvin called. He has to leave tomorrow, not Friday."

Liza fell backwards into the chair beside the door.

"He's on the way to the house right now and wants me to drive you over there."

"I think I'm going to be sick," Liza said.

"Come on, let's go. Once we get outside, the fresh air will help."

Liza needed Joanna's help to steady herself. She got into the car and rolled down the window. She stared straight ahead and did not utter a single word.

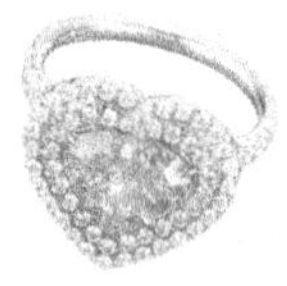

Chapter Thirty-Five

Never Was Not an Option

LIZA WALKED THROUGH the open front door into Melvin's arms. They could not deny their passion any longer. It was now or never, and *never* was not an option.

The clothes they shed fell faster and harder than their tears. *Goodbye tears* mixed with *don't leave me tears*.

He whispered, "I love you."

She whispered, "You're the only one for me."

Their passion took them to a place they had never been before. The intensity of their lovemaking transported them to heights of ecstasy neither knew were possible.

They lay exhausted in each other's arms. He stared at her. She stared at him.

He said, "I want to hold you in my arms forever."

She said, "That's exactly where I want to be."

As they lay in the after-glow, sleep fell upon them.

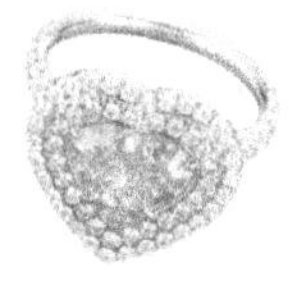

Chapter Thirty-Six

The Same Moon

"YOU LOOK SO PEACEFUL when you're asleep," Melvin said as Liza opened her eyes.

"How long have you been watching me?"

"About an hour now. I didn't have the heart to wake you."

"Melvin, hold me tight and don't let me go."

"I *never* want to let you go," he said.

"When I'm alone at night, I'll close my eyes and remember how it felt to be next to you and in your arms. Then I won't feel so lonely and the night won't seem so long."

He held her tightly and said, "When you look up at the night sky and see the moon, remember, we'll be looking at the same moon. We'll feel the same breeze and wish upon the same star. I'll be missing you a thousand different ways. No matter where I am, or how far apart we are, you will always be my Princess."

"I love you, Melvin."

"I love you too, Princess."

"I've decided to stay and continue working at the daycare. Joanna came to my room with tea when I got back yesterday. She convinced me to stay. She said I'm needed and it would be the best thing for me."

"I'm very proud of you, Princess. You're making the right decision. Aunt Joanna will look after you. You're like a daughter to her."

"Joanna would make a great mom. Maybe she could teach me to sing."

"I'm sure she'd be happy to. We should probably get dressed," Melvin said and kissed Liza on the forehead.

"I don't know about you, Melvin, but I'm thirsty. I'd like a glass of Champagne. The fact that you're leaving is nothing to celebrate, but our love definitely is."

"Truer words were never spoken."

Liza took two glasses from the cupboard, and Melvin opened the Champagne. "Pops wanted me to give you this. It's a bottle of his favourite Champagne. He thought you, Sarah, and Aunt Joanna would like to enjoy it one evening. I think he knew Aunt Joanna would talk you into staying."

"Your pops is really something else!"

"He sure is! Pops and Lola had so much fun with us this weekend. When they left this morning, they said to give you their love."

"That's so nice of them!"

Melvin nodded in agreement and handed Liza a glass of Champagne.

"Here's to looking at the same moon and wishing upon the same star," Liza said.

"Beautiful." He took her hand and said, "Let's go sit on the swing and enjoy the evening while we can."

"What time do you leave in the morning?"

"Someone will be here to pick me up at six o'clock. That's really all I can tell you."

"What about your furniture and all your things?"

"A moving company will be coming to pack everything and put it into storage."

"Do you think I could have your pillow?"

"You want my pillow?"

"Yes, because you were sleeping on it and it smells like you ... your fragrance is on it."

"Yes, Princess. You can have my pillow."

"One more thing ... can I have a bottle of your fragrance? I can sprinkle a little on your pillow and it will seem like you're still with me. I'll be able to sleep better."

"You can have both bottles. I only wear it because you like it."

Liza smiled.

"Aunt Joanna wants me to come in for a few minutes when I take you back to the house. I guess she wants to say goodbye."

"I'm sure I'm not the first one to ever say this, but there's nothing *good* in goodbye," Liza said sombrely.

"Then we won't say goodbye."

"I have a request," Liza said.

"Request away!"

"Would you play our favourite music? I'd like to dance with you."

He turned the music on, held out his hand, and said, "May I have this dance?"

"Yes, you may. Dancing with you will always be one of my favourite memories."

He pulled her closer and held her tighter. "The first time I saw you will always be one of *my* favourite memories. I was working from home, sitting at my desk, and happened to look out the window. That's when I saw you. You were going into the coffee shop. The wind was gently blowing your beautiful long hair, and then I saw your pretty face. That's when I knew you were the one for me. After a couple of weeks, I had your schedule figured out and decided it was time for us to meet. There was only one problem—I wasn't sure how to get your attention. There were so many people around, and you always took your coffee to go."

"You got my attention that first day when you winked at me. I basically inhaled you as you walked so close to me on your way out. That night I didn't sleep much ... maybe an hour at most. I couldn't stop thinking about you. The next morning, I put on my best dress and went back to the coffee shop, hoping I would see you again."

"I got to the coffee shop early and was watching for you from the back hallway. When you took your place in line, I hurried to stand behind you. I almost tripped on a table leg coming around the corner."

"I didn't see you when I came in, and I was so disappointed. I thought I got dressed up for nothing. When you came up behind me and stood so close, I could feel the heat from your body. I got a whiff of your fragrance and I *knew* it had to be you. I was so glad you asked to walk me to work. I couldn't concentrate on my work at all that day."

"When I got home, I couldn't concentrate on my work either! I could hardly wait to see you Saturday night. I actually went out and bought new clothes to wear on our date."

"Me too!"

"I thought I saw you in the mall that day. You were talking to someone, a girl I think. I was going in the opposite direction on my way to get my pants hemmed. I just glanced over and didn't really get a good look."

"I have a confession to make, Melvin. After we danced at Fast Freddie's and were walking off the dance floor, you asked if I was wearing new shoes. I lied. I said they weren't new, but they were. I'd bought them a few days before. I hadn't worn them yet, and my feet were killing me!"

"Mine too! I bought new shoes *that* day! All the time we've spent together adds up to one thing, Princess."

"What *one* thing would that be?"

"True love!"

"We're so lucky, Melvin. Some people *never* find it."

"I'm not sure if we found *it* or if *it* found us."

"The main thing is, we've got it!" Liza said.

"We sure do!"

"Melvin?"

"Yes, Princess."

"The music stopped ten minutes ago."

Melvin stopped swaying, stood still, and listened. "I guess it did. We've been dancing for a while. I think we may have to leave for Aunt Joanna's shortly."

"Can we just stay here forever?"

"There's nothing I'd like more, Princess."

***

Mr. Mittens was the official greeter, followed by Joanna, Sarah, Farley, and Sam.

"Come on in, you two," Joanna said.

"Hi, everyone! I can't stay too long, Aunt Joanna," Melvin said quietly.

"This won't take long," she said. "We have a small gift for you and thought we could have a farewell drink before you have to go."

"Pops wanted me to give you girls this bottle of his favourite Champagne. Why don't we have that?"

"That sounds lovely, dear. Sam has prepared the sitting room for us."

Liza put the tote bag with Melvin's pillow and fragrance around the corner in the hallway.

"I didn't think I would see you this evening Sam," Liza said as she re-joined the group.

"Can't let one of our own leave without a proper send-off," he said.

"I'm really glad you're here, Sam," Melvin said.

"On behalf of all of us," Joanna began, "I'd like to present you with this gift."

"Thank you. I don't know what to say."

They all watched Melvin unwrap his gift. Inside was a silver-plated compass with an inscription on the back that read, *This will guide you home.* "It's perfect. Thank you so much! How did you get it engraved so quickly?"

"Junior, did you forget your aunt has connections?" Sam said.

"And we're glad she does," Liza said, even though she didn't know anything about it, but she assumed Joanna bought it after she dropped her off at Melvin's earlier.

"I'm going to miss you guys," Melvin said. "I'll call when I can, though."

"We'll miss you too," Joanna said.

"Maybe you'll be back in time for our wedding," Sarah said.

"That would be nice, but we'll just have to wait and see."

"I'm going to say farewell for now, Junior. I best be gettin' home. You be safe out there! We'll be seein' ya on the flip side!" Sam said and gave Melvin a big hug.

"You too, Sam. Take care of everyone here for me while I'm gone."

"Will do. Night, all!" Sam said as he left.

"Lunch at the diner won't be the same on Fridays," Farley said. "I might have to get Hector to take your place!" he joked.

"Nobody can keep up to you when it comes to eating," Melvin said. "You'll put Ruiz to shame!"

"He doesn't know that!" Farley said.

"Say goodbye to Flo for me, will you?"

"You got it, buddy. Sorry to see you go. Sarah here is glad you're not taking Liza with you. She needs a bunch of help with the wedding stuff."

"That's not important right now, Farley. I'm sorry you have to leave also," Sarah said. "We were really enjoying our group of four."

"Me too, Sarah."

"It's time for me to hit the old dusty trail," Farley said. "Walk me out, Sarah?"

Farley and Melvin shook hands and slapped each other on the back.

"See ya," Farley said.

"See ya," Melvin said.

Liza closed her eyes to try to stop the tears from falling, but they fell anyway.

"Don't start that now," Aunt Joanna said, "or I'll start too. Come here, nephew of mine. Give your auntie a hug. You come back to us as soon as you can!"

"I will, Aunt Joanna. I promise."

"Call anytime! If it's in the middle of the night, that's okay. I've got plenty of coffee to keep me awake all day!"

Melvin laughed.

"I love you, dear."

"I love you too, Aunt Joanna."

"Good night, Liza, see you in the morning."

"See you in the morning."

"I have to go now, Princess. I have some packing to do when I get back to the house."

"If you have to," Liza said sadly.

When they got outside, Farley was gone, and so was Sarah.

"Sarah must have gone in the back door," Liza said.

Melvin took Liza by her shoulders, turned her toward him, and held her, neither saying a word. He stroked her long hair, pulled it back from her pretty face, and kissed her.

"I'll call as soon as I can, Princess, so I can hear your sweet voice."

"I'm counting on it."

"I won't say goodbye, only good night."

"Good night, Melvin. I'll see you later ... in my dreams."

"I'll see you there," he said and turned to leave.

Liza waved as Melvin drove away. She waved until she could no longer see his car and it faded into the distance.

The moon was full and seemed brighter than she had ever remembered. It shone down and illuminated the spot in which she stood. Hours later, she stood just as still, her tears glistening on the ground in front of her. She noticed a lone star in the sky and wished upon it, hoping he might see it and wish upon it too.

The night breeze swirled around and gently turned and guided her inside.

She pushed her own pillow to the floor and replaced it instead with his. She slipped her cold, tired body, still fully clothed, beneath the covers. His fragrance enveloped her as it had many times before and soothed her to sleep.

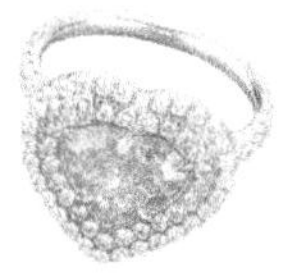

Chapter Thirty-Seven

Miss Liza's Love Day

LIZA WAS LATE FOR BREAKFAST, and Sam was worried.

"Hi, Sam. May I have toast please? Where's Liza?"

"Haven't seen Miss Liza yet. I'm gettin' kinda worried."

"Maybe I should go check on her."

"No need to check on me. I'm here and I'm starved. Can I have waffles with blueberry sauce, lots of whipped cream, and extra bacon please, Sam?"

"Comin' right up, Miss Liza."

"Someone's hungry," Sarah said.

"I'm playing catch-up. The only thing I had to eat yesterday was my snack at recess. By the way, Sam, thank you for my care package. Isaiah delivered it."

"You're most welcome, Miss Liza."

"How are you?"

"I'm fine, Sarah. How are you?"

"No, really—"

"Really."

"You said goodbye to Melvin last night, and this morning you're *fine*?"

"Technically we didn't say goodbye, just good night. As far as I know, the world did not stop turning overnight. I'm still here, and right now, I'm hungry. Sam, this coffee is extra-tasty today! What's different?"

"It's Mamma's special chicory recipe. She used to make it for Daddy when he was tired from workin' too hard and not gettin' proper sleep. Gave him energy, cuz the chicory makes it stronger and darker."

"I'm going to need a lot of your special chicory coffee today."

"I'll brew an extra pot so you can take some with you, Miss Liza."

Joanna came in carrying Mr. Mittens and sat down at the table across from Liza.

"Good morning, everyone. Sam, I'll have a half a cup of coffee now, and I'll take my thermos with me. I got up to get a drink of water late last night and found Mr. Mittens in his favourite spot, looking out the window in the sitting room, staring up at the full moon."

Liza put her fork down and looked over at Joanna. Joanna didn't miss a beat. "It sure was bright! Just about the time the wind started picking up, I went back to bed and Mr. Mittens followed me ... didn't you?"

"Meow."

"If you girls don't have any plans this evening, I thought we could go out and do a little shopping. There's a sale on at Gracie's. Sam is going to make one of his deluxe pizzas for our dinner afterwards. Lord knows, shopping gives me an appetite."

"I don't have any plans," Liza said.

"Me either," Sarah said.

"It's a date then," Joanna said. "Meet you girls here after work."

Sam handed Joanna a small thermos and her lunch bag.

"Thank you, Sam. Have a good day, everybody," she said. "See ya later!"

"Do you have an extra thermos for me, Sam?"

"Shore do, Miss Liza. I was just gonna fill it up for you."

"Shopping, huh?" Sarah said.

"I think it will be fun!" Liza replied. "What's Farley up to tonight?"

"He's planning to watch basketball. His favourite team is playing, but don't ask me who it is."

"I wasn't going to," Liza said.

"I really don't like basketball, and Farley knows it. He's happy he can have the whole couch to himself."

Sam gave Sara her lunch bag and said, "Have a good day, Miss Sarah."

"You too, Sam! See ya later, Liza!"

Sam gave Liza her lunch bag next, along with the thermos of coffee.

"Have a nice day now, Miss Liza." He patted her on the shoulder as he had done before. The kindness in his eyes touched something in her heart, and she knew deep down that she would be all right.

***

Liza put her thermos on top of the cabinet where she locked up her purse. Alice came into the classroom pushing a cart filled with library books.

"There you are," Alice said. "I see you brought a thermos with you today. Nothing like Java to *perk* you up!"

Liza smiled. "If you're wondering, I'm okay," she said.

"I *wasn't* wondering. I *know* you're okay. Do you want to know *how* I know?"

"Yes."

"Your eyes are kinda puffy today, so that tells me you've been crying all night. You did a good job of covering it up with makeup. You brought a thermos of coffee, not just a cup. Most likely, Sam's special chicory blend, which he makes when he knows someone is going to need it because they didn't get much, if any sleep. You showered, curled your hair, and wore a pretty dress today. You didn't stay in bed and hide under the covers; you showed up here. All those things tell me you're okay. To your first point, I don't *wonder.* I pay attention. Now, don't just stand there. Help me unload these books."

***

Alice and Liza weren't on duty, so when the children went out for recess, they went to the staffroom for coffee. Joanna came in carrying a large, white box.

"What have you got there, Joanna Jones?" Alice said.

"Let's go back to the classroom and find out," Joanna replied.

Joanna placed the box on Alice's desk and removed the card taped to the top. She turned to Liza and said, "I believe this has your name on it."

"My name?" Liza said.

"Your name is Liza, isn't it?" Alice quipped.

Liza opened it and read, "This scripture used to cheer up Momma: 'Weeping endures for a night, but joy comes in the morning!'"

"Go on, open the box," Alice said.

There were cupcakes covered with fluffy white icing and a pink heart in the centre of each.

"If that don't cheer you up, girl, I don't know what will," Alice said.

The recess bell rang. Joanna said she would go and get the children. She stood in front of them as they lined up at the door before coming in.

"Boys and girls, when you get back to the classroom, I want you to sit down quietly at your desks. We have a special treat for each of you."

All of the children followed Joanna's instructions, except Harvey. He ran to Liza, stood on his tip toes, and looked into the open box.

"Whose birthday is it?" he said.

"The cupcakes are not for someone's birthday," Alice said.

"Then what are they for?"

"It's to celebrate Miss Liza."

"Why?"

"It's a special day for her. Let's call it *Miss Liza's Love Day.* Today we're going to show her extra love," Joanna said.

"Should we sing?" Harvey said.

"We could," Alice answered. "How about if we sing to the tune of Happy Birthday? Everybody ready?"

Harvey slipped his hand into Liza's and stood beside her, singing the loudest.

"Happy love day to you. Happy love day to you. Happy love day, Miss Liza, Happy love day to you."

They finished singing and started clapping.

"Thank you very much, boys and girls," Liza said, holding back tears.

"I love you, Miss Liza," Harvey said.

"I love you too, Harvey."

"Who wants cupcakes?" Alice said.

A chorus of "I do's" rang throughout the class.

Alice whispered to Liza, "It will get easier, you'll see." She offered her the first cupcake. "There's nothing like a cupcake to make your heart happy ... and put some weight on that skinny little bottom of yours!"

As Liza watched the children enjoying their cupcakes, she realized Joanna was right. Being at the daycare *was* the best thing for her. She *did* feel needed and enjoyed observing the children learning and at play. Watching them reminded her of a simpler time, when she was their age. Life was good and she was happy.

"Go out and play," her mother would say. There were only a couple of rules: clean up your toys and put them away when you were finished playing with them. That was about it. The only responsibility she had was to have fun.

***

Liza and Sarah were waiting in the sitting room when Joanna came in and called out, "Are you girls ready?"

They came around the corner and surprised her.

"We're ready," Liza said.

"Gracie's got a summer sale going on right now. She put a few things aside for us. Here's a hundred dollars for each of you ... call it a J. J. House bonus. No need to thank me; you've both earned it." Joanna put her purse over her shoulder and said, "Let's go relieve Gracie of some of her inventory, shall we?"

Spending time with Joanna was comforting. Somehow it made Liza feel close to Melvin, and shopping *always* made her feel better.

After trying on almost everything in the store, they came away with a couple of bags each. This time, Liza didn't have to bring a red pen to mark the price down.

Mr. Mittens was waiting by the door as Sarah opened it. He inspected her bags when she put them down to take her shoes off.

"Trying on clothes is a humbling experience," she said. "Everything I tried on seemed a little tight on me."

"You look great in everything," Joanna said.

"Thank you, Joanna. That's very kind of you to say. I think I'll have to start watching my weight if I want to fit into the wedding dress I like come next June."

"I watch my weight every day," Joanna said. "I watch it go up and up and up!"

Liza started laughing, which was a welcome relief from all the crying she'd been doing.

"We can start watching our weight tomorrow. Tonight, we're going to stuff ourselves with pizza and drink wine.

Here's the wine, Liza; go ahead and open it. Sarah, the wine glasses are in the cupboard beside the pantry. I'll put the pizza to bake, and while we're waiting, we can go sit by the fireplace. Sam got it all ready for us. I just have to light it."

They watched the wood crackle and burn, drank their wine, and managed to eat the whole extra-large deluxe pizza.

"Sam could open up his own pizza joint," Sarah said. "This is the best pizza I've ever had."

"There's really nothing Sam could not do," Joanna said. "I don't know what I would do without him."

"I don't think you have to worry about that, Joanna. Sam is very happy here," Liza said.

"I'm really glad you girls have come to work here. You fit in perfectly. Not only with the children, but with the staff too. The house feels more like home now."

"It's a wonderful place to be," Liza said.

"Do me a favour, girls."

"Of course, just name it," Sarah said.

"Don't tell Alice we were drinking wine tonight. She thinks it should be reserved for special occasions and weekends."

"What happens at J. J. House stays at J. J. House," Liza pledged.

"I'll drink to that!" Sarah said. "Now, if you'll excuse me, I'm going to the little girls' room."

Once Sarah left the room, Joanna said, "Being away from the one you love is not easy, but you're surrounded by people who love you, and whether you realize it or not, are watching over you. It may not be immediately obvious to you, but if you look closely, you'll see. It's in all the little things."

Chapter Thirty-Eight

The Letter

LIZA'S FAVOURITE TIME OF THE DAY was early morning when she spent time with Sam, after Joanna had gone to work and before Sarah arrived for breakfast. Liza drank coffee and Sam cooked.

There was no shortage of conversation. They discussed the meaning of life, love, happiness, family, music, work, and any other topic under the sun ... and the moon and the stars.

It had been almost four weeks since Melvin left. No word yet. As each day passed, Liza grew stronger, and the feelings of emptiness and sadness were replaced with hope, purpose, and resolve.

During the day, Liza worked alongside Alice in the classroom. She focused on the children and tried to keep up with Alice, whose energy seemed boundless. Liza, Alice, and Isaiah would have coffee together at recess. Sam always made sure to pack extra snacks so she had enough to share. Sam happened to know they all loved cinnamon doughnuts.

At lunch, Liza and Sarah would meet outside at the picnic table. After they ate, they would walk in the flower garden before heading back to class.

Every day after work, Liza hurried home to change out of her work clothes, put on comfy clothes, find and carry Mr.

Mittens to the kitchen with her, sit down, and pet him while she told Sam all about her day. Sam would make an after-school snack for her ... just like her mom used to. Except the conversation she and Sam had was more meaningful. Probably because Sam had a wealth of life experience and wisdom to impart, which he did so willingly. Her mom didn't share easily and was quite reserved most of the time. Liza got the feeling her mom was only half-listening at the best of times and had the same feeling still. When her father was home, Liza would play outside after school until dinner was ready and go directly to her room afterwards.

The time Liza spent with Joanna was just as precious as her time with Sam. Their evening pastime included tea by the fireplace and lots of stories about Joanna's life. She told Liza about her life in the entertainment business. It didn't sound very glamorous. They were used to playing small-time clubs and being relegated to meagre accommodations. There were no fancy dressing rooms back then. Joanna and the other girls had to dress in a hotel kitchen pantry once, in between shelves that housed pots and pans, flour, sugar, and other supplies. One of Joanna's fondest memories was the night they entertained at a bar mitzvah. It was held at a pretty *swanky* hotel.

The dressing room was large, clean, nicely decorated, and even had a full-length mirror on the wall! They weren't always sure what would be provided, so they travelled with a lot of extras: their own mirror, clothes-hangers, small folding chairs, and believe it or not, toilet paper!

They dressed and were ready to go on stage when the rabbi came to invite them to dinner *and* said they had a reserved V.I.P. table. That was a first! He ushered them in and said, "First we eat, *then* we work!" Joanna recalled being paid quite handsomely that night.

Liza began attending church with Joanna, for the ten o'clock Sunday morning service. It was completely opposite to what she was used to. The church back home was very conservative. She found it quite boring and often dozed during the sermon. There was no dozing here! People were on their feet singing, praising, dancing, Amen-ing, and having fun. Liza came away feeling uplifted, invigorated ... and hungry. Sam had weekends off, so when they got home after church, Joanna used Annie Mae's recipe and cooked up some grits and gravy. They kept it a secret from Sam and Sarah. Sam didn't mention the fact that he noticed things missing from the supply cupboard; he just replaced them.

Liza and Joanna surprised Sarah and Farley one Sunday and joined them at the diner for the Sunday Special, much to Flo's delight.

Meatloaf Monday was still a regular occurrence. Farley was the guest of honour, and Sam would always pack up the leftovers for him to take home.

Tuesdays and Thursdays Sarah stayed at home with Liza and Joanna. After dinner Tuesday was set aside for wedding planning. Joanna was the official wedding consultant. Sarah hadn't made a decision about her wedding dress, so they continued to look through wedding magazines. They also looked for bridesmaid dresses, floral arrangements, bouquets, china patterns, honeymoon destinations, and wedding rings. They spoke to Simon about the possibility of custom design for the wedding rings. Since Joanna was a loyal customer and long-time friend, he offered to give Sarah the *friends and family discount*.

Twice a month on Thursdays, Joanna had meetings to attend: church council meetings on the first Thursday of the month, and town council meeting on the last Thursday of the month.

Sunday night was pizza night. Sarah would return early from Farley's and they would order from the diner. Joanna would do the pick-up. It wasn't as good as Sam's, but it did the trick.

Each night, Liza would sprinkle a couple of drops of Melvin's fragrance on the pillowcase. After she got into bed, Liza had taken to staring at the phone on her desk, trying to *will* it to ring. Needless to say, it didn't work.

Exactly a month to the day that Melvin left, Liza received a letter. It was on the kitchen table when she came in after work.

"What's this, Sam?"

"That letter came for you today, Miss Liza."

She inspected it but couldn't tell where the postmark was from.

"Do you think it's from Melvin?" she said.

"Only one way to find out, Miss Liza."

Liza opened the letter and recognized the writing immediately. It was from Marcus. Sam listened as she read.

> Dear Liza,
>
> I hope you are enjoying your summer and things are going well for you in Waterford. By now you have had the pleasure of meeting Flo and have eaten at the diner. I trust she has taken good care of you. I'm looking forward to hearing all about your adventures when you return. I'm sure the children are keeping you busy!
>
> Our African Safari has turned out to be the best vacation we've ever had. Unfortunately, we have to cut our time here short. The publisher has changed the deadline for submission. Instead of the original August

> deadline, it has been moved up. The deadline is now July 15.
>
> I'm sorry to have to ask you to change your plans, but it will be necessary that you return to the office for the beginning of July in order to prepare the manuscript. I will look forward to seeing you then.
>
> Sincerely, Marcus

Liza looked up from the letter and said, "I didn't want to go home for the August deadline; I definitely don't want to go back *sooner*!"

"Your boss needs you, Miss Liza."

"I want to stay here, Sam."

"I know, Miss Liza. I can't tell you what to do, but I'm sure Miss Joanna will help you to decide."

"Decide what?" Joanna said. "I know it's Tuesday, but we have to have our dinner first before we make any more decisions about Sarah's wedding."

"It's not about *that*; it's about *this*," Liza said and handed the letter to Joanna.

Before Joanna finished reading the letter, Liza said, "I don't want to go back. I love being here with you and Sam and Alice and the children."

"What about me?" Sarah said and sat beside Liza.

"Here, read this letter, Sarah," Joanna said.

"You can't leave yet!" Sarah said.

"I don't want to leave at *all*!"

"I understand how you feel, Liza. As much as I want you to stay, your first obligation is to your boss and your job back home," Joanna said.

"Wait a minute ... why can't Ethel type the manuscript for Marcus? Didn't she work for him before you did?" Sarah said.

"Very briefly. Marcus had to let her go. She made so many typing errors he couldn't submit his last manuscript. In addition to that, she didn't know how to work the switchboard properly. Instead of placing someone on hold and then transferring the call, she would accidentally hang up on them. She resorted to placing the call on hold and then walking down the hall and telling Marcus there was a phone call for him. Ethel would take messages for Marcus and then forget to give them to him. *That's* when he let *her* go and hired *me*."

"I guess there's no point in coming back here after you prepare the manuscript, since there would only be a couple of weeks left on the term," Sarah said.

"Once again, bad timing," Liza said sadly.

"It's an obligation you must fulfill," Joanna said.

"You're right, Joanna," Liza said.

"We'll just have to make the best of these two weeks," Sarah said.

"How 'bout some dinner to start your Tuesday night weddin' plannin'," Sam said.

"I'm not in the mood for wedding planning tonight," Liza said.

"Me neither," Sarah added.

"What *are* you girls in the mood for?" Joanna said.

"Wine," Liza said.

"Ditto," Sarah said.

"I'll go down to the wine cellar and see what I can find," Joanna said.

"You have a wine cellar?" Liza said.

"I have to entertain on occasion and need to have something on hand to offer my guests," Joanna explained.

"Would you like me to set the dining table?" Sam offered.

"I think we'll just eat right here at the kitchen table tonight ... just like we used to at home when we didn't have a dining room! You girls set the table and I'll see about the wine."

"I fried up some pickerel for you girls, so you might want to choose white wine to go with it," Sam said.

"Good idea! If you don't have to rush off, Sam, why don't you join us?"

"That's real nice of you for askin', Miss Joanna, but I'm headin' home for some of my wife's beef stew. Hers is better than mine, and I get to relax and watch television. I'll serve up dinner for you girls and then be on my way."

***

Liza didn't feel much like talking or laughing but managed to do both while Joanna and Sarah were telling jokes and acting silly throughout dinner. She knew they were only trying to cheer her up ... and it worked. She forgot all about the letter. The white wine tasted good but made her sleepy. When she started yawning, Joanna gave her a hug and sent her off to bed. Sarah and Mr. Mittens walked her to her room.

"I hope your phone rings tonight," Sarah said.

Liza fell asleep staring at the phone. She fell asleep quickly and began dreaming. She dreamed the phone was ringing. She answered and said, "Hello," but no one was there. She said "Hello" two or three more times and actually woke herself up talking in her sleep. Then she realized the phone actually was ringing. Liza got tangled up in her sheets, tripped, and landed on her knees. She pulled on the cord and the phone came toward her.

"Hello," she said desperately, hoping she wasn't too late.

She thought she heard Melvin's voice, but it was breaking up.

"Hello," she repeated.

"Princess?"

"Melvin?"

"Hello, Princess?"

"Yes, it's me!"

"Princess, can you hear me?"

"Yes, I can hear you! Can you hear me?"

"Now I can! I miss you so much!" he said.

"I miss you too, Melvin. How are you doing?"

"I'm okay. The project is going well. How are you doing?"

"I'm okay too. I was dreaming the phone was ringing. I woke up talking in my sleep, saying hello, and the phone really was ringing."

"I'm glad you woke up!"

"I have something to tell you, Melvin."

"I love you, Princess."

"I love you too, Melvin. I got a letter from—"

"Princess, I can't hear—"

"Melvin? Melvin!"

The line went dead. Liza sat on the floor with the receiver in her hand, listening to the dial tone. She hung up the phone, left it on the floor, and got back into bed. If by some miracle he called back, at least she could reach the phone easily.

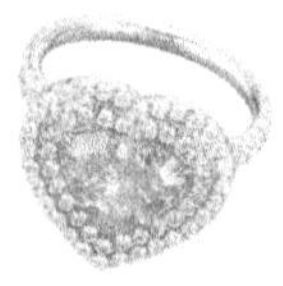

Chapter Thirty-Nine

Homeward Bound

SAM ARRIVED AT SIX-THIRTY every morning and typically fired up the griddle and then made the coffee. This morning was different. Liza beat him to the punch. The griddle was on and the coffee was ready.

"Good morning, Sam!"

"Miss Liza? What are you doing up already?"

"I don't know. I woke up and couldn't fall back to sleep, so I thought I'd get started on my day. Want some coffee?"

"I'm the one who should be askin' you that question."

"Here you go," Liza said. "Two creams, one sugar, right?"

"Yes, Miss Liza. How did you know?"

"Like Alice, I pay attention. By the way, Melvin called last night."

"He did? I was wonderin' when he'd be callin' you."

"You and me both!"

"Did you have a nice time catchin' up?"

"It was nice while it lasted."

"What do you mean, Miss Liza?"

"The connection wasn't very good. At first I could hear him, but he couldn't hear me. When the line finally cleared, Melvin said he loves me and misses me. He said his project was going well."

"Sounds like you covered the most important things, Miss Liza."

"There's only one problem, Sam. The line went dead before I could tell Melvin I'm going home in two weeks. Who knows when he'll be able to call again, and when he does, I won't be here. Then what?"

"If he doesn't get an answer when he calls your room, he'll call Miss Joanna. She'll explain that you went home."

"I suppose you're right."

"Now, you need to eat a little somethin', Miss Liza. What do you fancy?"

"How about French toast and bacon, please."

"I'll have it ready in a jiffy."

"Do you mind if I take my breakfast and coffee to my room? I should call my mom and tell her I'm coming home."

"I'm sure she'll be happy that you're comin' back. I'll put your breakfast on a tray for you."

"Could you please tell Sarah her wish for me came true. Melvin did call last night, and tell Joanna also. I don't want to have to repeat the story too many times."

"Yes, of course, Miss Liza."

***

Liza was surprised and taken a little off guard when she called home and Junior answered.

"Hello."

"Junior?"

"Hi, Liza!"

"What are you doing up so early?"

"I'm cramming for my final math exam this morning. What's up?"

"I got a letter from Marcus yesterday. I have to be back in the office on July 1. I was calling to let you guys know I'm coming home."

"That's awesome! It's Liza, Mom. She's coming home! Hold on, Mom, I'll give you the phone in a minute. Mom is trying to wrestle the phone away from me. See you when you get home—"

"Hi dear! You're coming home?"

"Yes, Mom. I'll be home in two weeks."

"That's wonderful news! Do you want us to drive to Waterford and pick you up?"

"That's not necessary, Mom. No point in driving all the way out here just to turn around and drive back home again. I'll take the bus home."

"Are you sure, dear?"

"Yes, Mom. The coach buses I've seen here seem quite deluxe, and I'm sure they're very comfortable. I can just relax and enjoy the scenery along the way."

"Call me when you make the arrangements. I'll plan to pick you up at the bus station."

"I will, Mom. I have to go to the daycare now. I'll call you soon."

"I love you, dear. I'm glad you're coming home."

"I love you too, Mom."

Liza brushed her hair, put some lipstick on, and decided to change into a more casual outfit. She glanced out the window and saw Joanna heading over to the daycare.

***

"Good morning, Isaiah," Liza said as she walked past the security desk.

"Good morning to you, Liza. Alice is already in the classroom."

"I figured as much. See you at recess."

Liza cut through the library. She walked into the classroom and called out, "Hi, Alice!"

"You look tired," Alice said.

"I am tired."

"Staring at the phone too late and for too long again?"

"I didn't stare at it too long. I fell asleep pretty quickly. It did ring, though. Melvin called." Liza told Alice about her short conversation with Melvin before telling her that she would be leaving.

"A *short* conversation is better than *no* conversation!" Alice said.

"You're right. It sure was nice to hear Melvin's voice. It's been so long."

"Treasure the moments you have. Even the little moments add up!"

"Your words of encouragement mean a lot, Alice."

"I get the feeling there's something else you want to tell me," Alice said.

"There is one more thing." Liza told Alice about the letter she'd received from Marcus.

"I'm sorry I have to leave before the end of the term. I'm really going to miss you and the kids."

"I'm sorry you have to leave too, Liza. I'll miss having you here, and I know the children will miss you too. They've all come to love you ... especially Harvey."

"I love them too. Especially Harvey!"

"Isaiah and I will miss having coffee and cinnamon doughnuts with you at recess. I'll have to talk Sam into sending some doughnuts over from time to time."

"When I'm back at the office, I'll take my coffee break at ten and pretend it's recess. I'll have coffee and a cinnamon doughnut and think of you and Isaiah."

"We'll have to get Sam to make one more batch of cupcakes before you leave," Alice said.

"Cupcakes?"

"We've had birthday cupcakes, Miss Liza's Love Day cupcakes, and now we will need *farewell* cupcakes."

"That would be very nice, Alice."

"In the meantime, we have young people to teach and destinies to shape. As one of my former teachers used to say, 'Put your thinking cap on. It's time to take on the day!'"

***

Joanna joined Liza, Alice, and Isaiah for coffee at recess and brought fresh cinnamon doughnuts with her.

"Sam told Sarah and me about your late-night phone call from Melvin," Joanna said as she dunked her doughnut in her coffee. "I'm glad he was finally able to call you. How did he sound?"

"He sounded great and said the project is going well."

"I'm happy to hear that," Joanna said.

"By the time he calls again, I won't be here," Liza lamented.

"Don't worry your pretty little self," Isaiah said. "You'll find each other. Just trust that he loves you and know that everything will work out in the end."

Chapter Forty

Flo and the Angel

LIZA WAS NOT LOOKING FORWARD to leaving her Waterford family—the new family she had grown to know and love. After Melvin left, she had to get used to being in Waterford without him. Now she had to get used to not being there at all. Even though it was difficult, leaving was easier than being left.

One week from Saturday, at seven in the morning, Liza would be on the bus going home. There were a couple of scheduled rest stops along the way, which meant arrival would be twelve hours later.

With only one full weekend in Waterford left, Sunday was set aside for church, then Liza's last Sunday Special at the diner. Joanna had plans to meet with the pastor and his wife for coffee after church, so Farley and Sarah picked Liza up.

The reserved sign was on their favourite table, just as it had been every Sunday. Sarah and Farley had never missed a Sunday Special since they'd started going there with Liza and Melvin.

"Ya'll are right on time!" Flo said, standing by their table and pouring coffee. "I hear yer goin' home and leavin' us all behind, girlie."

"Yes, that's right, Flo," Liza said sadly.

"Here ya go girlie; since I won't be seein' ya no more, I got ya somethin' so you won't forgit me."

"I could never forgit, I mean forget you, Flo!"

Liza opened her gift to find a beautiful little crystal angel.

"It's so pretty, Flo!"

"When ya look at her, remember ya got yerself a guardian angel watchin' over ya and keepin' ya safe."

Liza stood up and hugged Flo. They were both crying but trying not to show it.

"Thank you, Flo. I will treasure this angel and carry it with me always."

"Yer welcome, girlie. I better go and git yer food before Frankie starts ringin' the hurry-up bell."

"What a nice gift," Sarah said.

"Flo will surprise you when you least expect it," Farley said. "She surprised Hector with a gift for Harvey on Friday when Hector and I were here for lunch. It was a toy cement truck that looks exactly like the one Hector operates."

"That's so thoughtful. Harvey will probably bring it to school for show and tell," Liza said.

When Flo returned with their orders, they saw that Frankie had given them a double portion and an extra plate of bacon.

"Wow, Flo—" Liza started to say.

"Shh, don't say nothin'. Frankie was feelin' extra generous today. I'll bring ya some more hot coffee."

"I don't know where to start," Sarah said.

"I do. Right here in the middle." Farley stuck his fork into the centre of his food and came up with a large deep fried pickle.

Sarah and Liza followed Farley's lead.

Flo poured more coffee into their cups and whispered, "Yer Sunday Specials are on the house today. A present from Frankie. Don't nobody else plan on leavin' jest to git yer next meal free around here," she said.

"We're not going anywhere," Farley said.

"All right then. That's what I wanna hear."

Liza wrapped both hands around her coffee cup to warm them and drank from it the same way.

Sarah noticed and said, "Are you feeling okay?"

"I feel a little tired. I just haven't been sleeping too well."

"Maybe you should have a nap after we drop you off," Sarah said.

"I might do that," Liza said.

"Just think, next Sunday you'll be eating breakfast at home."

"Don't remind me, Sarah."

"I'm going to miss you when you go," Sarah said.

"I'm still here for another week."

"Six days," Farley said with his mouth full.

"Farley! Don't talk with your mouth full!" Sarah scolded.

"It won't be too long before you and Farley come home."

"Six weeks," Farley said.

"We can look forward to hanging out then."

"That will be fun. Thanks to you and Joanna, I can tell my mom all about the progress we've made with the wedding plans. We can start shopping for my wedding dress. Things are moving along quite well ... right, Farley?"

"Right. Pass the bacon, please."

"Don't eat it all," Sarah said as she passed the plate.

"I'm not."

"I'm going to miss Flo, eating here, and the deep fried pickles," Liza said. She paused and then said, "I just thought of something. I bet Aunt Sadie could get the chef at the hotel to make them."

"That would be great!" Farley said.

"All of a sudden you're joining the conversation?" Sarah said.

"It's something I'm interested in."

"Oh, you're interested in *pickles*, but not our *wedding*!"

"Of course I'm interested in our wedding. I didn't think you needed my input. You girls seem to have everything under control."

"Good answer, Farley," Liza said.

"You're off the hook this time, buster."

Farley kissed Sarah on the cheek and patted her hand.

"I won't be able to finish all of my breakfast," Sarah admitted.

"That's okay. We'll get Flo to give us a take-out container and pack up the leftovers. I'll have breakfast for tomorrow," Farley said happily.

Farley waved to Flo. She got a container from behind the counter and brought it over.

"Here ya go, Sparky," Flo said.

"Has he done this before?" Sarah said.

"Ya betcha. Every time he comes in for lunch. Frankie gives the boys extra, just so they kin take some home. Frankie has a soft spot for them guys workin' on them new roads they're buildin'!"

"Thank you, Flo, and thank Frankie too," Farley said.

"Yer welcome."

"If everyone is done, I guess we should head out," Liza said.

"I don't like sayin' goodbye. I'll jest say see ya when ya pass this way agin sometime."

"See you again sometime, Flo. It's been a pleasure spending time here with you," Liza said.

"Likewise, girlie. Take care of yerself."

"You too, Flo."

"See you tomorrow, Flo. Hector and I will be for lunch at the usual time."

"See ya tomorrow, Sparky."

"I'll see you next Sunday, Flo," Sarah said.

"Okie dokie."

Liza was teary-eyed when she got into Farley's truck. She wiped her tears on her sleeve, took the crystal angel from her purse, and held it on the way back to Joanna's.

"Thanks for the ride. See you later, Sarah. I'm going to take a nap now. I'm quite tired."

"When we get back to the apartment, I'm going to have a nap too," Sarah said.

"Bye, Sparky," Liza joked.

Four hours later, Liza emerged from her bedroom and went to the sitting room.

"Hello there, Sleeping Beauty. I was wondering what time you were going to wake up. It's almost time for me to go pick up the pizza," Joanna said.

Liza looked like she was still half asleep and couldn't help yawning. She sat in her usual spot beside the fireplace.

"I can't believe I slept for so long and I still feel tired. I'm glad you have the fire going. It gets cool here in the evenings. Back home it doesn't cool down as quickly."

"Here, this will help." Joanna handed Liza the blanket she always wrapped around her shoulders when she read before bedtime.

No sooner had Liza covered herself with the blanket when Mr. Mittens came around the corner, jumped on her lap, and started cozying up to her.

"Since you've been here, I've been playing second fiddle to you when it comes to Mr. Mittens. He's going to be a little lost without you."

Mr. Mittens looked up at Liza.

"I'll miss you too, Mr. Mittens."

"Sorry I'm a little late," Sarah said as she rushed in. "I had a nap and overslept. Farley had to wake me up or I'd still be sleeping."

"You're not the only one. Sleeping Beauty just woke up from her nap a few minutes ago," Joanna said.

"I didn't realize I was so tired. There's no reason for it. I haven't been staying awake half the night staring at *my* phone."

"Very funny, Sarah."

"You two try and stay awake. I'm going to get the pizza."

"We'll try," Liza said.

"It's going to be really quiet around here without you."

"I'm going to miss my conversations with Sam."

"He's going to miss you too. My conversations with Sam are different from the ones you have with him. I don't think I'll know what to say to him."

"You'll figure it out, Sarah. Ask him for some tips on marriage. He's really good at giving advice."

"Okay, I will." Sarah lowered her voice to a whisper and said, "I'm not supposed to say anything, but Joanna is planning a little going away party Friday at the daycare, and a dinner here Friday night. Farley and Sam are joining us. Joanna is ordering food from the diner so Sam doesn't have to cook."

"All that for me? Alice mentioned ordering cupcakes for the daycare, but I didn't know about the Friday night dinner."

For the next half hour, Sarah continued to fill Liza in on the party plans.

"Joanna's back. I just saw her car," Sarah said. "I better go get the plates and napkins."

"Pizza is here!" Joanna called out.

"Mmm, it sure smells good!" Liza said.

"Shall we eat here in front of the fireplace? Mr. Mittens doesn't look like he's going to be moving from your lap any time soon!"

"Meow."

"There's your answer," Joanna said.

Sarah came in carrying the plates, glasses, napkins, and a jug of water.

"I think I'll just have water with the pizza," Sarah said. "Anyone else?"

"I'd like some water," Joanna said.

"Me too," Liza said.

"Raise your glasses, girls. A toast to Liza. You've been with us for a short time, but it's been a good time. May the rest of your time be the best of your time! And may this water taste like wine!"

Chapter Forty-One

Solidarity

MONDAY MORNING, it was business as usual. Sam and Liza enjoyed their morning conversation and agreed to meet earlier for the rest of the week to maximize their time. Liza gave Sam a heads-up about the farewell cupcakes for Friday. She said Alice would be placing the order, but she wanted to request some with blue icing and white sprinkles. Sam said he would make sure of it.

At the daycare, the children followed their usual routine. Alice started each Monday with an overview of the week ahead. She began by explaining that Liza would be going home and this would be her last week with them. The children were visibly upset and voiced their sadness and disappointment. When Alice announced that they would be having a farewell party on Friday with cupcakes for a special treat, their disappointment suddenly changed to excitement.

She revealed plans for new enrichment activities to make the week fun and memorable. She went on to review the calendar with them as they recited the days of the week, months of the year, and practised counting. *Show and Tell* was up next. Three children were scheduled to present. Harvey was first. When Alice called upon him, he said he didn't have anything to share, which surprised Liza. She thought he would show the toy cement truck he'd gotten from Flo.

For the rest of the week, Harvey stayed inordinately close to Liza. Wherever she went, he went.

***

Friday at the farewell celebration, Alice presented Liza with a card the children had signed for her and a white t-shirt with *J.J. Daycare* in black lettering across the front.

"Thank you all very much. I will miss each and every one of you."

Penelope called out, "*Now* can we have cupcakes?"

Liza laughed and said, "Yes, we can have cupcakes."

After she and Alice served the cupcakes, Liza sat and ate with Harvey.

"Miss Liza?"

"Yes, Harvey?"

"Can I tell you something?"

"Sure, Harvey. What is it?"

"I'm gonna miss you."

"I'm gonna miss you too, Harvey."

"First my mommy left, and now you're leaving too, and I'm really sad."

Tears started to well up in Liza's eyes. "I'm sad too, Harvey."

"You know, you're kinda like my mommy at school, cuz you're always so nice to me and you let me hold your hand. When you have your own kid, they're gonna be real lucky cuz you're a good mommy. You can tell them I said so."

Liza could barely get any words out. She managed to say, "I will."

Harvey put his cupcake down and stood up. He threw his arms around Liza's neck and hugged her as tightly as he could. He didn't see the tears streaming down her face. She held on to him with one arm while she reached up to brush her tears away. Harvey let go, sat down, picked up his cupcake, and continued eating.

"I'm glad I got one with blue icing. Blue is my favourite."

"I know, you told me."

Penelope walked over and stood in front of Liza.

"Hello, Penelope."

"Miss Liza?"

"Yes, Penelope?"

"You have blue icing in your hair."

"That's okay. I'll be washing my hair later. Thank you for telling me."

"You're welcome, Miss Liza," Penelope said and went back to her table.

"I'm finished my cupcake, Miss Liza. Could you wipe my hands for me? They're a bit sticky from the icing."

"Of course, Harvey. I have a paper towel right here."

Liza wiped the icing from his hands. Harvey inspected them and said, "I have a present for you, Miss Liza."

"You do?"

Harvey reached into his pocket and pulled out his cement truck.

"Here," he said.

"That's your special toy, Harvey. I can't accept it."

"Yes, you can. It's a *present*. A present is when you give something to someone cuz you love them and you want to make their heart happy. That's what my daddy told me."

"Thank you, Harvey. You made my heart very happy. I have a present for you too." It just so happened that Liza was carrying the crystal angel in her pocket. She reached into her pocket and took it out. When she gave it to him, she said, "You have to be very careful with this, because it can break easily."

"I *love* it, Miss Liza! Angels are good. They come from heaven to protec you. My daddy told me that too."

"Yes, they do, Harvey."

"I think we should wrap it up in a paper towel and put it in my pac pac to keep it safe. When I get home, I'm gonna put it on my night table beside my bed. I won't be afraid of the dark anymore, cuz I will have a special angel watchin' over me. It's special cuz you gave it to me and when I look at it, my heart will be happy. It's good for hearts to be happy. Right, Miss Liza?" Harvey said, seemingly without taking a breath.

"Yes, Harvey, that's right."

For the rest of the day, Harvey was much happier. He played with the other children at recess and enjoyed the enrichment activities.

Liza stood at the door at the end of the day and hugged each of the children as they left. Harvey was the last to leave. He hugged Liza and said, "I can hardly wait to show my angel to my daddy. He's going to love it, just like me. I'll say my prayers for you to get back home to your mommy and daddy safe."

"Thank you, Harvey."

"Bye, Miss Liza. I love you."

"Goodbye, Harvey. I love you too."

"Bye, Miss Alice."

"Goodbye, Harvey. See you on Monday."

Alice handed Liza a box of tissues. "Thought you might need one or two of these."

"Thank you, Alice. It's been quite a day."

"They really grow on you, don't they?"

"They sure do."

"Harvey will be okay, Liza. His dad and his grandmother will make sure of that."

"He's an amazing little boy."

"He's got a very bright future in front of him, that's evident," Alice said.

Isaiah walked into the classroom and said, "Where's the deserter?"

Liza stopped wiping her tears and started laughing.

"It's not my choice to be a deserter," she said.

"We were just getting used to having you around, and now you're leaving us," Alice said.

"I would much rather stay."

"Even though we only had you for a little while, we're just glad we could have you," Isaiah said.

"You and Alice will always have a special place in my heart. You're my family, and I won't forget you," Liza said.

"We won't forget you either, young lady," Alice said.

"Anyone else coming through here gonna have some big shoes to fill! Our dinner talk is gonna be a lot shorter now. Alice won't have you talk about: Liza did this today and Liza did that today and Liza said this and so on."

"Isaiah! You're not supposed to spill my secrets."

Liza hugged Alice and said, "You're the best, Alice. I'm glad I was part of your dinner conversation. When I get home, you'll be part of mine!"

"Don't forget to mention my natural beauty!"

"That's the first thing I'll mention!" Liza said.

"Come on, beauty queen. It's time to go home to our castle," Isaiah said. Isaiah hugged Liza. "Be safe out there."

"You and Alice look after each other."

"Always do, always do," Isaiah said. "Let's go, girls," he said.

Alice and Isaiah walked ahead. Liza took one last look around the classroom before she shut the lights off and closed the door.

She was still thinking about Harvey, Alice, and Isaiah as she left the daycare. She walked next door and hadn't quite gotten to the front door when it flew open.

"*Surprise*!" Joanna, Sam, Sarah, and Farley jumped out in front of her. They were wearing party hats, and behind them she could see balloons and streamers everywhere. Liza really *was* surprised. She knew about the dinner, because Sarah had secretly told her, but she didn't expect anything like this.

"Hey, everybody! What's all this?"

"We wanted to surprise you with a farewell dinner party," Joanna answered.

"I had farewell cupcakes with what kids earlier, and now I get a farewell dinner too. How lucky can one girl get?"

"Here's your party hat," Sarah said. She gave Liza a fluorescent pink top hat. On it, the words *PARTY GIRL* were spelled out in silver sparkles.

As Liza put it on, Joanna said, "This calls for a toast. Everyone please help yourself to a glass of Champagne. Sam, please do the honours."

"To Miss Liza—may you touch the hearts of others the way you touched ours, all along the journey comin' your way."

"To Liza," they all said.

"That is so beautiful, Sam, thank you!"

"Come, let's sit down and enjoy our Champagne," Joanna said as she led the way to the dining room. "We have time before our dinner gets delivered."

"Delivered?" Liza said, pretending she didn't know the food had been ordered from the diner.

"Yes. Since Sam is joining us tonight, our dinner is coming to us courtesy of Frankie."

"This really is very special. I've never had a surprise party before. All the balloons and streamers make it so festive."

"Sam and I spent most of the day decorating," Joanna said.

"No wonder I didn't see you at the daycare today. It means a lot to me that you're all here and you went to so much trouble."

"No trouble at all, Miss Liza."

"We had fun planning it," Sarah said.

The doorbell rang. "That must be our food," Joanna said.

"Yay, the food is here," Farley said.

"Hi, Rocky. Come in. How are you doing tonight?"

Liza sat quietly and listened. Did she just say, *Hi Rocky*? she thought.

"Just fine, Ms. Jones. Been awhile since I been out here."

"Thank you for making the delivery for us."

"You're welcome. I help out from time to time. The regular driver was off sick tonight, so Flo called me."

"We're glad she did. Here you go, Rocky. No change necessary."

"Thank you, Ms. Jones."

"See you next time, Rocky."

"Farley? Can you come and carry a couple of these bags, please?"

"Be right there."

They carried them into the dining room.

"Just put them on the cart and we'll unload from here. Sam is our guest, so it's up to you and me."

"At your service," Farley said and saluted.

They put all of the containers on the table. Joanna said grace and announced, "Dinner is served."

"It feels like we were gathered around this table celebrating our first day at the daycare, and here we are commemorating my *last* day," Liza said.

"A lot has happened in a short time," Sarah said.

"Melvin was here that day, and now he's away somewhere," Liza said.

"We never know what tomorrow is gonna be bringin'. That's why we need to be here, now! They call today the *present*, cuz it's a *gift* to be livin' today. So don't waste your time thinkin' too soon about tomorrow; you can live tomorrow when it gets here. No sooner than that!"

"You're right, Sam." Liza put her hand in her pocket to get a tissue and felt the little cement truck. She held on to it for a moment. She decided against showing it to everyone.

"I guess it will be a big adjustment going back to work in the office and not having the children around you all day," Joanna said.

"That's for sure! There is one thing that will stay the same."

"Oh, what's that?" Joanna said.

"I told Alice and Isaiah that I'd have cinnamon doughnuts and coffee for my morning break and pretend it's recess."

"Let's all do that!" Sarah said.

"Great idea," Farley said.

"Here's to solidarity," Joanna said.

"Doughnuts for all!" Liza said.

"Looks like I got some bakin' to do," Sam said.

"You'll have to get up a little earlier each day, Sarah, and take my place for early morning conversations with Sam."

"I'd love to."

"I told Sarah you always give the best advice, Sam"

"You're bein' kind, Miss Liza."

"It's true! You've helped me *so* much, Sam. I should have recorded our conversations so I could listen to your words again and again."

"Anytime you want to call, you know where to find me, Miss Liza."

"Thank you, Sam."

"What time are you leavin' in the mornin'?"

"I'll be on the first bus out at seven, Sam."

"You'll be needin' a ride then," he said.

"I'll drive Liza to the bus depot," Joanna offered.

"I'd like to come along, Miss Joanna."

"Me too," Sarah said.

"Not me," Farley said. "I need my beauty sleep. Getting up at six every morning for work is enough for me."

"No problem, Sparky!" Liza said.

Joanna laughed.

Mr. Mittens quietly walked into the dining room toward Liza.

"Looks like you got yourself a visitor, Miss Liza."

"Mr. Mittens! Where have you been?"

He jumped up and sat on her lap, facing her.

"He's been helpin' us with the decoratin' today."

"I'm not sure getting tangled up in the streamers counts as *helping*," Joanna said.

"Meow."

"I'm very happy you guys will be going with me to the bus depot."

"I'll come in and make breakfast for you girls. You'll need a good start if you're travellin', Miss Liza."

"I'll sleep better knowing I'll see you all in the morning."

"Put something over the phone tonight so you're not tempted to stare at it," Joanna said.

"How does everyone know about that?"

"We've all done it at one time or another," Joanna said.

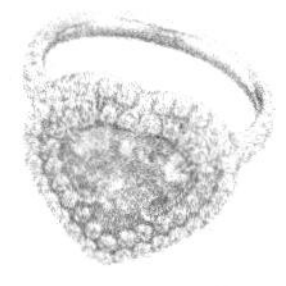

Chapter Forty-Two

Home Is Where the Heart Is

SARAH HELPED LIZA roll her suitcases down the hallway, out the front door, down the steps, and into the open trunk of Joanna's car. Sam came out carrying one more bag, which he also put into the trunk and then closed it. They all got into the car, slammed the doors simultaneously, and drove off.

"What a whirlwind!" Liza said.

"It's always hectic when folks are leavin' for a trip," Sam said.

"I had some last-minute packing to do, which took me longer than I thought."

"Packing *always* takes longer than you think, and when everything *is* packed, you always feel like you're forgetting something," Joanna said.

"Most of the time you are," Sarah said.

"I'm pretty sure I didn't forget anything."

"I'll check your room when we get back," Sarah offered.

Liza looked at her ticket and said, "When we get to the station, we'll need to find bus #71."

***

A supervisor was directing passengers to the baggage drop off area beside the bus before lining up to board.

Joanna gave Liza a carry-on bag with the blanket she always used in the evenings, along with a little something from Mr. Mittens. "I found Mr. Mittens sitting on the blanket in the bag. I told him he wasn't allowed to go on the bus with you and he'd have to stay with me. He had *this* in the bag with him and wanted me to give it to you. It was the squeaky toy he always played with."

"Thank you for the blanket, Joanna, and please be sure to say thank you to Mr. Mittens for me."

Joanna hugged Liza and whispered, "If I had a daughter of my own, I'd want her to be exactly like you."

"I'm honoured, Joanna. I love you and I'll miss you very much."

Sam stepped forward and handed Liza an insulated bag. "This is your lunch, snacks, bottled water, and your favourite chicory coffee."

"Thank you, Sam. You have no idea how much you mean to me and how much you've helped me."

"I do have an idea, Miss Liza. This is for you too," he said. "I wrote this poem for you. I had to get permission from my wife, since she's the only one I ever was writin' to before."

Liza took the envelope and clutched it to her heart. Tears already flowing, Sam gave her a white cotton handkerchief with the letter "L" embroidered on it. "Somethin' to wipe away those tears."

"I love you, Sam."

"I love you too, Miss Liza."

"I'll be seeing you soon, so this is just a little something for now," Sarah said. She unrolled a piece of pink construction paper. It was full of pictures, words spelled with some of the letters written backwards, glitter, and hearts. "The kids helped me with this. It's a list of all the things we're going to do together when I get back."

"Looks like we're going to be busy!" Liza said.

"That's right!"

"People are boarding now," Joanna said.

Liza hugged Sarah, Joanna, and Sam. Sarah turned and hugged Joanna and Sam next.

"Wait a minute ... I'm not leaving!" Sarah said.

It added comic relief to the sad farewell and made everyone laugh.

"I'll miss you all!" Liza said and climbed the steps to board the bus.

"Miss you more!" Sarah called out.

Liza chose a window seat in the first row, the same seat she always chose when she rode the bus to work. She liked to see where she was going. She was happy the bus was only half-full and no one sat beside her. The passengers were mostly married couples.

Liza's plan was to relax and take in the sights. She realized her plan failed when the bus driver woke her up to say they had arrived at the first scheduled stop, which meant she had been asleep for hours. She wasn't exactly sure when she fell asleep. Not having remembered much of the scenery, she gathered, sleep came quickly.

The bus was parked in front of a homestyle restaurant, with pretty curtains that hung in each of the windows, and flowers along the sidewalk in planters and in hanging baskets. Liza went in to use the washroom and noticed an area reserved for "Bus #71" in the section along the window facing the highway. She decided to sit outside at one of the picnic tables out front and enjoy the fresh air.

Liza looked through the lunch bag to see what Sam had packed. She took out a ham and cheese sandwich and underneath were two cinnamon doughnuts, of which she ate one. She was glad for the chicory coffee, so she should stay awake for the balance of the trip.

As she was eating her sandwich, she reached for a napkin but instead pulled out the envelope and remembered she had Sam's poem to read. She took the handkerchief from her pocket before she opened the envelope.

For Miss Liza
The love in her heart
Makes other people's start.
For those she loves
Are the fortunate ones.
She'll pass this way but once,
And you'll know it when she does.
Though you may not know her name,
You'll never be the same.
For it's the heart that knows
It's you she chose.
Forever love she sows.

No wonder Sam's wife fell in love with and married him, Liza thought.

As they neared the bus station, Liza stared at the beautiful sunset. Every colour imaginable was splashed across the evening sky. The scenery she'd enjoyed up until then paled in comparison.

Helga was front and centre when Liza stepped off the bus, waving and calling her name.

"Liza! I'm here, dear!"

She couldn't miss her, even if she tried. "Mom, so nice to see you! I thought Junior might come along with you."

"He's out with John."

"Is—"

"Your father won't be home until next weekend."

Liza took a deep breath and felt a sense of peace and calm come over her.

"You look a little thinner than when you left," Helga observed.

"I don't think that's possible, considering all the good food Sam was feeding us. You look good, Mom."

"Thank you. Your brother and John have kept me company, and I've been cooking more than ever! Those boys sure can eat!"

"I remember."

"Tell me all about your time in Waterford, dear."

"It will take more than the time it takes to drive home, Mom. There's a lot to tell."

"Tell me about your classroom."

Liza began by telling her about the children and how much fun they had. She told her about Harvey, Alice, and Isaiah.

"They sound lovely."

"They definitely are."

Helga pulled into the garage. Liza went around to get the bags from the trunk.

"Why don't you leave those for now. I'll get the boys to carry them in for you later."

"Okay, I don't really need anything at the moment."

"Let's go in and have a nice cup of tea, and you can tell me more about the daycare."

Liza was first through the door. Junior, John, and Aunt Sadie jumped out and yelled, "*Surprise*!"

Liza had a flashback to a scene from the day before.

"Welcome home, Liza," Aunt Sadie said and hugged her with her usual gusto.

"Hey, Liza," Junior said and hugged her.

"Hi, John," Liza said.

Liza felt like she was in some sort of time warp. Instead of balloons and streamers for a farewell party, there were balloons and streamers for a welcome home party. The table was set with Helga's best china, crystal glasses, and sparkling silverware. There were also lit candles. The aroma of food cooking permeated the house.

"This is all very beautiful," Liza said.

"We missed you and wanted to show you just how much!" Aunt Sadie said.

"Sit down and relax, dear," Helga said.

The dinner, conversation, and being with family helped to replace Liza's sadness with happiness and ease her back into being home again in a comforting sort of way. She shared some of her stories and listened to the others as they shared theirs.

"Let me help you with dessert, Helga," Aunt Sadie said. Sadie carried in a large banana cream pie.

"Gloria made this especially for you, Liza."

"It looks delicious, Aunt Sadie."

Aunt Sadie served Liza first. Liza took a couple of bites and didn't feel well all of a sudden.

"Excuse me, please. I'll be right back." She left the table and hurried to the bathroom. She felt a cold sweat come over her and then she threw up. *Where did that come from?* she thought. She washed her face, brushed her teeth, and rejoined everyone in the dining room.

"Are you all right, dear?"

"Yes, Mom, I'm fine. I just felt sick all of a sudden."

"I'm sure it's been a long day for you, travelling all those hours on the bus. You were probably up really early this morning too," Aunt Sadie said.

"I'm sure that's it. I feel fine now, but I'm really tired. I'm sorry, Aunt Sadie, but I won't be able to finish my pie."

"Don't worry, dear! There's more where that came from!"

"Junior, when you and John are done, go out to the car and bring Liza's bags in," Helga said.

"Thank you all for the wonderful party. If you don't mind, I'm going to go to bed now. Mom, I'm not going to go to church with you and Junior in the morning. I'd like to sleep in."

"Of course, dear. You just sleep as long as you need to."

"Good night, everyone."

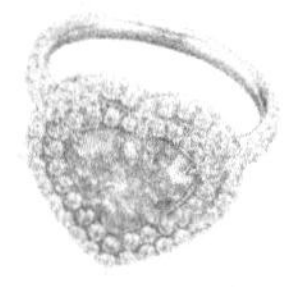

Chapter Forty-Three

The Signs

WAKING UP IN HER OWN BEDROOM, Liza couldn't tell if she was dreaming or if what she saw was real. She felt slightly disoriented. She slowly sat up and looked around, trying to get her bearings. As she sat on the side of the bed, the same cold sweat started again. She rushed to the bathroom and threw up. She brushed her teeth and went to lie down again. A few minutes later, the cold sweat subsided and she felt much better. *I've heard of "jet lag,"* she thought. Maybe this is "*bus lag.*" She chalked it up to being tired from the bus ride home, all the stress she had been feeling lately, and lack of sleep.

When Helga and Junior came home from church, Liza was drinking tea and eating toast. It wasn't Sam's deluxe breakfast, but it wasn't bad.

"I didn't expect you to be up yet," Helga said.

"Me either. Maybe I'll take a nap later."

"Sunday is a good day for taking a nap," Junior said.

"How was church, guys?"

"It was okay," Junior said.

"Your brother managed to stay awake the whole time, so I guess that makes it good," Helga said.

"I just made a fresh pot of tea, Mom."

"Just what I wanted," Helga said. She poured herself a cup, took a sip, and started making scrambled eggs.

"At dinner last night, I didn't get a chance to ask you about college, Junior. Which one have you decided on?"

"The decision was easy. The college I applied to here at home awarded me a full basketball scholarship!"

"Congratulations, little brother! Way to go!"

"Thanks, Liza. How does it feel to be home?"

"It's going to take a few days to get used to it. Going to the office tomorrow instead of the daycare is going to be a little weird. I'm going to be missing the children and my friends, but duty calls, so here I am."

"I know you didn't want to come back so soon, but we're glad you're home," Helga said.

Liza put her dishes in the sink and gave her mom a hug. "I better get started on my laundry or I won't have anything to wear to work tomorrow."

"I forgot to ask, are you feeling better this morning, dear?"

"Good as new, Mom."

Liza started unpacking her bags and sorting her laundry. She took the poem from Sam, the little cement truck from Harvey, the blanket from Joanna along with Mr. Mittens' squeaky toy, and the "things to do" list from Sarah and put them in her top right-hand dresser drawer. She wanted to keep all of her special things together in one place. She couldn't display any of them without having to offer an explanation, and she wasn't about to do that. She replaced her pillow with Melvin's, found the two bottles of his fragrance, and put them underneath Joanna's blanket in the drawer. She would only be able to put a drop of fragrance on the pillow before bed, so the scent wouldn't be too strong. Helga had a habit of tidying up Liza's room when she was at work or just out somewhere. She didn't want to answer any questions, so she decided to play it safe.

It took most of the day to get the laundry done and put away. By then it was late afternoon. Liza decided not to nap after all. She worried that if she did, she may not be able to fall asleep at bedtime, and she wanted to be fit for work in the morning.

She knew it wouldn't take her long to get back into her routine, but the first day she planned for extra time, just in case.

Sunday night dinner with her mom and Junior was peaceful and happy. She was thankful to have time together, just the three of them.

Liza went to her room, set her alarm, put a drop of fragrance on the pillow case, closed her eyes, and fell asleep immediately.

***

"There she is!" Marcus said. "Welcome back! What have you got there?"

"I went to the doughnut shop and bought a couple of cinnamon doughnuts and coffee for our recess … I mean coffee break."

Marcus laughed. "Recess? You're still on your school schedule. How did you know that cinnamon doughnuts are my favourite?"

"I didn't. My friends at the daycare and I made a pact to have cinnamon doughnuts for the morning coffee break. It will help me to continue to feel connected to them."

"Great idea! I didn't have time for breakfast. What do you say we sit down and have our coffee and doughnut now while we get caught up."

"Now it's my turn to say great idea!"

Marcus went on at great length about the African safari and described their adventures in great detail. He told Liza that elephants are his favourite animal. She could tell that by all the photographs he had taken.

"Which reminds me, I'll be right back." Marcus went to his office, and when he returned, he had a small wooden statue of an elephant in his hand, which he placed on Liza's desk.

"I brought this elephant back for you. It's heavy enough to use as a paperweight. That's not the only reason I bought it for you. If you notice, the elephant's trunk is up. That means you will have good fortune."

"I didn't know that, Marcus. Thank you."

Marcus was genuinely interested in Liza's stories about her time in Waterford and got a big kick about her stories about Flo. Their conversation was interrupted by a phone call from the publisher.

"I'll take it in my office, Liza."

"One moment, please. I'll transfer you."

Liza was looking through the files on her desk when Marcus emerged from his office about a half hour later, carrying the manuscript.

"Here's our next money-maker," he said. "I'm excited to submit it. I think sales for this one will surpass sales from the last one."

"I'll get started on it right away, Marcus."

"Thank you, Liza. I'm glad you're back."

Liza got up and ran down the hall to the washroom. Marcus stood by her desk and waited for her to return.

"Are you all right?"

"Yes, Marcus. I'm fine. I think I'm just feeling under the weather. The long bus ride home, stress from all the changes lately, and I haven't been sleeping well lately."

"You'll have to take it easy and get some extra rest. Ethel and I got back Friday, and since then Ethel has been suffering from jet lag. She's been sleeping late in the morning and then napping in the afternoon."

"I'll take your advice, Marcus, and plan to go to sleep early tonight."

That night, Liza turned in early and woke up the next morning feeling much better. When she got to work, Marcus was just on his way out.

"I forgot I have a meeting this morning. I should be back around two o'clock."

"See you later, Marcus."

Liza was making excellent progress typing the manuscript. Mid-morning, she stopped for coffee. She took a bite of her cinnamon doughnut, spit it out, ran to the washroom, and got sick again. She splashed some water on her face, rinsed her mouth, and walked slowly back to her desk. She didn't understand what was happening and why she was feeling sick. She thought she would close her eyes for a couple of minutes but fell asleep instead.

The phone rang a half hour later and woke her up. After her little nap, she felt better and continued on with her work, relieved that Marcus wasn't there to witness any of it.

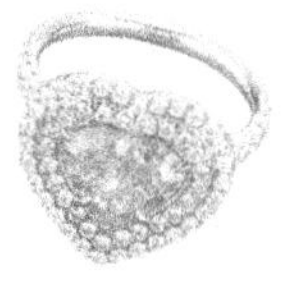

Chapter Forty-Four

Crackers

DURING THE TWENTY-MINUTE BUS RIDE home after work, Liza fell asleep. The driver knew Liza's stop, and when she didn't approach the front door to get off, he looked in his rear-view mirror and could see that she was sleeping. He called out to announce the stop, hoping that would wake her. It didn't. The second time he called the stop, she opened her eyes, blinked a few times, and looked out the window.

He turned to the front seat where she was sitting and said, "I believe this is your stop, Miss."

"Yes, it is. Thank you."

"You're welcome. Watch your step now."

***

Helga was making dinner, and Junior and John were watching television in the living room when Liza came home. The aroma of the food smelled wonderful at first and then turned her stomach.

"Hi, dear."

"Hi, Mom. Be back in a minute."

Liza hurried past her mom to her room. She dropped her purse on the floor and, once again, headed straight to her bathroom, barely making it in time before getting sick again. She couldn't understand why she was feeling this way.

"Dinner is ready," Helga announced.

Junior shut the television off and he and John basically flew into the kitchen and sat down, waiting impatiently for Liza so they could start eating.

"Junior, go and see what's taking your sister so long."

He got up, started down the hallway, and yelled out, "Liza, dinner! Are you coming?"

She opened her door and quietly said, "Yes, Junior, I'm coming. I'm just changing. I'll be there in a minute."

"She said she'll be here in a minute."

Liza managed a weak smile as she sat down beside Junior.

"You look a little pale, Liza," John said.

"Actually, you do look pale," Helga said. "Are you feeling all right?"

"I'm fine, Mom, don't worry."

"Nothing that food won't cure," Junior said as he stuck his fork into a meatball. He was just about to put the whole thing in his mouth when Helga stopped him.

"Junior! Put that down!" she scolded. "We haven't said grace yet."

"Oh ya, I forgot. Bless this food and bless us too, amen."

"Amen," John said.

Helga shook her head and said, "That's not the grace we usually say."

"I thought I'd try something new."

"That's new all right," Helga said.

Liza took a small amount of spaghetti and only a couple of meatballs. She ate slowly and made it through without incident.

Helga could see Liza wasn't quite herself. "If you'd like to make it an early night, the boys will help with the dishes."

"But, Mom—" Junior started to say.

Helga gave him the *don't-talk-back-to-me* look. He didn't say another word.

Liza went to sleep quite early and woke up feeling much better.

***

Marcus heard Liza come in. When the phone started ringing, she didn't answer it. He answered it and afterwards went to check on her. They bumped into each other as Liza was coming out of the washroom.

"You don't look well at all, Liza. You're so pale," he said.

"I'm not going to lie, Marcus. I am still getting sick."

"I think you should see a doctor. In fact, why don't you call right now."

Liza called her family doctor, and Marcus waited by her desk.

"You have a cancellation tomorrow at nine o'clock?"

Marcus nodded.

"Yes, nine o'clock would be fine, thank you. Thank you, Marcus."

"You don't have to thank me. It's best that you get to the bottom of this."

"I'll come in right after my appointment."

"Take all the time you need. The manuscript isn't going anywhere.

***

Liza made arrangements with her mom to use her car. She said she wanted to go to the dry cleaner at lunch to drop off a couple of her dresses.

The doctor was running a half hour behind schedule. Liza was nervously flipping through magazines as she waited. Finally the receptionist called her name. She ushered Liza into an examination room and said, "The doctor will be in to see you shortly."

A few minutes later, the doctor came in, carrying her file.

"Good morning, Liza. I haven't seen you in a while. What brings you here today?"

"I haven't been feeling well. I've been away working in Waterford and came home this past Saturday night. Sunday night during dinner, I started to feel sick and had to throw up."

"I see. Anything else?"

"I've been really tired too. I've been feeling stressed lately, and I haven't been sleeping well," she explained.

"I'm going to give you a check-up. Let's start with your blood pressure. Roll up your right sleeve, please."

After he completed the check-up, he filled out the requisition for the lab.

"Stop by the reception desk on your way down the hall to the lab. Make an appointment for Monday morning. I'll put a rush on this and have the results for you when you come in. By the way, if your stomach feels queasy, eat some soda crackers. They'll help to settle it."

"Thank you, I'll try that."

Liza's next appointment was Monday at ten o'clock. On her way back to the office, she stopped in at the grocery store and bought a box of crackers and a bottle of water.

***

"How was your doctor's appointment?"

"It was fine, Marcus. I had a check-up and then the doctor sent me to the lab."

"That's good."

"I have a follow-up appointment Monday morning at ten o'clock, to get the lab results."

"That's pretty quick," Marcus said.

"The doctor put a rush on it. I'll come in and work for a bit before I have to leave for my appointment."

"That's fine, Liza. I'll be in the office all day Monday. Don't worry about rushing back."

"Okay," Liza said.

Liza put the box of crackers in her desk drawer and some in her purse. For the rest of the week, Liza ate a *lot* of crackers and managed to subvert the nausea somewhat. Friday signalled the end of the work week, which Liza was relishing. Unfortunately, it also signalled her father's imminent return, which she was dreading.

Marcus left Liza to lock up Friday afternoon. Liza finished tidying up her desk and was just about to leave when the phone rang. In her haste to answer it, she accidentally knocked over the wooden elephant and sent it crashing to the floor. The elephant's trunk lay severed beside it. She picked it up and put the pieces in her purse, to repair at home. She was saddened to see the elephant that Marcus so happily had given her was now broken.

The caller had the wrong number.

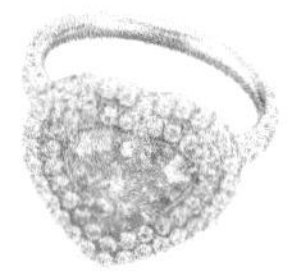

Chapter Forty-Five

The Inner Office

SATURDAY MORNING, Liza made her bed and ate some crackers before going into the kitchen for breakfast. She heard her mom and Junior talking to each other but was surprised to see her father.

"Hello, Liza. Would you like some coffee?" He was standing beside the counter pouring cream into his.

"Okay," she said hesitantly, wondering why he was being so pleasant.

He put a cup of coffee in front of her and then sat beside her.

"Tell me about your work at the daycare," he said.

As she explained all the programs at the daycare and told him all about what she and Sarah had been doing, he seemed genuinely interested. She started to tell him about Joanna and Sam when he interrupted her.

"I'm glad your experience at the daycare was good," he said. "Did you hear about Junior's scholarship? We have a basketball star in the family!"

"Yes, I'm very proud of Junior," Liza said.

As Helga served breakfast, Klaus went on and on about Junior. Liza started to feel nauseated again. She wasn't sure if it was the food or the conversation.

"Mom, may I use your car today? I've run out of a few things (crackers) and need to go to the mall."

"Yes, dear."

"How long will you be home, Father?"

"I'll be home for a week. We've just completed a big project and we'll be starting the next one a week from Monday, a little closer to home."

"You haven't been home for a whole week in a long time, Dad."

"It will give us a chance to spend some time together, Junior."

"Do you need anything at the mall, Mom?"

"No, dear; thank you for asking, though."

"I'm going to go now."

"Okay, dear. See you later."

As she drove to the mall, Liza was formulating ways to avoid her father. She had no idea how she would survive a week with him at home. She could go to work earlier and stay later. That would mean she would get more of the manuscript done in less time. She was wishing Sarah was back. Getting together with Sarah was always a great way to escape.

Liza spent time with Helga after church Sunday, while Junior and Klaus were tinkering in the garage, working on Helga's car. They came in long enough to eat and then went back to the garage.

Monday morning Liza went into the office for an hour and then left for her doctor's appointment. She told Helga she needed to use the car again, this time to pick up her dry cleaning.

When the receptionist called Liza, instead of taking her into the examination room, she took her into the doctor's private office.

He was sitting at his desk but stood to greet her as she came in.

"Good morning, Liza."

"Good morning," she replied.

"I have the lab results here," he said in a serious tone.

She felt the blood drain from her face and her palms began to sweat.

"What is it?" she said.

"Liza, you're pregnant."

"I'm what?"

"You're pregnant. The nausea, vomiting, and tiredness all make sense now that we have the results," he said.

Her thoughts drifted back to the night before Melvin left Waterford.

"Liza?"

"Yes?"

"Are you currently in a relationship with the baby's father?"

"Sort of."

"What do you mean?"

"The baby's father and I love each other deeply, but he's away working on a special project in a remote location somewhere, and I can't contact him."

"How long is the project expected to last?"

"It could be as long as a year."

"That answers my next question."

"What was your next question?"

"I was going to ask if you would have support from the baby's father."

"If he was here, we would get married. He made it clear to me that was the plan ever since we met. He gave me a promise ring to show his love for me and his plan for us to be together always."

"Knowing your parents the way I do, they're not going to be happy about this."

"That's the understatement of the year," Liza said.

"That fact that the baby's father isn't here may be a blessing in disguise."

"What makes you say that?"

"Your father would never let you get married at your age and would run the boy off."

"You're right about that. I don't know how I'm going to tell my parents."

"Your father is in town?"

"Yes, he got back a couple of days ago."

"I wish you good luck, Liza." He handed her a piece of paper. "Here's the name of a good friend of mine. She's an excellent obstetrician, and she'll take good care of you. I'll call her and tell her to expect you soon."

"Thank you. Your advice about the crackers really worked."

"Call me if you need anything else."

Liza called Marcus from a pay phone in the lobby and asked if she could take the rest of the day off. She explained that she wasn't feeling well. Marcus was more than understanding and told her to go home and rest.

Junior was fixing his bike outside when Liza drove up.

"Aren't you supposed to be at work?"

"Is Mom home?"

"You had her car, so of course she's at home. She's in the kitchen ... as usual. Dad is in his study ... as usual. You look really pale. What's going on?"

"I have something to tell them."

Junior followed Liza into the house.

"Hi, Mom," Liza said.

Klaus heard Liza's voice and came into the kitchen.

"Liza, what are you doing home?"

"I have something to tell you; please sit down."

"You really look pale, dear," Helga said. "Are you still feeling sick?"

"What are you talking about, Helga?"

"I've been really tired and quite sick. Marcus suggested that I go see the doctor."

"You were sick at work too?"

"Yes, Mom. I went to the doctor last Wednesday. He did a check-up and sent me to the lab also. I went back for the results this morning."

"What's wrong with you?" Klaus demanded.

"I'm pregnant."

Klaus flew into a rage and began yelling. "*What do you mean you're pregnant? Who is the father and where is he?*"

"The baby's father and I are in love, and ever since we met, we've been planning to get married."

"Ever since you met? How long has this been going on? Wait a minute. Helga, did you know about this?"

"I didn't know anything, Klaus."

"Where did you meet?"

"We were together in Waterford," Liza said.

"Where is he now?"

"He is away working and can't be reached."

"I forbid you to call him or ever see him again."

"I can't call him."

"That's beside the point," Klaus said.

"There's one more thing." Liza hesitated.

"What *else* could there possibly be?"

"The baby's father is black."

"That's it! Get out!"

"Klaus, what are you saying?"

He stood in front of Liza, pointed to the door, and yelled, "GET OUT! You are a disgrace to this family and you are *not* bringing a bastard child into my house!"

"Klaus, you can't be serious!"

"I am *dead* serious!"

"Where is she going to go?"

"I don't care where she goes, Helga, as long as she goes. I'm going out now. By the time I get home, she'd better be gone."

Klaus took his keys, slammed the door, and left.

Liza was sobbing uncontrollably.

"I'll talk to your father and get him to reconsider. In the meantime, I'll call Aunt Sadie. I'm sure you can stay with her for a couple of days until your father calms down and comes to his senses. I'll help you pack a few things. Junior, go and get a suitcase for your sister, please."

Chapter Forty-Six

On One Condition

AUNT SADIE WELCOMED LIZA into her home with open arms. She was kind, generous, and compassionate. She made Liza's stay comfortable, safe, and happy. Aunt Sadie provided Liza with a beautiful bedroom, *lots* of good food, understanding, and unconditional love. Liza had everything she needed ... except her family.

A couple of days turned into a couple of weeks. When Klaus would call home, Helga pleaded with him to allow Liza to return home. Her pleading was to no avail and fell on deaf ears.

Aunt Sadie lived across town, which meant it would take Liza an hour to commute to work by bus. To simplify things, Aunt Sadie rented a car and gave Liza the use of her own car. The commute by car would be much easier, and Liza was free to come and go as she pleased.

Liza took a couple of days to settle in at Aunt Sadie's before returning to work. She cried as she told Marcus about her pregnancy and what had transpired after she had told her parents. Marcus couldn't have been more understanding. He pledged his help and support and doted on her as if she was his own daughter. He bought her a new adjustable office chair to make sure she was comfortable. If he went out for coffee or lunch, he always brought something back for her. The cupboards in the lunch room were stocked full of crackers, which Marcus replenished on a regular basis.

Helga called Liza at work on a regular basis. After about a month had passed, she called and said she had something to tell her and asked if they could meet. Liza said she wanted Aunt Sadie to be present, so they agreed to meet at the hotel.

Helga was sitting at Sadie's private table waiting as Liza and Sadie came in.

"Hi, dear. You're looking well."

"Aunt Sadie and Marcus are taking good care of me."

"Thank you, Sadie."

"It's my pleasure, Helga."

"What did you want to tell me, Mom?"

"I finally convinced your father to let you come home."

"That's good news!" Aunt Sadie said.

"Somehow I feel that there's more to Father's sudden change of heart. What are you leaving out, Mom?"

"Your father said you can come home, but there is one condition."

"I knew it. What is it?"

"He said you can come home on the condition that you agree to give the baby up for adoption."

"Is he *crazy*? I'm not going to give my baby up for adoption!"

"That's what he said."

"Isn't there any other alternative, Helga?"

"You're his sister; you know him better than anyone else. What he says, goes. His decisions are always final," Helga said.

"Mom, can't we make this work somehow? I want to keep my baby. I'm nineteen. I have a job. We have plenty of money. With your help, Mom, we can figure this out. Won't you help me?"

"Right now, my hands are tied. I want you to come home, Liza. Once you're home, I'll try to get your father to change his mind."

Liza didn't really believe Helga could change his mind, but somehow deep inside, she had a glimmer of hope. As nice as it was staying with Aunt Sadie, Liza missed her mom and Junior, so she went home.

***

Klaus had just left for ten days when Helga brought Liza home from Sadie's.

Saturday afternoon, Liza had the house to herself. Helga went grocery shopping, and Junior was over at John's place. She was lying on the couch watching television when the doorbell rang. She went to the door to find Sarah standing in front of her. Liza threw her arms around Sarah and wouldn't let go.

Sarah could barely breathe but managed to say, "Liza, let go of me."

"When did you get back?"

"We got back last night. If you would have returned my phone calls, you would have known I was coming home."

"What phone calls?"

"What phone calls?" Sarah repeated. "I told your father to give you my messages."

"He didn't give me any messages."

"Why not?"

"I wasn't here."

"Where were you?"

"At Aunt Sadie's."

"Why were you there?"

"It's a long story."

"I've got time."

Liza began, "It all started when I got back from Waterford ..."

Sarah stared at Liza, not saying a word. She couldn't believe what she was hearing.

"My father doesn't know Melvin's name or where he is. I'm forbidden to ever see him or speak to him again."

"What if Melvin calls you?"

"He only has my number at work. I didn't give him my home number because I couldn't risk him calling here and having my father answer the phone. With everything that has happened, it's a good thing that I didn't. There's no telling what my father would say or do. Not only that, but my father pays all the bills. If Melvin called here, he would track the number from the statement. I'm afraid my father would do something drastic."

"Melvin didn't call again since the time he called you," Sarah said.

"I was just going to ask you if he'd called."

"What are you going to do, Liza?"

"I'm going to avoid my father as much as possible when he's home and find a way to keep the baby."

"I'll help you in any way I can. Now that I'm back, you can spend as much time at my house as you want."

"Thank you, Sarah. I'll take you up on that. I'm so happy to see you."

"I'm happy to see you, too."

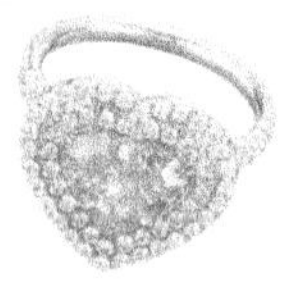

Chapter Forty-Seven

The Promise

KLAUS WAS BENT ON LIZA giving the baby up for adoption, and she knew it full well. In the days before he was due to come home, Liza did some research. She called an adoption agency and discovered that it was possible for her to fill out some preliminary papers without formally signing them, *and* she had up to twelve days after the baby was born to make her final decision. Armed with this information, Liza was prepared to deal with her father ... on her terms.

The day Klaus came home, he had only one thing on his agenda: to take Liza straight to the adoption agency. He ordered her to get into the car. There was no choice and no discussion. When she went along with it without putting up a fight or arguing with him, he almost seemed surprised. He waited in the car while she went in. On the way home, Klaus didn't say a word to Liza. He turned the radio on and listened to the news.

For the duration of her pregnancy, Liza did a good job of avoiding her father. When he was at home, she spent time at work or at Sarah's.

***

Liza was two weeks overdue and was scheduled to go to the hospital to be induced. It was nine o'clock in the morning when Helga drove her to the hospital. She made no attempt to park and go in with her. She pulled up in the drop-off zone and left her there. Helga didn't say a word to Liza. Liza was left alone to fend for herself, and Helga went home to prepare for a family dinner she and Klaus were hosting.

Liza walked up to the admitting desk. The intake nurse checked her in and called someone to take her to her room. She was taken to a segregated maternity ward for unwed mothers.

The room she was in had two beds in it. Hers was the one beside the window. Liza was happy to be able to look outside. It was a sunny, particularly cold winter day. They'd already had a record amount of snowfall, with more snow on the way.

Liza put some of her things in the cabinet beside the bed. There was a form on the bed to fill out for meal preferences. A food service worker came in and brought Liza a cup of chicken broth to drink, as she wasn't allowed much before the procedure.

Liza was sitting on the bed drinking her broth when she noticed someone standing in the doorway. The sun was shining so brightly, Liza could only see an outline of the person, illuminated by the bright light. It looked like the silhouette of an angel. As she walked toward Liza, the light seemed to follow her and became brighter the closer she got. It was though a heavenly angelic presence entered the room. Liza immediately felt a sense of peace she had never known before.

"Hi, Liza, my name is Celene. I'm your nurse and I'll be looking after you until you graduate out of here." Celine was tall, slim, and had beautiful long, blonde hair. She was so pretty. She spoke softly and kindly. Her smile warmed Liza's heart. She found just being in Celene's presence calmed her fears, and suddenly she didn't feel lonely anymore.

Celene picked up the chart at the end of Liza's bed and read it. "It says here you are a couple of weeks overdue."

"Yes, that's right."

"The doctor will be in to see you shortly. Is anyone from your family here with you today?"

"No, I'm here alone."

Celene put the chart down, walked over to Liza, and touched her arm. "Don't worry, you're *not* alone. I'll be with you."

Liza smiled and nodded.

Celene stayed with Liza until the procedure. Conversation flowed easily, and they discovered they had a lot in common. Liza told Celene all about Melvin, Waterford, Melvin's departure, and the events that had transpired since then. She told how her father was forcing her to give up the baby, and her mother was unusually silent throughout all of it. Celene was very attentive and listened with great compassion and sensitivity.

***

Liza had the baby at seven o'clock that evening: a beautiful baby girl weighing in at eight pounds, two ounces.

Helga answered when Celene called to inform them Liza had a baby girl. Helga seemed distant and cold. She thanked Celene for calling and said she had to return to her dinner guests.

Celene waited until Liza returned to her room and then brought the baby to her. It was time for the baby's bottle, since Liza wasn't breastfeeding.

"Here is your beautiful little girl. She looks just like her pretty mommy."

"That's so kind of you to say."

"What are you going to name this precious little bundle of joy?"

"Her name is Janet Lynn."

"Janet Lynn ... what a beautiful name! It suits her so well."

Liza started to cry.

Celene hugged Liza as she held the baby. "It's hard, I know, but you're strong; you'll be all right."

"I wish her dad was here. I miss him so much. I know he would love her."

"She's easy to love."

"My mother and father have a beautiful granddaughter and they don't want anything to do with her."

"That's certainly their loss. They don't know what they're missing, but one day they will."

"I'm not so sure."

"It's time to take Janet Lynn to the nursery, and you, my dear, need to get some sleep."

***

There wasn't much to do while Liza was in the hospital. Celene would come to bring the baby to Liza for feeding and get Liza up to walk around for her daily exercise. There wasn't a common room where patients could sit and visit or watch television. Celene was a gourmet cook and would bring Liza something delicious for lunch, and they would eat together in Liza's room. At the end of the day when her shift was over, Celene would stay with Liza until she felt tired enough to go to sleep, and then she would leave.

Only family members were allowed to visit. Each day Liza hoped that someone would come, but no one did ... until the fourth day. Celene had just come in to ask Liza if they could use Janet Lynn for a bathing demonstration, because she was the only baby who would stay awake long enough.

"I'll come back and get you in an hour for the demonstration," Celene said.

Just as she turned to leave, Helga came in. Celene said hello and left. She stood and watched from the nurses' station across the hall from Liza's room. She was surprised at how little time Helga stayed.

Celene went to the nurses' lounge and got some tea and took it to Liza's room. "Would you like some tea? I have a break now before the bathing demonstration, and I thought we could have tea together. I made these double fudge chocolate cookies. They dunk really well in tea!"

"That would be nice," Liza said quietly.

"Your visitor didn't stay long," Celene said.

"That was my mom. She came to make sure that I wasn't going to be bringing the baby home with me tomorrow. My father sent her. He doesn't want anything to do with the baby. He calls her 'that bastard child' and said I'm a 'disgrace to the family.' I told my mom I filled out some forms at the adoption agency, but I didn't sign anything, and I told her the baby is coming home with me. Needless to say, she wasn't happy about it. She said my father thought I was going to leave the baby at the hospital. He didn't know I have seven days left before I have to make any final decisions. Since she had no choice in the matter, she left to go buy some diapers and things for the baby."

"That's perfect. You'll be set for tomorrow when the baby goes home with you," Celene said cheerfully. "We have to go shortly for the demonstration, so drink your tea."

Celene's words comforted Liza. She felt better and quickly dunked her cookie in the tea and ate it.

***

First thing in the morning, Celene came to Liza's room with the baby. Janet Lynn was dressed in a beautiful pink sleeper with white hearts on it, wrapped in a matching blanket.

"I thought she needed a going home outfit and blanket to keep her warm. I searched for something with hearts on it, because hearts are my favourite. When I see hearts, they remind me we are surrounded by love all the time."

"Hearts are my favourite, too!" Liza said. Liza was wearing the heart-shaped ring Melvin had given her. She showed it to Celene.

"That is beautiful, Liza. It sure sparkles! I haven't seen you with it on before."

"I don't wear it because my family would have something to say about it. I don't want the love I feel when I wear it to be spoiled by their criticism and negative attitudes."

"I completely understand. Self preservation is very important. I have one more surprise for you," Celene said. She handed Liza a picture in a heart-shaped frame. "I thought you needed a picture of you and Janet Lynn."

In the picture, Liza had dozed off while giving the baby her bottle. The baby was looking up at Liza.

"When did you take this?"

"One night during the baby's last feeding. I couldn't resist."

"I love it; thank you, Celene."

"You're welcome, Liza. Now I have to escort you out. I know you're perfectly capable of walking, but I'm supposed to wheel you out. Hop in and I'll give you and the baby a nice ride to the front doors."

When they reached the front exit, Celene helped Liza with her bag.

"Do you see your parents out front?"

"Yes, their car is right there." Helga saw Liza. She got out and opened the car door for her.

"Good luck, Liza. It's been my pleasure to be your nurse."

"You've been more than my nurse. You've been an angel sent from heaven. I'll never forget you."

"I won't forget you either, Liza. Take good care of yourself and baby Janet Lynn."

Celene watched until Liza was safely into the car.

Klaus wouldn't even look at the baby. "I thought you were going to leave that bastard child in the hospital."

"Her name is Janet Lynn."

"Not for long. The adoptive parents will be naming her."

Liza ignored what Klaus said. "I have seven days before I have to make my final decision!"

The baby started to cry, and Klaus stopped arguing. Helga remained silent through it all.

***

Helga had fixed up a clothes basket next to Liza's bed for the baby to sleep in. There were diapers, sleepers, towels, lotion, powder, and baby bottles on top of Liza's dresser.

The first day at home, Liza spent most of her time in her room. Junior had been at John's all day and came to her room just before dinner. He knocked on Liza's door and said, "Mom wanted me to tell you dinner was ready."

She opened her door, "Tell Mom I'll eat in my room."

"Dad just left for a few days, so the coast is clear."

"Would you like to see your niece? She's asleep right now." Liza pulled the blanket back a bit so Junior could see her.

"She looks like you," he said.

"That's what Celene said too."

"Who is Celene?"

"My nurse at the hospital." Liza tucked the blanket around the baby. "You can hold her later if you want to."

Dinner conversation was minimal. No one mentioned the baby or the adoption.

The next morning, Helga came to Liza's room and announced she had visitors.

"I thought I wasn't allowed to have visitors."

"It's your father's friends from church."

Liza was suspicious but went to see them. "Hello, Mr. and Mrs. Dyck."

"Hello, Liza. How are you?"

"I'm fine. How are you?"

"We're fine," Mrs. Dyck said. "How is the baby?"

"The baby? She's fine, thank you."

That was the end of the polite conversation. They began telling her that she should go along with her father's wishes and give the baby up for adoption. They told her they thought she was too young to care for a baby and there was shame in being an unwed mother. They said the baby would be better off with two parents who could raise her properly with the right financial provision, and on and on.

Liza didn't respond. When they had stopped talking, she said, "Thank you for stopping by today. My mother will show you out. I have to go and feed the baby."

Each day the same thing happened. More church people. Each day Liza said the same thing.

Five days later, just after she ushered out yet another couple from church, her father came home.

"Have you come to your senses yet?"

By this time, Liza was so angry she couldn't contain herself.

She shouted, "I don't care how many church people you send here. I am not giving my baby up for adoption!"

"Yes, you are!" Klaus yelled back.

"No, I'm not! There's *nothing* you can say that will convince me otherwise."

"I have a feeling that what I'm about to say will *definitely* convince you. If you don't give that bastard child up for adoption, I will leave this family. That will be *all* your fault and yours alone!"

"Dad, you can't mean that!"

"I assure you I do."

"Klaus, you don't know what you're saying. You're talking crazy talk," Helga said.

"I know exactly what I'm saying."

By this time, Liza, Helga, and Junior were all crying. Liza heard the baby crying and went to her bedroom. Klaus stood in the middle of the living room with his arms crossed. The look in his eyes was empty and ice cold.

Helga walked over to him and tried to uncross his arms, but he stood firm.

"Klaus, you can't mean what you said."

"I mean every word of it, Helga. You better deal with the daughter of yours. She has two days. If she doesn't agree to sign those papers, I'm leaving." He walked away from Helga, went to his study, and closed the door.

Liza was still crying as she held the baby. The door to her room was open, and Helga and Junior went in.

Helga started. "Liza, you have to give the baby up. You don't want to break up our family over this, do you?"

Liza couldn't believe what Junior said next. "Liza, you're just being selfish."

"How can you say I'm being selfish? This is my baby. My flesh and blood. I don't want to give her up."

"Breaking up our family is selfish," Junior said and walked out.

Junior's words hit her hard and cut her to the core. For the next two days she didn't eat and barely slept.

With a broken heart and a battered spirit, Liza agreed to give her baby up. Klaus drove, Helga and Junior went along to the adoption agency.

Liza sat across from the adoption agent. She cried and cried as she signed the papers. The adoption agent was an elderly, kind lady who was very sympathetic. "Besides being adopted into a Christian family, I have one more request."

Liza gave the agent the box for the heart-shaped ring. Liza was wearing the ring and took it off, knowing she had worn it for the last time.

"Give this ring to the adoptive parents. Ask them to give it to her on her sixteenth birthday. This is a promise ring her dad gave me when he pledged his love forever. This is now my promise to her. *I give her my heart, and I will love her forever.*"

Giving Janet Lynn, her precious baby girl, to someone else was the hardest thing she *ever* had to do.

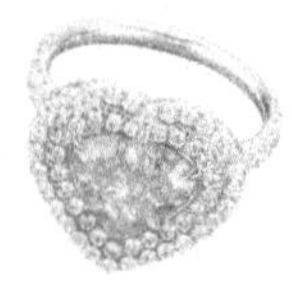

Chapter Forty-Eight

I Cry

I cry for her
I cry when I open my eyes
I cry when I still hear the sound of her breathing
I cry when the sound is gone
I cry when I remember how it felt to hold her
I cry because I cannot hold her anymore
I cry when I feel her near
I cry when she is distant
I cry when I remember how she cried
I cry when I remember her in peaceful sleep
I cry on my birthday
I cry on her birthday
I cry on a sunny day
I cry when I cannot see the sun
I cry on a rainy day
I cry on a snowy day
I cry when I hear her in the sound of the wind
I cry when the wind is silent
I cry when waves crash
I cry when they are still
I cry when I hear music
I cry when the music ends

I cry in silent moments
I cry on the inside
I cry on the outside
I cry silent tears
I cry when nobody knows
I cry when nobody hears
I cry when nobody cares
I cry when I walk
I cry when I run
I cry when I kneel
I cry when I stand
I cry when I fall
I cry when I sing
I cry when birds sing
I cry when they silently fly away
I cry when I see children at play
I cry when they laugh
I cry when they cry
I cry when they don't understand
I cry when I don't understand
I cry when I feel joy
I cry when I feel pain
I cry in a crowd
I cry alone
I cry when I am lonely
I cry in a church
I cry when I pray
I cry when I cannot pray
I cry at beginnings
I cry at endings
I cry at dawn
I cry at sunset
I cry at night
I cry when I close my eyes
I cry for her

Chapter Forty-Nine

Aunt Sadie

MARCUS KNEW LIZA'S HOME LIFE was unbearable during her pregnancy and worsened after the ultimatum and subsequent adoption. Liza told Marcus how she felt betrayed and abandoned by her family. She cried and said she just couldn't stand to live there anymore.

Through it all, Liza managed to fulfill all of her duties at work. Marcus wanted to reward Liza for her loyalty, dedication, hard work, and commitment. He gave her a raise and a substantial bonus. His second book became a best seller, and sales far exceeded the initial projections. Liza had a big part to play in the preparation of the manuscript, so Marcus thought it was only fair that she reap some of the rewards. As a result, Liza could afford to move out of her parents' house and get a place of her own. She rented a suite in a home owned by an elderly couple. It was in a nice neighbourhood, a good distance away from where her parents lived. She bought a second-hand car, which gave her freedom and added independence.

In the midst of all that had transpired, Klaus and Helga's twenty-fifth wedding anniversary had passed. Being Klaus' dutiful sister, Sadie thought she should plan a post-anniversary celebration. She called Klaus to share her plan and asked for his input regarding the menu and guest list. He told her not to bother and said he had no desire to celebrate.

Sadie found his reaction very disconcerting. She sensed there was a missing piece to the puzzle and decided to get to the bottom of it. She hired a private detective to follow him.

The detective followed Klaus for a period of four weeks. During that time, he discovered some shocking news. Klaus was having an affair. He took photographs and collected receipts for hotels, restaurants, and gifts Klaus paid for, dating back three years. There were many instances when Klaus told Helga he was away working, but in fact, he was not away *and* he was not working.

Sadie called Helga and told her she had some important information and she would be coming right over. She told her to make sure Liza and Junior would be there also. It was a Saturday afternoon, and Sadie knew Klaus was scheduled to return from "out of town" a couple of hours later.

***

There were three cars in the circular driveway out front when Klaus came home. He recognized them as Sadie's, Liza's, and the car he and Helga had just bought for Junior.

Klaus found them all sitting in the living room. Helga was crying. Junior was doing his best to console her, and Liza just glared at her father.

"What's going on? What are you all doing here?" he said.

"When you told me not to bother with the anniversary party and you didn't want to celebrate, I became very suspicious. It appeared to me something else was going on, so I hired a private detective to follow you," Sadie said.

"You did what?"

"We know you are having an affair," Sadie said.

"Nobody move," Klaus said. He went to his study, unlocked the cabinet that held his gun collection, and took out a shotgun. When he returned, he pointed the gun at them and said, "Do what I tell you to do or there will be four dead bodies in this room. I don't want to hear one more word out of any of you. Sit still and don't move."

He picked up the phone on the end table and dialled a number. "Hello, Sylvia ... listen to me. Tell Fred you're leaving him. Pack a few things, take the children, and go to our usual place. I'll meet you there."

With the gun still pointed at his family, he slowly started backing out of the room. He put the gun down, opened the door, and left.

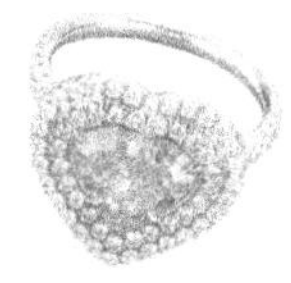

Chapter Fifty

New Beginnings

NO ONE HAD HEARD FROM MELVIN in over a year, until one day Liza was invited to Sarah's for dinner. They were just about to start eating when the phone rang. Sarah's mom answered it.

"Hello? Yes, Sarah is here. Who is calling please ... Marvin?"

Liza jumped up and said, "You mean *Melvin*! I'll take it!"

Liza grabbed the phone away from Sarah's mom. "Melvin!"

"Princess!"

"Yes, it's me!"

"Take it in my room," Sarah whispered.

"Hold on, Melvin, I'm going to switch phones."

"Go ahead, Liza. I'll hang up once you pick up in my room," Sarah said.

"Okay, got it!" Liza called out.

"Princess?"

"I'm here."

"I called you at the office yesterday. It must have been after hours, because no one answered. I still have Sarah's phone number, so I waited until today to call, hoping Sarah would be home and could give you a message."

"I have so much to tell you, Melvin. Where are you?"

"We just wrapped up the special project. We've been assigned to a new one, so we're moving to a new location tomorrow. I'm not sure how long I'll be at the new location, but I will try to call more often. I miss you so much, Princess."

"I miss you too, Melvin. I'll give you my new phone number. I'm not living at home anymore. Marcus gave me a raise so I could afford to move out and get a place of my own. I even bought myself a second-hand car!"

"That's wonderful, Princess. I know you weren't happy at home."

"Things at home got much worse after I got back from Waterford," Liza said.

"Why? What happened?"

Liza told Melvin everything. She could barely get the words out because she was sobbing. When she explained she was forced into giving their beautiful baby girl up for adoption, Melvin started to sob.

"I'm so sorry you had to go through all of that by yourself. If only work hadn't taken me away for so long, things would have been much different. We would have gotten married," Melvin said.

"If only," Liza said sadly.

"Do you know anything about the couple who adopted her?"

"They wouldn't tell me anything, just that she was going to a good home."

"That's good to know," Melvin said.

"I did give the adoption agent the promise ring you gave me, with instructions for the adoptive parents to give it to her on her sixteenth birthday."

"I'm so glad you did, Princess. She will have it forever, along with all the love that goes with it."

"And our hearts forever," Liza added.

"I'm sorry, but I have to go now, Princess. I love you."

"I love you too, Melvin."

Melvin wrote down Liza's phone number with a promise to call soon. Within the next year, Melvin was transferred a few more times and never did return home, although he did keep his promise and called Liza as often as he could. Time and distance came between them, and while working in a small town, Melvin met a local girl, fell in love, and married her within that same year. They had three children, all boys. Melvina and Liza kept in touch and always had a special love for each other.

The first five years after the adoption were the worst years of Liza's life. She felt lost and alone and missed her baby girl. Six years after the adoption, Liza fell in love again and had a baby girl. Liza continued to work for Marcus; as always, he was kind, understanding, and supportive. Liza's relationship with her family was never quite the same.

Without fail, every year on their daughter's birthday, Liza would call Melvin. They could comfort each other in a way only they could understand.

On the day her daughter turned eighteen, Liza went to the Post Adoption Registry to search for her. The same day, her daughter searched for Liza. Six months later, they found each other. Liza booked a flight to go and visit her.

They met for the first time ... again.

Liza got off the plane and saw a beautiful girl with long, dark hair, holding a sign that said, "My Mom, Liza."

Liza walked toward her. Her daughter dropped the sign and opened her arms to hug Liza. As she did, Liza caught a glimpse of something that sparkled.

Melvin flew out and joined them the next day. They went out for dinner and ordered Champagne to celebrate the momentous occasion.

"I'd like to propose a toast," Melvin said. "Here's to happy endings and new beginnings!"

Over the years, Liza and Melvin maintained a special friendship, and they each had a close, loving relationship with their daughter.

Printed in the USA
CPSIA information can be obtained
at www.ICGtesting.com
LVHW050336160823
755398LV00011B/68